Miriam

Vic Evans

Published by Accent Press Ltd 2014

ISBN 9781783756599

PART ONE

WREXHAM AND LONDON 1900-1957

Chapter One

Wrexham, North Wales, June 1957

It is early one June morning in 1957, not long after opening time for the market at Manchester Square, when a young man and a woman meet for the first time in the market café. The man, tall and not yet twenty, unwinds his college scarf and drapes it over the back of his chair before sitting down. Running his hand nervously through his fair curly hair he orders a pot of tea for two. The woman sits with her hands clasped. She is in her late fifties, though she looks younger, maybe because she is so slim, and her dark hair shows little sign of greying.

They watch in polite silence as the waitress sets out the tea things from a tray: a chrome teapot, a matching sugar bowl, and a milk jug all looking as outdated on the bare Formica surface of the spindly-legged table as her black dress and starched white apron. She places a small plate of rich tea biscuits before them and leaves.

'Nikolai, isn't it?'

'Nicholas, my name is Nicholas. Nicholas Wilder.'

Thrusting her hand into her jacket pocket she looks at him intently. Pulling out a box of matches she tosses it on the table with a red and black packet of Craven A cigarettes.

He shakes his head as she offers the pack. 'It feels strange to be called Nikolai. I've always been Nicholas although I've known for a short while that's how I was named.'

Lighting up and turning her head slightly she exhales through the corner of her mouth. As he watches her closely

1

her eyes narrow guardedly. How much does he know, this young man seeking her out like this? She holds his gaze. How much should she tell him? Why the hell did she agree to meet him in the first place? She could have dismissed the idea of meeting, made excuses, or simply ignored his letter. That was the sensible thing to have done. Yes, yes, she'd been through this many times before. It always came back to that unrelenting desire to see him. To find out about him, what he was doing and how he'd turned out. Perhaps to put to rest that question, did she do the right thing?

The new jukebox whirrs into life.

Briefly distracted she waits before responding.

Its brash chrome fins and flashing coloured lights look as incongruous as the tables in the insipid surroundings of the café. A record drops onto the playing deck with a clack. The Everly Brothers start singing 'Wake Up Little Susie'.

'I was taken aback when they gave me your letter at the police station; well, actually it was a bloody shock. How did you find me? Was it from the newspapers? They don't usually give out that kind of information.' There was a trace of the local accent.

'That picture of you jumping the wire at the Hungarian border last year was on all the front pages. You were a celebrity. Then I read about your defection. It was in –'

'My escape, dear, not my defection. Choose your words carefully, please.'

'It was the article on you in the *Picture Post* magazine that did it, photojournalist of 1956 and your full life story. Madrid, Moscow, Budapest, special correspondent on *Izvestia,* very impressive. I gave my college library as a reference and told them I was working on a project, a proposal for my thesis. They gave me a London telephone number.'

'Obviously you didn't tell them you were a nephew of

Esther Rabin. That would have put the cat among the pigeons.' She draws on her cigarette. 'Did you phone that number?'

'Yes.'

'You spoke to someone?'

'Yes. It was a man. He asked me a lot of questions. He said he'd get back to me and that I was not to attempt to contact you in the meantime. I remember he was quite firm about that. It was in March when I had a call at the college. I'd given up by then. I was told if I wished I could write to you but I was to leave the letter with the porter and not to post it.'

She draws on her cigarette again then slowly breathes out. 'The powers that be have provided me with a flat in Central London near the Embankment. They've been sending a charming man to see me every week, whether I want them to or not of course. He delivered your letter actually, last month. It's probably the same person who contacted you. They've certainly taken their time. He'd obviously read it. He told me if I wanted to meet you I should tell him where and when would be convenient.'

'Yes, I had a note at college about where and when.'

'He's been spending hours with me going over the usual routine, every detail, over and over, but I'm not supposed to mention that. I'll just say that the doctor, their doctor, said I shouldn't go on without resting for some time. Of course he meant I'd had a nervous breakdown. Go away somewhere quiet, he suggested. I could decide where but I had to report to the local police station every three days. Each time I've been it's a different officer so I have to go through the same routine, documents, passport, well, I haven't got any. Everything I had was taken from me as soon as I got into the British zone and I've never had a passport anyway.' She taps ash into her saucer then lifts her face to meet his eyes. 'I've been here, in Wrexham, about three weeks. Three publishers have

3

offered me contracts and I've had a generous advance from the *Telegraph* just to consider an exclusive with an offer of a regular column but I'm not allowed to take up anything yet. I told them I'm not ready. I took the advance of course. So! This was the only place I could think of where I could be guaranteed anonymity. It seems I was wrong.'

'Why here, Wrexham in particular?'

'Why not? It's as good a place as any.'

He stares at her. His eyes are drawn to her hand as she runs her little finger back and to around the inside of her watchstrap.

She sees he is not satisfied with her answer.

'According to the article you're from this part of the world.'

Licking a flake of tobacco from her lip she picks it off her tongue becoming aware of a slight tremor in her hand. There won't be a response to that sort of approach. No, there's been enough interrogation for one lifetime. After a pause she decides to go on the offensive. 'Well, are you working on a project? Is that why you asked me to come here today?'

'No.'

'No?'

'No, but I am working on an essay. Actually it's only my second term, a little early to be preparing a thesis.'

'Don't you have to do some form of military service, what's it called, National Service?'

'Yes but my call up's been deferred until I graduate. I'm reading Modern History but that's not why I'm here.' He takes a bulky envelope from his inside pocket. It is of a washed-out brown paper, discoloured in patches as if by damp, and its torn dog-eared flap is open.

Esther's eyes widen. The Red Cross stamp is unmistakable and the two red bands running diagonally across the envelope indicating it as having diplomatic immunity are still clear. She feels her heart beating against her chest. Could he see the pulse in her neck? Instinctively she draws her collar close.

'The solicitor gave this to me after my mother's funeral last July.' He places it on the table. 'I still thought she was my real – my natural mother then. The man who I thought was my natural father died some years ago. He was the manager of the bank on the high street where we lived. I'm the only one, no brothers or sisters. The house I grew up in and everything in it is left to me. It's empty. The place where I was so happy, all my childhood there, now I'm a stranger in it. I go through it room by room and see them so differently, cold, damp, empty; it's as if I haven't happened. I don't know how to live in it anymore. I don't want to go back to it.' Slowly he pushes the envelope towards her. 'This came with me. The Red Cross had placed it in my wrappings I was told.' He looks into her face. 'You know what's in it, don't you?'

For a split second her dilated brown pupils hold his in a cold stare. He sees they are flecked with hazel like the glass marbles deep in his boyhood memory. She blinks and abruptly averts them. An evasive shrug topples her cigarette ash.

'There's the letter addressed to me trying to explain why she's sending me away and saying she hopes we'll be together again one day. Then there's your typed note giving details and descriptions of events and some newspaper cuttings of articles by you.'

He waits for a response from her but she will not be drawn. Her eyes are still fixed on the envelope.

'I read these papers –' He is caught off guard by the emotion constricting his throat. He swallows then limply motions toward the envelope. 'I read these papers just before I saw the *Picture Post* article. I was –' Fumbling among his thoughts to find the expression of his feelings he gives up and then goes on. 'Do you know it was some days before I could believe it really was me being addressed in the letter? I read it over time after time. Then I retrieved the *Picture Post* magazine. Yes it was you, the person who wrote the articles and the note in that envelope. I still find it hard to believe.' His voice breaks slightly. Tears of suppressed anger well up. 'The idea I have of myself, who I am, who it is my friends think they know, it's shattered. Something I still find hard to accept. I have to find out who I really am.' He pauses again and breathes in before going on. 'That's why I'm here today.'

In the stillness that follows he reaches for the envelope takes out a photograph and gently pushes it over the table until it touches Esther's hand. She flinches as if pricked. 'Tell me,' he leans toward her, 'Tell me. What was she like, my – my real mother?'

Mentally shaking herself Esther stubs out the cigarette and leans forward to take the postcard-size sepia-coloured portrait. She'll just give it a token glance but she lingers over it longer to give her jarred feelings time to settle and to think of something to say.

How much should she tell him?

She gazes at the familiar likeness of her sister with her own strong aquiline features, heavy eyebrows, hair that looks dark in the style of the late twenties, and a lace blouse revealing a handsome neck and shoulders. The photographer's address is embossed on the bottom right hand corner: A. Percival Browne. Jamiesons Studios. 3A High Street. Wrexham. They'd had one of each and one both together, she recalled as she pushes it back to him.

Nicholas stares hard at her. 'How could she give me up? I must have been barely nine months old.'

How much should she tell him? Should she tell him what really happened? Best not to. Not yet anyway. Yes, that's it, she will play for time.

'Spain in November 1938 wasn't the best place for a baby, believe me. Especially if your mother was fighting

6

on the losing side.'

Nicholas looks at her closely. 'She's dead now, isn't she?'

Esther hesitates, 'I think you realised that before today but if you want to hear me say it, yes, she's dead.'

He lifts his teacup and finds it empty. He replaces it carefully on the saucer as the feeling of resignation swallows his thoughts. Momentarily he turns his face from her looking away and addressing nothing in particular. 'And my father, did you know him?'

'No. I knew of him but I never met him. He died before you were born. Look,' impulsively she places her hand on his arm causing him to turn back to her, 'children of all ages were being evacuated. Britain accepted thousands of them. The way she saw it, it was only for the time being.'

Perhaps that will close the matter. Yes it's best he sees it that way.

'Eventually many did go back but by then things had moved on. She was in the Soviet Union and you had been adopted.'

Why should she feel the need to justify anything? She swallows the feeling of resentment rising like bile in her throat.

Suddenly Nicholas leans forward and places his hand on hers. 'What kind of a person was she? Where did she come from? Where do I come from? Don't you see? I have to know what part I played in her life.'

She gently draws her hand away, folding her arms defensively. She would be wary of what she revealed and how she would put it.

'How much time have you got?'

'Oh, I can get the last train for Oxford at twelve thirty tonight if necessary.'

She pauses to gather her thoughts. 'We were very close, Miriam – your mother and I – do you mind if I call her Miriam; it makes it easier for me?'

7

'No, not at all. Go on.'

'Miriam and I grew up in Coedmawr. Do you know it?'

'No. I'm not from here. I grew up in Oxted, Surrey.'

'The village stands on a hill facing the mountain some five miles above here. In the winter the bloody wind always seemed to be blowing in your face. We never knew where it came from or where it was going but wherever it was it always called at the village on its way. There used to be a colliery below where most of the men folk worked. It closed for good after the miners' strike in 1926. There were collieries in most of the villages around the town then. Steam whistles announced the changing of the shifts and marked the passage of time for the townies and the villagers alike. There were only two years between us, see, and when Mam died in the flu epidemic in 1919, soon after Dad came home from South Africa, there was just the two of us, and Dad of course. As for you wanting to know where you come from –'

Esther pauses, reaches for the teapot, and pours for herself, offering to pour for Nicholas, but he shakes his head. She attempts a cautious sip without milk or sugar, makes a face, then puts the cup down.

'Well I suppose I have to go back to our roots.' Her eyes briefly look into the middle distance.

She will tread carefully.

'Over fifty years ago Dad, that's your grandfather Joe Rabin, used to come to this very market with his father every week. He's been dead, oh, it must be fifteen years now. In 1942 it was. We were both in Moscow then. It must have been over three years before we learned about it. We'd lost touch completely, you see.' She hesitates, 'Oh dear, I seem to be losing the thread. Where was I?'

'You were saying my grandfather used to come to this market.'

'Ah yes. Well anyway they took the train from Manchester Victoria and travelled in the goods van with a handcart loaded with clogs. Then after staying overnight in a lodging house they would catch the early morning train for the market at Oswestry. At the end of the day's trading they went back to Manchester.'

Manchester Square, Wrexham, 1900

Joe hated Mondays and Tuesdays when it was his turn to help Pa at the markets. He felt he should be working in his carpentry shop where he had a business of his own to look after, but Isaac employed emotional blackmail on his sons with the force and subtlety of a sledgehammer.

'So! The son doesn't want to honour his father alone in the world in his old age?'

Joe's mother had been dead two years and this was the response to Joe's protests every time he brought the matter up.

'Just two days a week,' he would whine looking up to heaven for support, 'is that too much for a father to ask?'

On Wednesdays it was the turn of Joe's eldest brother Maisky, who, despite being a married man with his own clogger's shop, was obliged to travel to the Oldham market and on Thursdays to Burnley. On Fridays Isaac's middle son Selwyn went with him to Rochdale and on Saturdays they went to Clitheroe. Joe also had an older sister, Reeny, the eldest child, who kept the accounts.

Though Isaac was a burden to his sons they never talked about it and to Joe who still lived with him he was also an embarrassment. 'You don't have to dress like that when we go to the markets, Pa.'

'Like what?'

'You know, the shawl and the cap.'

'It's tradition. You ashamed of it?'

'It looks foreign, Pa. People stare in the markets and you haven't been to synagogue since I can remember –' Joe broke off. A punter with a blue coal scar on the bridge

9

of his nose and a white silk scarf fixed at his throat with a gold-plated safety pin was showing interest in a pair of irons.

Isaac was well-known in Manchester Square, as the marketplace at Wrexham was called. If you were a steel worker or a collier needing clogs or irons to shoe them you looked for the announcement IKE RABIN FOR CLOGS gaudily painted on a board standing high above his cart. Often Joe was able to pick up some business of his own making a stool to order or such like.

When he was twenty-five Isaac Rabin the shoemaker as he then was, came out of the Ukraine with his wife Golda and one-year-old Reeny. Just occasionally, perhaps when he'd had too much cheese for supper, that day when everyone in his village ran away without even stopping to close their street doors came back to disturb his sleep. In his dreams they still seemed to be running when they got to the port of Hamburg.

They found their way from Hull to Manchester where Isaac worked in a clogger's shop. Eventually he did well enough to buy a shop of his own in Burnley. It was after Joe was born that Isaac had had the idea that changed the nature of the business and the lives of his family. He saved enough to rent a small warehouse in Manchester and instead of making the clogs himself he bought them in bulk from the cloggers in the city and took them to the markets in the mill towns and the Welsh Marches. When Golda died in 1898 the business was doing well. Why didn't he employ others to do the markets now, his family asked? Just sit back. You can afford it. There's no need to go around anymore.

'No,' he said. 'You can't trust other people and you never know what's around the corner.'

'But, Pa,' said Reeny, 'things have turned out well.'

'So! Things have turned out so well your mother dies?'

They didn't argue. In bringing them up he'd made too

10

good a job of instilling his own insecurities into them. One day it's going well. Next the Cossacks come through the village. The images that flashed into his consciousness when he was caught off guard by the smell of wood smoke or the sound of hooves on granite sets didn't help.

Joe especially had been sown with anxieties by his father, probably because he, being the youngest, was Isaac's favourite. Though his resentment of what he saw as the needless imposition on his life to satisfy his father's whims was beginning to overcome his underlying fear that danger was lurking around every corner.

Each Monday at around one o'clock Joe liked to visit the pie shop on the edge of the market hall, leaving Isaac to look after the stall on his own for an hour or so while he sat down to a hot pie. However on this particular Monday there was a reason why he was looking forward to his visit, one that wasn't just to do with hot pies.

Most Mondays two sisters, Edith and Sarah, came to town on the omnibus. Edith was seventeen and Sarah was two years older. When Edith left school at eleven there had been rare trips down to town with her mother and sister. They would climb up on the horse-drawn brake in the morning and take it back to the village in the mid-afternoon. Since then the omnibus had arrived, bowling down and grinding back up to the village every two hours from eight in the morning until eight in the evening each day of the week, excepting Sundays of course. While it was quicker than the brake, Edith had hopes that the motorbus she'd seen in Liverpool would one day arrive in the village.

It was part of the sisters' duties to come to Manchester Square on market days to buy what was needed at home. Their mother knew the girls enjoyed this weekly outing. 'It's quite harmless,' she'd assured their father Emlyn, a blacksmith at the colliery.

They had been visiting the pie shop for some time as

part of their treat and they often saw Joe there. Since Joe called after Edith when she'd once left her purse behind on the table they'd fallen to chatting, especially Edith. As for Sarah she saw nothing improper in it as Joe had introduced himself correctly without forcing his company upon them. And so for four weeks on the run they shared a table.

Today Joe came to join them, calling over to the busy pie man with a large tray steadied precariously on his head with one hand, 'Three meat and potato please.' Then he hung up his hat and sank on to the chair with a sigh before lifting his voice above the chattering market-goers and the scraping of chair legs on bare boards, 'Pa's even more stubborn than usual today.'

Edith looked at him becoming aware of the single dark curl he brushed in place across his high shiny forehead. 'You oughtn't complain about your poor pa like that.'

Joe could see she was joking. 'Ought I not? He wanted to take his lunch break before me today, says he feels faint. Can't go on much longer without something to eat, so he said.'

'Poor man. Perhaps you should've let him go. He must be getting on a bit.'

'He's fit as a flea. He never eats at this time of day anyway. He just has a glass of lemon tea over on the other side of market somewhere. He knows I meet people here at this time.'

To the girls Joe's Manchester accent with its flat vowels and harsh consonants was unfamiliar, and though he rolled his Rs like they did the slight lisping inflection and his pattern of speech sounded somehow exotic, especially to Edith. It contrasted with the Welsh lilt to which she was used, provoking her to tease him. 'People?' She feigned surprise and lifted her eyebrows. 'Who might they be?'

Before he could answer three bowls crowned with golden crusts were placed on the green-tiled tabletop. 'You know.' Joe paused awkwardly and taking up his spoon he broke into his pie, releasing the meaty aroma, before looking at Edith, 'You.'

'Do you mean the two of us?' said Sarah mischievously.

As the question hung in the air between them Edith became aware of the minute beads of gravy glistening on his moustache. Sarah persisted, 'Have you told him you meet two ladies for lunch?'

Edith noticed how full his lips were as he ran his tongue nervously around them.

Joe paused again with his spoon halfway to his mouth, looking her full in the face. He became aware of her eyes changing between green and grey as she moved her head in the dim light of the pie shop. Suddenly he felt uncomfortable, 'I've got to get on,' he said evasively through a mouthful of hot pie. 'Must get back soon but,' he swallowed, 'have you two ever been down to the river?'

They glanced at each other and shook their heads.

'Have you not? Well I could walk you there after the market today.'

'That would be nice but we'd have to take a later bus and Mam would be worried,' said Sarah.

'We could tell her we're getting a later bus next week,' suggested Edith.

'I suppose we could. I'd like a walk along the river.'

'It's settled then. I'll see you next week anyway and after the market I'll help Pa take the cart to the lodgings, then I'll meet you both at the bus stand.'

Chapter Two

Coedmawr, 1900

Ruth Hughes looked at her girls standing together in the parlour doorway as she straightened up from polishing the table. 'And why do you want to come back on a later bus?'

They told her about the gentleman who had offered to walk them along the river after the market but then they had to tell her how they'd been sharing a table with him in the pie shop every Monday for the past two weeks.

'Sharing a table, is it?' she gave each a searching look in turn. 'And both of you he wants to walk by the river?'

The girls kept silent.

'Or just one of you. Which is it I wonder?' then after a pause, 'What's his name?'

'Joe,' answered Edith. She felt her ears going hot under her hair and she knew her cheeks were scarlet.

'I'll talk to Dad when he comes home from work.' Then as an afterthought Ruth said, 'Best be when he's had his dinner.'

That evening Emlyn lit his pipe from the fire with a spill then sat back in his armchair looking at the two girls. 'What kind of a gentleman is he?' he asked pointing his pipe stem at Sarah to target his question.

'He's very respectable, Dad. Good manners.'

Emlyn paused his pipe half way to his mouth, 'I mean what is he, a clerk? Does he work in a shop? Not down the pit I hope?'

'He sells shoes in town, Dad,' said Edith.

'Shoes!' Emlyn shot a glance at Ruth.

'Yes. In the market.'

'In Manchester Square?'

'Yes.' Sarah was nervous, 'Well, it's clogs actually.'

'Clogs!' He's not that old man with the cart, is he?'

'No,' there was a pause before she added, 'That's his father.'

'His father!' Emlyn sat up, his pipe forgotten.

Edith explained, 'He helps his father in the market every Monday but I think he's a carpenter really.'

'They're from Manchester,' volunteered Sarah.

Emlyn turned to Ruth, 'I've seen that clog man in the market. He's a rum-looking Johnny, foreign if you ask me, like a lot of them from that Manchester place.'

'Well, Joe is not,' Edith snapped.

Ruth stood up, 'I think we'd better have a look at this young man. Ask him to come up for tea next Monday, then we will decide about walking by the river.'

The next Monday Joe and his father were pushing the handcart to the lodgings after the market. While Joe was doing most of the pushing Isaac was holding forth, as he usually did when he was irritated.

'So! He's going. That he's not going to eat with me, he says.'

'I've told you once, Pa: I've been invited to tea by two young ladies.'

Isaac raised his eyes heavenward, 'Invited, he says.'

Joe refused to respond, pretending to have difficulty in getting the cart over the cobbles.

'And am I not invited? Your own father?'

'Oh so you're speaking to me. I thought you were talking to God.'

'Not only does he leave his father to eat alone in a strange house while he chases after women, also he blasphemes.'

'Look, Pa, I'm just going out for a short time. I'll be back for supper.'

Isaac shrugged dismissively and sulked until they reached the yard of the lodgings. 'What kind of girl is she?'

'I told you, Pa. There are two of them. They're sisters that I meet in the pie shop on Mondays.'

'So they are two sisters but one of them is the one you would like to walk with most. Yes?'

'Well – yes.'

'And are you going to meet her family?'

Joe nodded.

'A goyishe family?'

'They're gentiles, yes. So?'

'A Manchester girl not good enough for you, eh?'

'It's not like that, Pa.'

'What was wrong with Trudy Marks?'

'With Trudy Marks everything was wrong, Pa, but it's nothing to do with you anyway.'

Leaving his father to store the cart in the stables behind the lodgings, Joe made his way to the high street, and after calling at the barbershop for a shave and a trim for his moustache he met the girls and they all took the bus up to Coedmawr.

Wrexham, June 1957

Esther flicks more ash into her saucer. 'So Joe and Edith soon started walking out together without Sarah. By the end of that December they were married, renting a cottage at the bottom of the village where Joe set himself up as a carpenter using the front room as his workshop.'

'What about his father Isaac?'

'He died the following summer. After that Joe turned his back on Manchester.'

Esther twists in her chair feeling restless, constrained almost. She looks out through the glass partition that subdues the hubbub rising from the floor of the market hall below. Broad beams of mid-morning sun strike down through the glass roof from a clear June sky. 'What time do the bloody pubs open; I can't stand any more of this tea.'

Nicholas feels a little irritated. He senses an attempt to change the substance of the conversation. 'It's another hour or so yet,' he snaps.

'I still haven't got used to the opening times in this country.'

He leans over the table, determined to maintain the thrust of his investigation. 'When was my mother born?'

At the sharp edge to his voice Esther turns her head and looks him up and down. 'It was in the November of that year, 1901. I was born two years later and four years after that Dad went out to Canada using some of his share of his inheritance. They wanted people to emigrate, especially carpenters. Work was scarce with some pits closed and prospects in the village were poor, so were the living conditions. I was only four but I can remember some children going barefoot except on Sundays. Mind you, it was never that bad for us. When he'd made enough money he would send for us, he said. We would have a new life. It was going to be wonderful.'

'And was it?'

'Two years later he came back without a brass farthing. Mam had pinched and scraped so that there was still some of the inheritance left but in early 1914 he used it to go off again, would you believe, like some kind of Gulliver on his travels.' She is surprised at how bitter she still feels about it. 'To South Africa he went. It upset me, I can tell you. Even though it must be over forty years ago I can still recall the shock. Well, I couldn't understand why he went, why he was so restless. Life didn't seem so bad to me that he would want to leave us, but things are seldom what they seem. He stayed there throughout the war. He was trapped there, I suppose. I think I can remember Mam saying we got just three letters from him in all that time.'

'The war?'

'You know: the Great War, the first lot. Don't you history students know anything these days?'

Nicholas ignores her question. 'How old was my mother when he went off the second time?'

'She'd be thirteen. Later that year I joined her at the grammar school. Things were tough from the middle of the war. We had nothing to take to school for lunch but mouldy cheese. Every day that's what we had. It smelled so bad it was left in a box outdoors where we had to eat it.'

Wrexham, March 1917

Miriam was sitting on the hard bench seat looking out of the rattling frosted window of the bus and feeling the welcome warmth of Mam pushed up against her. Leaning forward to tighten the strips of canvas wrapped around her boots to keep her feet warm and stop them slipping on the icy ground summoned up memories of playing in the snow with Dad all those years ago. Esther hated snow. She would refuse to come out. Dad used to wrap the strips around her tiny shoes, telling her that's what people did in Russia. She felt a sudden pining. What's he doing now all those miles away? Is he looking through a window at snow and feeling cold like me? She smiled. He'd laugh if he saw her feet.

It was the same early bus Miriam took to school on weekdays. She wasn't going to turn sixteen until that November, and she was the youngest in the matriculation class. But today was a Saturday, and there was a particular purpose to this journey, which was why she carried a large empty linen bag under her coat as did Esther, sitting on Mam's other side. The bus seemed unusually quiet, no gossiping in Welsh among the villagers muffled against the biting cold, just the occasional furtive glance here and there. It seemed Mam was not the only one to have heard there would be potatoes in town today. Miriam could bring to mind the smell as she peeled them, but when was the last time she'd eaten one? Sometime before the summer holiday, perhaps.

She turned again to peer through the window at the great iron-rimmed wheels of a heavy wagon rumbling over the icy granite sets as it left the railway goods yard. The pair of draught horses were straining against the mountainous load of potatoes bound for the market. Their breath was blowing in steamy blasts from distended nostrils as they crossed the lines in front of a bell-clanging tramcar crowded with steelworkers.

The bus, weaving in and out of the traffic, slowly overtook the wagon on Town Hill. Miriam puffed on the frosting window and scraped with her fingernails to get a better view of its burden. Then Edith drew the girls to her saying softly in Welsh, 'Keep close to me. We are staying with that load all the way to the market even if we have to hang on to it. If it is up to this lot,' she used the stronger Welsh term 'cythrauliaid', 'there'll be none left for us and it's the only load for this town until I do not know when.'

As Edith purposefully led her girls down from the bus Miriam noticed the horses at the top of the steep hill starting to turn into the street that led to the market, and she paused spellbound at what was happening. The near horse, unsteady on the slippery slope, was reluctant to make the turn and the driver was holding its head down and tugging its bridle with all the strength he could muster. It was then she caught sight of the colliers' women with shawls drawn tight around their thin shoulders silhouetted darkly against the low winter sun sidling along with the wagon. An image of hungry wolves stalking their prey sprang into her mind. Feeling the tension building up she hesitated before turning to follow Mam and Esther.

Suddenly two of the leaner women darted towards the wagon, and grasping the ropes securing the net that covered the load with an agility born of desperation they attempted to pull themselves up the high sides to get at the potatoes. The driver, startled in the middle of his difficult manoeuvre, gave out an irate yell as he twisted violently snatching the horse's head round in the opposite direction and bringing both to a dead stop so that the shafts thrust them forward. Taken by surprise their back legs slipped from under them. Miriam looked on in horror as their heads twisted up and their upper lips drew back over yellow teeth in a dreadful accusing grimace of pain and fear. Screaming their outrage at the sky they went down on their haunches and rolled onto their flanks, kicking and wrenching the shafts so that the load shifted and the great wagon slowly toppled on its side, throwing the women clear.

The net burst and Miriam and the others, who had spun round in response to the commotion, watched in amazement as an avalanche of potatoes poured down the hill. It streamed past the colliers' women, sweeping some off their feet. They waded into the torrent grabbing, scrabbling, and snatching in an attempt to fill their shawls. Workmen shinned down ladders filling their pockets, stuffing their shirts, and laughing as they did so. Two police constables shouted and followed, blowing their whistles. A haberdasher came out of his shop dancing around trying to fill a bowler hat as potatoes leapt from the granite sets. A cobbler ran out, nails between his teeth trying to scoop them into a bucket. A joiner left his saw in the timber and dashed to join the throng.

'Come on! This is what we're here for.' Edith set off at a trot with Miriam and Esther behind her as they joined the other villagers in the general rush. With her canvas-shod feet Miriam overtook everyone and reached the tail of the avalanche as more people were coming out of the side streets. She found herself shoulder to shoulder with the bus driver who was filling his cap and a soldier doing the same on her other side. As the avalanche lost momentum the pursuers became a mob on their knees picking up potatoes with one hand and clutching to them bulging hats, caps, shawls, and bags with the other. Miriam heard the sound of light-hearted laughter from men, women, and children and she shared the feeling of companionship as they rubbed shoulders, calling for onlookers to join in as if it were a game.

Then there was a blast on a police whistle.

A line of constables was standing across the bottom of the hill.

A weak sun went behind snow-threatening clouds.

The stillness that followed was broken by the pitiful grunting and squealing of the horses lying tangled in the harness among the splintered shafts.

A sergeant constable stepped out from the side of the street. He addressed them as a single body in his thin piping voice, 'This is private property. Put it down and move away.'

As of one mind the crowd turned towards the constables and stood still. From the corner of her eye Miriam could see Mam looking intently at the sergeant. Sharing her tension she waited to see what she would do.

The sergeant raised his whistle again and shouted, 'I'm going to tell you once more. If you do not do as you are told I will order these constables to draw truncheons and clear the street.'

There was murmuring and shuffling but still no one shifted. One of the children, a ragged looking boy of about nine years, tossed a potato at the sergeant. Miriam saw it describe a distinct arc through the icy sky and burst at his feet, splattering his shiny boots. The crowd exploded with laughter.

The sergeant blew two shrill blasts on his whistle.

The constables drew their truncheons and advanced at a walking pace. At first the people in the front fell back, pressing against their comrades who were reluctant to move, taunting the constables instead. Then amid shouts the air was suddenly filled with potatoes.

Miriam drew back her hand to throw but Edith seized her daughter's wrist and shouted in Welsh above the tumult, 'We have not come to throw them away, you daft cat. Let's get from here as quick as we can.' They turned and thrust their way through the throng, joining many others who were putting the disturbance behind them.

Another whistle-blast and the line prepared to charge. A roar of anger filled the air and another barrage of potatoes swept helmets from heads. The line broke and the constables scattered, leaving the street to the triumphant crowd.

It was over as quick as it started.

The joiner went back to his saw, still in the timber: his apron pocket bulging. The cobbler carried his bucket indoors and continued soling. The haberdasher tipped the contents of the bowler hat into a box under his counter. The crowd dispersed and the women slunk away with heavy shawls. Miriam looked back on a street empty except for some squashed potatoes, a discarded helmet, and an enduring image of the horses' blood running in the gutter.

Chapter Three

Coedmawr, 1920

It was just two years later, after Christmas 1919, when Miriam was the first to be confronted by Dad on his return. Throwing open the door and sweeping in from the street carrying a carpetbag, it seemed to her he filled the tiny downstairs room, carrying with him an aura of cigars and the sweet scent of the brilliantine oiling his abundant moustache and the dark curly locks that tumbled out of the bowler hat lifted in salutation. As he dropped his bag and opened his arms she threw herself into them and he pressed her to the heavy, diamond-set fob weighing down the gold watch chain spreading across his waistcoat. She felt her heart lifting. In the street the driver of a Great Western Railway motor brake was unloading a tool chest and a trunk plastered with shiny purple labels announcing Union Castle Line.

They had received the picture-postcard of the ship on which he would be sailing over three weeks ago and a telegram from Southampton saying he had docked only the day before, but they had no idea what time he would actually arrive. Miriam recalled how different it was before when she was just six years old. Then Dad walked in unannounced and sat down in his chair by the fireplace, clutching a blanket roll on his knees. It had taken him more than a day to speak and more than a week to admit failure.

Now their lives were to change greatly. Dad had made enough money to buy outright one of the newly built semi-detached houses. They were the first ones in the village and a mile from the primitive conditions of their tiny cottage in the colliers' row, notoriously known as 'Vron Offa'. The house had hot water, a bathroom, a flushing lavatory indoors, gaslight, and a gas stove. There was new furniture including a gramophone, a piano ordered from Cranes of Liverpool and Wrexham, and a glass-fronted bookcase ready stocked with books. Over the handsome mantle in the parlour Dad hung a framed picture of the ship that had brought him from Cape Town with its name, Gloucester Castle, engraved on a brass label. Miriam even had her own bedroom, as did Esther of course. The girls found many of their classmates now lived in the neighbourhood, in contrast to Vron Offa, where they had little in common with the girls of the cottagers who left the elementary school in the village when they were thirteen.

But despite this Joe still behaved as if money were tight. He had trouble finding regular work and when Edith pressed him at the dinner table in front of the girls he claimed all the money was spent on the house.

'So!' Miriam heard him exclaim, 'We'll have to tighten our belts.'

It seemed to her the highly charged seconds that followed lasted an eternity.

Suddenly Edith sprang to her feet sending her chair flying back. 'Tighten our belts,' she screamed, 'Tighten our belts. *Arglwyd*! Did you not notice the scraggy necks on these girls when you came back? Just skin and bone they were.'

Startled Miriam felt herself blink. In a flash she understood the saying to jump out of one's skin.

Further enraged by the look of incomprehension on Joe's face Edith shrieked, 'Well, didn't you?'

Joe shrugged, puzzled by this release of pent-up anger and holding out up-turned palms he turned to the girls. Miriam felt uncomfortable and looked away. Scornfully she heard Mam say, 'No you wouldn't, would you. You with your gold watch, tiepin, and ring. Looking a real toff you were when you walked in after all those years.'

Dad's voice acquired a clipped edge. 'Is it not enough, woman, that we have a house that's paid for so no one can take it from us?' He moved to the door, averting his eyes from the girls as he passed and turning in the doorway he added, 'So things were so bad. Is it my fault?'

Edith was calm now. Using words tinged with bitterness and talking in a laboured and measured way, for since Joe's return she had to express herself in English most of the time, 'You really do not know how bad things were, do you?'

Again Joe turned to the girls, particularly to Miriam, who had moved closer to Esther, placing a hand on her shoulder.

'That is because you do not want to know. You do not care.' She swept her arm around the room and shouted, 'Yes a very nice house it is, but we had to suffer for it too. Getting by on the crumbs you left us and now you tell us we must carry on with just crumbs. Well, we don't have to, do we Joe?'

Joe shrugged again shaking his head slightly. 'What are you getting at, Edith?'

Striding over to his tool chest standing in the corner by the chimneybreast Edith snatched away the brocade cloth with which she had covered it to soften its angular features and flung open the lid so hard it crashed against the wall loosening an inner panel, as she intended it should. The panel fell forward, exposing many gleaming yellow coins set flush into the wood. Miriam stared wide-eyed, her hand tightening on Esther's shoulder with the marvel of such a sight.

'There is at least a hundred Krugerrands there. That's what it says on them anyway. When I opened the lid to cover it with the cloth it fell against the wall and that is what happened.'

Dad's going to faint, thought Miriam; his ashen face engendered an instant of pity in Miriam's breast.

'They're gold, aren't they, Joe, solid gold?'

Joe's eyes turned from the chest to Edith as he struggled for words. 'It was to give us security,' he said limply. 'You never know what's around the corner.' Even as he finished the sentence he remembered how many times he had heard those words from Pa.

'Why did you not tell me, Joe, why?'

His lips worked but no answer came. Increasingly becoming aware that he did not know why and would never know no matter how hard he sought within himself he went over to the table and sat down heavily.

'Was it security for us, Joe, or just for you?'

Still he could find no answer.

Edith went and stood over him. Speaking over her shoulder in Welsh she told the girls to leave the room. Then after a pause she said, 'Now listen, Joe, I've got something to talk to you about that's more important than this business and now is the time for it.'

Joe lifted his head. There was a mixture of surprise and anticipation on his face.

'Miriam's teacher says she will pass the matriculation this summer and if we can afford it she should go to Aberystwyth. There will be a place for her.'

Joe looked at Edith blankly. 'Aberystwyth?'

'Yes. The university.' She nodded toward the chest. 'There is more than enough there to send her.'

'To a university, a carpenter's daughter?'

'Miriam is clever, too clever to go into service. There aren't many positions now anyway and staying at home in not for her. Do you want her to work in an office in town, a typist?'

'Young girls work in offices now?'

'Most of them in the village go to work in town. In the war they were driving the trams. There was a woman conductor on the bus some days but you wouldn't know that, would you, stuck as you were in the back of beyond.'

Joe got up from the table, and, going over to the chest, he stood looking at the coins for a moment before turning to her. 'I had to work hard to get that gold, Edith.' He shook his head. 'It nearly broke me.'

'I know that, Joe, but you should have told me what was in there. I should not have found it hidden the way I did.'

Joe went back to the table and slumped onto a chair before the words held back for too long came tumbling over each other. 'I would've come back sooner, after two years like I promised, but with the war I couldn't get a passage. It nearly drove me mad thinking about you, wondering what was happening to you, how you were managing, and the girls, how they were growing. Looking at your pictures every night frightened I was forgetting your faces. I worked from sunrise until sunset all through those extra years. That's how I got the money for the house.'

He stopped and put his head in his hands. Pa had done his job only too well, he thought. Those Cossacks are still around the corner. After a few moments he felt as if a weight had lifted from his shoulders. The burden of the guilt he had been carrying was gone. She had found out. Now he had to live it down. He raised his head. It was time to move forward. The pogroms belonged to the past. He turned to Edith, 'Maybe I'll think about Aberystwyth, just maybe.'

Early the following morning, when most of the village still slumbered in the peace of the Sabbath, Edith came downstairs to light the fire as usual, but after laying the kindling in the grate the feverish pains in her forehead, in her neck, in her back, and down her arms drove her to lie on the sofa. That's where Joe found her when he came down, shivering and too weak to raise her head. As he covered her with a blanket he looked into her eyes. They seemed empty, unknowing, as if he were a stranger to her. In a wave of panic he called up to the girls.

Miriam was first down with Esther close behind. Dad was in his chair. She had never seen him like that before. It set off a string of anxious feelings. He was so upset. Wringing his hands with his eyes fixed on Mam's face and why was it so flushed and wet with perspiration? Then shocked but calm, almost detached, she set to and tended the fire, telling Esther, 'Make a pan of porridge with milk and honey to get Mam's strength back and,' as an afterthought she added, 'make enough for us as well.'

That day Edith lay in a fever, restlessly moving her head from side to side, complaining of pains all over, and taking nothing to eat. In the evening Miriam helped her dad to carry her up to bed and arranged for the three of them to take turns through the night occasionally mopping her brow and moistening her lips from a bowl of water.

In the morning it was clear to Miriam that something more had to be done, but what? Esther and Dad were at a loss. Now calm anxiety turned to dread, almost panic. Dad would have to stay at home and Esther would go up to the village for a small bottle of brandy to mix with milk to drip through Mam's lips with a teaspoon.

The next day Edith was worsening, whimpering with pain between prolonged bouts of coughing and desperately sucking air into her bubbling lungs. Overwhelmed with desperation now, Miriam bound her chest with a towel in an attempt to ease her suffering, but try as she might she was not strong enough to draw it against the cough torturing her ribs. In desperation she left her dad to do his best while she hurried out of the house without closing the door running and stumbling by turns to the top of the village for the doctor.

Manchester Square, June 1957

Esther pours more tea for herself. Nicholas declines. 'You don't suppose they have a slice of lemon, do you?'

'I doubt it.'

'It was just a thought.' She takes a sip and makes a face before going on. 'Mam was the first in the village to die of influenza that year. The Spanish Lady, they called it. She was gone within five days. Many more from the village would follow by the end of the year. Miriam passed her "matric" in the summer and Dad found a regular job as a carpenter in a flourmill in town. Her teacher got her an invitation to Aberystwyth for an interview. I suppose that was too much for Dad to take. He'd just lost his wife, now his eldest daughter was to leave home.'

Adwy Coedmawr, 1919

'But what do you mean I can't go? Mam said you'd agreed to me going if I got a place.' Miriam held out the letter of invitation.

Joe, just in from work, was settling himself at the dinner table. 'That was before we lost her and now there's just the three of us I need you girls at home.' He opened his newspaper and buried his head in it deeper than usual as a sign the matter was closed.

Esther came in from the kitchen with a plate of stew for him.

Miriam spoke to her in Welsh, a brittle edge to her voice. 'Take it back and put it to warm.'

Esther turned about, careful not to spill any gravy, and disappeared through the door.

Joe closed his paper, folded it crisply and put it down on the tablecloth, giving Miriam a belligerent look fired by a surge of irritation. 'Did you tell Esther to take that plate back?'

31

Miriam advanced on him, emotion rising, her eyes flashing in defiance. 'You know I did and don't put on that attitude, as if you expected me to accept your word without question. You know very well Mam wanted me to go to college and,' she pointed at the tool chest, 'there's no reason why I can't go.' Her voice trembling she shouted, 'You never wanted me to go.'

Joe rested his elbow on the table pointing at Miriam. 'Don't you go putting on those airs with me, young lady. How that gelt is to be used is none of your business. Your job is to keep house while I bring in the wages.'

Esther came in from the kitchen, wiping her hands on a dishcloth. 'I can manage the house, Dad. You don't need two housekeepers.'

'So!' Joe raised his voice a level snarling, 'This is the gratitude I get. I provide a house like this, a palace compared to that,' he struggled for words, 'that hovel down in the village and you're both against me.' He rose to his feet bringing his fists down on the table so the plates rattled. 'Well,' he was almost shouting now, 'in this house you'll do what I decide and what's more you'll speak English. I'll have none of your sly Welsh talk.'

Miriam moved towards him, hands clenched. Dad was crushing her dream just as a matter of convenience. How could he do this as if her life was of no more importance than the household tasks?

There was a taut silence between them. Miriam could feel the tears pricking her eyes. Surprised by cold hatred she looked upon Dad. 'Very well then.' She was calm now with a hard edge to her voice. 'As you say this is your house and while I'm here I have to look after it, but I'll not stay in it a minute longer than I need to.' With that she threw the letter on the table and left the room.

Taken aback by this display of passion Joe sat down heavily. What had he said to bring about such a reaction? Perplexed, he looked to Esther as they listened to Miriam's footsteps on the stairs followed by the slamming of her bedroom door.

'She'll get over it – won't she?'

Esther denied him an answer. 'I'll bring your stew, Dad.' Then she turned away, leaving Joe to open his newspaper and stare blankly at it, aware of a deep feeling of unease.

That year autumn approached with Miriam attempting to reduce the drudgery of the housework by pestering Joe for money to buy some of the new labour-saving devices. If Edith had wanted a modern gas heater for the flat iron or a mechanical carpet sweeper or even to send the sheets to the new steam laundry to avoid the back-breaking dolly tub and mangling Joe would have looked upon it favourably as a way of improving efficiency. But Miriam, well she was just trying to get out of doing the housework, and Esther was colluding with her.

Matters came to a head in September. Unable to endure the daily regime of these mindless chores any longer without doing something about it she determined to go down to town to talk to her former teacher.

'With your matriculation certificate and my reference you can apply for a post as an uncertified teacher and after two years you will gain your teaching certificate,' she said. So that was it: she would apply to a number of positions confiding only in Esther.

Eventually an envelope arrived on the doormat addressed to her. She was first down every morning to clean the grate and lay the fire. It was an offer from a private girls' school in southern England at a salary of fifty pounds a year including accommodation. Feeling giddy with elation she sat down heavily on the stairs and read the letter through again with shaking hands to make sure she was not mistaken, and then she read it through once more to savour the words. What should she do now? Well, first she would dash upstairs to show Esther before preparing the breakfast and then give it to Dad when they were at the table.

Joe read no further than the words typed on the top of the page, Claremont School for Girls, Weybridge, Surrey. Miss Miriam Rabin, Brooklyn, Adwy, Coedmawr, Denbighshire. This was only the second time there had been a letter addressed directly to her. Suddenly she had gained a standing that was upsetting. He did not know why but it aroused a cold fury deep within him. 'What's this about?' he demanded without reading further.

She told him, aware there was a note of defiance in her voice and noting with satisfaction that it was not lost on him.

'You're not going off to the other side of England and that's it. This is where your home is and this is where you stay.' He brought his hand down on the tabletop emphasizing his words.

Miriam stood up. 'I'm eighteen in November, Dad,' her voice reflected her quiet but strong feelings, 'and I'm going away to earn my own money whether you like it or not.'

Esther rose and went to stand with her.

Joe sat back in his chair creasing the letter between finger and thumb. Pointing it at her he sneered, 'So! This house not good enough for you, eh. Too common for someone like you with your education and your clever mind.' He paused to let his words sink in. 'And how do you expect to keep yourself?'

'I'll have fifty pounds a year, Dad, and accommodation. I don't need your gold for this position.'

Joe read through the letter rapidly. A pound a week was more than enough, the thought struck him. With dismay he realised she was right. She didn't need his money. He was going to lose her. Throwing the letter down he glared up at them and folded his arms across his chest, hiding the anger and the dread rising in him. 'You knew about this.' He stabbed his finger accusingly at Esther. 'Both in it together going behind my back.'

Esther stood closer to Miriam, instinctively placing an arm around her shoulder.

'Well, go if you must, but Esther will have to leave school to take your place.' The glottal stops and flat ahs in his voice becoming more unfamiliar sounding to them as his feelings rose.

'She's got a scholarship, Dad. She starts the matriculation classes in September.'

'Not if you're leaving. Who's going to keep house?'

Miriam glanced at Esther then back to Joe. Dad had turned the tables on her, snatching away her triumph.

The smouldering anger in her eyes provoked panic in him at the prospect of losing her under such bitter circumstances. He had to find a way out, but how? If he gave in, let her go away, he would look foolish and weak and he would lose her anyway. But if he stood his ground Esther would turn against him as well. Such a victory, that he should lose both girls? He would bargain, allow himself to be persuaded, give way on something while aiming to keep her at home or at least from going far away.

Rising from his chair and holding out his open hands with fingers splayed he placed them on the table in a conciliatory manner and leaned toward the girls. 'Look! Let's sit down again and see if we can meet each other halfway on this.'

After a pause Esther looked to Miriam. She shrugged and they both took their places at the table.

Joe sat down, pausing to give his words some weight. 'If you take a position locally Esther can stay at school and with her help you could manage the house between you when you both come home at the end of the day.'

Miriam gave him a hard bitter look. 'And what will you do when you come home at the end of the day?'

He ignored her manner in his relief that she had taken the bait. 'I'll chop firewood and break the coal.'

What could she do? She couldn't leave Esther as Dad seemed to think she could. The unbroken drudgery she had come to know only too well would destroy her. She would have to make the best of it. 'Can we have a carpet sweeper and send the washing to the laundry?'

Hiding his relief Joe sat back as if considering the matter carefully. 'Carpet sweeper, yes. Washing to laundry, well – perhaps the sheets and maybe the towels. I don't see why not. But not my shirts, mind.'

Miriam made to stand up.

'Well – shirts. But not the collars.'

Miriam glanced at Esther and moved again.

'So! And the collars.'

Chapter Four

Black Lane School, 1921

It was a bitter February morning as Miriam stepped down from the bus and made her way past the sulphurous smouldering pit-bank louring over the school. Driving rain stung her face as she crossed the yard toward the arched doorway of the porch that bore the word 'GIRLS' carved in the sooty stonework above it. The bell clanked tonelessly from a cupola in the centre of the wet slate roof.

Two years ago she had given up her opportunity of a post in that genteel school in the south of England, starting as an uncertificated teacher at this elementary school in the rough pit village across the valley. She reflected how her former teacher had been horrified. Well now she had gained her teaching certificate and Esther had a job on the local paper. Dad had refused to pay for her to go to college of course but evening classes in typing and shorthand at the technical institute had got her a job that could perhaps be the start of a career in journalism.

Some girls scuttled past and disappeared into the porch seeking shelter. Others walked singly and listlessly up the yard. Boys were straggling across to the other porch, splashing each other from puddles, reluctant to go in despite the cold and wet. Two were kicking wildly at a stone, lashing out with their hob-nailed boots, elbowing each other, and nearly colliding with Miriam before she reached the door.

She passed the peg racks in the porch with their faint tang of disinfectant and arrived at the teachers' room down the corridor. Footsteps echoed on the woodblock floor at this time of the morning. The school seemed so empty and expectant. She was always first in the morning because the next bus was too late. In the teachers' room where it was always gloomy, despite the high windows, the gas was lit and the fan-jets spluttered with yellow flame. She hung up her coat and signed the time book. There was a chill in the room. Perhaps if she poked the fire into life it might help. Then she must put her dinner, a turnip and potato pie wrapped in muslin, into her locker to be heated in the oven when the children went home at the end of the morning session.

As she was putting on her black pinafore the heavy brass door latch clicked and Mr Rhys came in, acknowledging Miriam's presence with a nod. Glancing at the clock he went over to the cavernous wooden cupboard standing open to reveal large bottles of red and blue ink, boxes of pens, pencils, nibs, chalk, sheets of pink blotting paper, stacks of shiny red exercise books, and a bundle of canes. Taking out a pile of books he placed them on the table and removed his waterproof. Then drawing his watch from his waistcoat pocket he glanced at it. 'Oh dear, what a terrible morning it is.' Not waiting for a response he bustled away.

Miss Roberts came through the door took a fleeting look at the clock, then she went over to the pegs, removing her hatpin as she did so. Miriam watched her taking her hat carefully from her hair, placing it on a peg, shrugging off her coat, shaking it, and thrusting the hatpin into the collar. Then she draped it on a chair-back and announced to the room in general, 'Terrible weather.' Miriam nodded sympathetically and smiled to herself. The school was such a bizarre place. She didn't think she'd ever get used to it.

Mr Pritchard, the headmaster, entered. 'Ah Mr Rhys!' Mr Rhys heard the headmaster but was now settled in his usual chair reading the newspaper he'd taken from his small mock crocodile skin case. 'I want to talk to you about those standard six composition books.' Mr Rhys continued with his reading for some moments. It was sufficient so as to put in doubt, as he intended, whether he would respond. Then he carefully folded the paper and placed it in his case before looking up. 'Perhaps later, Mr Pritchard?' The headmaster cast a malevolent look upon him, holding his eyes for some moments as if about to react, then he turned to Miriam. 'Miss Rabin, it's time you were in the girls' porch. See that they wipe their feet this morning or the floors will be awash.'

Miriam was still smarting from the implied reproach as she stood at the door when the girls were coming in, swirling around her, and ignoring her calls to wipe their feet. She found herself swept aside as they streamed past, pushing and pulling their way to the peg racks. Miss Edwards was carried in with them. She was swept past Miriam, saying, 'I should just stand in the corridor and wait for them to form up.'

The girls formed up in Standards Five, Six, and Seven and waited unspeaking until the teachers marched them into the Big Room where they stood at their desks looking to the front. The boys were entering from the other door in suppressed silence.

Folding back the glass partitions of three classrooms formed the Big Room, with its many narrow windows rising to meet the lofty ceiling. The walls were tiled to the high sills in a mossy green, then they were washed a jaundiced yellow. A grey morning light fell from behind the children onto the blank wall facing them.

Miriam's class was at the end of the room, so there were windows along the side as well. A large clock hung on the wall behind the children. On the high teacher's desk was a single jar of wilting crocuses and snowdrops. She stood in front, adopting a severe look to ensure the girls kept their eyes on her as the boys took their places standing at the desks.

When the noise of studded boots on the block floor had died down the headmaster entered and stood upon the dais with his thumbs hooked in his waistcoat, as if to set the seal on the stillness that descended on the school. He was unmoving except for his eyes sweeping up and down the desks row by row subjecting them to the same malevolent stare he had used on Mr Rhys. Then he roared, 'That boy!'

Every boy stood rigid, hoping he was not the one being singled out.

'You. Yes, you, Jenkins. Stand outside my door.'

Grey-faced, the malefactor slunk away to await his fate.

Miriam flinched inwardly. That roar always gave her a start.

'School will be seated.' The headmasterly voice interrupted her thoughts.

There was a clatter of desks and a sullen silence fell upon the assembly. Turning to his assistant teachers he nodded curtly as the signal for the registers to be taken. Then he stepped down and with his hands clasped behind his back he strode from the room.

Miriam ascended to the high desk. Unhooking the cane from the side and assuming the authority it bestowed upon her she placed it deliberately across the top and opened the register. Taking up her pen she cast a stern look over her class of fifty boys and girls as she dipped it in the inkwell and held it poised.

Each day the sight before her assailed Miriam's spirit, threatening to overwhelm and crush her. There was the condition of the children's clothing, which smelled unpleasantly. The girls' ragged woollen jumpers and pinafores were crudely patched in a pathetic attempt at prolonging wear, and there were holes in socks worn by ill-fitting studded boots and shoes. Then there was their poor physical condition. The boys' scraped knees were the thickest part of their legs. Her eyes swept over dirty faces, necks, ears, continually running noses, and boils. And their attitude: a sly low cunning and insolence prompted by the poverty of their lives.

Today, when she came to John Jones' name and his recorded absence for two and a half terms, she recalled how, having lost his leg to a coal wagon last year playing on the railway, he told his classmate Bryn Thomas of his wonderful time in hospital with clean white sheets and dinner every day. Later a surprised shunter found Bryn lying with one leg across the line.

At Gwilym Probert's answer to his name the image flashed through her mind of him twisting and writhing under his desk in a desperate attempt to shield his arms and legs from the stinging strokes of her cane fired by the blind rage his unrelenting and insolent taunting had brought down upon himself.

Or was that it? Did her anger not come from the smouldering frustration waiting each day to explode? The frustration produced by the failure of the children to meet her expectations. To seize the opportunity she was offering and to pull themselves out of their dreadful existence so that they could escape the future that was waiting for them. Or was it the education itself just sufficient only to calculate their yardage down the pit or to operate the furnace charger at the steelworks.

This was not how she'd pictured herself at that school in the south of England. She was going to bring enlightenment and to instil the ability to appreciate fine literature, music and painting, to help children prepare for examinations and to get on. She'd imagined surroundings alive with stimulus, and of study and achievement that was much like her own school had been. Not the oppressive atmosphere of a school whose day is punctuated by the colliery steam whistle marking the two o'clock shift changeover, and where smiling was regarded as dumb insolence, reproducing the industrial tyranny that dominated the life of the village.

With school over she followed the last of the children through the gate and stood at the bus stop. The sky had cleared and the air had a frosty sharpness to it with an acrid bite from the smoke of coal fires. There was the headstock of the pithead winding gear at the colliery opposite. The two great wheels lit by the late afternoon sun were set a-quivering, as if straining at the leash slowly starting to turn against each other, one winding up and one down. Suddenly they started whirling so fast the sunlight flickering through the spokes fused the wheels into scintillating blood-red discs. After some time the spokes reappeared as the wheels gradually slowed before coming to an abrupt stop.

A motorcyclist coming out of the colliery gate regularly marked the imminent arrival of the bus and today was no different. Miriam watched the rider slowly weaving through several colliers crossing the yard from the lamp room. He called out, acknowledging their coarse remarks shouted in Welsh, their eyes and teeth flashing from faces grimy with coal dust. As the motorcyclist turned into the lane, his cap pulled down on his head with his goggles strapped around it, he waved to her as usual and as usual she waved back, but today he did not ride away. Instead he carefully circled his machine in the rutted lane, pulled up alongside her, and shouted over the rattle of the engine, 'Do you want a lift? I'm going up the top road.'

Chapter Five

Edwin's motorcycle rattled along the lane, swerving around the dusty potholes with the heavy acetylene lamp bobbing as if it were about to fly off its bracket. When he first offered Miriam a lift on the pillion she tried to sit demurely with her hands on the tops of her thighs, but finding that impossible she was faced with the choice of refusing or holding on to him so she chose the latter. Gradually, day-by-day, her hands moved further around his waist until she felt comfortable enough to clasp him tightly.

He lived with his family on their farm over the mountain at Bryneglwys. At first he dropped her at the top of the village without a word, just a cheery wave leaving her to walk home down the hill. He didn't pick her up in the mornings because he had to be at the pit by six o'clock. It was two weeks before she saw his face for the first time. When he stopped to let her off he lifted his goggles and pulled his muffler from his mouth.

'Your face isn't black,' she said in surprise as he turned to look at her.

'Why should it be? I work on land.'

'On land?'

'On top, not down the pit.'

'You're not a collier then?'

'I'm a blacksmith. I have to go down sometimes to splice cables and that but you won't find a forge down there. You can't even take a match down, girl.'

Their exchanges grew longer and as the days became warmer it was not lost on her that Edwin was now wearing a jacket and open shirt, revealing his powerful neck and chest, the source of his deep rich voice. Setting his cap on one side he would lean his motorcycle against the dry-stone wall that ran along the top road and they would sit on it chatting for some time before going their own ways. Esther did not seem to notice that she came home later or if she did nothing was said, and she was always home before Dad anyway.

One day Miriam told Edwin about Dad going overseas and the shortages and bitter cold of that January and February in 1917.

'That would be when my dad lost a lot of sheep even though they'd been brought down. Buried in the snow they were. Couldn't get to them, see. It was too deep. He told me that one morning the back door was covered in a sheet of ice on the inside. It must have been very cold.'

Intrigued she lifted her chin quizzically. 'Must have been cold. Where were you then?'

'In Egypt. It was a lot warmer there, I can tell you.'

She laughed. 'What were you doing in Egypt?'

'I was called up in 1916. On my eighteenth birthday it was. I went out to Cairo in the Royal Welsh the next January. That's where I learned to ride a motorbike.' He paused pensively. 'Then we went up the Sinai to the Red Sea.'

'Where Moses parted the waters?'

For a moment he seemed not to have heard her looking over toward the distant Cheshire plain. 'That's where the trouble started. I had a nasty time of it at Gaza. It was a mess. Johnny Turk chased us out. No getting away from that, but in June General Allenby took command and we beat them at Beersheba.'

'Were you in a great battle like Joshua crossing the Jordan to conquer the Promised Land?'

Slightly irritated by her persistent biblical allusions he turned to her, 'I crossed into Jordan all right and we had a battle. It was at Megiddo but Promised Land – you can

44

keep it if you ask me. Dust, flies, blisters, and fatty corned beef melting in the heat. I haven't been able to look at it since.'

'It doesn't sound very biblical.'

'In the October we were in Damascus and then Aleppo.'

The names had an exotic ring for Miriam. 'To think you've actually been to those places seen them and walked the streets. It must have been very thrilling.'

'Not for Johnny Turk. The war was over for him after that. In 1919 I was demobbed but I didn't get home before Mam died. I came out a corporal.'

One day she asked him about the farm.

'Well there's Dad and my sister Evelyn. Then I've two brothers but they've left, got farms of their own, see. We graze about a hundred ewes on the mountain, bring them down for the winter, and we've a couple of heifers and poultry.'

'Why haven't you a farm of your own?'

'I've been promised the tenancy of a place on the top. It's only got a temporary man for now, a bit of a rough place, needs a lot doing.'

'Then why don't you take it?' As she spoke Miriam leaned forward across his lap to pull the pink and purple flowers from the foxglove stems that were growing against the wall. Losing her balance slightly she leaned a little further than she intended putting a hand on his thigh to check herself, swiftly withdrawing it.

He coloured slightly. 'Well, I have to take a wife before I get it see. Can't keep a farm without a wife.'

She laughed, 'Where will you find her?' She had collected the flowers in the palm of her hand and was slipping then onto her fingers one-by-one. 'At the market perhaps?'

A little irritated, Edwin stared coldly at the gloved fingers held up claw-like. 'You know foxgloves are deadly

45

poisonous, don't you?'

'I know they're supposed to make your heart beat faster.'

'They'll stop it altogether. The green leaves will kill a cow.'

'Didn't you do this when you were a boy?'

'I remember Mam used the leaves to blacken the lines of the stone floor in our kitchen.'

Miriam drew the flowers from her fingers one-by-one and dropped them on his lap. 'The Tylwydd Teg make gloves from these.'

He brushed them off. 'I hope you don't tell the children such rubbish at that school.'

Folding her arms and setting her mouth in a firm line she fixed her eyes over toward the mountain as if to shut him from her. She would be setting off soon. There was no need for him to put her down like that. How dare he dismiss her work as rubbish? They didn't seem to have anything in common. He knew nothing about what happened in school no more than she knows about the pit.

For a few moments Edwin watched a kestrel hovering over the moors. Then as it plummeted into the heather he sought to recover her attention by reaching down and pulling a flat stone from the base of the wall to get at the white-flowered nettles that grew there.

It scraped with a hollow sound that made Miriam turn. 'You'll get stung.'

'No I won't. They're dead nettles.' He crushed the plants in his hand. 'See!' He plucked another and taking Miriam's hand firmly he pressed it in her palm before she could resist and closed her fingers on it. 'There you are. It doesn't sting does it?'

Startled she shook her head.

'Didn't you know about dead nettles?'

She shook her head again.

He was still holding her hand. 'I'll show you something

else about them.' Letting go of her hand he took another plant, and pulling two white flowers from it he held a single one to her face between his finger and thumb, 'Watch this.' He squeezed the end of the flower so that a milky bead was exuded. Bringing his face close to hers he captured it with the tip of his tongue, puckering his mouth and smacking his full lips. Then he brought the other flower up to her squeezing it. Putting her tongue to the nectar, she took it in, feeling the suffusing sweetness. Then holding her by the shoulders he pressed his lips to hers swiftly before moving away leaving her quite breathless.

It was not long before Edwin was coming down to the Adwy to drop Miriam off at the house. Then came the day when she invited him in to meet Joe and Esther, having prepared them beforehand. Joe took to him straight away and when they got engaged he was delighted.

Adwy Coedmawr, December 1922

They were married in the village church on Boxing Day morning. The wedding party was made up of Joe and Esther, their neighbours, Edwin's father, his two brothers, his sister, their children, their neighbours' children, and everybody's dogs. After the ceremony, with a bitter wind blowing off the mountain, a fiddler with chapped hands led them down to the house in the Adwy as they processed behind the bride and groom, drawn by a white-plumed horse in a brake decked with ribbons. At the house the guests found a big fire blazing in the parlour and in the living room a sea of glasses, scores of bottles, and a mountain of sandwiches. A forest of holly and mistletoe met their eyes as they crowded in, with Miriam and Edwin seated in the place of honour, facing a large frosted drum of a wedding cake on its wooden platter. Joe poured out the drinks and they raised their glasses as one of Edwin's brothers, acting as best man, led them in toast after toast each one getting more bawdy as lewd and rhyming advice was offered to the bridal couple by the men in turn, provoked by the women who were riotously feigning embarrassment.

Presently the gas was lit as the winter light failed and someone put a record of a popular dance tune on the gramophone. The younger people started to dance, stumbling over excited children and yapping dogs scampering between their legs. Then from the other room some notes of an air scraped on a fiddle drifted through until they were swallowed in the tumult.

Cushions had been piled on Miriam's chair so that she was perched above the table and from her place she looked over the throng as Edwin stood up to toast his new father-in-law for the fifth time at least. His tie was pulled down with his shirt undone, exposing the black hair on his chest and calling attention to the thick neck atop his powerful shoulders. She hadn't seen him like this before, with the flickering flames of the fire lighting his flushed face emphasising his hawk-like nose, full lips, and the tumbling curls of his black oily hair. He looked so satyr-like. She was aware of an unfamiliar prickling feeling in the pit of her stomach.

Then came the cutting of the cake. Taking a large knife from a bowl of hot water Edwin seized Miriam's hand in his, clasping it tightly around the bone handle. Then lifting it high above his head so that he yanked her arm in its socket he brought it down hard, thrusting the blade through the icing without cracking it amid great shouts of 'Da iawn!' The fiddler played the chord of a jig and Edwin drew her into the widening space in the middle of the room, leaving the blade standing in the cake. Tentatively at first she allowed herself to be drawn, then swaying her hips and quickening her pace she began following the dance steps.

Jig after jig was danced on unsteady feet until jostling

produced angry words, tussling, and badly aimed blows. The air became uneasy and the dancing broke up. The menfolk gathered in groups and the women busied themselves with glasses and plates.

Miriam felt her nerves tightening. The stuffy warmth of the house was becoming unbearably oppressive. She sought Esther but Esther was not to be found. Taking her going-away coat from the hall she went to the side door, and stepped out into the darkness, breathing in the keen fresh evening air.

'Hello!' Esther's face momentarily appeared like a carnival mask in the flame of her lighter. She drew on the cigarette, breathing out smoke slowly through the side of her mouth. Holding out her distinctive silver, green, and black enamelled cigarette case for Miriam to take one. 'It's getting a bit edgy in there, isn't it?'

Miriam accepted the light and folded her arms, looking up at the starry blackness with eyes half closed. Someone had started playing an accordion and its singing was coming through the closed door with the splashing sound of palms loosely clapping in time to the music. She allowed the day's images to tumble through her mind in no particular order.

'Are you happy, Miriam?'

The question grated somehow, breaking into her reverie. She was irritated though she didn't know why and she bit back. 'What about you?'

'What about me?'

'Well aren't you pleased for me?'

Esther pulled on her cigarette then breathed out slowly, 'No. Not really.'

Taken aback, Miriam snapped, 'Not really, what do you mean? Don't you feel happy for me at all?'

'Well if you really want to know how I feel, and mark you this is the first time you've asked me, I feel betrayed.'

'How so?' Miriam angrily stubbed out her cigarette on

the wall, breaking it in two and letting it drop to the ground.

'You inspired me. Do you know that? You showed me the importance of a career. I supported you against Dad in your fight for independence.'

'Esther! What are you saying?'

'Now you're barely twenty-one and you've given it up to marry a pit blacksmith and be a farmer's wife.'

Miriam's eyes flashed, 'Esther, listen to me. I have to give up teaching now I'm married. You know that.'

'No. You listen to me. You've given it up to marry that Edwin Moss to please Dad. Oh, I can see through him all right that – that ladies' man with his hair as oily as his motorbike.'

'Esther, I couldn't go on in that dreadful school. It would have destroyed me. I was trapped. Don't you see?'

'Now Dad really has won. He's got his way completely. You've destroyed yourself.'

'Esther!' Miriam screamed. 'Dad blackmailed me with you. I could have gone away, become a real teacher, but I stayed because of you. What else could I do after that? What else? Tell me.'

Esther threw down her cigarette and snatched open the door. With a backward glance she stepped into the enveloping stuffiness and din, closing the door behind her.

Breathing deeply Miriam struggled to contain her shuddering breast and the sobbing that threatened to choke her. Almost panting now she placed her palms against the door. That was it, she was gradually bringing her feelings under control. The sobbing subsided except for the occasional spasm. When her breathing steadied there was nothing else to do but to go in and join Edwin.

Later that evening the newly married couple left in a taxi amid great ribaldry to go down to town to stay the night in the best room of the Wynnstay Arms Hotel, where a bottle of the finest champagne to be found in the cellars awaited them. In the early afternoon of the next day Edwin's brothers came in their farm lorry to take them up to the farm and the newly acquired livestock where Evelyn was at the door to lead the way into the warm front room of the farmhouse.

The farm, Wrexham, 1923

The farm was the last one on the lane that climbed to the high desolate moor above Coedmawr. In the weeks before they were married Edwin had laid a pipe from the well on the top field to bring water to a tap in the kitchen. There were four cows to be milked when he came home from the pit. The milk churns were picked up each day by the dairy lorry. The sheep were grazed on the mountain except when they were brought down for wintertime. Poultry provided eggs for the market man and within a few months Miriam had learned to churn butter for him as well. The baker came up every other day in his van and the general grocery man came once a week with his horse and cart, bringing paraffin for the lamps and the kitchen range. Once a month a load of coal from the pit was dropped in the yard. There was a black and white collie called Tess who was supposed to sleep in the barn but Miriam pleaded on her behalf so that she was allowed in the house, and there were many cats about the barns keeping down the rodents that pilfered the cattle feed.

And so Miriam was sucked inescapably into the whirlpool of that first year's cycle. In early spring it was lambing before the sheep went back up on the tops. In June it was haymaking, shearing, and dipping. The coming of autumn brought the bottling of fruit from the kitchen garden and jam making filled the house with a hot and fruity aroma. Then the sheep were brought down. Beetroot was pickled. Potatoes, mangolds, parsnips, and carrots were lifted and laid up against the bleak austerity of winter.

Now Edwin was beginning to cast a dark shadow over Miriam, threatening to crush her spirit and stifle her personality as he became the personification of the farm with its unalterable and unyielding daily rhythm. Moving the cattle down the lane to the water and back up the field before daybreak, feeding the poultry and chopping the beet and straw for the cattle feed, separating the milk, and churning the butter before expressing it into pats ready for market, collecting the eggs and packing them in straw for the egg man, filling the lamps and trimming the wicks, doing the laundry and cleaning the house, mucking out the cow stalls and filling the mangers, chaining the cattle and washing udders ready for milking, scouring the pails and lighting the hurricane lamps on the dark afternoons just before Edwin came home. And while he milked, filled, and put out the dairy churns for morning, leaving enough for the butter making next day, Miriam prepared and cooked their meals on the paraffin range. Even so she still found time for Esther who came up to visit most Sundays, having become resigned to Miriam's marriage despite her disquiet and for Joe who, now that he was retired, popped up in the week for his two bottles of 'llaeth menyn', buttermilk.

In the evenings, after they had eaten, Edwin would sit in his chair by the fireside silently smoking and sometimes going over the weekly accounts or reading the newspaper he'd brought home from work while Miriam cleared away the dishes. Then she would join him and taking one of her library books from the shelf near her chair she would open it and start to read.

This had been irritating him lately. He didn't know why it should disturb him or when he first became aware of his irritation. He felt she should be doing something else but what it should be he could not think. 'What's that you're reading now?' It was not really meant as a question. He just wanted to express his feelings from behind his paper.

She raised her head. She felt he wasn't expecting an answer but she would give him one anyway. 'It's very interesting actually. It's about the making of the English working class.'

He lowered his paper. 'And why should you be reading about that?'

'Because it looks at how society works.'

'What's that got to do with us?'

'It's everything to do with us. This book is about how we came to be what we are today.'

'We're what we are today because I got this farm. You don't need to read a book to find that out.' He stood up in front of the fire, slackened his heavy leather belt, then putting his hands behind him on the base of his spine he stretched his full length before looking down at her and giving vent to his irritation. 'Society doesn't work, it just is. That's all you need to know, girl.'

Despite feeling the power of his looming bulk she retorted, 'Well that's where you're wrong. Society works according to economic laws. We are what we are because of them and because of what's happened in the past.'

'Ha! What's happened in the past's got nothing to do with us.'

'It's got everything to do with you for a start.'

'What do you mean with me?' There was an intimidating edge to his voice.

'This book describes The Clearances.'

'The what?'

'The Clearances. They improved farming, increased the growing of food. Less people needed on the land, more people available for the mills, factories, and pits. People lost their land but with the population increasing there'd have been famine. The end justified the means.'

'I asked what that's got to do with me?'

'You work in the pit because I work on the farm. You

can't do both at the same time. I free you for the pit just like The Clearances.'

He seemed to tower over her now. 'I work in the pit to keep this farm until we can take on more. You know that.' He poked at her book with his thick finger, 'If that's the sort of ideas you're getting from these books you'd better stop going over to that library.' He turned away as if to show the matter was closed but Miriam would not have it so.

She raised herself from the chair. 'There are ideas in these books that can bring about change.'

'Change?' He turned back to her.

She drew up to her full height and looked into his eyes, 'Society can be planned. We don't have to accept the mess it's in now.'

Edwin returned her look for some moments before turning away shaking his head and saying over his shoulder, 'I'm going to check the animals and the poultry. I think the fox is about tonight.' He paused to pick up the shotgun in its place beside the kitchen door.

On Saturday nights Edwin took to going over to the village. Sometimes he would visit a public house or he would go to the picture show at the parish hall. 'After all,' he reasoned, 'she goes to the public library in the village one evening a week.'

At first Miriam welcomed the opportunity for reading without the tension it provoked when Edwin was home but gradually she became unsettled. She felt a growing desire to talk and to express her newly kindled ideas but to attempt this with Edwin roused his oppressive desire and stirred a need in him to subject and control rather than to discuss and reason.

He in turn found the evenings wearing whether it was the charged silence of her reading or her abrasive responses to his remarks, and feeling the need for a break he started going over to the village in the middle of the week also. If he went out as many evenings as he liked, then so would she. Miriam placed a card at the public library announcing that she would hold a reading group for ladies on two evenings each week and she made arrangements for a room to be available.

The reading group soon gained regular members. Miriam set the reading list drawn from the latest political, historical, and literary works she would order for the forthcoming week and during their meetings they discussed the issues raised. When Esther heard about it she decided to go along and gradually she became one of the group's most enthusiastic members, being appointed secretary with responsibility for ordering from the reading list.

It was one evening that Miriam learned from two of her ladies, who had just acquired wireless sets, about the transmission of lectures, orchestral concerts, and opera by the British Broadcasting Company. They wished to introduce topics that had been raised and had also appeared in the new publication, the *Radio Times*. Having brought a copy with them both spoke in turn about the significance of the increasing popularity of broadcasting. Miriam decided to look into it before taking the matter up with Edwin.

Sometime later, after they had finished the meal, she handed him a sheet of paper across the table. On it was printed:

F.W. WILLIAMS ELECTRICAL
GOODS
REGENT STREET, WREXHAM

WIRELESS SET (PHILCO 135) £12-12s-00d
AERIAL £9-00s-00d
HIGH-TENSION BATTERY £1-01s-00d
ACCUMULATOR (WET CELL) TWO £1-00s-00d

CARRIER 10s-00d
FITTING £1-00s-00d

TOTAL £25-03s-00d

His eyes ran over it briefly before coming to a stop on the bottom line. 'What's this about?'

'Now don't try to tell me you haven't heard of a wireless set. That's what we need up here for the evenings.'

'What for? They're just for cranks. You'll be asking for a telephone next.'

'Miriam held up the *Radio Times* she had laid in her lap. 'It's all in here. There are regular broadcasts, even weather forecasts and talks on farming too, so there must be lots of farmers listening in.' She pushed it to him across the table.

He ignored it. 'Ah, but you need the electricity girl. Those things don't run on paraffin.'

'I know very well what's needed to run them and so do you. You can't tell me you haven't heard all about them down at the beast market or that you haven't been listening to broadcasts because I know they've got one at The Cross Foxes.'

Caught off guard he was silent for a moment so Miriam pressed home her advantage. 'I've been talking to the man in the wireless shop down town. We'll have one accumulator battery connected to the set and the other we'll take to the garage in the village. That's what the carrier's for, otherwise you get acid on your clothes. I've heard it costs a penny to get them charged and they last for over a week.'

'You seem to have gone into this a lot but there's one thing you didn't do and that's talk to me about it first.' Then he stood up and threw the paper onto the table dismissively. 'Anyway, you could've saved yourself a lot of trouble because we can't afford twenty-five pounds and you should know that.'

She opened her mouth to speak but he interrupted leaning across the table and wagging his finger at her, 'There's very few folk can afford that kind of money for a toy because that's all it is. A toy for the well-off like some of those so-called ladies of yours at that library where you get these daft ideas.'

Miriam fought back her rising irritation. She would not be drawn into a shouting match but she was not for accepting the matter as closed either. Standing up she rested her hands on the table, leaning across to him her eyes flashing dangerously so that he drew back.

'Now you listen to me, Edwin Moss. There will be no trouble with the bank getting the money for a wireless no more than for anything else we need on the farm.'

Edwin raised his finger again opening his mouth as if to make a point.

'Ah!' She checked him raising hers also. 'I haven't finished yet.'

His mouth closed.

'I'm going to start listening to broadcasts any time I want. I'll either do it here or somewhere else.'

'Where?'

'I don't know yet. Perhaps The Cross Foxes,'

'Ha! They won't let a woman in there on her own.'

'They do so on Saturday nights, as well you know.'

He remained silent.

'And I've heard the library may be getting one. That'll be another daft idea you won't like but one way or another if there's no wireless here I won't be here in the evenings either so you'll have the place to yourself.'

Bellevue Park, Wrexham, June 1957

Esther lights another cigarette. 'Well of course they soon

had a radio, as did most people by then, including Dad and I.' She coughs. 'As with Miriam I used coercion. It was like drawing teeth out of Dad but he was taken with it from the start. He would sit as if his ear were glued to the speaker listening to the news broadcasts though for some time he forbade me from tuning in to what he called "that jazzy music".' She leans her head back, pensively smoking.

At afternoon closing time for the pubs Nicholas has persuaded her to take him to the park: a short stroll. They sit on a seat facing the distant moorland rising over three hundred metres above sea level, four miles west of the town. It was turning purple in the mid-afternoon sun.

He was perched on the edge of the seat. 'And –' He says expectantly.

Her thoughts broken in to, she sits up with a start, drawn back to the present. 'As a result of Miriam's reading group I became an active member of the Labour Party in the town. In the General Strike in 1926 I went to Manchester, marching. That's when I had my first smack from a policeman's baton.'

Nicholas's eyes widen.

'Oh, it wasn't to be the last one, believe me. After that I was belted in Liverpool and London. Anyway that's beside the point. Throughout the miners' strike I organised soup kitchens in the pit villages. Miriam ran one in Coedmawr, in fact she did a lot of work then and that's when she joined the party as well. Edwin was on the farm full-time, there being no work for him at the pit of course. Then toward the end of the six-month long strike starvation did the owners' work for them. The local landowners had instructed their gamekeepers not to approach colliers who were poaching. They were just to leave them be. It was that bad.'

'Really?'

Esther nods. 'Pit by pit the men went back to work for

less pay. So the soup kitchens continued for a while. But that wasn't the end of it. Not by a long chalk. Edwin's pit had flooded in the strike so the owners decided to shut it down for good. After losing his job as a blacksmith in that pit he went down the Gresford pit as a collier.'

Chapter Six

The farm, Wrexham 1934

Edwin knelt naked over the small metal bath in front of the fire as Miriam rubbed the loose coal dust from his back with the piece of sacking that was kept hanging on the back door. His pallid buttocks contrasting with the black of his torso always fascinated her. The whites of his red-rimmed eyes flashed through lashes thick with coal dust and not for the first time his pink lips drawn back from teeth flashing against his blackened face reminded her of a picture of a leering satyr she'd seen somewhere.

These days he had to do the milking in his black, for the cattle would not wait on him washing. Then he would eat his meal with Miriam while the water was heating on the range.

She slapped his back lightly, 'That's it. Your back's done. I'm going over to the village with Esther after to get the bus for town.'

'Another meeting is it?' He stepped into the bath and eased himself stiffly into the steaming water. 'You're going to put the world to rights, I suppose.'

'There's a speaker at the miners' institute tonight talking about unemployment and economic planning. He wants delegate support for his memorandum at the party conference at Llandudno in October. Oh and by the way, Esther's been elected as a delegate for the local branch.'

'You're wasting your time, girl. Go to the pictures instead, for you can't do anything about unemployment. There's nothing anyone can do if the work's not there except keep looking. It will pick up eventually. It always does.'

'Something has to be done now. It can't go on like
this.' She leaned forward, bringing her face level with his,
sensing the warmth of his body and the musky scent of his
stale sweat. 'This man's memorandum is about
government taking responsibility for unemployment so
that it can do something about it. There are things that
need to be done. New roads, new houses, schools and
ships to be built, and slums to be swept away. Do you
know six hundred thousand jobs could be created and
instead of the government paying unemployment they
could be paying wages? There would be more money to
spend, more trade. It could turn things around.'

Edwin was not expecting a serious exchange. Taken
aback by Miriam's display of fervour and the intensity of
her argument he asked sullenly, 'And where would the
money come from?'

'Borrowing. It would be a planned programme of
investment by a board set up by the government.'

'You'd have the government taking over the country
like that man Mussolini,' he pronounced it Moosoleenee,
'or those men in Russia. What do they call themselves –
Bol-sheviks? Anyway what's this man's name when he's
at home?'

'Mosley, Sir Oswald Mosley. He's the Labour MP for
somewhere in Birmingham.'

After washing his face vigorously Edwin stood up,
briskly towelling himself, then in one swift movement he
stepped out of the bath, wrapping the towel around her
waist and forcefully pulling her to him. Leaning back she
thrust her hips against his, feeling the warmth of his body
through her skirt and smiling provocatively, almost
challengingly. She lifted her chin to look in his eyes still
black-rimmed with the mascara of coal dust.

'Listen, girl,' his voice was low and gruff, 'most men
are without a job for more than a month or so because it's

their own fault. The work's there if they look around and they're ready to go after it and take what's going such as I did. The trouble is they're too fussy, see. They'd rather blame somebody else like the owners or the government.'

She pushed him away. 'I must be going now or I'll miss that bus.'

As she shrugged on her coat he flicked the towel over his shoulder and stood with his hands on his waist, flaunting his body. 'You know what I think?' he called as she stood at the mirror in the kitchen putting on her hat.

'So!' She addressed the her reflection, 'He thinks as well.'

He ignored the remark. 'I ask myself why do these women meddle in soup kitchens and stick their noses in matters that are nothing to do with them?'

She clicked the latch forcefully and opened the back door.

'It's because they need an excuse to get together for a blether,' he shouted at it as it slammed.

The reading room was judged to be too small for the expected audience that evening so every chair in the institute had been set out in the ballroom. Even so there were still people standing at the back as a suspenseful hush fell upon the assembly when the chairman of the local party stepped out onto the stage to announce the Labour Member of Parliament for Smethwick, Birmingham.

Oswald Mosley had recently resigned from his position as chancellor of the Duchy of Lancaster in the government of Ramsey Macdonald in protest against the cabinet's rejection of his memorandum on action to deal with the rising tide of unemployment. It proposed government intervention in the form of central control of banking, raising of the school leaving age; road-building programmes and above all, state assumption of responsibility for economic welfare. Tonight he was hoping to convince his audience to send their delegate to conference with a mandate giving full support for it.

Miriam saw a tall, slim, dark-haired young man with a military style moustache step briskly up to the platform. When he started speaking his high-pitched voice captured her attention immediately, but it was his words that struck home. Speaking with a dark force that seemed to put over ideas that would brook no resistance or questioning. She felt as if he was taking her into his confidence, revealing the ultimate truth: there was a coming crisis with little time to avert it, so there was need for immediate action of a kind not tried before.

All the time he spoke he gave emphasis to the detail with powerful gestures. Now stabbing the air before him with finger and thumb together, now punching toward her personally from his shoulder, now sweeping with open hand over her head including her in his whole audience with his chin held up his eyes looking into the distance one moment then down into hers the next. Now clenching his hand into a fist above his head while shaking it to stress each syllable. It seemed to Miriam he was reaching into her heart and so it was with the other listeners as he carried everyone along with him.

He spoke for over an hour. At the end, his face pale with exhaustion and beaded with sweat, he left the platform to a roar of approval, stamping of feet, and applause that left no doubt of overwhelming support.

Bellevue Park, Wrexham, June 1957

'So you saw Mosley speak?'

'Yes.'

'What happened to the memorandum at Llandudno?'

'After his speech at the conference we rose *en masse*. The cheering went on for minutes on end.'

'Then?'

'Then – it was defeated. By a small margin admittedly, but defeated it was.'

'Why?'

'I still can't understand why. One or two union leaders with large block votes were late getting there, something to do with the trains. Perhaps that would have swayed the result. Who knows? But it was clear to Miriam and me that the chance for the Labour Party to do something was rejected. Looking back – even if it had been carried I doubt whether the government, any democratically elected government, would have adopted it as a whole programme.'

'And after that?'

'Well, after that we both became disenchanted with the Labour Party. We felt that in the coming crisis it would betray its principles and the people it represented. I think it was then we came to believe that democracy didn't have a future in dealing with a situation that seemed to be getting worse by the day. So did Mosley but while we joined the Communist Party he went other way. It wasn't surprising I suppose, given his background in the landed aristocracy. He never really belonged in Labour so he broke away to found what he called the New Party.'

'So what happened then? What did my mother do?'

'Over the next two years she was a regular at the miners' institute and her reports to the ladies' reading group became a popular feature. Meanwhile I became a well-known speaker at meetings as far away as Liverpool, becoming area secretary of the Communist Party. Soon after that Miriam was appointed local secretary, causing an inevitable split in the ladies' reading group with those supporting her breaking away to join the party that met three times a week in the reading room of the library at Coedmawr. She recruited from pitmen, steelworkers, shop girls, clerks, even insurance clerks, and she also took classes at the institute two evenings a week for the Adult Education Scheme.'

'Did you ever see Mosley again?'

'Oh yes, we saw him on a number of occasions after that. By then he'd formed the British Union of Fascists and was sliding into anti-Semitism, attacking Jews in his magazines and pamphlets and holding provocative meetings and marches. That's when we joined an action group.'

'An action group! What for?'

'Well it may be hard for you to understand today but then it really did look as if the democracies in Europe were finished. For us it was to be either a communist or a Fascist world. In Britain with the apparent failure of the national government it seemed as if it was going to be decided on the streets.'

'The streets of Coedmawr?'

She laughs, 'Not quite. We went to Liverpool and Manchester at weekends, at first just to take part in counter-demonstrations, in other words, street battles. The Blackshirts would march in Jewish areas where the event had been well publicised in the local press during the week before. Of course they said it was communists who attacked them. All Jews on the streets were supposed to be communists while all financiers in the city were supposed to be Jews. I never quite saw how they squared that. When there was a weekend with no meetings our action group used to train in jiu-jitsu and tactics. Miriam and I specialised in smashing chairs in meeting halls so the BUF would have to pay the owners for them. Your mother was good at that, I can tell you.'

Nicholas smiles in spite of himself. 'Tell me, what did Joe have to say about his daughters doing things like that?'

'Mercifully I don't think he ever knew what we got up to then. Within a couple of years he was to lose us forever.'

Chapter Seven

The farm, Wrexham, September 1934

Miriam held the oil lamp high above her head. It was the best one from the parlour. She took a fleeting look at its crystal globe etched with figures from Greek antiquity and the translucent blue Wedgwood reservoir with white classical cameos. Then she hurled it at the stone wall of the barn. A wave of satisfaction swept over her as it exploded into shards of glass and cast iron. The brass wick holder flew up into the air to fall onto the farmyard. Then giving herself over to an ecstasy of destruction she seized lamp after lamp from the row she had set out behind her, flinging them against the wall until there was nothing left but a mound of shattered glass, broken pieces of metal and lamp oil soaking into the loose grit of the yard.

Breathlessly elated with the overthrow of the lamps' tyranny she looked over the scene of destruction. Sensing movement behind her she turned. There was Joe standing with his thumb hooked in the strap of his haversack, his breath coming in wheezing gasps.

She smiled. 'That's it, Dad! Something I've wanted to do for a long time. Edwin can shovel that lot into a sack for the bin men. I've done with those damn lamps. No more glass cleaning and wick trimming every day.'

He was speechless with bewilderment and still panting.

She leaned towards him. 'Dad, we've got electric light now.'

Joe caught his breath and found his voice. 'The smashing I heard. I came up the lane as fast as I could. Thought something terrible was happening, I did.' He swallowed again, pointing to the wreckage and shaking his head. 'But so much ruin.' Then he looked at the cables strung from pole to pole around the farmyard, gently swaying in the light breeze. He knew that Edwin had installed a generator mainly because the milk now had to be pasteurised at the farm with a cooler according to ministry regulations before it could be sold to the dairy, but he hadn't realised the whole farm would be electrified, including the lights. 'Such improvement,' he murmured, more to himself, but then he addressed her. 'So the generator breaks down. What will you do then?'

'Oh, I've kept a couple of hurricane lamps and we've got candles. That's more than you've got down yonder. What will you do if your electric goes off?'

'Well, you know I've kept the gas. I wouldn't let them take it out when we had the electric just in case.'

'How many times has it gone off since you've had it Dad?' she asked indulgently.

'So it hasn't gone off yet except when the meter runs out, but the gas gives a better light, and you never know, it might only be a passing fad. For shops and factories there's enough, but for houses …' he shrugged.

'Dad, how can you say that? There's been electric trams down in the town for over twenty years. Most of the houses there are electric now and most of the street lamps.'

Joe shrugged again.

'I've got to get on now and do the poultry.' She turned toward the barn calling over her shoulder, 'Edwin'll be home soon. You know where the buttermilk is.'

'So you have electric light now.' They were sitting at the table. Joe had stayed for dinner when Edwin came home. He didn't usually do this but as the evening was closing in he wanted to see the farmhouse in the new illumination. The harsh brightness of the bulb hanging from the ceiling turned night into day and banished shadows from every corner of the room, unlike the soft glow of the lamps easing the darkness with their diffused circles of golden radiance.

Edwin dipped his bread into his scouse while spooning pieces of mutton into his mouth. 'That's why I'm going down the pit. It gives us enough to do up the farm. Now Miriam's got an electric separator she can churn double the weight of butter and I get more for the milk now we do the pasteurising ourselves. At this rate the generator will pay for itself in no time, man,' he licked gravy from his coal-blackened fingers, 'then perhaps I won't have to go down the pit.'

'Will you not? Such progress.'

Edwin pointed his spoon in the direction of the sideboard. 'Progress! I'll show you progress. See that wireless, it's going next week. We're getting a new set a third of the price that one was. Working off the electric and no more carrying batteries to the village for charging.' He laughed, 'There'll be something else for Miriam to smash.'

With dinner over Joe left Edwin to his bath. Crossing the yard he went down the lane under a darkening autumn sky.

Miriam switched on the wireless and tuned in as the chirruping and buzzing told her it was warming up. What had once been the embodiment of dissatisfaction and irritation in the home had now become a focal point, bringing them together listening to the broadcasts and sharing the interest and discussion they aroused. Notably their chairs were closer at the fireside and Edwin was content to listen in whether Miriam was at her branch meeting or reading with one ear cocked and sharing the occasional comment or response. As she had become more proficient in farm matters he had gained confidence in her. She in turn had begun to find him less overbearing and gradually there had developed a mutual respect and tenderness owed in part to the return of their affection.

Edwin eased himself into the bath. Closing his eyes he let his head fall back. 'On Friday evening, girl, when I've had a rest, I'm going back to the pit for the half past nine cage.'

'Why?' Miriam started to knead his shoulders.

'I've swapped shifts with Jack Bennion so that I can go to the match on Saturday. The town's playing Tranmere. It should be a good game.'

'You'll barely have time to get your head down.'

'Don't worry. A couple of hours will do me.'

'When you come in on Saturday morning you'll sleep for ever. You won't be fit for going to the match.'

'Of course I will, girl, never you mind. You can manage the milking this once, can't you? It'll be too early for me to do it before I go down to town.'

'I don't mind it now and again though it leaves me with a terrible backache.'

'That's 'cos you're not used to it.'

'I don't intend to be.' She massaged the back of his neck with her thumbs. 'Duw! You've got some terrible blackheads here. I couldn't see them before we had this electric light.'

He reached up behind him and took her arm, drawing her round so they were face to face. He touched her cheek gently then he cupped the back of her head in his hand and kissed her, pressing his lips on hers. She pulled away and gave his shoulders a squeeze. 'Take care when you go down Friday night, cariad. You'll still be tired from the morning shift.'

Gresford Colliery, Saturday September 22nd 1934

The town and the villages around slept under rank upon rank of slated roofs shiny with the unrelenting rain. In the lamp room at the colliery a fourteen-year-old lad and his much older workmate had just finished cleaning the lamps from the afternoon shift. It had just gone two o'clock in the morning. They settled down to have a smoke for half an hour or so. The harsh jangling of the telephone startled them. The lad dropped his cigarette. 'What the heck can that be about at this time?'

It was the fireman at the pit bottom, 'They're coming up!' There was a click. The phone was dead.

Bemused the lad looked at his workmate, 'They're coming up. Why? It's only half-a-shift.'

Almost immediately colliers started appearing at the hatches. Though he was busy getting the lamps in and handing out the safety tallies with no time to speak to them he noticed they were alarmed, even panicked. Soon it all went quiet. The lad looked at the board. More than half the tallies were still on the hooks, including his father's.

Then the fireman thrust his head through the hatch, demanding abruptly, 'How many lamps are you short?'

Unsure the lad turned to his workmate who shouted, 'Two hundred and sixty but,' his words hung in the silence.

'Well.' The fireman was insistent.

'Some passed the hatches without them, mind – so I don't really know.'

The fireman was gripping the ledge of the hatch. His knuckles were white. He turned to the lad. 'Get on your bike and go down to town for the ambulance, quick as you can.'

'I've got no lights. If the bobby sees me in town I'll be in trouble.'

'*Duw annwyl*! Get on that bloody bike.'

Miriam opened her eyes with a start, immediately wide awake. Something had disturbed her. Something was outside and it wasn't the rain beating against the panes. She sat up, throwing back the bedclothes. Hastening to the window she flung it open. The recurring blasts on a colliery steam whistle carried clearly from down below on the saturated air. It was the alarm signal at one of the pits, an accident of some sort. It could be coming from any one of them. She would go back to bed.

Which one of them? The question leapt into her mind. She sat up again. Clutching the sheets with both hands she went through the names: Llay Hall, Llay Main, Bersham, The Hafod, and Gresford. Gresford! She felt a cold chill. Unable to settle she dressed and went down to make a cup of tea. Her footsteps on the stairs roused the dog.

In the streets, lights appeared at windows and doors opened. Men in caps with collars turned up started walking hunched against the cold, driving rain, their boots clattering urgently on shiny wet cobbles, and women, too, stepped out, hastily shrugging on coats and pulling shawls tight around tousled hair and thin shoulders. Along the streets they went, drawn toward the insistent and repeated blasts of the steam whistle.

Miriam sat in the chair, her head nodding until the pre-dawn chill woke her. Remembering the poultry and the cattle she went out to attend to them and feed the dog. As she closed the gate on the top field the lightening sky in the east told her she should be hearing Edwin's motorbike coming up the lane. She would go back to the house now out of the wet and wait at the open door. It was some time before she forced herself to go into the living room to look at the clock, forgetting to take off her dripping waterproofs. It had gone eight. He should have been home an hour ago. She felt sick with anxiety and dread.

Then back at the door, what was that she could hear? Something was coming up the lane. Yes. Tess's ears pricking up confirmed it. Her heart leapt and almost swooning with relief she leaned on the doorpost, but the grinding of gears on the last bend told her it was not Edwin's motorbike.

She went out to meet the small van as it turned into the yard. The passenger threw open the door and strode swiftly over to her, splashing unheeding through the puddles. His companion stayed in the van keeping its engine running.

He touched his cap respectfully, 'Mrs Moss?'

She looked at him, her whole body feeling numb, as if it did not belong to her.

'We've come from the pit. Is Edwin Moss here?'

She shook her head, her mouth almost too dry to speak. 'What's happened?'

He nodded toward the door. 'Can we go in for a moment?'

She led him into the kitchen and sat down heavily at the table with hands clasped, her face expressionless, with eyes unblinking and fixed straight ahead.

Taking off his cap he looked down on her, speaking slowly as if he was giving time for the words to take effect. 'There's been an explosion.'

She turned suddenly to look at him.

'Your man's in the Dennis section, isn't he?'

She said nothing.

'Well there's a fire in that section, see,' he tried to sound as if he was explaining some simple, everyday matter something that he had done so often that morning he had almost got the hang of it, almost but not quite for he still had to pause before going on, 'and there's been a fall, a lot of falls.'

Miriam sat still.

'They're doing everything they can to get through to them, mind – everything.' He tried to sound reassuring but he couldn't keep it up. 'Trouble is, we don't know how many got out see. A lot threw their lamps away as they ran for it. That's why we're here. Yours is the last house. We've been going round to see if anyone's gone home. Anyone who might have –'

'How many are down there?' Her voice sounded hollow.

'Over a hundred at the last count when we left. We're expecting news at the pithead any time.'

She stood up, 'I must go there now.'

'Well we can take you down now, girl, but you'll have to find your own way back, see.'

'Take me down now.'

He took her arm gently, 'Come on, cariad.'

The van crawled along bumper to bumper in the queue of vehicles at the approach to the main colliery gate. The driver peered through the smeared windscreen. The wiper was struggling with the rain. RAC patrolmen lined the road, attempting to keep the traffic moving. As they were about to enter the colliery yard they were halted as lorry after lorry loaded with sand turned across their path to drive in.

Fraught with anxiety Miriam slipped out of the van and joined those going in on foot. Swept along by the silent crowd she stepped over the railway tracks between the halted wagons, each one bearing the word GRESFORD in white letters. Not knowing where to go to get information: she'd never been to the colliery before, she joined others pushing and edging over to the main red-brick building. She wormed her way to the front of the crowd but policemen were preventing anyone from getting nearer. There was a hushed and desperate stillness except for the low rumble of steam rising in a column above the winding house.

Suddenly she heard Esther calling her name. Almost unbelieving she looked amid the nurses, ambulance men, and the fire brigade in front of the main building. Then she saw her waving as she came down the steps of the offices towards her. After speaking quietly to a policeman who then stood aside she came over. 'I've been looking out for you, girl, in case Edwin was down on this shift. Now I know he is.' Taking her arm she spoke to her gently, 'Come with me.'

Miriam drew her arm back as if resenting her sister's interference. 'What are you doing here?'

'I'm in the press party. The paper knocked me up in the night, and Dad of course. They sent a car for me.'

Miriam looked bemused.

'I'm still a reporter, you know, even though I'm area secretary of the party.'

Miriam ignored her. She was looking over the yard where an endless column of lorries was inching its way through the crowd, tipping its sand onto a mound where men were shovelling it into bags with a dogged urgency. Some were stripped to the waist and some were in waistcoats, obviously unused to such labour, including a vicar and his curate. The bags were being built into ominous stacks near the pithead, rising from an area covered in fire extinguishers marshalled in their thousands. Both extinguishers and sand bags were loaded into the cages continuously winding up and down. A blue RAF truck had come through the main gate, piled so high with extinguishers that some tumbled off as it bumped over the railway tracks in an effort to circle around the column. A melody played by the colliery band was carried on the sodden air as it attempted to keep up the spirits of the hundreds of men waiting patiently, but as Miriam slowly swept her eyes over the sea of white faces under dripping caps rising up the pit bank, it seemed to her to be an elegy.

'How long have you been here?'

'Oh! Just now. I got here just now.'

'Well this is the way it is up to now: seven bodies have

been brought up about an hour ago and I've got the names. Edwin's not one of them. Six got out early this morning. You know Edwin wasn't one of them either so we have to accept that he's still down there, girl. The rescue party from Llay arrived at daybreak. They went down straight away. They seemed very well equipped.' She tried to sound optimistic. 'There's been an official statement before you came. It said the inspector of mines and the colliery officials are underground now. Four districts are involved and there are approximately a hundred men trapped. You can wait here. It's all right, I've seen to it, but I'll have to go soon. There's another official statement expected. If you do leave here this is where you'll find me.' She turned to go.

Before she could move away Miriam abruptly clutched at her arm as if Esther's words had suddenly broken into her consciousness. 'What's happening down there? What's going on?'

Esther's manner changed, clasping Miriam's hands tightly and seeking her eyes with her own. 'The roadway's on fire, girl, burning coal, roof falls, and it's full of gas. That's what the sand's for and the extinguishers. They're trying to smother the fire to get to the men see.' She released her hands, 'I must go now.'

Miriam turned to watch the spinning wheels of the headstock from the veranda of the main block. When they stopped rescuers came from the cage, carrying two of their comrades. Clambering down the steps she joined the others stumbling across the tracks in their haste to get some news. They passed the two fallen men. Doctors were working urgently on them. Then the rescuers trudged wearily across the yard, wrapped in blankets, their oxygen masks hanging limply by one strap from faces that were lined with exhaustion and sweat-streaked coal dust.

Someone called anxiously, 'How's things going?'

One of them paused briefly and shook his head,

'Things are pretty bad.'

As more volunteers were arriving Miriam and the others were asked to move away. She went back to her place on the veranda, keeping watch. Early in the afternoon an important-looking group crossed the yard and went down, causing a murmur of speculation in the crowd and a knot to tighten in Miriam's stomach.

Esther appeared at her elbow. 'That's the chief inspector of mines. He's just arrived from London. You saw those two being brought up?'

Miriam nodded.

'Well they've both died. In the Llay Main party they were. There's still no statement yet so I must get back now.'

Miriam continued to stand in the crowd keeping watch at the pithead for over an hour until Esther joined her again, bringing a mug of sweet black tea and a thick slab of fruitcake.

'I've brought you this and something to eat.'

Miriam refused to turn away. Her eyes were fixed on the headstock wheels.

Esther said, 'I've just heard the second official statement.'

It left Miriam unmoved.

'Do you want to hear it?'

Miriam shrugged.

'Well I'm going to tell you anyway. The situation's still the same. A hundred or possibly a hundred and two are still unaccounted for. They said there'll be another statement as soon as the extent of the fire underground is known.'

Miriam pointed to the tall stacks of sandbags at the pithead. 'What are all those for? They're going to seal the shaft, aren't they? You can tell me. I heard someone say it.'

'They've got no intention of giving up yet. That was

the first thing they stated earlier. No! You've still got everything to hope for, girl.' She let Miriam dwell on her words for a moment before changing the subject. 'I forgot to tell you, Dad was going up to the farm when I left. He'd know you were down here when he found you gone but what about the milking? He can do the poultry, the cattle, and see to Tess but he can't do that.'

Miriam twisted her head. 'They can't be left too long. Seven o'clock at the latest.'

'After we've heard the next statement we can decide what to do. You can stand with me to hear it then you won't have to wait until it's posted up on the boards.'

It was another three hours of watching and waiting before Esther came and took Miriam to stand in front of the manager's office to hear the third official statement read out for the press by the managing director's secretary. Standing on the veranda bareheaded and jacketless with his waistcoat open he held out a paper and clearing his throat he began to read from it in a thin reedy voice.

'The fire on the main road which is preventing exploration of the mine has been fought throughout the day and the latest report is that it is being overcome. It may be that beyond the fire men may be found alive and it is with this hope that no effort is being spared,' he paused to clear his throat again, 'but in any event the death toll will be heavy.'

Miriam allowed herself to be led to the press car. Esther leaned in and wrapped a rug around her, speaking slowly. 'Now listen, girl, after the milking you must come down with Dad and stay with us until the morning and bring Tess. I will be back sometime this evening. The car will come for me very early tomorrow and you can come back down with me then. Dad will go up to the farm later to look after things, don't worry about that.'

Joe was waiting for Miriam as the car dropped her off in

the farmyard, and then left. 'I've done the poultry and I've left word at the bottom farm to stop the milk lorry coming up.' He nodded towards the cattle at the gate. 'They've been there for the last three hours. They've stopped eating.'

Miriam walked past him without replying, staring emptily, distant and aloof. The dog followed, leaping up and licking her hand as she absent-mindedly patted it.

Sometime later the milk frothed and surged as it was poured away down the drain. The cows had needed no urging as they went into their stalls.

Joe stood by patiently waiting in silence until Miriam came out, carrying an empty pail.

Suddenly she hurled the pail at the wall screaming, 'You bloody fool. You didn't have to go down.' Turning she ran to Joe, collapsing in his arms sobbing, 'He's still down there, Dad – he's still down there – all because of that bloody football match.'

Joe held his daughter tightly. 'I know, my girl. I know all about it. I heard it on the wireless.'

'He wouldn't have gone down, Dad, if I'd asked him not to. He didn't have to go. I could've stopped him.'

She sobbed uncontrollably for some time then Joe led her across the farmyard. 'Come on. Come down to us and I'll be back up in the morning to see to everything while you go over to the colliery. There's still hope. It's not over yet.'

At dawn Miriam had been waiting on the veranda for over an hour. Before her the scene of disaster was unfolding. Vehicles of every kind were bringing people into a yard now packed with as many women and children as men with all eyes fixed on the wheels for any sign of movement. Pedestrians were queuing down the road on both sides of the main gate, waiting to get past a convoy of lorries bringing more volunteers from the surrounding collieries. In front of the main building fire-fighting appliances from all the factories in the area and the aerodrome near Chester were lined up.

Miriam felt a hand on her shoulder. It was a smiling Esther. 'There's good news. Progress has been made. They hope to reach the first batch of men by 3.30. It seems they've been able to clear the road so that a pony can work.'

Sceptical, not daring to hope, and trying in vain to suppress the surge of elation sweeping over her, Miriam asked, 'Are you sure?'

'I've had it from a rescuer at the pithead. It's definitely more hopeful, "Slow but steady progress had been reported,"' she quoted. 'It's official. Given everyone at the pithead new hope, it has. Bell-men were sent around Rhos for help and they've been coming by the lorry-load ever since so they've got more than they need. While I was there twenty volunteers were asked for and over a hundred came forward, pushing so hard they had trouble keeping them back. There are over two hundred men working down there now.' She nodded over toward the yard and the pit bank. 'This crowd's growing by the hour. They say there's over a thousand on the bank alone. There'll be even more coming when the good news gets around. Everyone will want to be here when the men come up.'

Time dragged on into the afternoon as Miriam waited and watched the clock on the front of the main building. 3.30 came and went. Where was Esther? The thought hung heavy on her mind. Beset by unease and irritation she looked around for some time before spotting her briefly among the press party at the pithead. The crowd become lively, even animated, as hopes had been raised, and Miriam had shared in that common feeling, but now her mood had given way to the foreboding that was spreading like a dark cloud before the sun, and with it came a heavy silence. Then news spread like wildfire. The first batch of men should be reached by six o'clock.

It brought no comfort to Miriam. A dull coldness had taken hold of her. She withdrew behind it to shield herself from the hope that may be cruelly false. At five o'clock the spinning wheels brought up another body that was quickly identified. It was not Edwin's. Soon afterwards a low murmur of alarm ran through the crowd and Miriam saw the volunteers loading the cages to capacity with sandbags. They went down and ominously came up for more. Some time later she counted six cage-loads of men coming up.

The minutes went by before Esther pressed through the crowd to reach her. 'I think you'd better come into the office with me where you can sit down.'

'No!' Miriam turned away and went back to looking at the pithead. 'I'm staying here. They're bringing them up at six. They said so, didn't they?'

'Miriam.'

Esther was getting to be a pest, maybe if she ignored her she would go away and take her bad news with her.

Now Esther took her arm, 'Miriam, listen to me!'

Miriam shook her hand away still looking at the pithead.

'Miriam, he's not coming up.'

'Of course he is.' She felt quite cheerful now, but how could Esther be so dim? 'Haven't you heard? They're bringing them up at six.' She turned to her. 'Do you think I should go back and get his dinner ready so that it'll be hot for him when he comes home?'

Esther gently took her arm again. 'No, but I think you should go back and do the milking. That's what he'd want you to do. Come on, girl, I've got the car waiting. Dad's up there and I'll be up later.'

Esther finally arrived at the farm late at night and sent the car off. Joe was standing at the back door, his finger to his lips. 'She's in the front room sleeping.' He spoke in a low voice indicating with his thumb. Then he led her to sit with him at the kitchen table in the light of a hurricane lamp. 'She wouldn't tell me anything. She seemed almost cheerful. After she'd done the milking and poured it away and seen to everything else she said she felt like a nap. That was more than two hours ago. She's been out for the count ever since.'

'Leave her for now. You know the latest, I take it?'

'Only what I heard on the wireless before she came but I couldn't make it out very well, it was faint and crackling. There's little juice left in the main battery with the generator not been running and I don't know how to work it.' He nodded at the lamp; 'It's back to this now.' Then he leaned across the table, 'So tell me, what's happened down there?'

Esther took out her reporters' pad. 'The best I can do is take you through the notes I've made.' She flipped it open and holding it closer to the lamp she read aloud from her shorthand. '5.30 p.m., it's been decided to recall the men. There is a continuing series of explosions and fire is raging. Six o'clock, every official concerned with making a final decision had gone down to give their opinion as to whether it is advisable to carry on with the rescue operations. 6.30, just heard they've gone right up to the fire.'

She paused and looked up, 'I stopped making notes here for a while but after some time I go on. The chief inspector is back at the colliery office from underground where he's been for some hours. He says that an agreed statement will be issued officially after all parties have conferred.'

She looked up at Joe. 'I've taken the official statement down, do you want me to read it word for word?'

Joe gestured impatiently for her to do so.

She turned over the page and read on formally with a detached edge to her voice. 'Statement issued eight o'clock. The attempt to overcome the fire in the main road has gone on continuously since yesterday. In spite of very strenuous efforts and although some progress has been made in this road the fire had got a further hold in the road to the right, through which it was hoped at first to reach any possible survivors.

'Today several explosions in the vicinity of the fire on the main road have occurred.

'This afternoon they became more frequent and closer to where the men were working on the fire. The return airway in both the main returns is carrying carbon monoxide in dangerous quantities and it is with great reluctance that all parties – the management, the representatives of the miners, and His Majesty's Inspectors – have come to the conclusion that no person can possibly be alive in the workings.'

She paused before concluding, 'In these circumstances and in view of the increasingly grave risk to the men engaged in combatting the fire it has been decided that it would not be right to continue to expose these workers to such serious risk, and all persons have been withdrawn from the mine.'

She closed her notebook and looked up at Joe. 'It was shortly after this I asked the managing director on behalf of the press how many were on the death roll.'

'And?' Joe asked

'He told us that as near as he could say the total is two hundred and sixty.'

Joe's face paled visibly even in the dim lamplight. 'I thought it was going to be about a hundred. That was bad enough but this – it's nearly the whole shift.'

'I can't say there weren't gasps from our group when we heard that. Some of them hardened journalists too.' She lit a cigarette. Shaking the match until it went out she leaned over the table towards Joe. 'Do you know, Dad, I almost felt sorry for that man? He had to go out and tell those people – those people waiting there in the rain for their men to come up – that there were more than double the expected deaths – that no one was being brought up alive, or even dead.'

She blew out smoke as if to punctuate what she had said. 'They've already started sealing the downcast and the upcast shaft. They'll be entombed down there for ever.'

'Almost,' Joe queried?

'What's that?'

'You said you almost felt sorry for him. Why almost?'

'Dad, it's no secret. They've been detecting gas in that road for six months and the management have ignored it. There's never been proper ventilation in there, despite it being a very gassy road. It would cost too much, they said.'

Suddenly she brought her fist down hard on the table startling Joe. 'Cost!' she shouted glaring fiercely at him. For some moments her eyes flared in anger. 'I saw the cost tonight and I was glad the yard was in darkness as I passed through that crowd to get to the car. It spared me having to see their faces at least.'

'Miriam doesn't have to know all that right now, girl.'

'What don't I have to know?' Miriam, roused by Esther's voice, was standing in the doorway.

Joe rose and took her arm gently. 'Come and sit down.'

She turned to Esther with resignation in her voice. 'You can tell me the worst now. I know he's not coming up. I suppose I've known since yesterday. I just didn't want to hear it.'

'The rescuers have been brought out, girl. They're sealing the roadway to save the rest of the pit. There can't possibly be anyone alive down there. I expect the gas got to them before the fire.'

Miriam slumped into a chair. 'There's no funeral then. He's already buried.' She looked up smiling brightly. 'That's handy isn't it?' But then grief refusing to be denied tore the smile from her face and she fell forward onto the table, convulsed with sobbing. Esther clasped her from behind and held her, pressing her face into Miriam's hair.

There was no future now. No point to all those plans for the farm, the cistern on the top of the well, the boiler for hot running water, the milking, the electric, and Edwin gone. She would never see him again. Gone as if he'd never existed. It seemed impossible. How could it be, never to feel his touch, to hear his voice, no more teasing, no more fun, just as things were starting to – starting to become so fulfilling?

The sobbing ceased and she looked up, casting her eyes around taking in the rough sack hanging behind the back door ready to rub his back when he came – but he was never coming home again – and his brown smock with the cap he wore back to front for the milking so that he could rest his head against the cow without getting his forehead rubbed raw. Then she rose and made towards the front room, pushing Esther's hands from her shoulders. Stepping down she looked around. There was the shotgun propped in the corner with two cartridges near to hand on the sideboard as if waiting for him. She touched the stock, where it was polished by his cheek, lightly with the tips of her fingers. And there was his chair with the copy of the *Farmers' Weekly* on the arm where he liked to keep it, and his slippers. She looked at his slippers. Sitting down limply in her chair she called Tess to her from under the sideboard where the collie had been curled up for most of the day. As she caressed the head resting on her lap she felt a numbness enveloping her and as her muscles relaxed all feeling departed, and she descended again into deep sleep.

Bellevue Park, Wrexham 1957

Esther fidgets. She is finding the park seat uncomfortable. 'So that was it but it didn't end there. Two days later another man was killed on the top when an explosion blew the seal off the shaft, bringing the final toll to two hundred and sixty-six.'

'It must have been terrible for my mother. How did she cope after that?'

'She carried on alone in the farmhouse over the next two years but she gave up the farming, just letting the fields for grazing and scraping by on her salary as a full-time official of the party.'

'But there must have been a disaster fund. She would have had money from that surely?'

'No. She wasn't entitled to any because she had another income and a little money in the bank.'

'And after that was she still a party activist? And what about Mosley did she meet him again?'

'Ah! Sir Oswald and his Blackshirts. Well the street battles continued all over the country and we were in most of them many times, battling with the police who always protected him. We both picked up a few knocks but at Cable Street something happened to Miriam, something ugly.'

'Tell me about it. What happened to my mother?'

Esther stands up stretches then she rubs her backside with both hands. 'This seat's getting bloody hard and I'm getting bloody thirsty.'

Nicholas sees he will have to settle her down before he is going get her to continue. 'Perhaps we could go up to the station. I noticed a buffet there when I got off the train.'

'With a bar?'

He nods. 'With a bar and it should be open now.'

She takes his arm. 'Lead on.'

Chapter Eight

Wrexham General Railway Station, Wrexham 1957

Esther waits for a shunting engine to clank past the window of the buffet, drawing on her cigarette. 'Well! Where was I?' She takes another draw. 'Well from about that August of 1936 Miriam and I followed the situation in Spain almost day by day.'

'In Spain?'

'Yes. You know, Franco's attempted coup? We discussed nothing else at the branch meetings and she even held daily discussion groups. They were packed with unemployed miners and steel workers and it became the main topic at the workers' education sessions. While I was writing articles for the *Daily Worker* and even had some pieces published in *Tribune*, Miriam seemed to be throwing herself into the movement body and soul as if she craved action, submerging herself, her grief perhaps, in work that took up her every waking moment. She became quite well known regularly addressing meetings at Chester and Liverpool, packing the St George's Hall to the doors on some occasions. Oh! And another thing I remember, just like Mosley she seemed to welcome the disturbances her meetings provoked. Her manner of speaking was almost a mirror of his, the other side of the coin so to speak. As if he had branded his personality onto her consciousness. Just like him she could hold a hall spellbound. I felt somewhat uncomfortable with that. I never had such an emotional commitment. No, not to such a degree. I'm more practically minded, I suppose.'

She takes a quick sip of her gin. 'So Franco had struck

at the democratically elected government and it polarized the situation bit by bit, becoming clear to us, particularly to your mother, that Spain was to be the battleground between the left and the right.'

Now Nicholas feels a stab of irritation with what he sees as an attempt to broaden the narrative, shifting the focus from his mother, and it fires his response.

'Democratically elected? The Left in Spain had hardly shown any real respect itself for the democratic process.'

'What do you mean?' Esther's retort is sharp.

'Well credit me with some knowledge of the time. I am reading for a BA in Modern History after all and the Socialist leader Francisco Caballero did threaten civil war if the Right won in the elections of February thirty-six.'

'Nevertheless the republican government was legally elected.'

'Would the Left have accepted the result if the Right had won? You said Franco polarized things but that had already happened. Ideology does that demanding total acceptance with no place for opponents. How long do you think the Marxist parties would have tolerated democracy if the Republic had won?'

Esther is taken aback but only momentarily. 'Ideology! Ideology, ha! What do you know? This wasn't about ideas, about socio-economic theories. It was a war of extinction. It was class against class. The Right: the great landowners who fed their sons into the command of the army, intended to enslave the workers using the Civil Guard and the Moroccan troops to dismantle the reforms gained through the democratic process. They wished to return Spain to the so-called glories of the fifteenth century, back into the mediaeval past de los Reyes Cristianos, the past of the Castilian Queen Isabella la Catolica. For them it was a crusade that justified the slaughtering of whole villages of agricultural workers, women, children, and babies throughout the twenties and thirties in their committed attempt to destroy any move toward the kind of modern society we take for granted.' She pauses, forced to draw breath. 'For them Fascism was something to be used to achieve these ends, not something to be embraced. This is where I differed with your mother. Like you she saw it as a war of ideologies too but as I said before, I'm of a more practical bent. You seem to be more like her. Put yourself in that time.' Esther places a hand on Nicholas' arm, 'Would you have been as neutral and detached as you are now? Ideology was important to her and I think it is for you too. You should beware,' she lifts her glass and points it at him momentarily, 'you may get yourself into something.' She pauses before taking a sip then, tapping the table with the finger of her other hand to give her words emphasis, she says, 'Either way that's what the Right intended in Spain, to use Fascism, and whichever way we looked at it we saw it as a tyranny and an international threat to the whole of Europe and modern civilization.' She takes another sip from her glass by way of punctuation. 'We were vindicated four years later.'

'How can you say that after what you must have been through in Budapest only last year?' Nicholas pauses to give weight to his words, 'For much of Europe Fascist tyranny has been replaced by the Soviet kind.'

'Fascism hasn't been replaced by anything in Spain.' Esther's words, though calm, have an icy bite. 'The defeated are still feeling the weight of Franco's spite. He obviously feels free to exercise his obsession for retribution. It shows no sign of slackening as far as I can see.' While she speaks Nicholas' eyes are drawn to her hands, twisting a matchstick into tiny pieces between her nicotine-stained fingers.

He didn't intend the discussion to go in this direction. Indeed he didn't want a discussion at all. What happened to his mother at Cable Street? That was the way he wanted it to go.

Patiently Esther goes on, 'What I'm trying to tell you is that Miriam, like me and many others, came to see Spain as the battleground that would decide the future. Oh, I have to admit that I don't know whether it did. Maybe a republican victory would have prevented the last war or maybe Spain was the first round in it.'

Nicholas holds his palms open in a pacifying shrug. 'I just find it hard to understand how someone like my mother could have drifted into that situation; a school teacher, a farmer's wife, becoming so militantly extreme, a demagogue.'

'After Edwin who knows what grief and loss she went through, unable to come to terms with knowing he was still down there? The party provided a social life for her. It made her feel she mattered. We all felt involved in great events on a world stage in the discussions we had long into the night.'

'Cable Street?' Nicholas is getting impatient.

London, Sunday October 4th 1936

'Miriam! I said we must stay here.' Esther was tugging at Miriam's coat and shouting at the top of her voice over the roar of the multitude massed in Trafalgar Square for the anti-Fascist demonstration organised by the Communist Party of Great Britain, but to no avail. As Miriam elbowed her way up the steps onto the street she pretended not to hear and when a tram with Aldgate on the board came grinding up she joined the mass of demonstrators pushing on with Esther close behind.

Although they were packed tightly in the aisle Miriam managed to wave the leaflet announcing the counter demonstration in Aldgate and Cable Street under Esther's nose. 'If you want to let the Blackshirts march wherever they choose then get off now. Go back to the square. Go on! Put your head in the sand and hope they'll go away. I'm going over to the East End because that's where the Fascists are, and that's where they've got to be stopped.' Heads were turning and she realised she was shouting but she didn't care.

Esther pulled her close and hissed in her ear, 'But we're not part of any group. We'll be marching with a mob of all sorts like this one. It'll be a riot with everyone for themselves.'

'Look,' Miriam was still shouting, 'I've told you what to do. You can get off if you want to but I'm going on.'

Esther turned for the door as the tram moved slowly through a horde of demonstrators scrambling aboard, overwhelming the conductor and jamming the already tightly packed car so that she could only shrug complacently.

The crowds at the end of Whitechapel High Street were so thick the tram became caught up in the throng. As Miriam and Esther were carried from it with the demonstrators they stepped into the roar of jeering and ironical cheers that greeted the arrival of a busload of policemen that soon became jammed in the traffic.

Somehow word got round over the deafening noise: the Fascist procession was forming in Royal Mint Street. The sisters found themselves swept along in the torrent of bodies until by chance an eddying current carried them against a barrier that had been thrown across the road by the police.

Beyond the barrier an extraordinary sight unfolded before their eyes as the Fascist contingents were arriving to take up their positions in their Blackshirt uniforms. Many of them were wearing jackboots and black-peaked military caps with red armbands. A number of men and women were lying in the roadway on the other side of the barrier and ambulance men were assisting them.

The catcalling of the crowd and the rhythmic chanting of, 'Rats, Rats, Rats' deafened them and as the police force at the barrier was strengthened by reinforcements with drawn truncheons, missiles were thrown at a detachment of Blackshirts and the crowd became even noisier, with the sisters being crushed against the toppling barrier.

Fortunately they both went over with it, sprawling under the swiftly launched police charge that passed over them, leaving them on hands and knees in the road amid screams and scuffles.

Suddenly, from behind the police lines, a motorcar swung across the road with wire netting in place of windows. Out of it leapt a group of Blackshirts and from their gauntleted hands they started flinging missiles into the crowd in a determined and measured way.

Esther called to Miriam, 'Stay down!'

But too late she saw the potato burst in Miriam's face and watched in horror as she was hurled sideways by the force of the blow, hitting the road and rolling over and over before coming to rest on her back, her eyes staring blue-grey from a mask of blood with three razor blades

94

embedded in it and her cheek and lip hanging in a scarlet and purple flap of flesh.

Someone was seizing her arms. There were two of them. She could see the pavement passing in front of her face. Intriguingly large splashes of blood were appearing on it. Whenever she stopped moving it turned into a red mist. It was a good thing she had her shoes laced tightly or they would be dragged off as they rubbed along, and why couldn't she get to her feet anyway? She attempted to struggle. Then everything became black.

She was awake. She tried to lift her arms but they were held tight. Everything was so white. She was in a bed and she was aware of an encompassing smell. What was it, disinfectant, carbolic? She could see the ceiling though her right eye was covered with something. This wasn't her bed. Where was she? She moved her head a little but when she stopped the ceiling kept moving and a wave of nausea swept over her as she sank into blackness.

She was awake again. A man's face appeared. 'Ah, you've woken up.' Then he seized her eyelid, rolled it up, and shone a light in her eye. 'Hum,' then he disappeared.

She suddenly realised the woman moving around her bed was a nurse. There was intense pain in the right side of her face. She managed to pull her arm out of the sheets to touch it but it was covered with a bandage. The rest of her face felt numb when she cautiously explored it. She was desperately thirsty. What was that nurse doing to her? She tried to put the thought into words but her lips wouldn't do what she wanted. Now the nurse was poking a straw between her lips. She sucked fiercely on it. There was someone else with her, two of them, all in white except one of them had a vivid red cape as well. It hurt her eyes. Now they were trying to push something into her mouth. It was porridge. After that – blackness.

'Miriam!' That was her name, she knew that, but she couldn't be bothered to open her eyes.

'Miriam!' This time she opened them and there was Esther. She recognised her immediately but why was she looking so grave?

'Hello. Don't speak, you'll disturb the stitches, they say. Do you know me? Just move your head if you can.'

Of course she did. Cautiously she chanced a nod.

'Can you remember what happened?'

Something happened. That's why she was here in this bed. She would only move her eyes this time.

'You've been here for two weeks. They've told me that tomorrow they'll know when you can leave.'

It had been two or was it three days since she first heard Esther's voice in this place. She was sitting in a chair now. As long as she didn't make any sudden moves the nausea remained at bay. She knew there was something wrong with her face. Esther had explained what had happened but she had no recollection of it. There was talk of stitches being taken out but right now she would just close her eyes.

She was a little girl in the night creeping out of the house while everyone slept. She wasn't dressed but it didn't matter, for no one would see her in the dark. She must find Dad. He had gone over to the pit at the back of the house. If she didn't find him he would never come home again. It wasn't the least disturbing to find herself floating over the field and down to the pit but it was now an entrance to a grotto choked in ferns. She must thrust her way through them even though they pulled at her hair because this is where Dad would be. Inside there was a stone labyrinth lit by a strange blue light. Its mossy walls led her round and round until she came to a circular well set in the slippery flags of the floor. Kneeling down she peered into the blackness then something small but dense dropped onto her head. It crawled in her hair, the tiny needle- like tips of its feet pricking her scalp. She plucked at it with both hands but it escaped and scuttled onto her forehead, its gossamer wings rustling like dried leaves. With tiny hands it lifted her lid and its golden orbs peered into her eye. The face below its antennae reminded her of the Tylwydd Teg in her picture book. She had to brush it off but she could not move. No matter how hard she tried her arms would not obey her. Then it is slowly climbed down her cheek. She could feel the minute hands painfully pinching her skin as it gained a hold. At last she was free of the paralysis and she wrenched the creature from her. With an angry rustling of wings it struggled thrusting against her fingers. She overbalanced and toppled into the well falling down and down and down and – she made to sit up but hands restrained her. She was awake.

'Yes, well with the help of an ambulance man I got you to this hospital.'

Esther was filling in the pieces of the jigsaw again. Things were coming back to her. They'd told her she'd had twenty-three stitches down her face from forehead to mouth. Her eye should be fine once the swelling went down, they said. She had not looked in a mirror yet. Esther had promised she would be there when she did.

'It's been almost three weeks now. The party arranged lodgings for me and allowed me the use of the telephone. Your medical bills are also being looked after.' She nodded to the nurses at the end of the white-tiled ward. 'You've still got concussion, they say, but you'll be well enough for me to take you home the day after tomorrow, then you must rest for a while. They're giving you a letter to take with you to the clinic at Wrexham. Edwin's brother Jim has been keeping an eye on the farm and looking after Tess. Can you understand me?'

Miriam nodded. There was no need for Esther to shout. It was still very painful to speak but that didn't mean she'd lost her marbles.

'Evelyn has been down to tell Dad what happened.'

She mumbled painfully, 'How did he take it?'

'Oh, as well as can be expected.' Esther said cheerfully. Dad hadn't been told how badly injured Miriam's face was yet. He'd have to know at some time though. God knew what he'd do when he saw her. And what would Miriam do when they brought her the hand mirror?

While the dressing was being removed Esther sat at the bedside, holding the mirror and shielding the glass with her coat as if Miriam's image was already captured by it.

The cool air felt good on the exposed skin. It had been itching for days.

'Now remember, the doctor's told you however bad it looks now it will soon improve. The flesh around the wound is still swollen but the inflammation will subside in a few days.' She turned to the nurse, 'It will look better day by day, isn't that right, nurse?'

'Yes, that's right, it can only look better each day now and the stitch marks will fade completely in time.' She nodded meaningfully for Esther to turn the mirror to Miriam.

'Are you ready, Miriam?'

Hesitating for a moment; this was something she had to do, she nodded and Esther held it up.

It wasn't her face. It couldn't be. She became conscious of a sustained moan that rose and fell. After some moments she realised it was escaping from her own throat. It should have been a scream but searing pain prevented her mouth from opening wide enough to express her disbelief, horror, and despair. Unexpressed these feelings were trapped deep inside her. In time they would feed a smouldering anger.

There was a furrow, swollen, inflamed, and lined on either side by the black dots of the stitch marks. Those obscene purple folds running down her temple were bridging her partially closed right eye and crossing her cheek to her lip where the slice of flesh had been sewn back before ending at the gash in the corner of her mouth, drawing it toward her chin.

She seized the mirror and clasped it to her as if to smother the image of her ruined face. Then she fell back on the bed, staring at the ceiling. There was a trickle of blood from the corner of her mouth. The attempt to scream had reopened the wound.

Chapter Nine

The farm, Wrexham, 1936

She pulled on her coat. It was getting chilly out, with the end of October only a few days off. Putting on her beret she glanced in the mirror before opening the door.

Oh that face!

Unhooking the mirror and holding it in her hands she slumped onto a chair at the kitchen table. Hesitantly and cautiously she forced herself to maintain her image in the glass.

It was nearly two weeks since she'd been home. The wound had healed surprisingly quickly. She ran her finger along the deep crease where her cheek and lip had been sewn back together. It twisted her mouth down at the corner. Thank God her speech hadn't been affected. The scar was yellowing in parts, taking on the colour and texture of ivory, but elsewhere it was still raw and red. This was her face now, mocking, her mouth forever sneering back at her and the rest of the world. Were these her true feelings on show, disdainful, contemptuous; surely not? But others may think so and they may respond so. That was what she was going to have to manage. When she went out today it would be the first time she would be meeting folk who knew her from before, apart from Esther and Dad. Would she be able to face them, with their eyes always giving them away? It was bad enough on the train with those people staring and trying not to do so and she not knowing where to look. She must develop the ability to stare back. Look them boldly in the face. Dad and Esther were still not used to it, tending to speak to her scar rather than to her.

Miriam had come to a decision about Spain. She would tell Esther about it and talk over the final details after today's meeting. Walking on the moor, stumbling through the heather, day after day, driven on by her thoughts and the need for a resolution had left her exhausted but composed. What else was there to do but to get into the fight? Those deeply serious meetings at the branch long into the night, the discussions, the lectures, and so on that were so much a part of her life, giving it meaning and making her feel important, as if she were involved in history: now they no longer seemed central to her world. Now was the time for action. That's what Mosley had been saying all along. Well this was it. There was nothing more to do on the streets of Britain. She'd turned the matter over time and time again. There was nothing for her here. Farming life was over and so was teaching. What future could she see? Any sort of answer would have to be suspended until Fascism was defeated. Her decision brought a tranquil readiness, and that was all that mattered to her.

She must get down for that bus or she'd miss it.

Esther stubbed out her cigarette in the ashtray, her eyes fixed on Miriam, though her mind was elsewhere. It had been a difficult meeting for Miriam but nevertheless it had gone well enough, and now she said she had something important to talk over. Esther had an idea what was coming from the way Miriam had been speaking. Going out to Spain had occurred to Esther too as a journalist, of course, but the paper had made it clear that they could get all the information they needed from the news agencies. However to go out to fight – to take up a rifle – to kill and by so doing to – what, to save Spain from Fascism? Was a Socialist republic worth fighting and killing for? Maybe. It seemed Miriam thought so, but for her how much was it to do with revenge, to get back at the Fascists for what they'd done to her face, to her as a person? For there was no doubt she had changed, not too obviously on the surface but deeply nevertheless. It was there in the way she spoke, her tone, her bearing, even her eyes, especially her eyes. They'd become cold, steely, and hard, as if she herself had been tempered.

But what of herself, why had she decided to go? Well her first-hand accounts may even be able to influence public opinion, alert people to the danger. She would certainly gain the authority of personal experience. But there had to be more than that behind her decision. Did she really believe it was worth taking up arms? She couldn't be sure but if she didn't go she would never find out. That's why she must go too.

Miriam rapped the table to get Esther's attention. Lifting her voice above the lively spontaneous debates in the crowded reading room, she said, 'You know they've been calling for volunteers since September. Hundreds are going over there.'

'Yes, I know,' Esther snapped out of her reverie. 'Go on.'

'You heard them talking about it at the meeting today. I wouldn't be surprised if many of our members went.'

'It was you who was doing most of the talking.'

'Well.' Miriam shrugged.

'The recruitment started while you were in hospital,' said Esther. 'The International Brigades, they're calling them, but do you realise this is foreign intervention on the part of the Soviets? They're the ones who are doing the calling in the first instance, not the republic.'

'Yes, I know about the brigades, but that's what I'm saying, Italy and Germany are already in there supporting Franco. The democracies are not going to be taking part. Non-intervention, they're calling it. They're finished. We've said that many times.'

'You're going to volunteer, aren't you? That's what you're trying to tell me.'

'I've thought of nothing else since coming out of hospital and I've worked it all through in my mind. They're forming women's battalions within the brigades. There's a number I can telephone in Liverpool at the offices of the Transport and General Workers' Union. Unofficially they can tell me how I can get to the recruiting centre in Paris and I think they issue some kind of identity card.'

'You haven't talked any of this over with me.'

'I'm talking it over with you now, aren't I?'

'I shouldn't have left you up there on your own. Are you certain this isn't to do with your concussion, and what about poor old Dad, and the farm, and Tess?'

'I've thought about that too. I've been speaking to Jim, you know, Edwin's brother? He says he will see to the farm. He can sell it or keep it going for himself, whatever he wants. His cattle are grazing on it anyway and he'll have Tess. She'll be happier with him at his place. She misses the work. As to the question of concussion, in other words my judgement, and of course you mean this too,' Miriam ran her finger down her face, 'well I can't say for certain this has nothing to do with it but I believe strongly enough that I would come to the same decision whether I'd got this at Cable Street or not. Now the struggle has moved on. Spain is bigger than Cable Street. It's the battleground that will decide the future of Europe. This fight has been inevitable for some time and I want to get in it.'

'And Dad?'

'What can I say about Dad? D'you think I haven't thought about him? But he'll have you. He won't be on his own.'

'So that's it. I wondered why you haven't asked me to go with you. You want me to look after him while you go off to fight.' Miriam opened her mouth to object but Esther went on, 'Well there's a problem about that.'

'What's the problem?'

Esther remained silent.

'Esther! You don't mean –'

'You're not the only one whose been thinking about it. I'll tell Dad I've been sent on an assignment and I'll be able to look after you. You can tell him you're just going as a nurse or something non-combatant like that.'

'But you do know we'll be going as combatants, don't you, and you know what that means?'

'Yes. I'm quite clear about that.'

Chairs were being put up on tables. It was time to leave.

PART TWO

PARIS, MADRID, MOSCOW, 1936-1939.

Chapter Ten

Paris, November 1936

The engine slowly panted into the Gare du Nord. A weak November sun sent it shafts slanting onto the echoing concourse through the smoke and steam rising high to the glass roof as Miriam and Esther climbed hesitantly down from the car. The walk along the platform seemed endless. With only a day excursion ticket and no passport they evaded the glances of their fellow travellers. They were mostly men carrying brown paper parcels under their arms or, like them, with haversacks slung across their shoulders.

When they went out to the taxi rank according to their instructions their attempt to remain inconspicuous seemed in vain. They felt everyone was watching them.

'This way, comrades.' The voice barely audible above the commotion of the traffic came from a figure cautiously emerging from behind a pillar and gesturing towards a taxi already filling up. It started to pull away even as they were cramming into it.

The driver called out in English, 'It's just a short journey to the reception centre.' After that nobody spoke. With her face pressed against the windows by someone's back Miriam had no choice but to take in the unfamiliar street scenes that flashed by. This was the first time she or Esther had set foot on foreign soil. The taxi swung off Rue Montmartre, climbing a steep cobbled street before turning into a gloomy passage and lurching to a stop behind a small bus disgorging more comrades from its rear door.

After squeezing out of the taxi in the constricted space they followed the driver through a narrow opening cut in a

109

pair of ornate but dilapidated doors giving onto a dingy courtyard that smelled of rotting vegetables and drains. The sisters exchanged uneasy glances as the driver ushered everyone into a side entrance before disappearing.

They found themselves in a room filled with rows of chairs. It was dimly lit from small windows high up near the ceiling. At the farthest end of the room a man in a dark blue seaman's jersey was seated at a table, sorting through papers. The flag of the Spanish Republic had been hung on the wall behind him, partially covering a large crucifix. A tall man whose skeletal features and long black leather coat gave him a reptilian appearance was standing at the table. He waved to the chairs; many were already occupied, before sitting down. Miriam and Esther took a seat with the others, their feet echoing on the dusty floorboards. As they sat another taxi was arriving with its cargo of volunteers. When the clamour of footsteps subsided a brief glance told Miriam they were the only women in the room.

The man sorting the papers looked up. He had a bandage around his head holding a yellow pad over one eye. He asked, '*Qui parlent le francais*?'

Two hands went up. He nodded, asking again, '*L' Espanol*?' There was no response. A bell started tolling somewhere in the building. He gazed around the room, waiting for it to cease before speaking. 'How many have had military training?' His English was good. He nodded in acknowledgement as many hands went up. 'Has anyone used a machine gun in action?'

Two hands went up.

'It was the Lewis gun, yes?'

Both nodded.

He made a note of their names and then looking up he said, 'You will shortly be taken from here to the Gare d' Austerlitz. When you are there, do not group together. Spread out so as not to draw attention. As you leave here you will be given a ticket for Marseille. Once there you will be hidden up for two days or so until we can get you over to Barcelona by ship. With the ticket there is a slip of paper with one sentence in Spanish. It says that you are a Spanish worker going back home. This is your first lesson in the language. Learn it well, for if the police stop you and you do not sound at least half convincing even though they are tending to, as you say in English, turn a blind eye, you will be spending some time in a French prison.'

He passed the papers to his reptilian colleague, speaking briefly to him in French, then he turned back to the room. 'At Barcelona you will enrol in the Eleventh International Brigade of the Army of The Republic of Spain.' He addressed Miriam and Esther, 'You will both join the Women's Battalion of the Brigade as militia women.' Then he continued to address the whole group. 'Parade ground drill and weapons training will start immediately. Soon after that, very soon after that, you will go up to Madrid where you are urgently needed. By then you should have a fair grasp of Spanish.' Then he paused, leaning forward to give emphasis to his words. 'Finally, I must tell you this, the moment you enrol and receive your first pay you come under military discipline. The penalty for disobedience or cowardice is death.'

In the silence that followed Miriam's thoughts turned inward. Dad had been shocked when they told him they were going to Spain. That look of resignation in his eyes when he stood at the carriage window made it clear he didn't believe they were non-combatant. No. Not for a single moment, and when he collapsed onto the platform seat at the guard's whistle, bringing his hands to his eyes in his desolation so that he wouldn't see them go, it was unbearable. As the train jerked into motion she'd forced herself to watch for as long as possible as he sat with his coat pulled over his head. The memory still brought pangs of remorse and sorrow. But now she would put the past behind her. Her life was going to depend on people like these in the room. They were to be the principal factors in her existence from now on. She would immerse herself in action.

There was a loud knock on the door. 'That is the signal,' the reptilian man said. 'The transport is here. Collect your tickets from me then on your way out you will find food and drink for the journey. *Bonne chance*, comrades.' He gave the clenched-fist salute.

At the door people were clustering around large baskets in which were loaves of bread, shallots, and bottles of wine with the corks partly drawn. They filled their haversacks with the loaves and shallots and Esther took two bottles of wine as well.

'What are we supposed to do with these?' Esther was holding one of the shallots. Darkness had fallen and they were standing on the platform in the dim glow of a gas lamp.

'Do what I've done. Peel it and pop it in, but fill your mouth with bread first.'

They were both very hungry and Miriam found her shallot quite sweet as she munched it after taking a bite of the large loaf she was holding with both hands. Pulling a face, Esther did the same. Soon their hunger was satisfied and both feeling thirsty they turned their attention to the wine. Esther pulled the cork and put the bottle to her lips, expecting it to be sweet and thirst-quenching, like lemonade. She spat it out, 'It's like bloody vinegar, girl. However do they drink it?'

Miriam took a sip and rolled it around her mouth before swallowing. It made her thirstier. She noticed a railway worker filling a can from a waterspout. 'Come on.' She pointed to it, 'We'll wait 'til he's gone.' Then they went to the waterspout, cupping their hands to slake their thirst.

They were washing themselves down at the waterspout

as best they could when an engine puffed slowly past them, drawing their train along the platform. Soon they were on board travelling south through the night, singing the *Internationale* with those they had recently been so carefully avoiding, sharing bread, cheese, shallots, olives, wine, and pungent Gauloises Bleu cigarettes.

Chapter Eleven

Madrid, December 1936

Almost immediately the fighting started Miriam became separated from Esther when she was allocated to a different section. On her first morning in action she was positioned in a shattered doorway. Her section was pouring volley after volley into the windows of the building opposite. Suddenly a short burst of heavy machine-gun fire raked the wall at her side, splashing stinging and cutting fragments of brick in her face, causing her to double up instinctively. A longer burst relentlessly drove her back into a room filling with explosions of plaster and dust. She dropped her rifle and fell to her knees, hands covering her head. When it stopped she lurched to her feet. Tottering and numb with shock she took hold of the rifle and was attempting to aim through stinging tears when arms seized her shoulders and pulled her back, still clutching the stock of the weapon. She was the only survivor of the machine gun attack on her section. It was then she experienced for the first time what it was to be on the receiving end of an artillery barrage. With a terrifying sound the shells crashed into the building, making the ground rise up with every explosion and causing her muscles to contract with an involuntary rigor. Splinters and shards of metal whined and buzzed through the air while giant hands seemed to clap on her ears. Under cover of the barrage the nationalists were crossing the river, breaking through and establishing themselves deep in the Universita Faculta de Arquitectura.

While still recovering, Miriam was re-allocated to

another section and found herself taking part in the battalion counter-attack, charging across open ground in the face of intense fire, scrambling into rooms through windows after grenades had been thrown and blindly exchanging shots through ceilings before moving on house by house, each time leaving behind casualties. By that evening a front line had been established through the libraries in the universidad. The nationalists had been driven back. Their attempted breakthrough had failed.

Carefully Esther cleared the fragments of brick and tile that obstructed her field of fire so as not to raise the dust that would give away her sniping position. Then setting the back-sight of the rifle to the range she looked along the barrel and covered the machine gunner's head with the front sight, lining up the slot while allowing for the kick up and to the right. Framed by the slot his head seemed twice the size it should be. The fore and aft cap with its tassel was pulled down at a rakish angle, nicely presenting the side of his temple. That olive-smooth skin, the thought flashed through her mind, yet to feel a razor. His eyes were squinting through thick black curls as he aimed the gun. She pressed her cheek to the cool metal of the breach and caught the faint smell of oil. Taking up first pressure on the trigger she let her breath out gently and held it feeling her heart slowing, slowing and – she squeezed.

Immediately she rolled on her side over and over to get to a prepared position behind a breastwork of sandbags and peered out across the rubble through a narrow slit. The second man serving the Maxim had pulled the body clear of the gun and was directing his fire accurately to where she had been, throwing up pieces of tile and dust. She resolutely worked the bolt to reload and aimed again. He fell across the breach, tipping the silenced barrel so that it pointed up at the smoke-filled sky.

Flattening herself against the ground with a grunt of

satisfaction she waited as the battalion counter-attack opened with grenades and mortars exploding in front of her. She had moved up well ahead of her lines under cover of darkness to take up this sniping position. Her comrades were now joining her at the breastwork, firing furiously at the nationalists who were falling back across the open ground of the Universita Faculta de Arquitectura. Experience of the last few days told her that this would only produce a temporary lull. Soon they would attack again, probably when the planes and the big guns started their bombardment.

Just over two weeks later Miriam was in a frontline trench, slumped over a low breastwork of heavy volumes from the university libraries; the ancient books gave better protection than sandbags. Exhausted emotionally as well as physically, with lips blue with cold, hair caked in brick dust, her cordite-reeking clothes clung to her by a mixture of cold sweat, dried blood, and plaster that made her skin smart. The old and obsolete rifle had become almost useless through constant use. It seemed as if every other round was a stoppage. She marvelled at how expert she had become at clearing the breach and making each shot count, as well as finding opportunities for cover. She felt as if she'd been soldiering all her life and her rifle and haversack had always been part of her night and day. Further to the west she could hear shelling and aircraft. How indifferent she'd become to those sounds. When she first came up to the front they filled her with apprehension. She saw the medical orderlies going forward shouldering their rolled up stretchers, shrugging mentally on realising they aroused only the mildest interest in her even when they returned carefully and laboriously carrying their burdens. She was empty of feeling, at least for the present.

Wearily gazing around at what was left of her battalion occupying this section of the line she could recognise no one from Albacete. They were strangers to her, talking in all the languages of Europe. She'd become adept at working out what she could not understand and her comrades in the battalion, she noticed for the first time, were now made up of men as well as women.

She allowed her thoughts to surface. It had been several weeks since they were at sea out of Marseille. Their destination had been changed from Barcelona to Alicante. No one had told them why but in the cold grey light of morning they could see a warship shadowing them on the horizon. A diet of nothing but beans, olive oil, and bread washed down with sour wine had left them with dysentery, and those barracks at the induction centre on the Calle de la Libertad: what a disgusting state they'd been in when they arrived, until the German communists came and they'd set to cleaning them up. Then it had been on to Albacete.

Oh that first day, lined up on the parade ground after they'd had their hair cut short, all women recruits ignorant of the most elementary military skills; she'd been issued with what was supposed to be a uniform, khaki beret, jerkin, breeches, men's shorts, thick socks, and those crippling boots. During long lectures by the commissars and the group discussions they were told they'd be properly trained soldiers with good rifles when they went into action with the Brigade.

Then it had been about how to salute an officer and marching in step. Her feet had become badly swollen. She recalled the trench digging. Ah, the trench digging and the awe on feeling the weight of that rifle when weapons were issued. This was quickly dispelled as it became clear that it was from a batch of ten obsolete sorts from eight countries sent from the USSR. Together they scrabbled in boxes of assorted ammunition of different calibres to find the right bullets. Some of them were so old they were breaking away from their cartridges.

The following days were taken up with weapons training; how to operate the bolt, how to aim, how to clear a stoppage. There was political indoctrination, more marching in step, ammunition discipline, and more trench digging. Then almost before they drew breath they were up to Madrid and into the line.

Heavy fighting by the government militias in early November had failed to stem the nationalists' advance. They had arrived with their battalion as the Eleventh Brigade was forcing the nationalists to retreat just a few hundred metres in the central part of the Calle de Campo, suffering severe losses as they did so.

The smell of hot food broke into her consciousness, arousing a great hunger, and reminding her she had not eaten since the day before, which seemed so long ago. Looking to the rear through the dust still suspended in the smoky evening air she saw a line of handcarts being pushed from the direction of the Calle de Velazquez, bringing victuals from the cafés nearby. She pulled out her mess tin and held it up for a ladleful of steaming stew and a hunk of bread. Her canteen was filled with a mixture of water and wine. The food and drink brought with it a return of feeling that prompted anxiety as well as a bout of shivering. Where was Esther? She felt a pang of guilt. She'd not given her a thought for some time. Had she been wounded? Was she alive?

The next morning in the icy chill of first light Miriam's section was quiet, but the noise of savage fighting and heavy shelling was still coming from the west, and by mid-morning the monotonous droning of motors heralded the arrival of the bombers.

The planes attacked the densely built up areas to the east of Miriam's position. Each time the explosions and crash of masonry crept closer she lay on her back in the trench, watching the silver Italian Savoia 81s and the German Junkers 52s glinting in the weak sun, until the din ebbed, then she peered over the edge of the trench at the columns of oily black smoke rising above the rooftops. Everywhere there was the acrid scent of burning in her nostrils and a rubbery taste in her mouth. This was the first time the city, and indeed she herself, had experienced aerial bombardment on such a scale.

During a lull in the bombing and shelling the movement of a militiaman stirred her curiosity. It was a sargento crawling down the line, examining the faces of those he came to. With some he pointed to the rear, prompting them to scuttle across open ground to take cover in a shattered building. Behind him a column of troops had entered the trenches, moving along to take the places of those who were leaving.

He squeezed past the man nearest to her and crept up, putting his dark stubbly face close to hers. '*Mujer?*' He smiled revealing the stumps of black teeth.

She turned her face aside from the garlic fumes, momentarily bemused.

He made to snatch at her beret and expose her hair.

Slapping his hand away instinctively she realised what he was asking and nodded. After all, she reasoned to herself, she could hardly blame him for not being able to tell whether she was a woman or a man given the way she must look.

He prodded her in the middle of her chest and pointed over to where the others had gone, '*Dejar!*'

She hesitated.

'*Rapido! Entiende?*'

Climbing out of the trench, she hobbled stiffly over to join the other militiawomen in a large roofless building, keeping out the low sun. Everyone was smoking, stamping their feet, and rubbing their hands against the damp, cold air.

'What's going on?'

'We're being pulled out of the line.'

'Can't say I'm sorry,' a voice from the corner.

Eventually the building became packed to overflowing so that there were more outside than in. When it was clear the air raids had stopped for the day, although the shelling had increased, the sargento turned up and formed them into a long column, straggling across the open rubble strewn ground. After two false starts, due to incoming shells, he marched them off through the smoking ruins of the university city into the narrow streets of a residential area. The column became increasingly ragged as they stumbled over fallen masonry or took cover during a spell of shelling.

This was the first time Miriam had been in the city itself or seen the effects of the siege. Across her path was the skeleton of a mule killed in the bombing. Housewives had stripped it bare and a pack of starving dogs was gnawing at the bones. She was curious to see people emerging from cover to resume strolling after the last round had fallen, with street life going on almost normally. Impressed as she was by this nonchalance in the face of shellfire, Miriam realised that she herself had stopped flinching or instinctively doubling up at the sound of every incoming shell. She had also become as proficient as they in gauging how close it would land. As the streets opened onto the Calle de Bravo Murillo she could see people were still going to work on tramcars that were running, with gangs continually repairing the damaged tracks.

The column was bunching up and shuffling on its heels now, and Miriam could see it was turning sharply into an archway in the high wall of a large building. From the end of a dark passageway leading from the arch came shrieking and raucous shouting, drowning the continuing rumble of artillery and the explosions of shells.

Stepping out of the passageway and squinting at the bright sunlight she was met by an astonishing sight. The building had been a large cavalry barracks. The column was pouring onto a great cobbled square where horses had formerly been washed and groomed. It was not horses that were being washed today though. In the centre was a tightly packed group of some hundred or more militiawomen, naked except for their boots. They were being hosed by men on the periphery roaring with laughter as they watched the women scrub their pallid bodies with lye soap amid the noise that Miriam had heard coming through the passage. In a corner of the square a smouldering mound of clothing sent noxious wisps of white smoke to hang in the air. Women were emerging from a doorway dressed in clean items of uniform that were ill assorted and mismatched, as if they had been snatched up in a poor light and hastily pulled on.

Taken aback by the spectacle Miriam stood still for some moments as she became aware of unintelligible instructions in many languages blaring metallically from a loud speaker. By taking note of what the others were doing Miriam was able to make out the gist of them. She went over to a wall with a long line of benches set against it and placed her pack, ammunition belt, and rifle on them Reluctant to part with things that had become so much a part of her she took care to see that her name and number she had painted on each was still legible. Then after some hesitation she started to undress for the first time in over two weeks. Dropping her jerkin and beret she hesitantly pulled at her shirt. It separated reluctantly from her back. The cold sharp air felt clean on her skin, out-weighing any remaining modesty, especially when she saw the pale, faintly luminescent globular bodies of the lice pulsing in the seams. She had known for some days that they were in the lining of her beret. She had been popping them every night with a match flame. Peeling off the rest of her foul-smelling clothes and stepping back into her boots she joined those at the fire, watching the legs of her breeches kicking and dancing as they sailed through the hot air onto the pile as it suddenly flamed up.

The initial shock of the icy water from the hoses made her gasp and for a moment took her breath away but she soon followed the others, vigorously working the disinfectant soap into the hair on her head, under her arms, and between her legs, enthusiastically scrubbing away the body lice and smaller parasites. She felt reborn as she revelled in the feeling of clean flesh. Walking over to the bench she picked up her kit and carrying her rifle by the sling she strode toward the clothing room. The icy air tautening her skin renewed her confidence as she treated the men with the hoses to a contemptuous and defiant stare.

She passed through the door and looked around what had once been a barrack room, dimly lit from narrow windows and a couple of electric lights flickering with each salvo of shells. There were tables down the middle of the floor where clothing was being issued and around the walls women were dressing before being ushered out by an orderly who pointed them in the direction of another building across the square. A large multi-lingual sign over a doorway at the opposite end of the room caught her eye. COMRADES, BRING YOUR PARTY CARD AND PAY BOOK THROUGH THIS WAY. She delved in her pack and holding the papers in her teeth she picked up her kit and weapon and stepped through the doorway down into a smaller, even gloomier chamber.

Her eyes adjusted to the poor light struggling through the wire mesh of a chipped enamel shade in the ceiling. Against the far wall there were boxes containing more clothing. Despite the dimness she could see it was clearly of a better quality than that in the barrack room. Apart from a male orderly seated at a table in the middle of the floor shuffling papers she appeared to be the only other person in the room. He held a list up to the light and crosschecked her card and pay book. Satisfied, he copied down her name and details then passed them back to her.

'Get dressed, comrade.' He indicated the boxes behind him with his thumb before returning to his papers, seemingly unaffected by the spectacle of a woman standing before him naked except for her boots. As Miriam turned and went over to the boxes a figure moved from the shadows, holding out a hand for the orderly's list and without looking at him scanned it then passed it back.

She started selecting items of clothing that included a tunic of serge and a heavy greatcoat.

'You are allowed two sets of underwear and socks, Comrade Moss.'

Startled she spun around. The voice, a man's, came from the table behind her, but it was not that of the orderly who continued diligently working on his lists.

'And a blanket.'

The owner of the voice moved out from the shadows and came over to her. He was tall and probably in his late thirties, with cropped fair hair showing from under his blue beret. The nine millimetre heavy automatic pistol on his cross belt and his black leather jacket marked him as a Soviet commissar.

'How do you know my name?'

His almond-shaped eyes above high cheekbones skimmed over her breasts, her stomach, and down to her pubic hair before he lifted his face to look closely into hers. There was a glint of curiosity in his bright blue pupils as he took in the scar.

He jerked his head in the direction of the table behind him. 'It is on that list.'

She met his gaze steadily with eyes flashing and breasts rising and falling as her breathing deepened with the barely suppressed fury prompted by his impertinence. He continued to stare. She turned her back and picked up the shorts and vest she had selected and pulled them on before facing him again. He was holding a sheet of brown paper and a length of twine for her to wrap the spare underwear and socks. An almost insolent smile played around the corners of his thin-lipped mouth. She snatched them from him, nearly tearing the paper.

'You will leave the rifle and ammunition in the next room.' He had a strong Russian accent but his English was good.

'Why?' She picked up the gun.

He smiled, pointing to it contemptuously. 'Do you think that will last another day?'

'Will I get a better one?'

He shook his head. 'You are not a soldier anymore.'

She threw the parcel down. 'What do you mean?'

'The Women's Battalion is disbanded. That's why you've been pulled out of the line. The Anarchists have forced this decision on us. They have too much of their own way, but not for long.'

'What will happen to us – me?'

'Women are to work in an auxiliary role,' his tone made it clear he was quoting from some official statement he held in contempt, 'not in the front line.'

Remembering she was still half-dressed Miriam started to pull on the breeches, 'What kind of a role is that?'

He shrugged. 'Nursing, making bandages, taking hot food to the front, working in a canteen, serving on a committee –'

'I came here to fight.'

He waited while she finished dressing, thoughtfully watching her lacing up her boots. 'Your battalion was taking heavy casualties day by day. If you'd stayed at the front I guarantee you would be dead by next week and of no use to the party at all. We have special tasks for certain party comrades, very important tasks. You do not have to re-muster as an auxiliary. I can arrange that.'

She looked at him thoughtfully. A commissar, he was obviously in an important position. She had seen how officers deferred to them at the front. It was clear they could make decisions about equipment and resources. Maybe he could help her to find out what had happened to Esther.

He passed her an elaborate card; 'You will come to the Hotel Gaylord this evening. There I will explain.'

'Hotel Gaylord! Where the bloody hell's that?'

'It's a hotel in the Salamanca district, very luxurious, and the only one not being used as a hospital now. Ask for me at the desk.'

'Before I can meet you this evening I have to find out about my sister. We came out here together and we've been split up. I don't know where to go to find out about her.'

'By what name is she known?'

'Rabin, Esther Rabin, she's in the Women's Militia, the Eleventh International.'

He thought for a moment. 'Ah yes, your sister, of course. I don't know where she is right now. I will find out by this evening but it may not be good news for you.' He took a tiny tin containing an inking pad from his tunic pocket and a thick pasteboard card. Signing it he authorised his signature with a small rubber stamp. 'Here is a pass. Keep it with you always in your pay book. You will be asked to show it wherever you go in the city. Don't give it up to anyone.'

She read the name printed on the top: Major Nikonov.

'And here is a chit that will get you rations for one day and a bed for tonight at the barracks.' He nodded to the table again. 'The orderly will show you the way. Now I must go.' He strode across the room and through the door as the rush of a shell forced Miriam to drop to the floor, her hands over her head. It fell nearby. The concussion filled the air with dust from the floorboards and flakes of plaster from the ceiling. She scrambled to her feet, patting her tunic and ruffling her hair as she went to the door. The yellowy-green smoke cleared enough for her to see his black leather jacket. He turned and waved briefly before disappearing into the passageway.

Chapter Twelve

The Hotel Gaylord, Madrid, 1937

Miriam tentatively pushed through the revolving glass and chrome door of the hotel, and entering the foyer she paused momentarily as her eyes adjusted to the contrast between the bright light and the blacked-out streets. It seemed a world away from the devastation of the poorer residential areas and the squalor of the front. Beneath an enormous chandelier the room had the décor of an ocean liner. It was busy with the coming and going of foreign correspondents and fact-finding groups, but clearly identifiable were the uniformed Soviet advisers and commissars moving purposefully across the crowded floor. The air was thick with the smoke of perfumed cigarettes and expensive cigars. She elbowed her way through to the curved reception desk panelled in yellow wood with speed lines of ebony and chrome.

Major Sergei Nikonov, NKVD, was sitting at a table where he could see the entrance. As he sipped his drink he relaxed, becoming lost in his thoughts. It had been a long and tortuous path since he was a twenty-year-old student fighting in the Ukraine. After the Polish army was driven back over the River Bug there was that posting to the Kremlin Military Academy shortly after his brother had been arrested in Leningrad, or Petrograd as it then was, and never heard of again. He recalled the last time he'd visited his family home in Moscow. It must have been in the February of 1922. Was it as long ago as that? He'd found it wrecked and stripped bare of wood for heating. It was too late to save his mother from cold and starvation, so too his father, whose rigid and wasted body he'd carried to the burial pit. The rest of his family had been scattered and he'd not had word of them since. Unbidden, the faces of his wife of only two years and their baby girl lying together in a single coffin, both carried away by typhoid, brought a pang of long-suppressed grief. He sighed. Now it looks as if this business has become another damned civil war. The assignment to Madrid at the beginning of the year was unlucky to say the least. Still, given what was happening in Moscow just now, he was probably in a safer position than back there.

He saw her coming through the door, attracting attention as she wound her way across the crowded lobby toward the desk. She looked out of place in the elegant setting. The new greatcoat was slightly large on her, with the haversack strap across her chest crossed by the blanket roll tied at her waist giving her an odd, almost awkward look, and – such a scarred face. He let his breath out through pursed lips. People turned their heads as their eyes followed her, glancing circumspectly over their shoulders when she passed them. A vision of her leapt into his mind, clumsily pulling her newly issued shorts over her pallid buttocks with her small breasts swaying as she leaned forward. Well, would she accept the part he had for her?

Miriam leaned over the desk, pointing to his name on her pass but he was already at her side. He took her arm, 'I have a table in the restaurant. Let us go through.'

Shrugging off her blanket and haversack she gave up her greatcoat and allowed herself to be seated before she asked about Esther.

'The news of her is good.' Sergei shifted the leather holster on his belt as he sat down. He took out a pack of black and gold Balkan cigarettes and offered one to Miriam before taking one himself. He inclined his head, almost touching her temple with his hair as he held the flame of a silver lighter bearing an enamelled star in red and gold to her cigarette. Carefully he placed the lighter on the white cotton tablecloth. He had long hands, soft and tanned with finely tapered fingers and naturally pointed nails.

Miriam coughed once. 'Well?'

Sergei blew smoke at the ceiling before bringing his eyes to hers. 'Did you know your sister volunteered to be a sniper?

'A sniper! No I did not.' She took an agitated pull at her cigarette. 'That's good news?' she snapped angrily. 'For you perhaps but for me, no.'

'I've heard she's very good. Women make good snipers, shallow breathing. Breathing is important. She was picked out in target practice for special training. There is extra pay.'

'Extra pay! Ha! What good's that if Franco's men get hold of her?' She turned her head aside. 'The bloody fool,' she muttered under her breath. It was bad enough they were separated. Suddenly she felt alone, exposed, on a limb. What was Esther thinking of taking unnecessary risks like that? It was very selfish of her too. 'What would become of her if the worst should happen, and what would become of me,' she asked herself.

He patted her hand, attempting to reassure her. She watched the ash topple off his cigarette as he did so, then she stared at him coldly for a few moments until he broke the silence. 'Yesterday she was known to be in a section on the western part of the front. I can get a message to her if you wish.'

'I can go to the front and see her myself, can't I? You can arrange it. Yes?'

He turned his head away, slowly blowing out smoke before turning back to her. 'That's not practical. She's difficult to locate. You'll have to wait until she comes out of the line.'

'Really! Well just send to tell her I'm well and want to

meet her as soon as possible.'

'Of course. I will see to it tomorrow.' He motioned to the wine waiter. 'I trust you will like this wine. I have ordered steak.'

'Steak!'

'Yes. It is the best here. From cattle, not horse.'

She nodded to the door, 'Out there they're cutting up mules that fall dead in the street.'

Ignoring her remark he leaned toward her and touched her cheek lightly with his fingertip.

Against her will she felt herself flinch, but she did not recoil.

'How did you get this?'

She could feel the touch of his finger as he let it dwell on the livid wound.

A distant crump set the chandeliers jingling. She drew away from his hand.

'Don't worry. Franco's supporters live here in the Salamanca district. If you'd come in daylight you'd see it's very fashionable. He's given the order: it is not to be shelled or bombed. Some say he has a room booked here for when he enters the city.'

The waiter poured the wine and when the steak arrived she set to making it clear that no words would be exchanged once knives and forks were taken up.

Miriam finished eating and wiped her mouth with her napkin as Sergei watched her with a slightly amused smile. 'When did you last eat meat?'

'I had some goat stew at the front. Apart from that I can't remember. Some months before I came out here, I suppose.'

He sat back. 'Now first tell me about your face then I will tell you why I asked you to come here tonight.'

She touched her cheek impulsively. 'I got this fighting the Fascists on the streets.'

'London?'

'Yes. Cable Street.'

'So! You came to Spain to fight Fascists.'

Miriam did not answer.

He sipped his wine. 'Why?'

'Why! To save the Republic, of course, and the legally-elected government.'

There was another crump. She sat still.

Sergei leaned over the table towards her. 'Do you think the Soviet Union intends to help a government controlled by Liberals, Anarchists, and Socialists?'

Miriam thoughtfully ran her finger and thumb up and down the stem of her glass, 'When are you going to tell me why you asked me to come here tonight?' She looked at him from the corner of her eyes. 'It wasn't just to tell me about my sister, was it?'

Sergei leaned back in his chair, watching her for some moments as if to clear the board before getting down to the real business. 'We need someone to work in the rear, leading a band of comrades. Someone like you, perhaps.'

'Doing what?'

He folded his arms and rested them on the table, looking at her closely with his startlingly blue eyes. 'It's clear that Franco's coup has failed. Now he has to fight a war and we have to do whatever is necessary to work towards a Comintern victory. Comrades like you are needed to ensure that our so-called left-wing allies have no influence on the direction of the war. If you accept you will organise political actions, arresting our opponents and holding tribunals, and you will of course be given an appropriate rank. Occasionally you will lead attacks –' Miriam was about to respond but with a slight movement of his hand and without unfolding his arms, he stilled her, 'and enforce discipline with executions when necessary. You will be prepared in party matters, for you will be writing and making speeches for recruiting and boosting morale. You will also have a tutor to improve your Spanish, and if you wish you will be given lessons in the Russian language, which may be very useful to you later.'

'How do you know I can write speeches, let alone address meetings?'

'Comrade Miriam Moss,' he paused, unfolding his arms, 'you may call me Sergei. You are known to us. You regularly produced papers for your party branch. I've read some of them myself.' He brought his hand down lightly but emphatically on the tabletop. 'So! Do you think I invited you here tonight just to feed you? The truth is, comrade, you are an intellectual who has been forged on the streets and at the front whether you like it or not.' He grasped the edge of the table, leaning toward her. 'Well, what is it to be? Do you stay in the fight as an activist or as,' he shrugged contemptuously, 'an auxiliary?'

She looked down at the table. It swam before her eyes. She was being swept along. Everything seemed to have led to this, everything that had happened to her. The hardships of the Great War, the teaching and the farm then losing Edwin, the experience of running the branch, addressing meetings, the street fighting, Cable Street, she winced mentally, and the soldiering. Where would it lead if she accepted? There would be no going back, that's for sure, tribunals, executions, bloody hell! But still it was up to her whether she stepped over that threshold, accepted the offer to be groomed, which she found quite flattering, and committed herself, inescapably. And in return –? In return a chance to shape events, to further the fight against Fascism, to take a more active part in establishing Communism in yet another country – and to be giving orders rather than taking them, which she had begun to find rather irksome.

She looked up. 'An appropriate rank?'

'Yes. You will start as a captain immediately.'

'When do I report, Comrade Major?'

He leaned back, eyeing her keenly. 'Come here tomorrow, same time. Everything will be arranged then. I have to leave you now. In the meantime give some thought to a pseudonym, an alias. You would be wise to adopt one as a *nom de guerre*.' He rose and paused, 'But no. Let us wait. The brigades will have a name for you soon enough. Whatever it is it will tell me how well you do your work.'

Chapter Thirteen

Madrid, April 1937

They brought the man into the crowded room. Two militiamen held him before the table with his arms pinioned. They pulled his beret from his head and tossed it onto the floor. Miriam sat flanked on either side by officers dressed like her in blue tunics and peaked caps with red stars. She leaned forward and spoke to him, no longer addressing him as comrade. 'You have been found guilty of the charge.'

He objected forcefully, refusing to accept his guilt. Hurt, angry, and with his chin lifted arrogantly he refuted the charge. He had never possessed a torch, he insisted. How could he signal to the enemy giving away his comrades' position? 'Where is the evidence?' he demanded of the tribunal in a loud voice.

Miriam nodded to the two militiamen. They pulled him through the doorway onto the yard, still shouting repeatedly, 'Where is the evidence?' until a single shot silenced him.

The militiamen returned immediately. One of them tossed the man's watch and a few coins onto the table. Miriam spoke to her two subordinates, 'That's the last of this batch for today, comrades. Dismiss your men until tomorrow. I have some work waiting for me.' She closed her file to indicate the tribunal was adjourned, then waited until everything was cleared away and the last person had left before taking off her cap and tossing it on the table. Then running her hands through her hair she clasped them behind her head, placed her feet up one by one, and tipped her chair back slightly. Lifting her eyes to the ceiling she closed them, letting the rigor seep from her muscles bit by bit, allowing her mind to drift.

It had been nearly six months since she had taken up Sergei's offer, though she'd seen nothing of him since. She had done well. Word of her had reputedly reached the ears of the chief military adviser himself, so that even Moscow may have heard of her. In fact it was said that he himself recommended her promotion to major only a short while ago, and since then she had striven to impress even more. Her work was satisfying, almost enjoyable. She never expected that. She had also been complimented on her grasp of Russian that was increasing almost by the day.

Sergei had come out to the yard to smoke one of his Balkan cigarettes. He watched the limp bodies being tossed on a lorry while the wet sticky flagstones were being sanded. He muttered to himself, 'Oh you bloodthirsty woman. What have you become?'

It had reached his attention that since her promotion the new major was carrying out her duties with unnecessary and disturbing fervour. The senior adviser described it as fanaticism that could become out of control, suggesting he should investigate. In the last hour, unknown to Miriam, he had been observing the proceedings of the tribunal through an arabesque screen in the shadows of a gallery high up on the wall, opposite the panel of three. There she sat flanked on either side by two roguish characters, unshaven and in unkempt tunics, showing their black and yellow teeth each time they leered at the prisoners. He had seen and heard enough to confirm his unease. He should have kept in contact with her and not left her to herself. That time in the restaurant when he'd recruited her he'd detected the necessary steel that would enable her to carry out whatever action was necessary, but something else seemed to be at work within her here. Some emotion surpassing ruthless logic and it wasn't just that promotion had gone to her head. Was it anger perhaps, smouldering from within and driving her, demanding more and more victims for execution? This was not good. He would have to do something about it, something to take the edge off her steel. He had come prepared for an attempt to get through to her face-to-face.

As Sergei entered Miriam dropped her feet to the floor in surprise and stood up, pushing against the chair with the back of her thighs.

He strode up to her so there was just the table between them, withholding his recognition and greeting. 'How many out there were really guilty as charged, Major?' He spoke quietly, turning his head abruptly and nodding to the yard before looking back at her.

It took but a moment for her to recover her poise. She leaned forward. 'Is that important? Surely what matters is how many were Anarchists or trade unionists, our left-wing allies, as you called them.'

'I understand this has been going on for some weeks, since your promotion, in fact. I don't think it necessary for so much shooting. When I said to remove political opponents I did not have so many in mind.'

'Indeed! Then exactly how many did you have in mind?'

His eyes flashed and he shouted angrily, 'Look at yourself. Look at what you've become. When you're sitting at this table you're enjoying it and those villains either side of you, your so-called aides, where did you find them, the local jail? You've surrounded yourself with desperadoes. The senior commanders of the brigades would have them shot out of hand if they could see what they get up to.'

She nodded to the crimson tabs on her shoulders, 'I hope you're not thinking of interfering with my work, Comrade Major. I'm the same rank as you now.'

139

He thrust his face toward her. She could feel his breath with every word as he hissed, 'Surely you can see this could chase the middle classes into Franco's arms. Major – be careful.' There was a trace of menace in his voice. 'You are a major, *da*, but a commissar?' He paused before spitting out the answer, '*Nyeht!*'

There was silence between them for some moments. He hadn't meant to become so angry. To let it take him by surprise like that was foolish. He broke into an icy smile, intensifying the steely blue of his eyes. 'Do you know how you are called?'

Of course she knew, but his intimidation slowed her answer.

'*El Azote*. The Scourge. Oh, I'm not displeased with that, but you must always have before you the ultimate goal: power. Until the bird is in the net we have to move carefully so as not to startle it. We cannot afford to indulge ourselves. In future I shall watch your work with interest.' Swiftly he lightened his attitude and relaxed his bearing. 'I have a note from your sister.' From the breast pocket of his tunic he took out a paper folded into a tiny envelope and passed it to her.

Miriam's eyes lit up. She unfolded it and scanned the scrap of YWCA notepaper. Esther was well and hoping they would be able to meet soon. There was little else. She was sorry she could not give an address for a reply.

Miriam looked disappointed.

'Don't worry. She was fine yesterday, according to my aide who brought me the note. She's been at the front continually. That's why you've not had anything from her. It's dangerous to send letters from the front. The censors may get the wrong idea.' He drew his hand across his throat then he thrust it into his haversack. 'I have this also for you.' It was a tablet of French toilet soap.

Hesitantly she leaned over the table to take it, impulsively holding it to her face breathing in the expensive scent through the deluxe wrapping.

'And this too.' He brought out a tube of lipstick.

There was an uncomfortable pause as she took it.

'I was going to ask you to have dinner with me this evening, comrade.'

'This evening?' Another dinner. What was he up to?

'Yes. At the hotel, would you like that – Miriam?'

There was only one way to find out but she would have to be careful. They had both crossed that killing threshold, killing in cold blood. They could be dangerous to each other.

'Yes. Yes I would.'

'Until this evening then, Miriam.'

She nodded. 'This evening, Sergei.'

It was a warm evening at the beginning of May as Miriam made her way to the hotel. People were strolling along the ruined streets as if the hardships of the siege lay behind them for the time being at least. Coming out onto the stylish avenidas of the Salamanca district, which was untouched by the bombardments, she found herself walking with a light step anticipating the evening. She'd made a special effort back at her billet, washing down in a bowl with Sergei's soap. Her still-damp hair was pinned up under her cap. The lipstick was a little too bright, she thought, and using a mirror had still given her some trouble, but her skin was tingling in a way she'd not felt for a long time. It made her feel on tenterhooks, almost forgetting about her face.

Sergei was waiting at his usual table, boots and cross belt freshly polished, pistol and holster left in his room. She looked very slim in her neat blue tunic with the crimson tabs on her shoulders and high collar as she came across the floor. His almond-shaped eyes widened as she smiled. The lipstick clashed with the grey-blue of her eyes. He stood and pulled up a chair, signalling for the waiter.

'What will you have to drink?'

She hesitated for a moment, becoming conscious of her naiveté. 'Oh, I don't really know –'

'A martini?'

She nodded, wondering how it would taste.

They talked throughout the meal. Losing her reserve she told him about the farm, Edwin, and the pit. He told her of his wife and their baby, of his boyhood outside Moscow fishing in the lakes with his father and hunting in the birch woods with his brothers. She talked of growing up in the village and about Dad coming home from South Africa, and the gold coins. Then she tried to explain the Welsh language to him. He called for a pencil so that he could help her with her Russian, covering the tablecloth with Cyrillic letters as he did so.

Gradually, with the table cleared and empty glasses between them, they became aware they were the only people in the room except for the waiters putting up chairs.

He leaned over to her. 'I think it's time to go to the bar for coffee.'

Coffee at the bar, the moment had to be seized now. It may not come round again. Who could say day-to-day whether they'd even be alive for a next time? Besides she still hadn't found out why he really asked her to dinner that evening.

He took her arm gently, feeling it quiver under his hand, and unbidden it engendered a warmth within him and again aroused the memory of her unclothed. As he led her over to the bar he let his hand slip down gently to clasp hers.

She returned his hold with mutual warmth, and putting her lips close to his ear she muttered, 'We could have the coffee brought to your room.'

As he turned from closing the door she pressed her lips on his, putting an arm around him and pulling off her cap with her free hand, she tossed it behind her. He responded, returning her kisses as he drew her into the bedroom, unfastening her belt and holster before letting them thump heavily to the floor with the weight of the revolver. She pulled off her boots and breeches and lifted her tunic over her head, startling him as she stood boldly and incitingly before him. He struggled with the tapes of his blouse and his trousers, stumbling awkwardly as he did so. Then they fell on the bed in each other's arms. Miriam straddled him, taking him into her, and setting off a full thrust as he sounded her deepness.

It seemed they had enjoyed each other for some time before the knocking on the door announced the arrival of the coffee. They both ignored it. Sergei was now over her, his hips driving at her buttocks as she squealed with each stroke, until with a succession of spasms he was still.

The knocking had stopped. 'I think the coffee's gone away.'

'Maybe it's left on the table outside.' Sergei rose and padded over to the outer door. Returning with a tray he placed it at the side of the bed.

'You went out into the corridor like that?'

Sergei chuckled. 'Let us drink it before it gets cold.'

They lay together listening to the sporadic artillery fire from the western outskirts of the city, their cigarettes glowing in the darkened room. He cupped her chin and lifting her face, brushed his lips over her scar before gently kissing it. 'How did this happen?'

She told him about the potato with the embedded razor blades, her speech faltering as drowsiness overcame her. He took the cigarette from her loosening fingers and propped himself with his elbow and gazed at her face thoughtfully for some time as he finished his own cigarette. Reflecting on the evening he intended to produce some kind of impression of her but his heavy eyelids prompted him to turn over and settle down to sleep.

She was falling down the well, falling, falling and she

was going to die. There was no one to help her. This was it. Swiftly her death was coming at her.

She sat up, clutching the sheet to her pounding heart, bathed in perspiration and panting in short gasps. Her tongue was clinging painfully to the top of her parched mouth. With eyes staring wide she saw items on the dressing table along the far wall sharply outlined despite the gloom and the shifting perspective pulsing near and far, near and far, distorting the angles of the walls and floor and assaulting her senses.

She was coming to. She was not going to die.

The familiar feeling of release swept over her, leaving her weak and drained. Slowly she breathed in and out as the terror subsided.

He had taken her shoulders and was holding her. Gradually she allowed the relief to bathe her, to still her heart and breathing. Keeping her eyes closed, knowing the room would take longer to settle and the memory to fade, she shuddered at the feel of the damp sheet and the chill of her drying sweat.

He gently lifted the hair from her clammy face with one hand as he supported her. 'How often does this happen?'

'Often enough to make it too often.'

'I know about this condition. I've seen it before. Wounds heal as much as they ever will but the mind – who can say?'

'Sometimes it occurs during the day when I'm wide-awake, only fleetingly but vivid and immediate. It's terrifying, really terrifying. Strange though, I never had it when I'm was in the line. I wonder why?'

'Have you told anyone else about it?'

'No. Not even Esther. Why should I? You're the only one who's seen it. How could I tell you about it if you hadn't? It's impossible to put into words. As for what it's like on the inside: I don't think I have the language to describe it even to myself. You know, like trying to describe the colour red to a person born blind?' Now she was talking about it perhaps her words would give it substance, and if they did then perhaps it could be captured and locked in a chest.

He lit two cigarettes and passed one to her. 'I have to go soon. There is a special operation today.' He blew smoke at the ceiling then he looked at her. 'I think we should meet often. What do you think? Shall we see each other again, like this?'

'Yes. I would like that'

'I will contact you soon but now we must dress.'

Chapter Fourteen

During the following weeks Miriam was wrapped up in her duties, speaking at meetings to raise morale and aid recruitment, rounding up opponents of the Comintern, and even leading an attack in the western part of the front. She was not really inclined to make contact with Sergei believing herself far too busy to be concerned with marginal matters. However no matter how hard she tried not to do so she was thinking of him continually, especially as she supposed he was keeping her under observation.

He too found her intruding into his thoughts in an almost irritating way. It was very difficult if not impossible to put her from his mind as he was having reports of her work sent to him regularly. He decided to get in touch, after all, he reasoned, he needed to discuss certain aspects of these reports just to let her know he was keeping an eye on her, but before he did so there was a note for him at the hotel desk.

It was from Miriam, written in Russian. There were one or two mistakes where the lower-case letters had caused her some problems but it showed her grasp of the language was progressing well. She was crossing the city tomorrow afternoon and it may be that she would have time to call at the hotel. It would be nice if someone she knew were to be in the bar around then. It was signed 'M'.

He sat watching the revolving doors, only half expecting her to turn up because her note read only that she may have time to call, giving him to understand that on the other hand she may not have time, or perhaps reserving the option to change her mind, or did she use the wrong Russian term, intending to mean she would have time?

She appeared just as he was thinking about giving up and moving to the bar. Her eyes caught his immediately. He rose from his seat as she came up to him. 'You look different.'

She laughed, nodding and clearly feeling pleased to see him after what seemed an age, though it was only some four weeks. 'I don't look exactly as you remember me when you last saw me, I suppose.' She leaned closer to his ear so that he felt her breath on it. 'For most of the time I didn't have my clothes on.'

His eyes widened. 'So! You came. Let's sit over there.'

They had coffee, their hands touching frequently as they talked, both expecting only a short time together, exchanging small talk before going their separate ways, perhaps arranging to keep in touch, neither looking any further than that but that was not the way it was to be. After they'd finished their coffee and cigarettes, as if by unspoken agreement, they left the table and took the elevator up to his room. This time they made love gently, slowly, taking their time, each sure of the other and expressing their feelings more in tenderness than in drive and enthusiasm. They never got round to discussing her work.

After that, as their relationship unrolled, they seized any opportunity to spend time together, all too briefly, and always at the hotel before she had to return to barracks or to the front. Together in the warm closeness of his room they used Russian and as her competence grew she began trying it out on the Soviet advisers in the hotel lounge where they were becoming well known as a couple.

Gradually she came to feel a bond had grown between them greater than the feeling of direction and ruthless commitment they shared. Both had known tragedy and experienced violence at first hand. Was this happiness no more than short-lived? Did they enjoy each other while they could, a fleeting enactment between them before they went on their way to separate destinations? It was not what she wanted, but where else could it lead? Eventually he'd go back to Russia. For the first time she found herself thinking about what she would do when this war came to an end. She didn't want to lose him, she knew that. With a jolt she realised that for her, he and the war had become one. She wanted everything to go on as it was.

He in turn questioned what he should do about this comrade major. It wasn't good party practice to become emotionally entangled with someone for whose performance he was responsible, but he did not seek for this to happen. His feelings for her had got the better of him. He realised this, but why, he attempted to reason. She seemed vulnerable, arousing a protective instinct in him, but to protect her from what? Possibly from what she may become, had perchance already become. He'd seen it before, people becoming so absorbed with a sense of purpose they lost the ability or even the willingness to think coolly and logically, going on until they are destroyed by their fanaticism, but not before they finally recognize too late what monsters they've become. That still didn't explain why he felt for her as he did, why he didn't want this to happen to her. Why didn't he just take what was available while he could without this disturbing and inconvenient emotional attachment?

Because the sisters were yet to meet up, only being able to exchange notes through Sergei's aide, it took some time for Esther to find out that the notorious Scourge and Miriam were one and the same. It happened when she was riding a tramcar in a devastated area near the front. An enormous and instantly recognizable black and white portrait of Miriam on a propaganda mural covering the entire end wall of a tall fire-blackened building confronted her. Emblazoned vividly across it in red and yellow dynamic lettering was the legend *El Azote*.

Esther was now a major in charge of sniper training. She was also well known abroad through her articles in the foreign press, vividly describing life in the siege, but she was never called upon to report live on the fanatical exhortations of *El Azote*'s speeches, though she had read the texts and knew of her fearsome reputation for dealing with the enemy within as well as the enemy without. Unable or not wanting to believe her own eyes she jumped off the slowly moving tramcar and ran back to stand looking up at the mural. Yes, there was no doubt about it. It was Miriam's face. With her eyes staring over the heads of her audience she was portrayed standing with her head thrown back, one arm raised with fist clenched, the other hand at her waist with her thumb hooked in her belt. A shocked Esther had to accept that Miriam was *El Azote*. Those fervently over-obsessive speeches she had read, that was Miriam. *El Azote* and her squads striking fear in the brigades, that was she. The revelation came as a shock, leaving her emotionally numb. She would see Miriam as soon as possible.

Despite the urgency in Esther's notes they remained unanswered until after some persistent attempts Miriam arranged to meet her at a café. With Esther's token response to her greeting over, they settled themselves onto rickety chairs facing the avenue under a tattered awning offering some shade from the fierce heat of the late-afternoon sun. Somewhere deep in the café a radio was barking out a propaganda speech. Miriam, attempting to break the uncomfortable silence that lay between them, referred to the tabs on Esther's shoulders. 'I see you're a major as well now.'

Esther ignored Miriam's observation. Instead she turned her attention to a military convoy picking its way slowly along the broad rubble-lined avenue, trying desperately not to raise dust in the shimmering heat lest it attract the attention of the Luftwaffe's Messerschmitt BF 109s of the Condor Legion, newly arrived over the city.

Still looking away she said, 'This man who sends his aide with your notes for me, Major Nikonov, is that right?'

'That's right.'

'A Soviet advisor, yes?'

'Yes. He'll be along shortly. We've arranged to meet here. That's if he can find it. The landscape changes every time the Junkers come over.'

Esther turned to her. 'He's your lover, isn't he?'

'Yes he is, as a matter of fact.'

'I see.'

Miriam paused, waiting for the clanging of tramcar bells and the grinding and squealing of wheels on the metals of the intersection opposite to subside. 'What do you see?'

'That will be what's done it.'

'Done what?'

'Turned you.'

'Esther, what are you trying to say? He hasn't turned me into anything. You're wrong.'

'Then who has? What has? What has turned you into this – this Robespierre spreading terror in the brigades?'

'Where terror is needed it has to be imposed. How else can we achieve victory in these circumstances?' Miriam took time to light a cigarette, lifting her chin and releasing the smoke, 'Besides, you kill people often.'

'They happen to be the enemy.'

'The enemy is not just at the front, you know that very well. They are in the city, around us, everywhere.' She waved her hand sprinkling ash on the table.

'You mean anyone who's not working for the Comintern?'

'Well, yes. Those who are actively working against it

anyway.' She pointed her hand at Esther, the one holding the cigarette, 'If the defeat of the nationalists doesn't lead to a Communist republic, it's not a victory. Where does that leave you, Esther? You can't sit on the fence. Surely we haven't come out here just to fight for the restoration of the old democratic system?'

'We came out here to fight Fascism, remember? Because no one else would.'

'No one except the Soviet Union.'

'Which means Comrade NKVD Major Sergei Nikonov.'

'You're prejudiced. Do you know that? You still see the Soviet Union as czarist Russia, just like Dad.'

'"We are going to fight for the legally elected Republic." Do you remember who said that? Do you?' She slapped the tabletop, 'You did! You! *El Azote*!'

Miriam did not answer. Instead she looked out over the tram intersection and east up the avenue lit by the lowering sun through the jagged skyline of wrecked buildings behind them. If he could follow her directions Sergei should be making his way from over there. This was the first time they'd met outside the hotel and he was a little late. Esther had insisted on this place. The Salamanca district was too inconvenient, she'd said, and she wanted to meet urgently. Miriam had wondered why. She still felt irritated. It was the only time she could arrange to see him this week. This meeting with Esther was intrusive. She knew she was pregnant. Although she'd suspected for a couple of months she hadn't told Sergei yet, but now she was certain, and she was going to tell him today. However with Esther here it would be difficult. She might have to put it off unless Esther left them together afterwards.

'Oh, I know Russia provides the planes and the tanks, Miriam. Miriam! Are you listening?'

'And the advisers,' Miriam retorted, still looking up the avenue.

'Yes, I know, those too, but that's my point: the new rifles, the boots, even the rations, they're only for party members. We're fighting for Russia, Miriam, not the Republic.'

At that moment Miriam thought she spotted Sergei. Was it –? Yes it was. She rose from her chair, waving.

Shading his eyes he thought he could make out the café across the intersection in the gutted building outlined against the harsh light. Yes. That would be it, with the battered sign and ragged dusty awnings. Crossing to an island in the intricate network of tracks he waited for an opportunity as the tramcars lurched over the diamond points, the clanging of bells rising and falling as they passed him. Squinting against the sun he thought he saw her. He waved and she waved back. He stepped out. There was the screech of metal on metal in his ears.

A carafe shattered on the paving, swept from the table as Miriam sprang up. It left a splatter of red. She ran down to the avenue. Esther followed. It was clear something had happened in the centre of the intersection. Many tramcars had stopped. There was a crowd gathering around the front of one of them.

Miriam dashed across the tracks and reached it before Esther caught up with her. In vain she tried to get through but as she pulled and pushed people just closed up tighter. 'Let me through. Please let me through,' she implored in Spanish but there was no response. Esther drew her pistol and fired in the air. As one they turned to her a sea of startled faces. 'It is her man,' she shouted. Sullenly they made way.

Two drivers were crouched over a figure, the upper part of its body under the front bogie. There was a widening pool of blood spreading in runnels around the granite sets.

Lifting her palms to her mouth as if to smother or perhaps postpone her screams Miriam walked slowly

153

towards the tramcar. It seemed to her she was the only thing moving, as if time itself was holding its breath. She sank to her knees at the bogie. Perhaps it wasn't him. She must see. As she leaned forward to peer under the frame her breeches soaked up the blood. She couldn't see his face or even his head but there was his blue shirt, his belt and pistol. With a dreadful coldness she knew it was he and the spell was broken. Movement started up again. One of the drivers stooped to take her shoulders in his hands, shaking his head. Police officers were already ordering the crews to send for maintenance men so the body could be freed.

Esther lifted Miriam to her feet, and wrapping her arms around her she walked her back towards the café. Twice without speaking she attempted to turn round and go back to Sergei but Esther held her firmly. 'No, Miriam. Leave it to them. They know what to do.' Miriam struggled. 'No. Come with me. You can't do anything for him now. We'll go over to the Soviet Embassy later. The police will hand over his papers to them and they will arrange things.'

Esther's words echoed over and over in her mind. What did they mean? There she was at the table again where she'd been only a short time before. The tramcars were moving, bells clanging wheels squealing. People were going on as if nothing had happened. Perhaps it hadn't happened. Perhaps she'd just imagined it. Oh, if only she had, but there was the wine and the broken glass on the paving and there were the crews busy at the front of that tramcar. If only she could turn back time just for a few moments. God, is that too much to ask? She would not wave to him, not distract him, let him pick his way across first. He would be here at the table, smiling the way he does – did. The suddenness of loss overcame her.

For a moment Esther looked on helplessly. What had she to do? Everything had happened so suddenly. She had to do something. Miriam had got herself into this mess, but she couldn't leave her with someone else. There was no one else, just the two of them. Then, as if stirred by some primal instinct, she stood up and took her sister's arm, lifting her gently from the chair. 'I'm taking you back to my room, I've got three more days leave. Do you hear me?' Miriam, her senses deadened, turned her blank eyes to Esther as if she was seeing her for the first time that day. 'You can stay with me for a few days. You can't go back to barracks. I'll try to get a message over to them to get you some leave.'

It was two days later, sitting in Esther's room after they had returned from the burial pit, that Miriam told her. She had to tell someone. Only the other day she was wondering when to tell him, but now there was just Esther to tell.

'I thought you couldn't …'

'Just Edwin, I suppose.'

'I see. How long?' asked Esther.

'Now he'll never know.'

'Miriam, how long?'

What was Esther asking? How long? She wished she'd leave her be and stop trying to drag her out of herself, leave her to her own thoughts, to what she wanted to think about and what she wanted to say. Miriam looked at her blankly for a few moments then she answered, 'Three months.'

'Miriam, what are you going to do?' There was an urgent tone in Esther's voice. 'You're not going to keep the baby, are you?'

'That's what Sergei would want me to do. It's all I have left of him, and it's more than I had last time, isn't it?'

Christ! She was in a far bigger mess than last time. 'By the winter you're not going to be able to take part in any sort of action. You could easily get discharged as soon as possible, get to Valencia, the road is still open, and then go back.'

'Go back. Go back to what? A country that's ready to put its neck on the Fascist block?' Miriam turned to her, grasping the arms of her chair, clearly resolute, 'By this time next year the victory will be ours. The Fascists will be crushed and then perhaps it will be time to go back and bring up a child, his child, but not till then.'

'Miriam,' Esther stood up and nervously lit a cigarette, leaving the sentence hanging in the air before continuing in a voice straining to express a patience she did not feel, 'the nationalists are building up their forces for another big offensive on the city. You know that yourself. Sooner or later, probably later in the year, it will come. There is nothing surer. Then all the roads will be cut. There'll be no way out.'

'The brigades will hold them.'

Esther shook her head with all semblance of patience lost. 'You know the state they're in. Their weapons,' she sighed heavily, 'they've no idea how to keep them clean. Rifles, I've seen them. They're filthy. There's no discipline and the squabbling,' she shook her head again, 'I'm telling you they can't be counted on. This will be no place for you when you're six months gone in the depths of winter and when there won't be a roof left in the city, let alone any food to speak of.'

'I'm staying, Esther. There's work to be done. I'll manage somehow.'

Esther looked down at her, drawing on her cigarette and cradling her elbow with the other hand. Miriam's mind was made up. She might see things her way by the winter but it would be too late then and anyway, the thought suddenly occurred to her, she didn't want her to leave. She didn't want to be left on her own out here. They came out together and although they only saw each other rarely the idea they weren't both in it together, that Miriam wasn't somewhere in the city, was disturbing, even unbearable. She would have to report this to the offices of the military advisor and the senior commissar.

She ground out her cigarette on the table. 'Well, I'll see you as much as I possibly can. You must tell me where you work from and keep me up to date with your movements. Things are bound to get lively for us both soon.' She delved in her tunic pocket. 'Here's my card. I've got yours. Everything you need to know to get in touch with me is on it but things will change almost day by day. Try and use the telephone, it does work most of the time.'

Esther went down to the street door with Miriam and kept her in sight until she turned the corner without looking back.

Chapter Fifteen

Wrexham General Railway Station, June 1957

Esther's story is interrupted by the engine of a train drawing along the platform outside the refreshment room, bringing its carriages to a halt as the station bustles into life. Doors are thrown open as the guard calls over the hiss of steam, 'Paddington train. Shrewsbury next stop.'

Nicholas rests his folded arms on the tabletop, looking down. So that was his beginning, but his mother, oh God! His feelings are overwhelming him. What kind of a mother was that? Getting herself mixed up with a Soviet commissar who fathered him and this woman, her sister, his aunt, both of them – monsters. He is about to express his revulsion but people rising from their tables and leaving for the train hold him back. Others are entering, bringing with them draughts of sulphurous smoke. Then with the slamming of doors and the guard's whistle the train slides out, leaving only the rumble of a baggage trolley along the platform. The noisy chatter of the room, the clatter of crockery, and the singing of the tea urn fade from his perception.

No longer able to contain himself, he leans over to his aunt, hissing, 'My mother: a cold-blooded mass murderer and you, oh I don't know what.' Exasperated he turns his face away.

Esther inclines her head to one side, taking a sip of gin from her glass, and coolly studies him. 'You asked me what kind of a person your mother was. I suggest you wait until I've finished before passing judgement, or perhaps granting forgiveness.'

'Forgiveness! Surely it's for the surviving relatives of her victims to do that?'

'Nevertheless, for your own peace of mind, absolution lies with you. Listen!' She tries to take his hand but he pulls it away. 'This is something you have to understand: in acute situations people can change, become a different kind of person capable of extreme acts that seem right at the time. History itself, the society of the time, the lived human experience, all these factors were as much responsible for her deeds, our deeds. Believe me, we are all capable of those deeds. No one has a fixed character that can't be altered given the circumstances. We are driven by forces of the time in which we live. They act upon us whether or not we are aware of them. You may find that difficult to accept but until you do so you will not be able to set your mind at rest regarding your mother.'

Nicholas snorts, expressing his disgust at the idea, and contemptuously looks away.

She places her glass down firmly. 'Do you want me to go on? I don't have to. It was you who asked me to come. You who wanted to know. If you find the truth too morally repugnant then I shall go now and you can get the next train back to the secluded shelter of that college of yours at Oxford. There's the platform.' She makes to rise.

'No!' He reaches out and grasps her sleeve. 'Stay. I have to know everything – please.'

She settles back in her chair. 'So! The winter came and with it the expected launch of the nationalist assault down the Zaragoza road at the end of that December.'

Madrid, 1938

The front was held for the time being, but life in the city had changed for the worse since Sergei's death. Mothers prowled the ruined streets looting food for their young, seeking water frozen in the fractured pipes, and breaking up furniture to provide firewood to melt snow and to keep away the freezing cold.

As the winter ran on into early February Miriam now had a desk job commanding squads committed to dealing with people roaming the city in search of fuel, tearing down and breaking up anything that would burn, and threatening to do as much damage as the bombardments.

Laboriously she toiled up the stairs to her office and sat down heavily at her desk. Recently she had taken to wearing a long heavy skirt and a black leather greatcoat. Easing her belt down below her stomach she tightened it slightly to support her back. She was breathing hard. Her eyes fell on the fine plaster dust covering the surface of the table lit by the pale sun shining through the paper-covered window. She wondered how much longer she could go on. There was a surge of that deep sadness again and some guilt when she couldn't bring to mind the last time she heard his voice. Even his features were fading. It was an effort to recall his face. She had no photograph to recharge her memory. He had filled up her life completely. Now he was gone without trace leaving an emptiness, a void. To die like that after all he'd been through, not a bullet, just a bloody tram. At least other people knew Edwin and she could share her memories with them but there was no one to do that with Sergei. Esther had never met him. He was gone as if sunk in a bog that had closed over him. Gone as if he had never existed, but she knew only too well he had. He had not sunk without trace. He had left something behind. Something far more precious than Edwin had and this time she'd make sure she had a photograph as soon as possible.

Esther was due to come over this afternoon, if she could get through that was, with some information about arrangements she'd made with the sisters at a convent, though she'd warned it was not going to be easy. All maternity facilities were taken over for the wounded, as were the hotels.

The handset jangled discordantly. Some youngsters were barricaded in a building and refusing to come out. Would she come over?

'Shoot at the windows or put a grenade in, that should bring them out,' she shouted into the receiver. 'You don't need me for that.'

There were people watching. The *sargento* was not going to take responsibility, implying she should be there. He wouldn't have dared take this stance six months ago.

'Send a car,' she shouted.

The *sargento* protested. He did not have one.

'Then commandeer one and get it over here as soon as possible,' she barked before cradling the receiver hard.

Cautiously standing she made for the door, shifting the weight of her bulky holster round behind her hip. She met Esther on the stairs. 'I have to go out. There's some trouble.'

Esther looked her up and down, 'I think I'd better come with you.'

'I'd be glad of that, and you can tell me whether you've got any news.'

They picked their way over the rubble towards the street where they waited for the car. 'The sisters will take you in when your time comes, but only then, not before. The main problem we're going to have is getting there. I don't suppose you have a car standing by?'

Miriam shook her head. 'You must be joking.'

'Then we'll just have to seize one. By the way, the convent is on the western side of the city, so the area comes under regular artillery fire. It's had one or two near misses.'

As the open car pulled up at the scene of the trouble she assessed the situation with one look. It was a typical apartment block with its roof destroyed and its windows empty, like the eye sockets of a skull. The youths had been foraging for timber, probably to sell for fuel. Defiantly they refused to come out, shouting abuse from the darkness of a second-floor window. Unbeknown to them the steam from their breath was marking their position. A small crowd of mildly curious onlookers stamped their feet against the cold. The *sargento* had deployed his militiamen so they covered the front of the building. That was good at least.

The reluctant driver was hoping to be released from this duty by the militiaman beside him so he could go about his business. Instead Miriam tapped his shoulder and ordered him to take the car over to the *sargento* who was standing near the building with his hands in his pockets, making it clear he wasn't coming over on the orders of a woman and a pregnant one at that, but the hapless driver was even more reluctant to take his vehicle off the road and over the broken ground. Miriam leaned forward, awkwardly drawing her heavy-calibre Russian revolver. He watched the chambers turn as she slowly thumbed back the hammer in front of his face until it clicked twice. Taking her thumb away she left it held on the trigger and curled her finger around it. He could smell the oil on the sleek blued steel of the barrel under his nose as the hairs prickled on the back of his neck. Then she jabbed the muzzle in his ear.

The car drew up to the *sargento*. Miriam gently released the hammer down on the chamber, holstered the gun, and made to get out, but a cramping pain doubled her and she fell back onto the seat. Esther looked at her anxiously as she shouted, '*Sargento*, I want sustained fire on those windows, thirty rounds each. Is there enough ammunition for that?'

He shrugged. 'Just about,' he said churlishly.

'Just about! Have you or haven't you?'

He shrugged again.

'Do you have a machine gun?'

'*Que es eso*?' He did not understand or he was pretending. She had used the English word.

'*Maquina*?'

He shook his head scratching the stubble on his chin.

She sighed. '*Grenadoes*?'

He nodded. '*Si.*'

She pointed. 'Open fire, then put two in that doorway. Make sure you have enough rounds to finish them off after.'

The *sargento* looked blank.

'*Me Entiendes*, si?' she barked.

He continued to look deliberately obtuse, rolling his eyes towards the bystanders.

'Don't concern yourself with them. They need a demonstration of what happens to looters.'

Miriam ordered the militiaman out of the car and the driver to move it away from the front of the building. Then she covered her ears against the deafening fusillade of rifle fire. In the following silence she waited until the two deep explosions from within the building told her the grenades had gone in.

There was some screaming that went on for some seconds before five youths came out with their hands held up, one with his jacket smoking seemed to be shouting something. Another fusillade and they dropped except for a young boy who stood looking at them as they lay, his face holding an expression of puzzlement. With a single swift movement Miriam thumbed open her holster, drew the revolver, and fired. Esther cried out in surprise at the unexpected muzzle-blast of the heavy pistol close to her face. The soft-nosed bullet sent fragments flying from the top of the boy's head, hurling him to the ground with limbs flung loosely like a carelessly tossed rag doll, and leaving a fine scarlet mist in the air.

In the stillness that followed Miriam called to the *sargento*. 'Go in yourself and finish off any you find, then send for the Gardia to clear up.'

Looking at her and the smoking pistol with newfound respect he saluted. '*A sus ordenes, mi Comandante.*'

The driver, sweating profusely, his hands shaking on the wheel, followed Miriam's directions to move the car carefully through the sullen mob of bystanders, '*Despacio, despacio,*' she hissed in his ear while flourishing her pistol, 'Give them time to make way.' Another cramping pain doubled her up with her hands wrapped around her belly.

'I'll take this.' Esther's ears were still ringing from the pistol shot as she carefully eased it out of Miriam's tightly clenched fist. 'Have these pains just started?'

'Yes.' Miriam spoke through gritted teeth.

'I think we'd better go over to the convent now while we've got this car.' Pointing the pistol at the driver she climbed onto the seat beside him, and gave the name of the place, but he shook his head, his eyes wide with fear. He did not know how to get there and could he go now for he had business to attend to. Feeling a rush of irritation Esther brought the barrel down on the bridge of his nose, just a gentle rap breaking the skin so that it bled lightly. Then angrily wrenching his hands from his face she pointed at a map in the door compartment and ordered him to hand it to her. Having located their destination she gave directions using the pistol as a pointer.

As they moved further west Miriam's contractions became more frequent. Progress was slow along streets that a renewed nationalist offensive was filling with refugees moving into the city, despite the shortages and the shelling. The driver, taking advantage of a flock of sheep bringing the car to a stop, was topping up the tank from a can of fuel on the running board when Miriam's waters broke, bringing her to her knees on the floor. The sheep surged around the car, a stream of nodding heads, the pounding of their feet drowning out all other sound.

Eventually the car was able to move again, making slow progress against the surge of refugees with Esther holding the windscreen with one hand and the pistol in the other, threatening those who were slow to move out of the way.

A salvo emptied the street as they arrived. Miriam was on her hands and knees, panting and gasping for breath. Esther ordered the driver to go in and bring help while she opened the door on Miriam's side and attempted to get her into a sitting position. Then, in case they needed the car later, she lifted the bonnet, and taking the rotor arm out of the distributor, she slipped it into her jacket pocket.

Two sisters came down the steps of the convent, followed by the driver, and together they lifted a collapsed Miriam by her arms and legs and hastily carried her into the building before the next salvo. They went up a flight of steps and into a room bare except for a canvas stretcher on a large table. She was laid on it with a straw-filled pillow under her head.

In case the driver attempted to slip away Esther held up the rotor arm for him to see and pointed to a corner, telling him to wait there.

One of the sisters, clearly experienced, tugged off Miriam's coat, rolled up her skirt, and tucked it under her arms, stripping off her soiled flannel undergarments, and pulling off her boots. Then she rolled her woollen stockings down around her ankles.

The pains were coming regularly now in searing red contractions. She could hear herself screaming in prolonged outbursts that left her gasping and panting, her mouth dry and burning with the gritty plaster dust. She must have begged Esther for water because she turned to a sister who shrugged, pointing to a large enamel jug on the floor. The small amount of water at the bottom was frozen solid.

Esther called to the driver, asking his name. 'Luis,' he replied.

'Luis, she needs water.'

He shrugged.

'The car, get some water from the radiator,' she handed him the jug. '*Rapido!*'

The rust-coloured water was quite hot but cooling fast as it melted the ice at the bottom of the jug. Esther cupped her hand, and after dipping it into the water, she dripped it slowly into Miriam's mouth. At first she pursed her lips at the bitter metallic taste but she thirstily took more as Esther held it to her.

After some hours one of the sisters lit three candles which cast lengthening shadows across the room. She placed one near the jug to stop the water freezing. Miriam's labour continued, her exhaustion deepening, with no sign of the baby. The other sister slipped out and brought back bread and a small jug of wine for Esther and the driver. In between Miriam's screams the rumble of artillery could be heard, with occasional explosions nearby, creeping worryingly nearer and filling the air with fine dust and tiny flakes of plaster from the high ceiling. Suddenly she was being driven forward by a series of powerful and violent contractions. With each one she felt her back arching in an involuntary spasm. The sisters held her arms and shoulders as the top of the baby's head appeared. Just at that moment a rushing of air heralded the arrival of a shell, plunging the room in darkness, cracking the ears of everyone with its concussion, and driving in the window shutters, leaving them hanging crazily on their broken hinges.

Esther, scrabbling frantically with matches, managed to relight the candles. Through the dust that filled the room burning the back of her throat she caught a glimpse of the driver lying face down with his arms covering his head. Two more shells bracketed the building as the baby rushed out in a stream of blood and slime. One of the sisters took it in a piece of canvas and with practised hands, holding it face down, and started massaging until at a single cry she turned it upright until it cried again then carefully examining its mouth she placed it on its back at Miriam's side, cutting and tying the cord.

'It's a boy,' Esther told Miriam.

Too exhausted to move her head she just smiled.

'What are you going to call him?'

'Sergei would have wanted him to be called Nikolai after his father.'

A sister was attending to her, gently massaging her stomach as the last of the placenta was expelled. She spoke for the first time, 'As soon as possible we will get the priest to baptise him. Maybe tomorrow.'

'Piss off,' Miriam snarled in English.

Esther rolled her eyes at the sister by way of apology and taking the jug she used the water to clean Miriam up as well as she could. When she had finished the sister put the baby to Miriam's breast. She cradled the tiny head and felt him tentatively dabbing at her nipple with his mouth, then eagerly clasping it in his lips. The sister covered them both with a thin cotton sheet, indicating that Esther and the driver take a handle of the stretcher each. She drew the greatcoat over them and placed Miriam's boots at the bottom. With the sisters taking the lead they moved off down damp slippery steps to enter a large crypt. Esther retched at the shock of the warm fetid air. The dim light of flickering lanterns revealed figures huddled around an oil heater, their shadows thrown grotesquely across the vaulting. The crying of babies coming from the dark corners beyond the thick pillars did little to suppress the low growling of the bombardment.

They put the stretcher down in a corner and a straw filled mattress, some squares of cotton sheeting, and a lantern were brought. Then they lifted Miriam and the baby onto the mattress. Esther placed the pillow under her head and whispered in her ear, 'Are you awake?'

Miriam nodded, her eyes closed.

'I'll have to go soon. I'll give the sisters money for food, water, and candles for the lantern. They'll look after you both. You're safe from the shelling, or safer than the hospital anyway.' Esther rose to leave but paused, 'Oh, and keep your boots under your coat or they'll be gone by morning, and I'd better put this back.' Checking the safety catch was on and making sure the hammer was down on the empty chamber, she slid the pistol into Miriam's holster.

'Come on, Luis.' One of the sisters had put a plaster dressing on his nose. 'Let's go, you can give me a lift.' When they picked their way over the rubble to the main door they could see the carcass of the car peppered with holes and flattened against the wall across the street. 'Sorry, Luis.' Esther fished the rotor arm out of her pocket. 'You won't be needing this now.' She tossed it away.

Within a week Esther arranged a room for Miriam through the Soviet embassy. It was over the garages at the rear of the Hotel Gaylord. She also secured help for her from a party comrade on the kitchen staff, and a special fuel ration card, letting it be known that Miriam was an important member of the Comintern.

Twelve weeks' leave had been granted on condition that, as it said on the warrant, it was only a temporary situation with the baby. When it was nearly up she asked Esther the question she had been putting off even from herself, 'What does it mean by "temporary situation"?'

Esther sat down at her side, speaking slowly. 'Miriam, when it expires you are due to go back on duty. It means you won't be able to look after him then like you do now. Even if you have someone to do that for you when you are on duty you won't know when you will be home or how long you may be away. You could be at the front or anywhere.'

Esther was telling her what she already knew. She'd been over it many times in herself and even though she'd tried to push it to the back of her mind, it wouldn't go away. Her eyes fell on the baby, restlessly twisting in his basket, his chubby fingers clasping and un-clasping a small furry rabbit. She should've left and gone back six months ago, when Esther said. The awful truth swept in on her. She would not get out of the city now. It had not gone well. The nationalists were far from crushed and Madrid was being increasingly cut off from the rest of Republican Spain. Worse still, she knew more Italian troops had been pouring in over the last month since the British Government's tacit acceptance of Italian intervention in the newly signed treaty. She'd never get through the lines in one piece, neither her nor Nikolai, and even if she did the nationalists had put a price on her head. The Comintern wouldn't let her go anyway. She was too important to them. She'd be shot as a deserter if she even tried, baby or no baby. She brought her hands to cover her face, submitting to the despair that swept over her.

Esther took Miriam's hands and held them tightly. 'I'll see what I can do. I might be able to come and see you in two or three days. Whatever happens it's for the sake of Nikolai. We must do the best for him. Do you understand?'

Reluctantly Miriam nodded her head, still looking down.

Esther wouldn't tell her the price of the twelve weeks' leave. She'd had to guarantee the baby would go. The

Comintern and the Senior Commissar had demanded this, in fact they had given her the task of 'freeing up Comrade Moss' as they'd put it. They had their eyes on Miriam for the future and they'd let it be known things would not go well with Esther if she failed to achieve this. On the other hand, if she succeeded, there may be a position for her on a world-famous Soviet journal.

The warming sun of early May felt good on Miriam's back. She was returning from a walk in the park, carrying Nikolai in a shawl wrapped around her. He'd enjoyed watching the pigeons with his back against her legs as she sat on the grass. Now he was asleep. As she approached the hotel she saw Veronica, the kitchen girl who helped her. It seemed odd for her to be standing across the avenue at that time of day especially when she looked away at her wave.

Back in her room she started to mix the milk powder. He would wake soon.

There was a crash as the door was thrown open slamming against the wall with great force. Nikolai's little body shuddered into wakefulness, his eyes suddenly wide open. He began screaming in fright. Miriam dropped the milk jug. Two women in Red Cross uniform strode in past her. One of them took up Nikolai while the other, anticipating Miriam's response, seized her from behind, pinning her arms to her sides while her colleague left swiftly down the stairs, followed by Miriam's shrieking as she struggled violently against the arms that held her in a vice-like grip.

'It's for the best, Miriam.' Esther had followed them into the room. Miriam was now trying to bite her way free. She took her by the shoulders. 'It's only for a while,' she shouted over her shrieking. 'There's a train leaving the Chamartin station with a safe passage north to the coast where a ship is waiting to take them to a British port.'

Miriam continued to thrash about, screaming and pushing both her captor and Esther toward the door. Esther caught the eye of Veronica as she appeared from the top of the stairs. She came over and took the Red Cross woman's place so she too could leave. Together they forced the threshing and kicking Miriam down on her bed and held her until her screams turned to wild sobbing.

Then again Esther attempted to talk to her. 'He's being evacuated by the International Red Cross along with a trainload of other babies and children. I have seen to everything, his identification, everything. He'll be well looked after until you can join him.'

Exhausted Miriam quietened, lying limp on the bed. Esther slipped some notes into Veronica's hand as she left. 'Don't you see? It's for the best.' Miriam gave no response. 'He would never get through another winter like the last one.' Miriam continued to stare at the ceiling. Nikolai's framed photograph on a shelf above the bed caught Esther's eye. She picked it up and held it for Miriam to see. 'How long do you think he'd last if the Moroccan Regulares enter the city?'

She turned away to replace the photograph. Seizing her chance Miriam leapt from the bed, slamming the door behind her as she bounded down the stairs two at a time and into the street, followed closely by Esther. Frantically she dodged around passers-by, making it difficult for Esther to follow. Then as Esther was beginning to catch up she turned suddenly onto the avenida, dashing across the tracks in and out of the slow-moving tramcars until she reached up and pulled herself aboard one that would carry her to the railway station. Esther sprinted to catch it up but it was gathering speed and with a curse she gave up the chase to look for another one so she could follow, for it was obvious to her where Miriam was going.

Miriam ran along the crowded concourse as fast as she could, frenetically pushing and pulling people out of her way, glancing quickly through each gate until, there it was, its cars painted white and bearing the Red Cross emblem on the sides and roofs.

They must not hold her at the gate. She would get through. No one was to get between her and Nikolai. Clawing crazily at their faces, biting their hands, and twisting her way free she reached the cars as the engine started to pull out. She ran along beside them frantically beating at the sides with her fists, oblivious to the shouts of the uniformed men on the crowded platform, until stumbling she fell to her knees helplessly, holding her clasped hands up to the windows entreating each car to stop as it slid past her, powerless to do anything until the rear of the last one disappeared into the distance, leaving the track empty.

Wrexham, June 1957

'And that's how I found her, kneeling on the platform, her head buried in her hands.' Esther has stopped drinking. The bar is closed.

Nicholas sits unmoving. He feels distanced from the clamour and clatter of the refreshment room, as if he is looking down on a stage scene from high up in the circle: a table and two people under the glare of the fluorescent strips.

There is silence between them for some moments. Esther nervously plays with her watchstrap. 'So there you are: she didn't actually give you away.'

Nicholas remains silent.

'Did she?'

'No. You did.' His accusation surprises them both.

'You wouldn't be here now if I hadn't arranged your evacuation. It was for the best, you know.'

Nicholas looks at her hard, meeting her eyes with his and holding them. 'This is the first time you've told this story – even to you yourself. Isn't it? That letter in the package, it wasn't written by her, it was by you.'

Looking away Esther does not respond. She's gone too far. Damn the gin and damn him for being right.

'Up to now, right up to this point in your story, you've let me believe she packed me off. That it was she whom I had to forgive.' Nicholas closes his eyes and takes a deep breath before opening them, saying, 'You had me abducted, sent out of the way.'

Esther is about to protest.

'Oh, don't tell me it was for the best. Why didn't you have my mother taken on the train as well?'

'She was a wanted person. The nationalists would have shot her, Red Cross or not.' She reached over the table and took hold of his hand. 'She was trapped. Don't you understand?'

He snatches his hand away. 'She could have been disguised, perhaps as a nurse. You could have arranged forged papers, got her out on that train as well as me.'

'I couldn't have forced her against her will.'

'She would have followed me on to that train.'

'I couldn't have made her dress as a Red Cross nurse,' Esther snarls.

The room has become stilled. Nicholas realises he has been raising his voice. People are looking. 'Let's go outside,' he mutters.

They sit on a seat unspeaking, their eyes adjusting to the failing light, allowing their feelings to settle. The tink, tink tink, of a bell in the signal box breaks the stillness.

Nicholas looks away across the railway lines, shining like silver threads in the last of the sun, 'You didn't want her to leave at that time. You thought it best in the interests of the party that she should stay, send the baby off, carry on with her work.'

'No. That's not how it was.' Damn him again. What choice did she have at that time?

'Yes it was. You want me to believe she was dedicated to the cause far more than you.'

'I've already told you I tried to get her to leave as soon as I knew she was pregnant. It was too late at the end of May 'thirty-eight. The nationalists had Madrid in a ring that was tightening by the day.'

Esther waits for a response, becoming aware her head is slightly fuddled with the gin, but Nicholas is still staring across the tracks, so she goes on, 'Oh I know with the benefit of hindsight it's just possible that I could have got her out on that train, but at the time that's not how it seemed. It all happened so quickly. The opportunity came up. It was children only. I knew she would never put you on that train herself.'

Nikolai's silence is unnerving, after all, what else was she to do? How could she tell him she had her orders?

175

Miriam was to stay no matter what it cost.

Nicholas breaks into her thoughts. 'What happened after that?'

Esther shrugs. 'Soon after that her leave expired and she took up where she left off, but with more fervour than I would have thought possible. Using her work to deaden her loss I suppose. She'd made many enemies by then and she set to eliminating them. It was a civil war within a civil war over the next six months. I rarely saw her during that time, kept out of her way, in fact.

'I'm surprised she didn't eliminate you as well. How was it she could find it in herself to even speak to you again?'

'Well, she did, and that shows you how she came to see it my way to some extent despite her feelings. That November Moscow ordered the Russian advisers to stand down and started to pull them out. By then our relationship was starting to get back to its former state, though I don't think it was ever the same again. We were both offered the chance to go to Moscow and we took it up. Your mother, in recognition of her zeal, was one of only six women recruited into OMSBON.'

'OMSBON?'

'Separate Motorized Rifle Brigade for Special Designation of the NKVD of the USSR, Moscow division.'

'NKVD.' Nicholas draws in his breath before letting it out in one exclamation, 'Christ! They were every bit as bad as the SS, worse if that were possible. Stalin's murder squad.'

Esther looks back at him, her eyes glass-hard, before going on, 'It was an elite formation, a sort of Praetorian Guard, a key unit in Moscow to defend the Kremlin. We both had to drop to the rank of captain, of course, and I had to take up lessons in the language, though I never achieved the spoken competence of your mother.'

'And you. What did you go as?'

'They offered me a position on the newspaper *Izvestia,* special correspondent.'

'Was there no other way she could have got out of Spain, got to France, perhaps, then back to Britain to re-join me?'

'It was out of the question. The Comintern wasn't going to let her go. They'd invested too much in her and even if she'd made it to the border, the French already had an agreement with what was obviously by then the new future regime. We knew they were turning people back or interning them in what amounted to concentration camps.'

Yes, that's what they'd had in mind for Miriam for some time. She could see now how she'd been groomed for it. Of course, the Moscow offer to herself as a special correspondent on *Izvestia* was the reward for her part in it too, but to tell him that – no. He mustn't know that. She'd done it to save him, that was what he must believe, and who knew, it may be true. She may have done that anyway without coercion. That's what she herself must also believe. On the other hand, who could say whether in her heart of hearts Miriam didn't come to see it as a fortuitous way of having him sent out of harm's way so that she could carry on with the good work?

'What could you do in Moscow? The civil war was all but lost then, wasn't it?'

'That's not how we saw it. The fight was to go on by other means.'

'The fight! Your zeal was as strong as my mother's, maybe stronger, and you're still trying to conceal it.'

'Really?' She lights up again, taking her time. Shaking the match to put it out, she flicks it away. Her hands trembling she draws deeply on the cigarette, then she turns her collar up against the chill of the night air, slowly exhaling before saying, 'Tell me, how successful do you think your more –' she pauses giving a sarcastic edge to her voice, '– Liberal approach would have been against Fascism? Indeed, how successful was it to be in the war to come?'

Nicholas remains silent, waiting for Esther to make her point.

She turns to him. 'You sit there at the cost of other people's blood. Do you know that? Other people who were,' she pauses again, 'more than zealous, as you would say.'

'What do you mean?'

'Well, what good would your Liberal approach have been in 1941?'

'Now I see what you're getting at, but you're wrong. It was the democracies that ultimately overcame Fascism, not Communism, nor Marxism, nor any other ism.'

'Ha! It was Russia that brought down Nazi Germany, the Russian people and Stalin's leadership.' She points a wavering hand at him, the cigarette between her fingers, 'Oh, the war would have gone on longer without the democracies, I give you that, but eventually the end would have been the same.'

'And the rest of Europe would have exchanged Hitler's yoke for Stalin's.'

Esther springs to her feet and strides a little unsteadily to the platform's edge. Taking one more pull on it, she tosses her cigarette across the lines, then turns on her heel so sharply her coat flares out. Glaring at Nicholas for a brief moment, she swiftly retraces her steps to stand over him. 'Stalin,' she growls. 'Don't you talk to me about Stalin. What can you know? I was there on Red Square in November 'forty-one. I saw him on the Mausoleum in the falling snow. I saw him, I tell you; from the press seats along the Kremlin wall at the anniversary parade with the front line less than half an hour's drive away. That was his answer to the German Fascists while the rest of Europe cowered under their heel.' Then she turns, lights another cigarette, and paces along the platform until she disappears into the shadows of the footbridge.

He shouts after her into the encroaching night, 'What happened to my mother after that?'

The glow of a cigarette lighting up her face as she draws on it tells him she has turned and started back. He watches her emerge into the lamplight until she slumps down at the opposite end of the seat. They both sit facing the tracks.

Chapter Sixteen

The Sea of Marmara, 1939

Miriam stood at the rail as the ship approached the Bosphorus. She welcomed the cold drizzle of the first days of the new year on her face, causing droplets to form, before running down her forehead and her cheeks. It made a refreshing change from the stuffy oil-laden air below decks with its smell of boiled cabbage and the constant throbbing of the engines. Esther was down below in the cabin, still feeling the effects of seasickness. The Russian vessel was cautiously negotiating a sharp bend in the waterway, bearing round to port so that across the shimmering blue-grey water Miriam could see the brooding skyline of the Old City on the European side. Istanbul, there it was, silhouetted through the thin mist against broken rain clouds lit faintly from above by a watery afternoon sun. Occasionally the mournful hooting of ships moving in the opposite direction towards the Dardanelles strait was carried on the damp air. As they closed on the western shore her eyes took in the bulk of the Blue Mosque amid its slender minarets, standing over the city. Then, swinging to starboard, the vessel settled on its course past the mouth of the Golden Horn that would take it into the Black Sea and on to its destination at Odessa.

Odessa: the Soviet Union, the Old Russian Empire, and the very place from where her grandfather and his family came. The only contact with him she'd ever had was the large and ancient cigar box and its contents that Dad had kept in his tool chest. She recalled the rainy Sunday afternoons when as little girls she and Esther had been allowed to slide open the lid and rummage in it. There were old and water-damaged photographs of people in exotic clothes taken at a portrait studio. Their grainy sepia faces stared out intently at them through time. Somehow she had come to understand that these were her grandparents and their family. There were also thick cards with tattered and worn edges, which had once been gold, with Cyrillic lettering printed on them, or was it Hebrew? She couldn't remember. Among the shipping labels with indecipherable lettering: hatpins, hairpins, coloured ribbons, silver thimbles, and strange-shaped buttons, there were small keys and a tiny silver case whose lid sprung open to reveal a scarlet silk lining and nothing else except a small knob of beeswax and a faint sweet scent of honey. Then there was a chunk of a marble-like substance that they were told was from a piece of wedding cake. Apart from that nothing was ever said about the box or its contents, and they never asked, for the mystery was part of its attraction.

With her destination approaching she wondered for the first time what life was like for those people in whose silt, the detritus of their lives, she once rummaged? Those people who lived somewhere in the land where she was going. What would she have called her grandfather had she known him, Granddad or Grandpa? Who knows? Dad just referred to him, if at all, as Pa, as if he didn't belong in this existence, but was a remnant of another world, a world always referred to as dark, menacing, with all connection to it broken and yet here she was. What would it have in store for her? She would have to converse in Russian all the time now, except perhaps if she was alone with Esther. Would she come to think in that language, or still in English as she had with Spanish? Mam never did come to think in English, always having to translate from the Welsh in her mind before speaking. Recalling Mam prompted a twinge of doubt and helplessness, for there was no going back. The decision she'd made in Madrid was irreversible now, if it had ever been possible to revoke it. She felt she'd been carried along by events as inexorably as this vessel was carrying her to whatever awaited her in a Soviet future.

This was the nearest they'd been to land since leaving Barcelona, steaming at full speed to avoid the Italian submarines off Sardinia and rounding the Sicilian headland. The flight from Madrid to Barcelona on a Douglas transport aircraft crammed with Russian military advisers had been very uncomfortable, having to change direction and altitude many times to avoid patrolling nationalist planes. Now within a day or so they would be docking. They had received their food cards and rail warrants for the journey to Moscow, filled in the immigration forms, and an application for Soviet citizenship. You will have to give up your British passports when you get to Moscow, they were told. At first the official didn't believe they'd never possessed them. He'd sought higher authority before reluctantly stamping their application permits, still refusing to initial the stamp until NKVD clearance for the passenger list was telegraphed from Moscow.

The early afternoon air in Odessa was mild and damp as they climbed aboard the train of sandy brown cars with just their canvas duffel bags and haversacks as luggage. Heeding the warning of the Russian winter ahead both had acquired heavy quilted jackets to wear under their uniform greatcoats, and exchanged their officers' caps for felt hats with earflaps. They had been required to report to the administrator of political travel at the central rail office at Serednofontansky 12A. A small, weasely man with heavy black eyebrows and pince-nez above a Chaplinesque moustache, he told them the train would carry them on its journey of two full days across Ukraine to Moscow, with only one intervening stop at Kiev, apart from a halt between Kiev and Moscow to take on coal and water. There would be no food provided on board but they were allowed to take the official rations sufficient for one day only. They had to be bought from the administrator himself of course. It was strictly forbidden, he warned them sternly, to buy food or anything from the villagers at the halt, or from the platform at Kiev, and it was not permitted for them to leave the train until it reached its destination at Moscow's Kurskiy station. As an afterthought he also warned them they would need adequate gloves. Did they have any, he asked? It was very important to have the correct kind, soft and strong so as not to hinder the hands because it was dangerous to touch metal in sub-zero temperatures. As it happened he had a supply of sealskin gloves confiscated from a capitalistic profiteer just recently. He let them have a pair each for a small payment.

They were crammed into a sleeping compartment with six bunks. Sailors of the Black Sea Fleet already occupied four. They were lying on them, still wearing their greatcoats, cradling their boots in their arms and studying their bare feet. The car was under the care of a stocky attendant. Her open flat face with enormous freckles looked out with startling blue eyes from under a peasant kerchief confining, with limited success, a shock of red hair. She was resplendent in her uniform of an olive green flannel blouse, baggy trousers, boots, and a cap precariously balanced atop her kerchief. Smiling brightly to one and all she introduced herself as Lina and for a few kopeks she issued damp sheets to Miriam and Esther with the advice to hang them over their bunks to dry. The sailors spurned the sheets. They would use their greatcoats.

Soon the entrance doors were secured shut and the train

pulled out as Lina locked the interconnecting doors. After an hour or so snow appeared on the high ground and when the air became progressively colder she was prompted to ensure all windows were screwed fast. Finally she stoked up the great boiler at the end of their car and the sailors stripped down to their grubby shorts and flannel undershirts. A greasy pack of cards was produced and a vodka bottle was passed around. The sisters declined the offer of a mouthful and retreated to the corridor. When the bulky radiators heated up the air became as humid as a bathhouse and rank with the stench from the lavatories at each end of the car that had ceased functioning as soon as they left Odessa. Undeterred by this Lina pulled out two bundles of straw from her cubbyhole and spread them liberally on the floor of each lavatory, placing a small bucket of thick black disinfectant in each with the injunction to, 'Use it.' Little spirit stoves and iron teapots appeared on the floor of the corridor with which their fellow passengers interminably brewed the thick black tea that they topped up in their glasses from a hissing samovar at the side of the boiler, steaming up the windows so that it was impossible to see through them. When Miriam attempted to clear a patch of window with the end of a lace curtain to relieve the claustrophobic atmosphere she found the outer pane covered in ice.

In the middle of the first night, about four o'clock, the train arrived in Kiev. Miriam lay in her bunk listening to the slamming of doors, the thumping of footsteps in the corridor, and the shouting of orders above the roar of steam from the locomotive. Searchlights played on the curtains, temporarily throwing everything in the compartment into sharp relief with its white light. In the bunk above her Esther had stopped snoring, a sure sign she was awake. Should she reach up to take her hand and give it a squeeze? She would have to sit up. It was too much trouble. Then with a jerk the train moved off to continue its journey.

During the following day they spent most of their time in the corridor, driven out of their compartment by the foul fumes of the makhorka home-grown tobacco smoked continually by their travelling companions.

With very little else to do Miriam laboriously cleared a patch on the frosted window to look out on a vast, clean, white, empty landscape of unchanging windswept steppe. It seemed so repressive, making her feel insignificant, as if without existence. She wanted to curl up in the snow to become so small she would disappear into nothingness. Turning away from the window she broke the melancholy that was threatening to overwhelm her and kept her eyes focussed on the interior of the car.

By late afternoon they had consumed most of their meagre rations and practised their Russian on Lina, who constantly supplied them with tea at a price. Miriam expressed her concern that their food was all gone but she told them not to worry. Arrangements would be made. When the train stopped at the halt sometime in the night they were to put all their clothes on and bring their duffle bags and haversacks into the corridor, leaving nothing behind.

Once again the train jerking to a stop disturbed Miriam's sleep. Sitting up in her bunk she shook Esther awake and pulled on her coat, boots, scarf, and hat, not forgetting her gloves. Lina unlocked one outer door and tugged it open. Then with a ham-sized fist she smashed an exit through the ice sheet covering the side of the car. A small group of peasants clustered around the steps and paid their inducement for her to allow her passengers out to visit their food stalls. Lina turned to the sisters. 'Do not speak of this to anyone. It is illegal to produce anything to sell or to buy food from the peasants. Come on.'

'But what are we going to do?' asked Miriam.

'We are going to buy some food from the peasants.

Let's go.'

Surly-looking militia guards standing under a spotlight looked on without objection. They would get their share of the takings later. As the peasants moved on car by car to make their payments passengers were disgorged under swirling snowflakes, dancing in the yellow electric light barely penetrating the vaporous haze. A train was drawing into the rail yard from the opposite direction, the rhythmic beat of its exhaust sending out clouds of condensing steam and sulphurous smoke as it passed. In the murky air more locomotives were taking coal and water into their enormous tenders from the great tanks and bunkers towering above the billowing smoke clouds.

Miriam and Esther were among the first to climb down onto the rough icy planks. The air was so biting cold it seemed to scorch their lungs as they breathed it in. They quickly followed the example of their fellow passengers, wrapping their scarves around their mouths and heads so that just their watering eyes were left clear. Everywhere there was steam. Steam in columns and in clouds. Steam from breath freezing on nostrils and beards. Steam from cooking fires and from the locomotives. Lina, acting as their guide, led them over to the food stalls, urging them to shoulder their way through the milling crowd. Miriam could feel her eyes stinging from the smoke and her senses were sharpened by the scent of a pan of potatoes frying in oil. Lena urged them to take out their mess tins to hold a spoonful as they paid with a few coins. Then there was a copper vessel of boiling cabbage and beetroot soup. Miriam took a ladleful. Seizing her arm Lina drew her over to an iron tray of steaming apples baking over a charcoal brazier. Helping herself to one Miriam came upon a table of salt beef slices and smoked sausage. Lina helped herself to a large pickle from a tub and took a fistful of sunflower seeds from a hemp sack, stuffing them in her pocket without paying. Then taking three loaves of coarse black bread from a basket she thrust one in each of their haversacks and one inside her coat. As they passed a large basin of fermented buttermilk with ice floating in it Miriam took in the sour, acrid smell and declined a bowl. When they came to the crude green glass bottles of vodka with rag stoppers, freshly distilled that morning, Lina cautioned them with a wagging finger.

Miriam's eyes had been so fixed on the food that the peasants were just shadowy figures to her, but when she had taken all she wanted and was satisfied that Esther had sufficient she began to look around the stalls as she spooned her hot soup. She could see them carrying out their transactions with a desperate urgency, stuffing the money into canvas bags hanging around their necks. The fires throwing up light from below onto their gaunt faces enhanced their high cheekbones and hollow feverish eyes. Their woollen hats distinguished the men from the women in their thick kerchiefs wrapped around heads, necks, and mouths. Tattered quilted overcoats with kapok poking through splits were tied at the waist with cord, and on their feet were wooden-soled felt boots.

Then she saw the bundle. She felt her stomach constrict. Swaddled in a blanket and furs it was carried in a shawl slung around the woman's shoulders, allowing her to conduct her dealings with one arm cradling it. The urge to lift her arms in imitation of the woman overwhelmed her. Scarlet soup splashed on the packed snow as she dropped her mess tin and spoon. Esther picked them up. How old? She would go closer just to take a look. Perhaps it was not quite twelve months. His age. She would be able to see how he looked now. Slowly approaching the stall step by step she leaned over the table and held out her hand openly, almost imploringly. 'Let me look please – *pahzhalstah – pahzhalstah.*'

The woman was unsure of what she wanted. She didn't like what she saw in her eyes. Instinctively she held the baby closer with one hand, turning away slightly, almost shielding it, and standing back she spoke in a strange language. What was it, Yiddish? Ukranian? Clearly by her gestures it meant go away.

There was a hand on her arm. It was Esther. Clasping it she spoke softly with her mouth to her ear, 'Come on. It's time to get on board.' With one arm around Miriam's waist she led her to the train. As they hauled themselves up the steps Miriam looked back over her shoulder but there was nothing to see through the smoke, the steam, and the tears. Their locomotive gave a deafening blast on its whistle, and with a roar jerked forward as the frozen wheels came unstuck from the rails, spinning before gaining a grip, then snatching the couplings car-by-car it started them rolling.

By late the following afternoon they were obviously approaching the outskirts of Moscow. The temperature had lifted enough for the ice cladding to loosen its grip, dropping in great sheets to shatter on the trackside. The windows had cleared so that they could see in the twilight the poorly lit dilapidated settlements, partly obscured by dense factory smoke, that were gradually joining up to form the shabby suburbs. There was a stirring in the car as people were getting their possessions together, and Lina busied herself with a pitchfork at the open door, tossing out the steaming straw from each lavatory in turn, laughing as it took flight and dispersed in the air.

Soon the train was drawing along the shiny wet platform under the harsh station lights. It was on time to the minute. They descended into the bustle of the platform and the sound of stirring music from the loudspeaker system as they made their way, pushing through the jostling passengers and the crowds of people anxiously waiting to meet loved ones, friends, and relatives. Edging past a mother embracing her sailor son on his first leave they entered the Office of Political Travel where they presented their papers as arranged. A solemn-faced youth in NKVD uniform officiously consulted his passenger list and stepping smartly forward ordered them to follow him out and across the congested main concourse. He occasionally glanced back to make sure they were still with him as people stepped aside at the sight of his uniform, pressing back to make way.

'It looks as if we've been arrested,' Esther muttered nervously in English.

'We shouldn't have got out at that halt,' whispered Miriam, feeling an irrational cold chill of fear creeping up her spine. Maybe buying food there was a trap and Lina had denounced them.

Leading them through the exit to a covered lorry waiting in a poorly lit part of the station approach, the youth indicated they were to climb into the back.

Hauling herself up Miriam peered around in the gloom. Faces partly obscured by steaming breath were turned to her. There was something about their look, dejection, helplessness, or just plain misery that she found catching, almost overwhelming, or was she imagining it? Suddenly, with a kerchink, a powerful lamp was switched, on shining in their eyes, blinding them through their closed lids and raised palms. Miriam could feel her heart thumping against her ribs. 'Hands down,' a voice demanded harshly. A uniformed figure compared their features to a sheet of photographs. The light went out and she heard footsteps moving away, leaving them in complete darkness until her sight slowly adjusted to the gloom. In the sustained tension no one felt able to speak in case they drew attention to themselves.

After a muscle-tensing age with her pulse racing Miriam heard footsteps again and a figure, his face shadowed by the peak of his cap, appeared at the tailboard. It was slammed up and fastened. 'Welcome to the Soviet Union, comrades. You are being taken to the reception centre where there is food and a bath waiting.'

Miriam felt the sudden release of tension flow through her. She realised how the sense of helplessness and foreboding had subjugated her feelings but now, oh the relief of it, she needn't have worried.

As the lorry pulled away Miriam looked back at the impressive and monumental entrance of the Kurskiy Railway Station. Above it was a giant floodlit portrait. The avuncular features of First Secretary Comrade Stalin were unmistakeable. Below it an electric clock and calendar board reminded her it was Moscow time, the tenth of January, 1939.

PART THREE

MOSCOW

Chapter Seventeen

Moscow, January 1939

Miriam entered the immense openness of Red Square. Facing her through the thin freezing fog loured the Kremlin wall, and before it the crouching bulk of the Lenin Mausoleum. As she turned to her left she could just make out GUM, the famous department store, and on the south-eastern end of the square Saint Basil's Cathedral appeared through the haze. People crossed her vision like spectres or emerged out of the icy vapour as they came towards her, ghostly figures hunched in the cold air. The muffled clop-clopping of hooves marked the passing of one of the many horse-drawn vehicles still to be seen on the streets, with their pneumatic tyres slicking over the smooth granite sets. As she neared the great entrance to GUM she could see the leafless plane trees along the front of the incongruous stuccoed arches, encrusted with ice and forming a delicate tracery. Guttering paraffin flares were struggling against the failing afternoon light at the junction of Ulitsa Ilinka, and the flames in the oil drums at the traffic police posts were adding a sulphurous yellow glow to the murk. It all reflected her morose mood, probably due to tiredness and overwork, she told herself. Things would look different in bright sunlight.

This would be the first time she'd seen Esther since they had been sent to their separate quarters on their arrival two weeks ago. Given a few hours out of the NKVD barracks in the granite-walled building on the northern end of Lubyanka Square, housing the People's Commissariat of Internal Affairs and the newly built NKVD underground prison, she was going to meet her at GUM where Esther's postcard told her there was a café where they could take tea. It was a relief to be free of the intense atmosphere of the induction course, eighteen hours a day of lectures, interrogation training, weapons practice, and tightly structured debates ,with meals being taken without a break.

The café was in the dimly lit entrance hall and Esther was sitting at a table waiting for her. 'Do you feel as exhausted as you look?' She drew up a chair.

Miriam collapsed onto it, nodding weakly. She suddenly realised how tired she was. The feeling that she could just sit down for an hour or two without having to do anything or think about anything in particular or respond to questions with an immediate and appropriate answer was overwhelming and it made her head swim. She mustn't get used to it, she cautioned herself: it's only a momentary pause.

'Let's speak Russian, especially in public like this.' She spoke in English. 'We might as well now and when we write postcards to each other it may be unwise if we didn't use it as well.'

'Postcards! It's always postcards, never letters.'

'And quite right. There are still spies and counter-revolutionaries about. Everything has to be kept above board. There can be no private correspondence. No sealed envelopes containing private thoughts.'

Esther took a sip of her tea. 'Tell me, Miriam, do you think in English all the time, or have you started thinking in Russian?'

'It depends what you mean by thinking. If I go up a flight of steps looking for an address on an arresting operation counting each floor to myself, it will probably be in Russian, but when feelings or ideas spring to mind, you know, spontaneously, and I express them to myself or when I reflect it's still in English, or even when I think of something to say I often have to put it into Russian before I speak, but that's getting less and less.'

'I couldn't have put it better myself. By the way, I'm still struggling with the Cyrillic keys on my typewriter, but it's coming along. What have you been doing since we last saw each other?'

Miriam explained in as few words as possible, 'I've had to attend talks on political awareness too and I have a political officer who meets me for two hours a day. He takes me on tours of the city and I have to memorise everything and turn out a summary when we get back to the *Izvestia* offices on Pushkin Square. You should see them, all glass and concrete. This goes on for the next three weeks, I've been told, and then I have to complete a detailed questionnaire. I told him I filled one in when I joined the party but he said I have to do it often, on a regular basis, so that it shows the evolution of my political consciousness.' She made a wry face.

'I have to produce a short autobiography at the end of my induction so you're getting off lightly.' She wasn't looking forward to this. She couldn't think why it should be so other than it being a chore. It seemed to loom before her like a black cloud. She finished her tea. 'Perhaps we'll take a look at the shops here before I go back. Is this place anything like Lewis's in Liverpool?'

'Not any more. It must have been much bigger once, but all the shops have been requisitioned for offices. The roof is worth seeing though, all glass and a mass of wrought ironwork. It's a bit late for a sightseeing tour now but next time we must meet up earlier and I'll take you to the Tretyakov Gallery. It's said to be the finest collection of Russian art in the world.'

'I'm too exhausted right now for anything like that and I've only got a couple of hours anyway. It's just nice to sit down and do nothing. By the way, we've been taken to visit Lenin's tomb to see the great man there. They stand for hours in the queue but we went straight in.'

'Yes, well, that uniform will get you to the front of any queue.' Esther opened a packet of cigarettes and they both lit up.

Miriam drew gratefully on her cigarette. 'You said in your card you're in a hostel or something. What's it like?'

'Well it'll do for the time being. It's very close to the offices. I'm in a room with fourteen others, including four men. We all share the same washbasin and lavatory, it's warm and the water is hot, but I use the excellent facilities in the offices most of the time. They tell me I'm getting a room to myself in an apartment block soon that's also nearby, with a bathroom and a scullery on each floor,' she raised her eyes to the ceiling, 'bliss.' She pointed to Miriam with her cigarette hand, 'What are your barracks like?'

'There's only six of us women in the whole special unit so we're all in one room, showers, laundry, everything, all taken care of. Better than in Spain. We eat in the main dining hall. It's enormous, seating hundreds, except those of us on the induction course. We have to grab our rations on the run.'

'Before you go back to barracks you must see the new metro station at Revolution Square. It's just off the northern end of Red Square over there.'

Presently, after strolling through the arcades and marvelling at the glass-roofed interior, they buttoned up and Miriam was led outside to walk briskly in the biting evening air across the wet cobbles, shining in the dim street lamps and outlined by the fine powdery snow, to the recently opened metro at Revolution Square. Esther led her into the main hall with its marble lined arches and heroic bronze figures of Red Guards, workers, sailors, sportsmen and women who were depicted as having made the Revolution possible and subsequently helped to build the Soviet State.

Esther took her arm and stopped her in the milling throng on the vast shiny marble floor. 'What do you think of it?'

Miriam swept her eyes over the high vaulted and multi-arched ceiling with its gigantic glittering chandeliers as she searched for the Russian words. 'It's truly magnificent.' She nodded at the bronze figures and inspiring architecture. 'Are all the stations like this?'

'I think there's only about five been built up to now, but yes, they're all palaces like this one, each different in topic and style. Eventually there'll be a city network and a district line. I've heard women and the Communist Youth League volunteers built this one.'

'Marvellous! Is it deep enough to be used as a bomb shelter?'

'A bomb shelter! Whatever for?'

'Have you forgotten why we're here? War is coming. There's nothing more certain. This is the theme of most of our lectures at the barracks. Perhaps not soon but it's inevitable at some time in the future.' She placed her mouth close to Esther's ear so she could make her hear above the bustling crowd in the echoing hall of the station concourse without raising her voice. 'There is talk of letting the European countries fight it out, stand back, keep out of it until they exhaust themselves in a long, drawn-out war like the last time. Then the Soviet Union can clean up, re-build the whole of Europe free of capitalism and its Fascist by-product.'

'You're talking about Britain and France as well as Germany, aren't you?'

Miriam nodded, drawing back.

'What if they don't go to war with Germany? They don't show any signs of being warlike any more than they were with Spain. Quite the opposite if you ask me. They may just stand back, come to an accommodation of sorts, and keep out of it allowing Germany to attack us. It's set its sights on the USSR and the capitalist countries may let it do its dirty work for them. It seems a terrible risk to me, to stand back and not try to come to some agreement with the democracies against the Fascists.'

'Yes, I agree, but the general opinion among the lecturers on my course is that Britain wants no agreement with us, and who knows what approaches it's made to the Germans. France has not honoured its existing arrangements, using the excuse that Poland would not allow our troops to cross its borders to aid Czechoslovakia. When it comes to it the democracies back down. We saw this in Spain and with Czechoslovakia. When push comes to shove,' she used the English term, 'they won't fight, but it won't save them from war. A day of reckoning will come. We must be ready for it. Capitalism inevitably leads to collapse, then Fascism and war. It can't exist side by side with the Soviet Union. Sooner or later Germany will invade us with or without the western democracies. As to when, then we must trust to the judgement of the Central Committee.'

'In other words the General Secretary Comrade Stalin. You may be right but can we afford to stand back? According to Reuters news agency, this is just between you and I you understand, there is a conflict with Japan, military activity of some sort at a place called Khalkhin-Gol.'

'Where's that?'

'It's a disputed zone somewhere on the Soviet-Manchurian border, and there's trouble brewing with Finland over some territory or other in the gulf, but none of this will find its way into the Soviet press or radio, so keep it to yourself. As you know there are harsh penalties for spreading rumours, and quite rightly so.'

'Of course. This is still a great experiment we are involved in, still in its early days with much to be done. We must guard against negative thoughts, even within ourselves.'

The great octagonal clock hanging from the ceiling within its Soviet red star gleaming with chromium-plate and enamel finery caught Miriam's eye. 'I'll have to be going back now. Will you take a train from here to your place?'

'No, the Metro doesn't go that far yet. I'll take a trolley bus.'

As they parted at the entrance to the station and arranged to keep in touch by postcard Esther took Miriam's arm, saying, 'Oh and by the way, the new stations can be used as bomb shelters.'

With a wave Miriam made her way back to Lubyanka Square. Esther seemed settled, she mused. She was obviously throwing herself into her work. How typical of her to be enthusiastic yet still analytical, not accepting anything at face value. She would have to take care who she shared her thoughts with, though.

The Lubyanka, headquarters of the NKVD, February 1939

The Chekist ushered Miriam into the room. It was large and bare. The walls and high ceiling were a pale patchy yellow. In the middle of the brown linoleum there was a small green baize-topped table. On it was a carafe of water but no glass, a box of pencils, and a writing pad. A chair with its back to the door had been placed in front of the writing pad, facing another chair across the table. On the far wall opposite the door there was a radiator as big as a small car. The only window was an open glass panel above the door from the corridor. The harsh light came from a single bulb hanging from a long flex so that it was just over a metre above the tabletop.

'Please sit down, comrade.' The Chekist stood with his back to the radiator, his hands clasped behind him. 'To remind you, comrade, you must write in the first person. Leave nothing out. Start from your family background, analyse it in terms of Marxist theory, then show your developing political consciousness from your earliest recollections. Discuss your decisions and actions and relate them to the events that shaped your life. Show how they influenced your decision to join the party and become an activist, and the evolving train of thought that led to you accepting a commission in this branch of the NKVD. Take as long as you like but remember you will have to demonstrate the truth of what you have written line by line in a dialectical debate with your political officer. Then we will see if your political consciousness is evolving in a way suitable for a party comrade in an elite organisation. When you have finished take your papers to the desk at the end of the corridor, then come back in here and wait.' So saying he walked to the door and stepped out, closing it behind him.

Miriam looked down at the water in the carafe for some

moments. There was a film of dust on its surface. The room was warm but not unbearably so. She took up a pencil and addressed herself to the coarse, grey, unlined paper of the writing pad.

There was a rising tension as the pencil approached the sheet of paper, as if an invisible barrier lay between it. Mentally she pushed. It seemed to give like a clear membrane until it tore and the pencil thrust through onto the page, but her thoughts were uncoordinated. As they rushed at her she struggled with them, but they were dominated by the feeling of dread that something awful would be released if they were fitted together into an ordered pattern. Instead she would put them down at random as they occurred, like pieces of a jigsaw scattered on a table.

She started writing. The loss of Mam, the privations of the war, the mean village school, teaching at Black Lane School, Dad's refusal to let her take her place at college, her earliest memories in the cottage at Vron Offa and the contrast with the new house when Dad came home, the grammar school, then Edwin. Suddenly, she felt a tension building up. Now she would begin at the beginning, taking each topic in order, and relate them to Marxist theory showing, to herself as much as to anyone else, how these events determined the development of her political awareness.

The radiator broke into frenzied ticking, like some angry cricket, and became silent again. The farm, the arguments, the reading group, the Labour Party, the Miners' Strike, and becoming area secretary of the Communist Party; the writing was fevered and erratic until Gresford when it became difficult and uncomfortable recalling the experience, but she would go on despite the beads of sweat falling on the page. Cable Street – There was a chill on her back. Her shirt was saturated. Her breathing had become heavy, and her mouth was dry as if it had been filled with salt. She would put the pencil down for a moment. Taking the carafe in both hands she slaked her thirst with a long draught, then waited until her heart settled.

She took up the pencil, feeling an urgent need to write about Moseley, until again she stopped, unconsciously lifting her hand from the page and running her fingers lightly down her disfigured face and closing her eyes against the searing memory. Then she went on, Spain, Sergei, she realised she was grinding her teeth, Nikolai – There was just emptiness. She couldn't find it in herself to dig deep enough to write about him. Better to keep the emptiness, keep it buried. Her hand was shaking. The pencil dropped. It rolled and fell to the floor.

The tension was so great she had to keep writing. Taking up a fresh pencil she wrote about the contradictions within the Spanish Republic, the treachery of the Anarchists and Socialist groups, and how this contributed to its defeat as well as the non-intervention of the capitalist democracies, and concluded that war between them and the Fascist powers was inevitable. She felt easier writing in this vein but she knew the picture was incomplete. Nikolai was a gaping hole in the narrative of herself, a piece of the jigsaw that only when it was fitted in could give the picture meaning, and she knew she could not bring herself to confront it. This would have to do. It didn't have a bearing on her political development anyway.

She went out to the desk in the corridor and gave the papers to the typist, then used the lavatory and washed her face in cold water before she went back in the room and sat in the same place waiting for him: Major Chernov, her political officer. They'd been meeting as part of her induction at least twice a week, but not in this situation, nor in these conditions.

She'd left the door partly open. There was the clacking

of a typewriter, low voices, the slamming of a door, footsteps coming and going, each time raising the expectation they could be his until she became accustomed to them not being so. As time passed sitting with her back to the door became uncomfortable. She shifted uneasily. The empty chair facing her was disturbing. Why didn't she sit on it? She was about to do so when he came in, pushing the door gently until it clicked shut.

His feet made no sound and as he moved to the chair she caught the scent of carbolic soap he carried about him. A tall lean man, he sat down, placing her papers before him and looking up at her. She always felt his eyes were the palest blue she'd ever seen. They had white lashes and eyebrows and he had high, almost gaunt cheekbones. His nose was sharp above thin, colourless lips.

Taking up her papers he turned them and placed them down in front of her. He had a disconcerting way of starting without any form of greeting. She could never be certain whether this was intentional. He tapped them. 'Starting at the beginning, read to me what you have written, but slowly.'

And so she started sentence by sentence, occasionally being stopped, especially when she had expressed an opinion, to investigate and substantiate the logic of each premise in terms of Marxist theory. It was hard going through the main events in her life, the analysis, demonstrating her developing political thought, until finally ending in Spain.

'Comrade Captain Moss, why have you stopped?'

She did not answer. Try as she might it would not come out. Her lips trembled. She did not want to answer.

'You had a child. Major Nikonov, your lover, was the father. Was that not so?'

She turned her face away.

'Look at me.' His voice was calm and soft.

She turned back. His eyes seemed compelling and even

paler, almost grey.

He placed his finger on the paper. 'There you write of the tragic death of Major Nikonov. Sergei was his name, was it not?'

She gave a mechanical nod.

'You go on to mention that you had a baby, then nothing more, nothing at all.' He looked at her. His eyes seemed to pierce her skull right through into her mind. 'There's just a gap until your enrolment in the OMSBON section of the NKVD.'

She would keep her emotion bottled up. Restlessly shifting and changing her position on her chair, clasping and unclasping her hands.

Chernov leaned forward, his face close to hers. 'He is a little boy, isn't he? What is his name?'

She looked up at the ceiling, trying to stifle the shuddering in her chest, then down at him as he leaned back in his chair.

'His name!' He shouted suddenly, startling her. 'Tell me!'

Racked with sobbing she cried out, 'Nikolai!' Her hands tightly clasped and her arms held rigid she said it again, but in a whisper, 'Nikolai.'

'He was taken from you, wasn't he?'

There was no answer. She wouldn't respond to this. Her jaw was set as if to shut out the memory of that time. She didn't want to let it in. She wouldn't allow it. It was far too painful.

'Comrade Captain.'

Through the mist of tears she fixed her eyes on the tabletop.

'Miriam Osipovna look at me.'

He'd used her patronymic. How dare he get so familiar and how did he know Dad's name anyway? Of course, it was on her citizen application papers. He was making the point she could keep nothing from him. She would look at his face but not into his eyes.

She heard him saying as if from some distance away, 'I want you to do something for me, something very painful, but it must be done. Before you can move forward in your political thinking you must re-visit that dreadful time.'

She shook her head.

His tone was calming and persuasive. 'Listen to me. That's all I ask. You don't have to say anything. Keep looking at the wall in front of you.' He got up from his chair quietly and placed it at her side before sitting down again.

She remained still, her expression impassive.

'Now let us both look at the wall.' He spoke softly in her ear.' What do we see? There you are in that room in Madrid. They are taking your baby. You hold him. You hold him tightly. But it is no good. They are dragging him from you, tearing him from your hands. Can you see?'

Oh God she could, she could. She cried out, 'Yes!'

'Now look, they are taking him away. And now at the railway station, the train is leaving. There he is in the window. You can't get to him. The train is leaving. The cars are starting to move. They are passing you one by one. You can't get to him. What do you do? Look, the last car is going away into the distance. He's gone, Nikolai, he's gone, your baby boy.' He paused and turned to speak softly in her ear again. 'Tell me now, not what you see, tell me what you feel, those feelings pent up for so long, you must let them out.'

He sat back.

They came welling up, the horror and the despair as if for the first time, even worse than the first time. She struggled to put them into words but then she fell forward onto her forearms, her shoulders heaving with deep irrepressible sobbing. Overwhelming her it continued unabated. The grief seemed to be pouring out of her endlessly.

Chernov got up from his chair and went over to the radiator. Leaning on it he lit a cigarette, staring reflectively at the ceiling while he smoked and waited patiently. Occasionally she would raise her head and let it fall again as she collapsed into more sobbing. After some time she felt it subsiding and she sensed him returning and placing his chair to face her again. She sat up, composed herself, breathing deeply and remaining silent; a sense of release suffused her body, but to him she presented a cold and unfeeling exterior.

He dropped his cigarette in the carafe and took out a pack. Placing it on the table he slid it to her then he moved to stand looking at the back of her head his hands clasped behind.

She ignored the pack, looking fixedly at the radiator opposite.

Leaning over her he spoke in her ear. 'Our meeting today has been connected with your interrogation training as well as your autobiography. You have just had an object lesson in breaking down a personality; oh, don't be disturbed, you came through it well. It is very important; the psychologists tell us, in reconstructing a subject's consciousness so that they will make a full verbal confession in court and willingly accept their guilt for their misdeeds. During the last five years we have developed our techniques quite successfully as we stemmed the attempts to overthrow Comrade Stalin. Even our former chief, the treacherous Yezhov, was involved in the villainy, but now we move forward with a new leader, Comrade Beria, although there are still some vermin in the NKVD to be rooted out. So you see successful interrogation has to be carried out in a thoroughly ruthless manner to probe deep into the subject's psyche and one of the chief factors in this is information. You have to know the key events in a subject's narrative, the traumatic events that are too disturbing for the consciousness, becoming pent up like volcanic forces waiting to be released, and of course for our purposes, controlled.'

He paused for some moments. She wondered if he was going to leave but he went on, 'You will conclude your autobiography by showing how Fascist intervention in Spain led to you losing your little boy.'

'That's ridiculous.' She turned on him, 'Fascist intervention was the reason I was there in the first place, and without it there would have been no Nikolai.'

'That's very good, but nevertheless you must make it clear where you stand. You must show how his loss has affected your thinking. You have accepted your role in a way you could not have done if you had kept him. Do you or do you not think what happened was for the best? You must answer this in your writing, showing how your consciousness has evolved under the party's tutelage. In that way you will demonstrate that you understand the guidance of Comrade Stalin.' He got up from his chair. 'This concludes our talk today, Comrade Captain. We will meet again next week for a final discussion of your completed autobiography.'

She turned back to face the radiator.

He went to the door and paused. 'You may go when you have finished. Leave your papers at the desk at the end of the corridor and report immediately to your superior officer.' He left the room, leaving the door open.

Her breathing had steadied. Was she glad Nikolai had been removed? The question had the force of a hammer blow. After all, Esther was right. He wouldn't have survived in Madrid. Was she glad for him or for herself? Perhaps it depended on whether she believed she would ever see him again. Could she have got out of Madrid and back to Britain to find him sometime after he had been taken, instead of embracing the Soviet Union? But the future did not lie with Britain, not as a capitalist country. It looked as if it would either be crushed by the Fascists or swept into the Soviet Union. Nevertheless the question had been in her subconscious ever since, but she'd never put it into words before. Oh, if only she could have held on to him, brought him with her, but that was never possible. Perhaps one day she could get him back, one day when the Soviet Union prevailed over Fascism. Right now she would complete her autobiography.

Chapter Eighteen

Moscow, March 1939

Miriam strode purposefully through the Aleksandrovsky
Gardens beneath the Kremlin walls, her boots crunching
on the broken ice. She intended to take a short cut through
to check on the disposition of the NKVD guard unit on
duty under her command at the Kremlin Palace, where the
Eighteenth Communist Party Congress was being held, but
she reckoned without the faint warmth of the pale March
sun on her back, bringing out the colour of her uniform
and the blue tabs on her shoulders and the cuff bands on
her sleeves. How it changed her mood, almost
imperceptibly. As if it had crept up on her, catching her off
guard. Gradually she began to stroll at a more leisurely
pace, turning aside along pathways among the water
gardens where the ice was beginning to relinquish its hold,
and the tentative trickling of the streams joined the
splashing of the fountains and the dripping waters of the
early spring thaw. The sight of snowdrops and violets in
bloom lifted her heart. She paused to admire them and the
pussy-willow twigs with their swelling buds. As her
skirted coat tails brushed the bushes she caught the scent
of lavender.

Things were not turning out so bad after all. The
thought arose stealthily without warning. Suddenly the
cawing of a large flock of rooks reminded her, Russians
take their arrival as a sign of the coming spring, a sign of
hope. She watched them swooping to settle on the Central
Exhibition Hall, jarring her mood as they turned black the
yellow and white neo-classical portico. Swiftly she turned

her back on them to continue her walk. Nearing the children's playground close to the Borovitskiye Gate Tower the sound of an accordion and screams of laughter fell on her ears. With her hands clasped behind her she approached the low surrounding hedge of the play area with cautious steps. Curiosity overcoming her hesitation she looked into the compound. A soldier, his tunic blouse carelessly unfastened, was balanced precariously on a rustic seat surrounded by an arc of small boys and girls bundled up in furs and quilted smocks like bear cubs, sitting on tiny chairs with a very young kindergarten assistant standing behind them. They were spellbound by the soldier's antics with glove puppets. Arms held out at full stretch on either side of him, his knees slightly bent, he turned his head to each puppet in turn, attempting to give them voices to sing to the accordion while he tried some dance steps, his feet moving delicately and swiftly despite his soft, calf-length boots. The children were helpless with mirth, clasping their little hands between their knees and rocking back and to with delight. Four or five of his comrades squatting on their heels watched from a distance with broad smiles, obviously enjoying the sight, bobbing up and down, clapping in time to the music and adding their hoarse voices to the joyful cries as they joined in the responses with a child-like spontaneity. Turning away she found herself chuckling as she resumed her walk to the Kremlin Palace, still purposefully, but with a lighter step.

Having discharged her duties at the Great Hall she made her way back up the hill to her quarters at Lubyanka Square, where she found a postcard from Esther suggesting that she let her know when she had time off duty so that they could meet up at the Perlov Tea House on the corner of Myasnitskya and Bobrov before visiting the Tretyakov Gallery.

She made her way down from Lubyanka to meet Esther at

the Perlov. The street was quite crowded with people taking cautious steps on the semi-frozen slush, huddled against the biting wind, and keeping clear of the aged trams whining along the icy rails and clacking and lurching over the points, blue sparks spurting from the frosted overhead power lines. Winter had returned with a defiant blast, making a mockery of the early spring weather of the last few days. She was glad of her full-skirted, ankle-length uniform greatcoat with its thick felt lining. Stopping briefly at a crossing to take her bearings and looking out at the junction under a light dimmed by the overcast sky, the disappointment cruelly provoked by the false spring enveloped her in a sense of deep isolation. She felt as if she were just a spectator, separated from these people and invisible to them, huddled into the wind as they were or leaning forward with it to their backs, scurrying on their way. They all had someone to talk to, to spend time with, and to exchange thoughts or ideas. People surround her on the streets and back at the barracks but their eyes seemed to see through her. She couldn't make contact with them except in the course of her duties. She supposed Esther had a more fulfilled social life. She must have to interact with her colleagues at *Izvestia*, not just give or take orders.

Using Esther's description Miriam easily identified the exotic Chinese façade of the tea house. As she approached the door it was held open and a waiter addressed her with a short bow before taking her coat and leading her to Esther's table near the window. She found that the Perlov was actually a shop for selling tea, with lacquered columns, shelves, and counters painted with green and gold dragons and serpents, but there were also tables and chairs where tea could be taken. After greeting her with the announcement that Madrid had finally fallen Esther ordered for them both.

Miriam took off her gloves and removed her cap,

shaking her hair free.

'Yes. Yesterday Franco made his entry into the city according to Reuters.' Esther paused while the waiter set two glasses before them in their silver holders with a silver dish of lemon slices and small lumps of grey-black speckled sugar, then moved away. 'Ciano, the Italian foreign minister, calls it the greatest victory for Fascism up to now.'

The waiter returned with a silver teapot from which he poured their tea, then set it on the table, and with a brief bow, left them.

'Up to now. It sounds as if he's got a list of victories up his sleeve. Maybe someone should ask him to show it,' Miriam said.

'I'll have to leave you around two thirty this afternoon. I hope you don't mind but we should be able to get around some rooms on the first floor of the gallery before then. It's impossible to see all the paintings in one visit anyway. There's well over a hundred thousand, covering the most ancient Russian art chronologically decade by decade. This will be my third visit so I know my way around a little. I find it very restful. It helps me to clear my head.'

'Clear your head, do you have a lot to think about then?'

Esther squeezed a lemon slice into her tea. 'Well, I do actually.' When she finished with the lemon she took out her cigarette case and offered one to Miriam, taking one for herself. The waiter appeared at her elbow with a lighter then moved to Miriam before disappearing.

She kept her eyes on Miriam while she turned her head to breathe smoke from the side of her mouth. 'There's a man. An editor on the foreign desk.'

There was an awkward silence. 'Well?'

'And he's married.'

Miriam froze with the glass partway to her lips. 'You're having an affair.'

'Of course. That's what an affair is, isn't it?'

'Please don't tease. This is serious and that wasn't a question.'

'Well, I'm just telling you. I didn't ask whether you approved.'

'Indeed!' She drew on her cigarette. 'What about his wife?'

'What about his wife?'

Miriam waited expectantly but in vain. 'If it goes wrong – if she finds out.' She sought the words in Russian but she went on in English, 'Your goose is cooked. She'll want you out of that office.' Then she drew deeply on her cigarette, turning her head as if to gaze through the window. She felt even more isolated now, more loneliness, that's what she felt, a deep loneliness. Now Esther had a man it just left her feeling even more shut out, as if she was looking in through a plate-glass window.

'Penny for your thoughts?' Esther used the English term.

Reprovingly Miriam replied in Russian as she gathered up her gloves and cap. 'Oh nothing. It's time we were off to the gallery if you're going to meet him later this afternoon. That is why you have to go at two thirty, I assume?'

Esther stubbed out her cigarette without replying and went over to pay at the pagoda-style kiosk. Then they both took their coats and shrugged them on before stepping out through the door respectfully held open by the waiter. Walking uphill to the corner with Ulitsa Lubyanka they took a trolley bus south over the river and the canal to the Tretyakov.

Buying their tickets in the basement they declined the offer of the cloakroom and kept their coats on as their steamy breath told them the gallery was unheated, then they went up to the first floor. Esther fished a tattered guide sheet out of her pocket, 'Although it can be quite

215

difficult at times it is worth sticking to the numbered sequence,' and so they started at the room numbered one nearest the stairs from the basement. It was the first of a series of fifteen dimly lit rooms with spotlights tightly directed at the paintings themselves, hung in chronological order and dedicated to the eighteenth and early nineteenth centuries.

As they strolled casually through one room after another Miriam was prompted to murmur, 'I must say I expected to see more works of a religious character, icons and the like, but these could be from anywhere in Europe up to now.'

'The religious works are held in the ground floor rooms. Before the eighteenth century Russian art was entirely religious but from then on, under European influence, it became almost exclusively secular.'

Leaving room twelve they passed through two large rooms to enter thirteen. Suddenly Esther quickened her pace. 'There's nothing much of interest in here, we'll go through into the next one.'

But Miriam had already seen the portrait as soon as they entered the room. Gently releasing Esther's guiding hand from her arm she slowly approached it. It was of a boy of four or five years with delicate refined features, rather sentimentally painted with tousled fair hair falling over his forehead, the face lit on one side, the rest in shadow dissolving into the fine gold of the background. The eyes looking wistfully to the side were perhaps too large and the lips a little too full for modern taste. She felt her throat tightening but she suppressed the tears. 'It's all right, Esther. I can manage this sort of thing now, but thanks for thinking about me anyway. Does the sheet give his name, the little boy I mean? '

Esther held the sheet up to the light over the painting. 'It's titled *Portrait of Arsenii Tropinin, the Artist's Son* painted in 1818. It says here this painter was a serf for

216

forty-seven years before he gained his freedom from his master.'

Conscious of the time she guided Miriam to the door and they resumed their stroll through the rooms with Esther peering at her sheet in the poor light and reading out the titles of each painting as they passed. 'I'm sorry, I didn't think you would spot it so quickly.' Esther, still feeling uncomfortable, paused before a landscape with trees in the foreground. 'We came upon it sooner than I expected, you see.'

Miriam seemed not to have heard. 'Look! What is that painting called, the one with those blackbirds in the trees?'

'Let me see.' Esther fumbled with her sheet. 'Here it is, The – something. I can't translate that word, Have Come. That's it. The, something, Have Come.'

'It's not the word for birds, is it?'

'No. I know that word.'

Excitedly she lapsed into English. 'The Russians say when the rooks come it's a sign of the coming spring, a message of hope. The word must be rooks. Oh Esther! What a coincidence.' She reverted to Russian. 'I saw them the other day at the Alexandrovsky Gardens, a great flock of rooks, cawing and swooping, and I thought about the saying, a message of hope. Did you say that was the title?'

'No. You said that. The title is *The Rooks Have Come*, that's if you've got the right word.'

'Yes.' It was a man's voice from behind them. 'It is the correct word.'

They both turned round. The owner of the voice had also been viewing the painting. He was quite tall, almost six feet, and although his cap was held before him in both hands his uniform showed he had the rank of colonel in the NKVD. 'And it is a message of hope,' he added. 'So powerful a message on a day like this when winter is reluctant to give up his cruel grip and seems to hold on forever, and so clever a painting. See the spire of the bell tower in the middle ground behind the trees with the rooks?'

They turned to the painting.

'How it connects the church, and by implication the institution of the Church with a time of hope, with Easter on the way. Good propaganda, is it not?'

'Indeed it is,' said Miriam, partly turning back to him but keeping the damaged side of her face away from the light.

There was an awkward pause. 'Excuse me, I am Dmitri.' He paused expectantly as she swiftly pulled off her glove and offered her hand.

'Miriam. My name is Miriam and this is my sister Esther who has brought me here: she comes often.' Esther received an arch look. 'She tells me she finds it restful.'

He took her hand and gave a short nod to them both. 'Pleased to meet you.' Then he turned back to Miriam, still speaking formally, 'I too come here often for the same reason. You both have good Russian.'

She modestly accepted the compliment over Esther's murmured thanks.

'Have you been in the Soviet Union long?'

'Since the beginning of this year. We came from Spain, Madrid actually.'

'But you are English?'

'Ah.' she was about to correct him but she realised she did not know the Russian for Welsh. She'd look it up later but for now, better to take the easy way out, 'Yes.'

'And in Spain, you were fighting?'

'Yes we were both majors with the Eleventh International Brigade.'

'Indeed!' He nodded to her blue shoulder tabs. 'Now you are a captain, NKVD and,' he saw the crimson bars on her chest, 'OMSBON?'

'Yes, OMSBON,' said Miriam. His eyes widened, he was clearly impressed. 'And Esther is a journalist on

Izvestia.'

'So! Comrade Captain and Comrade Journalist, let me show you both a painting that I find particularly interesting and typically Russian. It's just along here.'

Esther broke in, 'I'd love to see it but I have to go now, I have an appointment, so if you'll excuse me I'll leave you.'

'Of course,' he gave a short bow.

'Enjoy your afternoon,' Miriam said slyly as she left them.

He held out his arm. 'It is this way,' and led her to stand before a very large, almost monumental work. The subject was a ragged column of people moving across the middle of the picture. He turned to the painting and spoke without looking at her. 'It is titled *Religious Procession in Kursk Province*, painted around 1880. The painter, Ilya Repin, wants to show us the different attitudes of those in the procession to the icon being carried at the head of it. See the blind faith in the faces of the priests struggling along with that large and heavy object on their shoulders. Look at the one holding his face up to the sky, religious ecstasy written all over it and the face of the female peasant following, the one in the kerchief. There is complete trust in her eyes, as if the icon was the very saint himself who was leading the procession. See her clasped hands, her shoulders hunched as if she awaits the blow on her back. But the bishops, ah, look at the bishops. Have you ever seen such smugness, especially the one peering over the top of the open book of the gospels he is holding in front of him, and the mounted soldiers of the Czar, their chests thrust out aggressively. Yes, all the ranks of the old regime are here and the organs of repression, the soldiers and especially the Church and its instruments, the icons.'

He spoke with surprising intensity, she mused, and he was quite attractive when he lost his stiff formality. His hand, as he used it to explain the picture, was so broad and powerful, a labourer's hand, and yet the fingers stressing the features of the picture with such precision were a craftsman's fingers. This work clearly meant something special to him. It was gigantic, amazingly well executed, very colourful, and so compelling.

Suddenly he turned to her. 'What do you think of –' He stopped his voice trailing off.

She knew why he faltered. Her face was caught fully in the light shining on the picture. Instinctively she turned it away.

Intrigued more than shocked he continued, 'What do you think of it, Miriam?'

Startled out of her self-consciousness but at the same time her mind sharpened more by the suddenness of his familiarity than the question, she came out spontaneously with her impressions. 'That figure in the foreground, the lame youth in the thick felt coat, I find him quite disturbing, hobbling with his staff, almost staggering in his desperation to keep up with the procession while his eyes are fixed intensely on the icon, his hope of salvation. It makes for a very powerful image.' Surprised at how he had brought forth this comment from her she went on, 'And the peasants, they look exactly like those we saw from the train as we travelled here from Odessa.'

He nodded. 'That is what makes the work timelessly Russian, not the Church nor the monarchy, they belong to the time when it was painted, but by the way the peasants are depicted, they are still with us today, a legacy of the past, not changed, I'm afraid, not yet anyway. There is much more work to be done.'

Miriam remained silent. He was somewhat outspoken for one in his position, especially considering they'd just met. Surely the current party line was on what had been achieved, not what had not yet been done, but she would keep her thoughts to herself on this.

He looked at his watch. 'I'm afraid I too have to go

now.'

There was a moment's awkward silence. 'Maybe you would like to walk back to Headquarters with me?'

'No thanks. I still have some time to kill. I think I'll just stay here a little longer,' she gave a weak smile, 'look at some more paintings.'

'Very well.' He took some steps back, awkwardly lifting his hand in a clumsy gesture of farewell and conscious that it was inadequate muttered, '*Sveedanya*,' before turning to go.

'Bye.' She stood looking at his receding back. Why did she do that, just let him go? She could at least have given him her address. Or even walked back with him, that's all she had to do. Now the moment was lost. She felt a strong impulse to call after him.

She was about to do so when he stopped and turned.

Mentally she took a step toward him. It may have shown in her body language.

'If you will tell me how I can contact you we could arrange to meet, to visit this gallery again or – somewhere else perhaps.'

She nodded.

He brought out his notebook as he came back to her and they exchanged addresses.

Then he gave a heartier wave as she let him go, but she still felt she had somehow handled things awkwardly. There was no reason why she couldn't walk back to Headquarters with him. She was not that keen to continue around the gallery anyway. Perhaps she was afraid of him seeing her face in broad daylight.

The People's Commissariat of Internal Affairs, Moscow, May 1939

If anyone thought of NKVD Colonel Dmitri Alekseevich Ignatov at all it was his cool external presence, not his intense inner life, that struck them, but just occasionally and startlingly it would break through his hardened exterior. His manner gave his comrades the impression of tension and the strength of spring steel and to his victims his lean frame conveyed the flexibility and suppleness of a python. When they first met his wife-to-be found his blue eyes with their almost white lashes under a thatch of fair hair striking though at first she found his pale skin a little repellent.

On the day of Dmitri's arranged meeting with Miriam he was striding down the long and wide wood-panelled corridor with its grey carpet runner leading to wooden double doors. Officers and secretaries in NKVD uniform were bustling back and to. He hoped his card had got through to her. Would she recognise him? After all, it was two weeks into May before they'd been able to coordinate their time off, nearly eight weeks since the Tretyakov. He would have no such trouble recognising her. Impulsively he drew in his breath at the memory of her scarred features suddenly revealed in the spotlight. Such damage to a face that should be so good-looking. Yet despite that he was aware of a strange sense of attraction and repulsion that she prompted in him. Should he take her to his usual sites? Not much chance of conversation in the gallery and she may find the polytechnic boring: it was a specialised interest, and they both had only a few hours leave. In which case he decided he would suggest a restaurant and as he knew of only one it would have to be the private place called Café Margarita that had re-opened after many years of being closed down. It was really a cheap café trying its best to be a restaurant in the area around Tverskaya off Pushkin Square, but as he had just invited her out for a drink it would do. He pushed open the heavy doors to the echoing marble entrance hall. Would she be there? He looked over to the waiting area with seats. There she was.

Dmitri had said it was one of Moscow's oldest restaurants. It looked it, she thought, after they were seated. There was an acrid smell of cheap tobacco, boiled cabbage, and onions in vinegar. Her spirits fell as she peered around the smoke-filled room. It was tiny and poorly lit with dark wooden walls. Two soldiers, quietly subsiding into an alcoholic haze, and a pair of gnarled old men playing chess with knotted and twisted hands were the only other customers. He was unknown to her but she kept that to herself as he seemed to take it for granted that she should be familiar with him. Had he brought her to this gloomy place to avoid the attention of other diners? It would seem he didn't want to be seen with her.

'What would you like to drink, Miriam?'

He startled her. She hesitated, unsure. She hadn't drunk alcohol since before Nikolai.

'I shall order konyak. We'll have a single drink to warm us up, yes?'

She nodded. It seemed a good idea. It might lift her spirits and help to cope with this place. Alcohol was about the safest drink here as long as it was not made out at the back.

The waiter, a Belarussian in an embroidered skull cap, a greasy silk blouse, and wide scarlet cummerbund that enhanced his enormous belly, set an opened bottle of Armenian brandy, two tiny glasses, and a small dish of zakuski on the table. Wiping his hands on a dubiously stained cloth slung over his shoulder he filled the glasses before giving a short bow from the waist that made his jowls quiver. Then he left them.

Dmitri Ignatov took out a pack of American cigarettes, placed it on the table, then sipped from a glass. 'So Miriam, tell me about yourself, not what you do, but where you come from, your family, and why you are here?'

He meant, how did she get her face in that mess? That's what he really wanted to ask. Well, unless she walked out on him he was entitled to know, she supposed, and anyway it was nice to have someone's attention. He was good-looking and it had been some time.

As if he read her thoughts he reached over the table and placed his free hand lightly over hers. His touch was so fine she barely felt it and she recalled how she first noticed his hand at the Tretyakov. 'I don't just mean how you got that injury.'

As they smoked and sipped their drinks she told him her story, including her full name, how she became a teacher, was widowed, joined the party, how she got her injury, and Spain. She left out the finer details as well as Sergei and Nikolai, ending with her arrival in Moscow. 'And you, now it's your turn Colonel Dmitri –?'

'Alekseevich Ignatov.'

She inhaled her cigarette, enjoying the luxury of the cool, sweet Virginia tobacco, and the brandy that had become quite pleasing on the palate, producing a mellow feeling that lightened the surroundings. 'Tell me everything, where you were born and grew up, what has happened to you, how you came to be in the NKVD, and,' she held out her glass as the thought occurred to her, 'are you married?'

'I was born in 1899 to a peasant family in Kursk Province, that's why I found the Ilya Repin painting at the Tretyakov interesting. I was working with a pitchfork when I was seven and stacking stooks at haymaking when I was eleven as well as being responsible for a flock of geese. Despite this I managed to finish the three-year course at the local school.

'When I was fifteen I was sent here to Moscow as a servant to a corn merchant, a distant relative of my father, who fitted me out in a black suit and tie, had my photograph taken, wrote on the back 'Dmitri Alekseevich, his master's servant' and sent it back to my father. Also in that year the German war broke out. After a while my master sent me back to school where I became a top student in mathematics. At the beginning of 1917, aged eighteen, I was called up. After six months, perhaps because I was tall and strong, I was chosen to train as a junior NCO. By August 1917 I was sent to the front where I was concussed by a German shell and sent to hospital. I was there when the Revolution broke out in that October. Then I was elected on to the regimental committee there, I served until the regiment disbanded itself at the end of the year. We were told to take our weapons if we wished and head for home, so I went back to my village in Kursk Province until August 1918 when I was mobilised into the Red Army.

'Then I was sent to the lower Volga region near Tsaritsyn where I was wounded by a grenade and back in hospital in July 1919. Because of my exemplary record I was accepted into the Russian Communist Party and by 1921 I was promoted to a red officer.

'As the Civil War came to an end my regiment was sent to fight the rebel Kuban Cossacks. Conditions were terrible and there was great slaughter. My commander, Tukhachevsky, ordered the harshest measures. The forests in which the rebels were hiding were cleared with the use of poison gas. Calculations had to be precise to ensure that the cloud of asphyxiating gas was thoroughly dispersed through the entire forest so as to destroy every living thing concealed within it. Was that too harsh? I have asked this question many times but I always conclude that a great commander cannot manage without harsh measures.

225

'Then in 1932 I was sent to study at the Leningrad Mountain Engineering Institute where I learned about explosives and where I met and married my wife, Irena. Graduating in in 1934 after a two-year artillery course I was called to serve in the recently founded NKVD and told to report to the Lubyanka, Moscow.

'In 1934 to '38 I took part in the Purges. Some call that time the Terror. I believe they were necessary.

'My wife obtained a divorce in 1937. Since then I've led a quiet life buried in my work although I've recently acquired an interest in Russian literature. During any short breaks I have sometimes visit the chess club at the Smolny Institute, the Tretyakov, where met me and the Polytechnical Museum on Novaya Ploshchad just off the north side of Lubyanka Square. I find the huge collection of gadgets, clocks and devices from ancient times an engrossing diversion."

He re-filled their glasses. He'd told her what he wanted her to know, just as she had done with him, leaving out the details of his divorce. Then he stubbed out his cigarette, picked up a small slice of rye bread from the dish, dipped it in the sour cream, and sat back, chewing it reflectively. He had been watching the effect on her as he skipped over his activities in the Terror, on her hands, on her face. Tempted as he was to go into detail he held back, though it would be interesting to get a response, some indication of her inner feelings, perhaps use her as a mirror to his actions, but that would have to wait. He was uncertain how to go on or even why he wanted to do so, but he was curious. He was attracted to her. Yet he shouldn't be, not with that nasty disfigurement. It was her personality as much as anything. Yes, that was it. There was something about her that he admired. What was it? That she'd been in combat, carried out some ruthless actions? He knew she was the famous *El Azote;* he'd looked her up. He wouldn't let her know that yet. Her reputation was probably part of the attraction but there was something else that attracted him, something he couldn't put his finger on, but why be so introspective about it anyway? That was his trouble, he was too analytical; just take things as they come. On the other hand, it might be dangerous to pursue this sort of thing much further. She was a westerner, after all.

He became aware that Miriam was waiting expectantly for him to continue. Hastily he swallowed and put the piece of bread down. 'How long since you have left England?'

'It's been three years at least, but actually it's Britain. I'm British, not English.' He looked blank so she tried to explain about Scotland, Ireland, and Wales. 'Therefore it is the British government, the British foreign secretary, and so on.'

'So! What is Britain like?'

The question took Miriam aback. Had she understood the Russian word for like?

He could see she was groping for the meaning. 'The people, how do they look?'

'They look much the same as the people on the streets in Moscow.'

'They do? But here they are from all the Russias, all over the Soviet Union, different races and colour.'

'In Liverpool they're from different parts of the Empire. You see them from all over the globe, much the same, I suppose. That's what struck me when I first went there, but in the rest of Britain they look, well, British.'

'And they are well off with plenty to eat?'

'No, actually. A large number of British people have been close to starvation for some time. I've been to residential streets in Liverpool that would shock anyone. They're as bad as anything in the worst parts of Bombay or Calcutta,' for a moment a rush of feeling challenged her command of Russian as she sought the words and phrases, 'and I've taught children dressed in ragged clothing, shoes

227

worn and broken, almost *naket un borves*.' Surprised, she heard herself drawing on the Yiddish phrase for naked and barefoot she'd heard Dad use in the past.

Dmitri's eyes narrowed a little. 'You are Jewish?'

'My father is.' She went to move on but he interrupted.

'So, and where is he from?'

'He was born in England, Manchester. His parents were from the Ukraine.' She was curt with him. This was irrelevant to her point.

'Ah.'

'You know, Dmitri, Capitalism really had failed in – What do you mean, ah?'

'That is why you speak Russian so well.'

'That's nothing to do with it. It wasn't spoken in my home and I doubt whether my father can speak a word. I speak Russian because I learned to speak it. I'm still learning actually.' She'd had to work hard at it. It didn't come easy to her. How dare he make it sound so?

He felt a twinge of amusement as her face coloured and her eyes glinted with irritation. 'I'm sorry,' he was smiling, 'But you did use a Russian Yiddish phrase.'

She met his eyes with hers.

'Go on.' The corners of his mouth were twitching.

'As I was saying, Capitalism has failed in the West,' she regained her enthusiasm, tapping the table to emphasise her words. 'Do you know, I have seen able-bodied men on the streets of Liverpool and London, lines of them, begging, with mines, steelworks, and shipyards standing idle. So much for the mighty British Empire.'

'But there are no peasants.'

'That's true in theory but although there's been no serfdom or peasantry for hundreds of years, the lot of people in many parts of British society has been little better, and now with the break-up of Capitalism –' She shrugged.

'You were a teacher. What did you teach?'

'They were very young children. I taught them to read, write, and do arithmetic.'

'Did you teach them about Russian literature?'

She laughed. 'They were too young and I don't know anything about Russian literature anyway. I've heard about it, lectures and talks on the wireless, the BBC, and listened to two Chekhov plays, read a little about it as well and about Tolstoy, *War and Peace* and such, and I saw the film of his book *Anna Karenina*, played by Greta Garbo, before I went to Spain.'

'You've read it?'

'No. I'm struggling with him at present; mainly I read the newspapers, *Izvestia* and *Pravda*.'

'I like to visit the Tolstoy House and Museum occasionally. It's only a short trolley ride from Lubyanka Square. Perhaps you would like to come with me?' There was a pause. 'I could show you around.' He spoke rather bashfully.

She found that engaging. 'Yes. I would like that.'

'And Russian history?'

'Russian history?'

'What do you know of Russian history?'

'Again, I met it on the wireless and some articles in the *Listener* magazine, Alexander Nevsky, Ivan the Fourth, the Terrible that is, and Peter the Great. We had a little about the Revolution at the party branch.'

'Comrade Stalin has written the definitive work published last year, the *Short Course*.'

'Oh yes, I had to study parts of that on my induction and we had lectures on it.'

There was an uncomfortable pause. She felt he was framing a response.

'Tell me,' there was tension in his voice, 'why do you think the Boss is changing his ministers?'

A scruffy accordion player lurched into the café and peered unsteadily around the room. With their eyes they

229

followed him as he shuffled over to a dark corner. Shrugging out of the straps he placed his instrument on the table and slumped down heavily at it. The waiter put a small glass of vodka before him and moved away, rolling his eyes and wiping his fingertips on his blouse as if to remove any form of contact that may have occurred.

She turned back to him.

He smiled at her, inclining his head gently towards the musician. 'He won't be playing for a while.'

She returned his smile, feeling the intimate warmth of shared amusement as the tension between them dissipated. 'I didn't know Comrade Stalin had made any changes in the Central Committee. Has he discussed this with you?'

He chuckled. 'Well, no, actually, but it's talked about openly in my office so something's going to be announced very soon. I thought that perhaps as a student of Russian history you might be able to make a guess.'

He was teasing her she knew but she didn't mind. 'Tell me more.'

'Well the main change that's startled my colleagues is that the commissar for foreign affairs, Maxim Litvinov, you may recall, was sacked this week and replaced by Vyacheslav Molotov.'

'So?'

'Well this follows quite a lot of contact with trade delegations at the German Embassy and economic talks are still going on, I believe.'

'And?'

He leaned toward her so that she felt his breath on her lips. 'Former commissar for foreign affairs Comrade Litvinov is a Jew. Are Jews going out of favour in the USSR too, like in Germany?' He leaned back. 'It's just something to think about: the USSR moving closer to Hitler.'

'It's unthinkable. I came here to continue the war against Fascism.'

He shrugged. 'Let's have a final glass of brandy.'

They talked for some time, becoming more relaxed in each other's company, before leaving to make their way back to the Lubyanka, he to enter by the main reception hall, and she through a discreet side door that led to her barracks.

It had been a pleasant afternoon. Despite the surroundings she had enjoyed his company. His attention was flattering and it was quite a thrill when he suggested they meet again to visit the Tolstoy House and Museum, though it would have to be in three or four weeks as he had been placed on continuous duty at the Commissariat for Foreign Affairs. The prospect was exciting.

Chapter Sixteen

Moscow, June 1939

Shyly he held her arm as they got down from the trolley
bus on Ulitsa Tolstovo. After not seeing each other for
four weeks they were both a little self-conscious at first,
especially on the crowded trolley where they had to sit
pressed up shoulder to shoulder. The bright June sun shone
in their eyes as they approached the wooden house that
looked out of place, evoking the city of a hundred years
past.

Dmitri nodded casually to the woman attendant as they
entered into the warm stuffy atmosphere; the windows
were kept tightly shut to keep out dust. He exchanged two
American cigarettes for the loan of the key to the garden
door. 'For later,' he explained to Miriam. It seemed as if
the warm weather had persuaded Muscovites to stay
outside, for the house was empty of visitors. 'The family
only spent the winters here. The house is designed with
two thicknesses of wood to keep in the heat. The summers
were spent on the ancestral estate.'

He led Miriam through to the dining room on the
ground floor. There was a large table laid with crockery.
'The whole household sat together here. It is laid for the
evening meal which began promptly at six.' With the
confidence of someone who, from frequent visits, knew
his way around he lost his self-consciousness as he led her
into a small room where Tolstoy's elder sons played
billiards, pointing out the portrait of his eldest daughter
Tatyana by Ilya Repin, 'Do you remember at the
Tretyakov?' he prompted, '*Religious Procession in Kursk*

233

Province?' Then they went into the bedroom of Tolstoy's youngest child, Vanya.

Miriam looked over the room at his high chair, small bed, rocking horse, and books. Suddenly she felt an overwhelming sadness. 'He never grew up, did he?'

'No, he didn't. He died of scarlet fever at the age of seven.'

Tears welled up in her eyes. 'And the room with his things was kept preserved like this,' she choked. 'He must have been much-loved.'

Her response aroused an air of curiosity in him. It seemed overly sensitive. Suddenly she was peculiarly vulnerable. Why was that? His analytical nature was aroused. He took her arm gently. 'So much so that for a short time he and his wife were reconciled but only for a short time. Mostly they quarrelled violently.'

As they went through Tatyana's bedroom with the walls hung with her talented paintings and sketches, Miriam began to feel more comfortable and relaxed in his company.

He took her up the stairs to the first floor where they came to a large hall. 'This is where his guests were often given supper, including the young Sergei Rachmaninov and Ilya Repin.' They went into the bedroom of Tolstoy's favourite child, Mariya.

'It's so bare, almost spartan,' observed Miriam.

'That's because she shared his ideals and passion for an austere way of life.'

At the far end of the passage was Tolstoy's study. The presence of the great man could be felt in every corner of the plainly furnished room. Candles had been placed at his simple solid desk as if ready for him to start work. His chair seemed strangely out of proportion and low. When Miriam pointed this out Dmitri chuckled. 'He wouldn't admit to being short-sighted, instead he sawed off the ends of his chair legs to bring himself closer to the desktop.'

She laughed out loud at the thought. 'How much did he have to saw off each leg before he got it right?'

He smiled broadly. 'Perhaps he only wanted to take a fraction of each but he ended up with his chin on the desktop.'

They both broke into peals of spontaneous and irreverent laughter at the thought.

Still chuckling as they walked along the passage past the washroom containing Tolstoy's bicycle and his shoemaking tools, they came to the backstairs and the door to the garden. 'This is normally only accessible to special visitors.' He held up the key and winked. Then he unlocked the door, and, taking her hand, he drew her out. As she stepped onto the flagstones the heady scent of mimosa and lilac almost overwhelmed her. Locking the door he led her along a path to the boundary wall with its brickwork golden yellow in the sunshine. They came to a rustic arbour set in the shade of the lilac trees, and a willow. He stooped at the low doorway as they entered into the gloom momentarily blinded after the bright sunlight. They sat side by side on the small bench seat.

The air was heavy with the mustiness of the bare earth floor and the heat of the sun slanting through the foliage and beating on the wood-shingled roof. He took off his cap and tossed it on the ground, then he undid the top clip of his tunic and sat back. 'It's warm, don't you think?'

She nodded, becoming conscious of his shoulder pressing on hers, and she felt the weight of him sending a tingle through her arm and a fluttering in her stomach. In the few tense moments that followed she could hear the bees among the flowers. Aware he was reaching for the peak of her cap she turned her face to him so closely she was looking into his eyes. Slowly he took it from her head. As her hair fell out she felt his hand on the nape of her neck as he gently pulled her face to him. They kissed over and over, each time awakening her hunger. She hadn't realised how much she'd missed the contact. She'd almost forgotten what it was like to have her lips crushed, opening her mouth to receive such passion. How could she have forgotten this pleasure? She let him clasp her tightly to him, pulling her around and crushing his lips on hers as she returned his kisses, pulling him to her as if to urge him on and on until he brought his hand down to her buttock, tightly clasping it while kissing her neck as she moaned lightly. Simultaneously they eased away from each other to draw breath.

'Shall we go to my apartment?'

'Yes,' she breathed, panting lightly.

It was off Lubyanskaya Ploshchad on Neglinnaya Ulitsa, quite close in fact to the Polytechnical Museum. They went through the lobby, passing the concierge at her desk, and took the lift to his floor. In the entrance hall of his apartment she gave up her cap, tunic, belt, and holster, then he removed his. She had thought he would offer coffee or tea, and indeed he may have originally intended to do so, but instead he put his arms around her and she responded with the fervour of the garden. Then he drew her into his bedroom, walking backwards and guiding her to his narrow bed. Pulling off her boots he ran his hands up her legs to her waist, plucking at the trouser fastening until she had to help him undo it. Sitting up she eased them and her knickers over her buttocks, allowing him to draw them off while pulling her blouse over her head as he stood up to undress. He plunged forward, burying his face in her stomach. Lifting his mouth up to her breasts he stabbed at her nipples with his tongue. She felt herself convulse with spasms almost too exquisite to bear. Oh, it had been so long, and she wanted him in her. Drawing her knees up she pulled her thighs down toward her face so that he could enter her as deeply as possible. His thrusts were urgent and powerful, continuing for some time, but she urged him on deeper, deeper still, clasping his back and drawing him harder and harder until finding the narrowness of the bed difficult to manage, he turned sideways, pulling her onto him as he lowered himself to the floor. She straddled him, taking him into her deeper still until he sat up, clasping her to him in his ecstasy, and rolling her over so that he was on top of her again, and she was overcome by the suffusing relief as the congestion was loosed in a burst of warmth and release.

They lay in each other's arms for some time, their bodies striped with the late afternoon sun slanting through half-closed window slats, until Miriam, becoming aware of the hard wooden floor pressing against her hip, gently freed herself and clambered inelegantly onto the bed, leaving him to follow, rather awkwardly wrapping his arm around her. After some moments he appeared to be dozing so without moving her head she attempted to look around the room through half-closed eyes. There was a single window, a tall louvered closet, a chair, and she was conscious of a bedside table behind her with a lamp. As she lifted her head slightly to take in more of the room she disturbed him, and he attempted to roll over, almost falling off the bed. Clearly there was not enough room for them both to lie in comfort, so as if by mutual consent they rose and padded around, recovering their clothes and dressing rather self-consciously. Leading her into the living room he made tea for them both on a gas ring and they sat at a table that, with its two chairs and a wireless set, was the only furniture in the room.

They agreed to meet again, though they knew it would be three or four weeks before they could get time off together. 'We could go out to Kolomenskoe village. It's to the south of the city, not far by bus, a beautiful place, a favourite country estate of the czars. I could show you Peter the Great's cabin.'

'I would like that, and what will we do after?'

He placed two cigarettes in his mouth and lit them both,

giving one to her before releasing the smoke slowly. 'You tell me,' he said slyly.

'Well, we could come back here later and I could spend the night.'

'Good idea, but you'll need a sleeping out pass.'

'Oh. I forgot about that.'

'Don't worry. I can arrange it.'

He wanted to escort her back but she declined. She needed to stroll along in the warm early evening air, before becoming immersed in the clamour and clatter of the barracks, to reflect on the day and on her feelings. Had things got out of hand? She didn't think so. After all, she should have been able to see it coming. Strange how, looking back, it all seemed to be so – inevitable. To have someone attracted to her was exciting. He did ask to see her again. She'd never thought this would ever happen again, and she did find him attractive. There was no doubt about that. She found herself looking forward to the next meeting with some eagerness. In fact she was becoming quite aroused at the prospect. What would Esther think? She hadn't heard from her for some time, despite sending her a card every week.

Kolomenskoe, July 1939

Miriam was glad they were going out of the city. The late-July heat was almost unbearable. 'I've brought you a present,' Dmitri said smiling as they took their seats on the bus for Kolomenskoe and laughing at her consternation when she unwrapped it: 'It's a mosquito veil. You'll need it when we get there. You put it over your head and shoulders. Don't worry, you'll see others doing the same.'

Despite not seeing him for five weeks she immediately felt relaxed in his company, as if no time at all had passed since they last met, and she was amused at the way he chatted on the journey like an excited schoolboy anticipating the day out and showing off his knowledge of the country estate of the czars.

Should she go to the *Izvestia* offices? Best not to. It may raise questions. Should she voice her concern with Dmitri; perhaps ask him if it was wise to make enquiries? Not for the first time she felt a stab of annoyance with Esther. What could have happened? She was a pest impinging on her life like this when she should be carefree and enjoying herself. Instead there was this constant nagging concern.

They spent the whole of the afternoon at Kolonenskoe village. Dmitri acted as a guide as they visited the museum at the front gate, the Falcon Tower, the Church of Our Lady of Kazan built for Czar Alexis in 1650, and the log cabin of Peter the Great, recently brought from Archangel and restored. Then they strolled in a shady grove. Miriam was grateful for the mosquito veil. It was very thoughtful of him. There were clouds of them under the trees, obviously a pest and a torture for the unprepared, yet they didn't seem to trouble him.

Eventually they took to the refectory to sit down, cool their feet, and have a dish of chilled borsch and two tall glasses of black tea with a slice of lemon, sweetened with varenye. Afterwards Miriam had morozhenoe: ice cream served with fresh fruit, and Dmitri, a vatrushki: a cheese-filled tartlet.

While they ate they chatted about each other's work, their heads gradually becoming closer across the small table so that he could feel her hair occasionally touching his face as she moved her head. He was looking forward to the evening. It was a pity he wouldn't be able to see her for some time after today, maybe even for five or six weeks or more. This special detail at the embassy was unfortunate. Perhaps she would get bored with having to get to know each other all over again each time they met. He hoped not. He was getting fond of her; in fact he had to admit, he was getting very fond of her.

'How is your sister, Esther, isn't it? How is she finding things at *Izvestia*?'

'Yes. Well I haven't heard from her since we met at the Tretyakov. I really don't know why. I've been sending a card to the address she gave me every week but I'm getting no reply. I'm very anxious. Actually I've been wondering whether to ask you what I should do. Is it wise to get in touch with her office do you think or will it cause trouble for her?'

'Maybe, but wait. I'll try to find out what I can as soon as possible and I'll get information to you somehow. There's something big on at the embassy, something very big. She may be assigned to it. If so there'll be a clampdown on any contact.'

Miriam's face darkened. 'Something big?'

'It's probably nothing to worry about. This is normal when something is developing. The government keeps things close until it's ready to release information, often sealing people who are involved from contact with friends or relatives, which brings me to something I have to tell you.'

He didn't want to see her again. The thought hit her

with some force.

'From next week I'm on attachment to the embassy for at least six weeks or more. I'll still be working at the Lubyanka but I'll be forbidden to leave the building except to go to the embassy when required.'

The relief was so palpable her face gave it away.

'Is anything wrong, Miriam?'

At his unexpected use of her first name she became self-conscious and she coloured slightly. 'No. It's nothing. Well, it's just that I thought you were going to tell me you didn't want to see me again.' It was then she realised how much she would miss him despite the long time between meetings previously.

He took hold of her hand. 'I hope you don't mind too much.'

She shook her head. 'No, no. I don't mind. It can't be helped.' She took her hand from his and lit a cigarette.

He noticed her hands trembled slightly. 'In five or six weeks I should be getting some leave.'

She breathed out smoke. 'That will be nice. So what is going on, can you tell me?'

His mood became grave as he leaned across to her as close as he could get. 'I've heard that as a result of a meeting in Berlin last week between the Russian charge d'affaires, the head of the Russian trade mission, and the chief economic negotiator for the German government, a high-ranking Soviet personage will discuss extending the trade agreement into the political sphere with a high-ranking German personage as soon as a visit to Moscow can be arranged. That's why I've been attached to the embassy in charge of security.' He sat back. 'I'm afraid I've burdened you with a dangerous secret. I hope you don't mind.'

'What on earth,' she started in English before going on in Russian, 'What can the two countries have in common, except the stated desire to tear each other to pieces?'

'Just one thing: opposition to the capitalist democracies.'

'Who are these high-ranking personages, or aren't you allowed to tell me?'

'Molotov and Ribbentrop.'

'Oh my God!' She used English again.

'So as you can see there is a need for great security.'

They sat in silence for some moments. She felt anger flaring in the pit of her stomach. Suddenly it rose to her head. 'Well, this will be something for the Russian people to swallow,' she drew deeply on her cigarette, 'and the German people too, I shouldn't wonder.' She exhaled the smoke violently as if to spit it across the room.

'It should be interesting. I shall be liaising with German military personnel. They start arriving next week.'

'Interesting,' she snarled. 'I'll say it is. I may well have been fighting them in Spain.'

'Look, Miriam, there's nothing you or I can do about it. Europe, even the world, is in a state of flux. Although it looks as if the Japanese forces have been held in the Khalkhin-Gol zone on the Manchurian border, it was an attempted invasion of Soviet territory, and there's trouble brewing with Finland. The USSR needs some years of peace to complete the great work. It can't afford to take an aggressive position with Germany of all countries, not yet anyway. It may be that in the short term some ideological sacrifices will need to be made to buy time.'

'Even so, if you shake hands with the devil you get them burned.'

He took hold of her hands in his. It was a pleasant sensation that calmed her.

'We must trust to the Soviet government and in the meantime remember you haven't heard anything about this. Don't speak to anyone about it, not even to Esther when you make contact with her. Do you understand that?'

She nodded. A feeling of resignation flowed over her.

He was right, there was nothing that could be done.

'I will find out what I can about her, why she isn't contacting you, and so on though it will be too dangerous to write to you about it, even sending a message by word of mouth is too dangerous: there's no one I can trust. So this is what I will do: I will send you a card each week, it will be read by the censors, just a few words to keep in contact.' He took her hands again and looked into her eyes. 'Now you must listen to me carefully. I'll not tell you how to contact me and you must not try to get in touch under any circumstances. If I have something to tell you about Esther I will end my sentence on the weekly card with two full stops instead of one. It will look like a mistake. You will have to wait to find out whether it's good or bad news I'm afraid.' He squeezed her hands tightly before letting them go and looked to her. 'Do you understand why this must be so?'

She nodded and in the gradual release of tension she found herself looking out through the open doors, over the well-kept lawns, past the bell tower, all that remained of the Church of Saint George, to the woods shimmering in the heat.

'It will be time for the bus soon,' he said. 'I thought perhaps we could get some street food and some wine and take it back to my apartment. I have a gramophone, you know, and some records. We could listen to music.'

She brightened up in anticipation. 'That sounds good.'

Suddenly he leaned toward her and clasped her head in his hand. Drawing her face to him he kissed her lightly on the lips. She felt her body warming and pressed her mouth to his to express her anticipation.

He sat back. 'When I get leave we'll have more time together. Next time we meet it will probably be late August, early September. The air in the city will be very humid. We could escape to the country, perhaps to visit Borodino, the Napoleonic battlefield, and the village. It's a

two-hour bus journey. It may help you with your Tolstoy.'
He smiled playfully.

She nodded.

Next morning she signed herself through the guardroom at the barracks in time for breakfast. The thought of the kasha sat heavily on her stomach. It had been a wonderful evening. His taste in music was a little heavy for her but they didn't spend that much time listening to it. They were in bed after two gramophone records. Recalling the bed was so arousing that she let her mind drift. The images arose in turn by their own volition so that the ripples and contractions in her stomach took her by surprise. She longed to see him again soon. Five or six weeks were almost too many to wait. To be without for so long now her appetite was aroused was exquisitely painful.

Chapter Twenty

Esther stands up stiffly and stretches. 'I'm getting too old for waiting on cold railway stations. What time did you say that last train is?'

'Twelve thirty. In just half an hour.'

'It's very cold,' she rubs her arms. 'The refreshment room's closed and there's nowhere else to go except home. There's not enough time to finish the story anyway.'

Nicholas looks up at her as she lights a cigarette. She's going. She can't go, she mustn't. He is about to speak but he can't think what to say. The feeling of powerlessness overwhelms him.

She prepares to leave, to say goodbye, time had run out, a good enough reason to leave it at that. No point in going on with it.

'Why did you come today?'

'Why did I come today?' Caught off-guard she needs time to think. 'Why do you ask that?'

'Well you asked me why I wanted to meet you. Now I'm asking you, why did you come today? You didn't have to.'

In a flash of insight she realises the real reason why. He was the only way she herself could alleviate some of her own guilt. Through his reactions, his responses, he may even be the instrument of absolution setting both their minds at rest. That's why she will try and get him to understand how it was. She is no longer a reluctant narrator with something to hide. Perhaps she never was. She has to go on. She has to complete the account if only

245

to put her own mind at rest. He's been using her to seek his peace of mind but has she not been using him also?

'Look! There must be an early Paddington train that'll get you to Oxford in plenty of time. Why don't you come back to my rooms, that'll give me time to finish the story in some comfort? At least it's warmer than sitting out here.'

He is taken aback. 'I have to be at my college for tomorrow morning. I have a tutorial at ten o'clock.'

'So! If you're not you can tell your tutor whom you spent the night with. That should impress him, I've no doubt.'

'Do you think he'll believe me?'

'What! A note I should give you? Come on, I'll get us a taxi.'

Her rooms are in a large terraced house in the town. Opening the front door quietly she switches on the light and takes him down the hall. It smells of stale tobacco and boiled cabbage. One wall is graced by a picture of a serenading gondolier executed in the gaudy metal foil of chocolate biscuit wrappers. They go into the front room, once a parlour in better days. Another slightly open door tells Nicholas it leads to a bedroom.

She puts the light on and goes over to the bay window and draws the dusty curtains. 'Drink?' She brings out a Gordon's gin bottle from behind a row of books.

He shakes his head.

'Tea then?'

Reluctantly he nods.

Lighting a gas ring she pours herself two fingers of gin and places a kettle on the sputtering blue flame. 'Sit down.' She nods at two shabby easy chairs facing each other as she spoons tea into an enamel teapot.

Pouring the whistling kettle into the pot she swills it around and sets it to stand. 'I'll leave you to pour and help yourself to the sugar. I haven't got any milk but I've got some of the condensed stuff if you want.'

He shakes his head.

With a sigh she sits down in the chair opposite, takes a sip from her glass, and looks at him thoughtfully for some moments. 'I don't suppose you've ever been arrested?'

Nicholas is no longer surprised by what she says so he just shakes his head again.

'The man was so friendly but I knew what was happening. On my way to the newspaper office it was. You know what I found so terrifying?' She waves her glass expansively. 'The not knowing, you know? Not knowing why.' She inclines her head towards him. 'They don't tell you that, not there. Not at first anyway.'

Nicholas leans forward to pour his tea. It looks as if she is losing the thread. What had this got to do with his mother? He decides to go along with her for a while hoping she'll get back to the main story.

Esther takes another small sip and looks up at the ceiling as she slips back in time. 'It was the end of April in 1939. My first spring in Moscow, and Miriam's too of course.'

Moscow, April 1939

There was a black van waiting at the kerb in front of the *Izvestia* building. She could see it from a distance facing towards her. Becoming aware of a sense of foreboding like a dull ache she hesitated, nothing to worry about. Everyone feels this when they see the black crows, she reasoned. Then she walked on.

As she came up to the van on her left hand side the passenger window was lowered. 'Good morning.'

She froze. Her stomach turned to water.

He got out and went to the rear door, holding it open. Dressed in his grey suit, he was tall, slim, and very young. 'Captain Simonov. Would you mind coming along with me, Comrade Rabin?' His voice was pleasant and respectful. 'There is a matter you may be able to help me with. I shouldn't think it would take long.'

She hesitated.

'If it's too inconvenient then another time will do but perhaps it's best we go along now and clear things up. Don't you agree?'

Numbly she nodded and almost in a daze allowed him to take her arm and help her into the van. After closing and locking the door he went around to join the uniformed driver in the front, curtly ordering him to move off into the traffic on Tvertskaya Ulitsa.

She didn't ask where they were going, she didn't want to hear the words, but when the van took a left turn at Okhotny Ryad and moved up the hill to Teatrainy she broke into a cold sweat. Now she knew for certain.

They turned sharply into a side opening in the Lubyanka building, drove slowly through a tunnel, and stopped at the tall double gates at the end. When they opened they moved through into a small courtyard and waited for another van to leave before pulling up at a rather ordinary entrance. As the gates closed with a jarring clang the young man got out, unlocked the rear door, and held it open for her.

She stepped out on to the mossy cobbles and looked up at the rectangle of blue sky far above the six-storied building with its deep-set empty windows facing onto the sunless yard on all sides, and felt a deep cold dread that prompted a spasm of trembling. As he took her arm gently she blurted out, 'Why am I here?'

'Please, come to my office and I will explain.'

He walked her over to the entrance, stopping at a hatch to bark out a code through the opening as they went through into a long wide windowless passage dimly lit with a stone-flagged floor and bare walls. 'Come. Follow me.' They moved along, making their way through the uniformed NKVD men who were busily passing back and to and in and out of doors.

What if Miriam came along? That would be a shock for her. Maybe she could sort out this misunderstanding. But then she remembered Miriam was in the barracks, somewhere else in the building. At least she hadn't been brought to the prison. She knew that was in the cellars below.

Eventually, opening one of the doors, he took her through into a large room with a carpeted floor and many typists at their desks in their smart grey uniforms. The luminous glare coming from long tubes hanging horizontally from the ceiling dazzled her momentarily. She'd never seen fluorescent lights before, not even in the newspaper office.

'This way.' Leading her to a glass-panelled door and into what was clearly his office he pointed to a chair at a table while he closed the door, softening the clacking of the typewriters. 'Sit down, and please don't smoke.' He sat on the other side, facing her. The room was also windowless with a fan on the ceiling slowly sweeping the air with a gentle whisper. On the wall facing her were the familiar portraits of Comrades Lenin and Stalin.

'You asked me why you are here,' he paused for a moment, looking intently at her. 'Have you no idea at all why you have been asked to come?'

She shook her head slowly.

'Are you certain, comrade?'

She sat still saying nothing. He'd called her comrade. That was a good thing at least.

He got up and went to a filing cabinet in the corner, took out a manila folder, brought it over to the table, and sitting down, he opened it and looked up at her. 'Grachev,' he said without forewarning.

She felt her heart stop. Every part of her stopped still. All of a sudden she knew what this was about.

'I can see you know who I mean. You know him more familiarly as Andrei. Is that correct?'

She nodded. He had not used the prefix 'Comrade' this time.

'A colleague of yours at *Izvestia*?'

Again she nodded. 'What has happened to him?'

'He has been very cooperative and so has his wife. She was understandably concerned at his bourgeois and extremely immoral behaviour, conducting an affair in his workplace before his colleagues. It must have been very demoralising and diverting for them. She suspected there was more to it. His behaviour toward her changed. He became argumentative, talking loosely about events, making rhetorical and challenging statements counter to government and party policy. Naturally, being a faithful party member. she decided to inform us of this.' He folded his arms and leaned on them. 'Comrade Rabin, during the course of a series of –' he paused for the most suitable word, '– searching interviews, he revealed some conversations you had together. You shared certain counter-revolutionary views, it seems; in fact it seems to me you were the chief instigator in this,' he leaned back, 'but I could be mistaken.'

She could hear the typewriters faintly through the door and a voice plaintively complaining about something. They must have tortured him. He wouldn't have let her down otherwise. They'd put words in his mouth.

'Now, this is only my second case. I want to make a good job of it. So I do hope you will help me to clear this up.' Suddenly his voice became brittle and hard. 'You will, won't you?'

She nodded yet again.

'Yes, of course. After all, we only have his side of the story. We've yet to have yours. It may be there's nothing to it.'

What could she have said? The question emerged in her mind to dominate her thoughts. She wouldn't admit to anything. No, that was the thing to do. Besides, what had she said? What had they got out of Andrei? What had they got him to say? Miriam had warned her about his wife. It was too late now.

'I must say it's a relief to work with someone who wants to cooperate. I do dislike having to fall back on the services of my more muscular comrades. Would you like some tea? I'm going to order some sandwiches. You might like to join me.' He picked up the phone without waiting for her to answer. Then he continued, 'Now, what we need to do is to get down on paper exactly what you have been saying, every word. It's very important you remember every word. Then it can be decided whether you were just expressing frustration, anger, or some trivial irritation, or in fact whether there is something more to it, that you were perhaps seeking to corrupt or recruit for counter-revolutionary purposes or perhaps being on the verge of doing so without realising it. It does happen, you know.'

She felt her mouth become dry.

'You will have to satisfy us on that, I'm afraid, and if you were on the point of becoming a counter-revolutionary without realising it you will no doubt be glad to purge the tendency before it becomes something extremely serious.'

The door opened with a bump and a clatter of crockery. A dumpy woman wearing a white smock and a kerchief covering her head bustled in pushing a trolley. She served the tea and placed a plate of tiny sandwiches on the table without once raising her eyes. As she made to leave Captain Simonov got up and politely held the door for her before resuming his seat.

The pause gave her time. She struggled to muster her thoughts but she was overtaken by a wave of indignation. How dare he accuse her of this? Who did he think he was, this lad still wet behind the ears? She'd shot men like him, in fact his smooth face reminded her of that first boy she'd killed in Madrid. Her feelings flaring up into fury she shouted, 'Whatever I'm supposed to have said I am not a counter-revolutionary, do you understand? I fought Fascism on the streets and in Spain. I was asked to come to the Soviet Union. I left Capitalism behind, that's more than you've done. Look at yourself in your bourgeois clothes; you'd probably lap it up if you had the chance. What am I supposed to have said? Go on, tell me. What does it say on that paper? I demand to see it.'

Taken aback, he did not answer, but closed the folder as if to conceal it.

Driven by her anger now she continued, 'So I was having an affair, when you've grown up you might understand what that is. His wife finds out and –' she shrugged. 'That's what it's about in that file. Nothing more.'

He recovered his poise. 'Esther Rabinovitz, let me make your position clear, you are not here because of your affair, but because of what is written in the file. Do you understand? You have been denounced.'

Denounced, the word shocked her into silence, lost for words, her breast rising and falling with barely suppressed feeling.

His voice was cold. 'You must understand, comrade, I am all that stands between you and the cellars. They don't serve sandwiches there. Please have one, by the way.' He pushed the plate towards her.

In an explosion of wrath she swept it from the table to shatter the glass door panel, scattering fragments of bread and pickled sprats. There was silence. The typing had stopped.

Wrexham, June 1957

Esther rises from her chair with some difficulty and stands in the bay window, still holding her glass. Clasping her arms across her chest she turns to Nicholas. 'Well, I found out what the cellars were like. I was stripped, examined, fingers poked up me, my hair cropped with shears, stuck in a cell for three months, naked, the light on continually, no window, no bed, no furniture of any kind, every now and then a bowl of potato soup, a chunk of bread, and a mug of water through the hatch, no toilet facilities, the floor under inches of stinking water, and not knowing what was going to happen to me. That was the worst part.'

'Three months!'

'Yes, three bloody months.' She comes over to him and sits down again, looking at the floor. Talking had brought the memories back and with them the emotions sweep over her, the self-loathing at her physical condition and her animal-like screaming and moaning as she splashed around her cell, sometimes on her hands and knees, sometimes upright beating the walls. 'I didn't know it had been three months until after.'

'After?'

'Every so often they would drag me out, pressure hose the place as of it was a cowshed, and hose me down as well. The freezing water was like needles piercing my skin. I was left in shock after. Then they'd throw me back. One day when they didn't throw me back but took me to the hot showers instead I thought that was it. They were going to shoot me. I'd heard somewhere they shoot people in the showers because it makes it easier to wash away the blood but no, they threw some liquid soap over me and left me to wash. It was bliss. I didn't care if I was going to die, at least I'd experienced some pleasure for the last time. I remember I was too weak to stand up against the weight of the water so I just sat on the floor. Then they gave me my clothes back, would you believe it, just as if nothing had happened? I couldn't understand why my skirt kept falling down. Even my feet had shrunk. My shoes seemed to belong to someone else. Two of them took an arm each and helped me into a room, sat me in a chair, and left me. All the time I was confused. I was trying to understand why they would go to this trouble if they were going to shoot me. Then he came through the door.'

'He? Who came through the door?'

'Colonel Dmitri Ignatov. I didn't recognise him. Why was a high ranking NKVD officer going to interrogate me? After he reminded me who he was he started to beat me up.'

Moscow, the last week of July,1939

It had taken him all of two weeks to find her and take over her case. Now he had to go through the motions of close interrogation so that he could get her out with no case to answer. She was very lucky. If it were up to him she would be left to the chekists and she would suffer the same fate as that lover of hers. He'd found her apartment and got it ready for her. He dared not contact Miriam, except by the arranged method. Stick her in bed for a few days, that should do it, and then it would be up to her while he made sure her office was contacted in the usual way so that she could be back at work as soon as possible. Meanwhile he had to convince the chekists a robust questioning had been carried out. It would need all his skill not to finish her off. She was in poor shape, just a couple of black eyes, a bloody nose and mouth. That should do it.

It was the end of the first August week that Miriam received the coded card. She had been tortured by doubt. Would Dmitri keep to his word? Or would he break off communication with her, deciding she was too much trouble? Was it really a second dot? Still in the habit of doubting him she looked at it many times. Yes there it was; he had found out something about Esther. What was it, she wondered, good or bad? She fostered the card with mixed feelings, for it also brought the delightful news of his impending leave coinciding with hers following the completion of her advanced training. He was still thinking of her after all. It gave her a warm feeling. She would see him in two weeks or so. They would visit Borodino on the 31st. Until then she would have to endure this intense anxiety about Esther. A week later she was relieved to receive Esther's card asking her to arrange a meeting. It took another week for them to get together at the Perlov.

Miriam arrived first and was sitting at a table when

Esther entered. Was this her? No it couldn't be. Oh God! It was. The shock was like a blow to the stomach. Her eyes: they were sunk into her head with blue patches under them and she shuffled, hunched like the old peasant market women, clutching her bag. Her clothes were just hanging on her and her face, she couldn't bear to look at it, her cheekbones standing out like that and so deeply lined with tufts of her hair sticking out from the beret she had pulled on in an attempt to hide it. Without acknowledgment Esther lowered herself gingerly onto a chair, looking beyond Miriam to the far wall.

'What happened?' There was a tremor in Miriam's voice.

With eyes unfocused, dull, and lifeless, she flicked a glance toward Miriam's face whose appearance reflected her condition as clearly as any mirror. 'I looked worse than this when I came out. You were right about his wife.' Her voice was flat and weak. 'She found out, cooked my goose all right. She knew someone high in the party and reported him for uttering anti-government statements. They got him to confess. He implicated me.'

'Oh no! You were taken in.'

Esther nodded.

'After a couple of weeks I was worried about you,' Miriam said, 'I tried to get in touch, sent a card every week. I didn't know what to think and as time went on I feared the worst.'

'Dmitri got me out, no case to answer, saved my life, I suppose. I find it difficult to believe I'm out of it. Sometimes I think it's a dream. It catches me unawares during the day then I'm terrified I'm going to wake up and find I'm still there.'

Miriam thought she was going to break down but she managed to compose herself before going on.

'I keep telling myself how lucky I am. I've still got my job and my apartment. I've been back at work a week now;

in fact they've given me the foreign desk, even though I collapsed twice the first two days. They've been very good to me. Dmitri's had something to do with that. That reminds me, when do you see him?'

'In three days. He's got leave. We're going to visit Borodino.'

'Thank him for me. I never had the chance. In fact I can't thank him enough. I didn't recognise him at first then he put me out like a light.'

Miriam looked puzzled.

'Oh, never mind.' Esther was tired. She was becoming weak. 'I'll tell you some other time. I had a hell of a surprise when I realised it was him.'

'I asked him to find out where you were. He sent a coded message that he'd found something out. He couldn't tell me what and – the husband?'

She sighed then shrugged hopelessly. 'Gone.'

'What happened to you in there?'

'Can't tell you any of that. I had to sign an undertaking.' She tried a smile but her face was still painful and the effort was too much. 'You should have a good idea anyway. I was in the same building, couldn't have been far from you at any time.' She sat for some moments vacantly looking at the floor before lifting her face as if remembering Miriam was there. 'I must take a break for a minute and gather my thoughts. I'm afraid I still find it hard to keep my mind on things.' She took out a pack of cigarettes. After the match had stopped sizzling she lit one, taking a long sucking drag, then pushed the pack toward Miriam.

'Where's your lighter?'

Esther shrugged, shaking out the match flame before tossing it in the ashtray. 'They never gave it back to me. I don't think I'll complain. Do you know, for a couple of days back at work I couldn't read anything? It's coming back to me slowly. Talking like this helps but occasionally

I just have to stop. My mind seems to shut down.'

'Just take your time.' Miriam sat back. She would let her get herself together. It was disturbing to see her like this. As if her soul had been taken away. She'd seen it so often, even been part of it, and it had never affected her, but Esther? She felt a stab of anger. The silly cat! She should have known what she was letting herself in for.

Esther finished her tea, then she spoke as if she'd forgotten the last thing she'd said, as if there'd been no pause. 'There'll be a bombshell in the news tomorrow. Tass has cleared it for publication so it's safe for me to tell you. In fact it's been all over the papers in the West for nearly a week, including the German papers, especially the German papers.'

'I think I know what you're going to tell me. I had some indication of what was in the air from Dmitri.'

'Even so,' she shrugged wearily, 'I've been cut off from the world for some time, I know, but I didn't think things would advance so far and so fast.'

'Well, tell me, what has happened?'

She spoke slowly and quietly as if remembering one word at a time. 'Last week a pact was signed between the USSR and Germany. It's called a non-aggression pact. In brief it means that both sides undertake to guarantee a state of peace between each other for at least ten years. There are economic and trade concessions on each side too. I've read a copy of the preamble, guarantees of tons of grain, oil, tungsten, and other rare metals to be transported to Germany by the USSR every week and agreements on areas of interest along the Baltic where each side gives the other a free hand to do as they please.'

'In other words to give Hitler a free hand to do as he pleases as long as he doesn't bother us. It goes against everything the comrades have been fighting for.'

'It's been signed by Molotov and Ribbentrop last week and Stalin and Hitler this week.' She spoke with a weary resignation. 'We are now the best of friends, well, not actually. It's not a treaty, just a formal agreement on certain things, but it does give each side the assurance of non-intervention in specific areas and ten years of guaranteed peace.'

'The best of friends with Hitler? What will people think when it comes out tomorrow?'

'Oh it's going to take some swallowing, I agree. I've been given the line to take over the past two days and I've finished the copy for tomorrow. It's already gone to press but there you are. What else could the Soviet Union do? The democracies haven't stood up to Germany. What's done is done.' Suddenly her mood lightened becoming sunnier in outlook. 'I have to say there are enormous benefits to having peace between the USSR and Germany guaranteed. It shows deep foresight and creative thinking on the part of the Boss and Molotov and that's what the Soviet Union needs now that all counter-revolutionary forces have been destroyed. People tell me things are beginning to move forward, there's more to buy in the shops and so on. We, us both that is, haven't experienced what things were like under war communism or the old economic plan. Russia is starting to move forward. There are matters on our borders that can now be settled without the fear of Germany at our backs. It's quite a masterstroke really.'

'And how will the rest of international Communism, the Comintern, look upon this – masterstroke, other than as a betrayal?'

'That remains to be seen. It could be the end of the Comintern. After all Comrade Stalin does promote Communism in one country. That's always been his stand. You know that.' She giggled momentarily despite the pain in her ribs making her wince, 'Can you imagine how embarrassing it will be for the comrades in London?'

'I expect they'll find a way to accommodate it. It'll be

rather difficult for them if it comes to war between Great Britain and Germany though. The USSR will be committed to support the German Fascists and – Esther, what will happen to Dad? He will be on the side of the enemy.'

'Oh, it'll never come to that. Anyway Russia isn't committed to join in anything, only to stand aside and keep to the trade agreements. That's the genius underlying the Boss's masterstroke. Let the Capitalist countries tear themselves to pieces. Don't you see? Every sack of grain given to the Hitlerites is a nail in their coffins.'

Sustaining the conversation had obviously exhausted Esther. Her face had become even more slack and lined. She looked so old, aged almost. 'I think it's time you went back to your place now.' Miriam said. 'You look as though you need a rest.'

Esther nodded feebly.

'I'll try and get in touch with you early next week.'

She nodded again as they got up from their chairs and made to pay and leave.

Later in her room Miriam was suddenly overcome as the realisation returned: things could come to war with Dad on the side of the democracies and she and Esther on the side of Germany. What had they been doing in Spain? Weren't they supposed to be fighting for democracy against Fascism? But she had resolved that some time ago. Hadn't the democracies proved weak, unfit to go on existing? The end justifies the means and time must be bought. Let the German Fascists do the dirty work. All the same, what would happen to Dad? And then she sat down weak at the knees at the thought that drove out all else: what would happen to Nikolai?

Chapter Twenty-one

Borodino, August 31st 1939

It was a humid last day of August, a cloudy and sunless Thursday. The air on the crowded autobus was close and reeked strongly of unwashed clothes, stale sweat, cheap tobacco, and poultry. It was obvious to Miriam and Dmitri that they were the only battlefield visitors among the passengers. The windows were closed as tightly as possible in a futile attempt to keep out the white dust that gritted between their teeth and enveloped the vehicle in a great cloud as it swayed and pitched along the un-made road making it impossible to see out. Miriam contented herself with letting her eyes wander along the aisle, taking in the diverse appearance of the travellers. Some were city folk, perhaps factory workers, on their way to the market at Borodino village with sacks containing live poultry or rabbits raised in their apartments. The cackling of geese down at the front drew her attention to an aged babushka with the crated birds on her lap.

The atmosphere was fuggy with cigarette smoke but Miriam didn't mind it. As far as she was concerned everything was fine with the world for the time being at least. Dmitri had a few days leave from yesterday and they would spend as much time together as possible. Lost in her own thoughts she let them run and the chattering and raucous banter of the bus faded from her consciousness. She'd thanked him for his help, for saving Esther's life in fact. It was gratifying to think he'd done it for her, certainly not for Esther, whom he didn't seem to like very much. The last few weeks had been irksome. Intense

263

training for the defence of the Kremlin, carrying out operational exercises, forming and re-forming around tactical points in the city, all had left her and her squad physically exhausted. She also realised how emotionally drained she had become by the double anxiety aroused by Esther and by her doubts about Dmitri. But now both issues appeared to have been resolved. She felt calm and relaxed.

It was late morning when they got down from the autobus in the main square of the village, with its boardwalks and quaint buildings walled with rough-hewn horizontal timbers, their doors and window frames painted in white, green or yellow. Most of the other passengers joined the throng in the local market. Taking her arm Dmitri walked Miriam a kilometre to the south, passing the battlefield museum. 'It contains only tired-looking models.' He was dismissive turning Miriam to view the battlefield itself from the high ground near the monument to the fallen.

'Where exactly is the battlefield?' Miriam's question was prompted by the sweep of the landscape that seemed to go on forever in all directions, a vast amphitheatre of wheat stubble with occasional groves of silver birch and pine. In the far distance a train, dwarfed by the open space so that it looked like a child's toy, was leaving a trail of smoke and steam as it moved across their line of vision. Above the horizon purple and black clouds were rolling and swirling as if churned by some turbulent force. Overhead the sun was striving to find an opening in the overcast, occasionally breaking through and bathing the monuments strewn around the area in a sulphurous yellow glare. The impact of the space unrolling endlessly before her seemed to arouse a mood of melancholy in Miriam.

As if sensing this Dmitri took her gently but firmly by the shoulders and faced her to the west while standing behind so that she could feel the pressure of his chest and hips against her. 'That's where Napoleon's army came from, about a hundred and twenty to a hundred and thirty thousand men.'

'And the Russian army?'

'About the same.' He swept his hand around in a semi-circle. 'All this is the battlefield as far as you can see in any direction and further. Look! You can still make out some of the earth works of the field fortifications. It covers over a hundred square kilometres. What is that in English miles?'

'I – er – don't know.'

'I think it's about forty square English miles. Much greater than Waterloo but like Waterloo it lasted all day, about fifteen hours with around eighty thousand dead in all. It was the bloodiest single day of battle in the nineteenth century.'

'And who won?' She thought she knew but felt mischievous.

He enjoyed her teasing and entered into the spirit of it. 'I can see you haven't read Tolstoy's account of the battle. Once you have done so you'll never forget it. Actually it was what you call an impasse. A French word you English use, though why you don't use your own language is a mystery to me.'

English: he'd used that word again. Irritated she turned to him, snapping, 'Oh, come on! The French rightly claimed a victory because the Russian army withdrew beyond Moscow.'

'Actually Field Marshal Kutuzov swung around to the west behind Napoleon, blocking his communications and, as you know very well, the city was abandoned by the citizens and Napoleon found a ghost town with no people to supply his army. Soon fires were started all over and the city and it was burnt to the ground, denying the French shelter against the coming winter.'

'There's no need to be so –' She sought the Russian

word in vain and came out with the English, '– smug, about it.'

'Smug,' he mimicked his face creasing into a broad smile enhancing his high cheekbones. 'Smug.' He pretended to savour the word.

'What time of year was it?'

'August the 26th in the calendar before the Revolution but in the new calendar, the 7th of September. That's next week actually.'

'To burn a city, just abandon it, what a crazy thing to do. Wouldn't it have been better to come to some kind of agreement?'

He became serious. 'Is that what you would have done, Miriam? That doesn't sound like the ruthless *El Azote*.'

She was taken aback momentarily. 'So! You found out!' Turning away she paused for a moment before changing the subject, her eyes looking into the immense unbounded space and over to the haze-obscured horizon. He felt her body quiver with a sudden light trembling that passed like a brief draught. 'Do you think an invader will come this way again?' she asked.

He looked thoughtful. 'I don't think so. Today is not the same for an army. Then it was about horses, farriers, blacksmiths, wheelwrights, oats, and barley, all freely available in western Russia and the Moscow region. Now an army is about machines. Without petrol, oil, components, and spare parts the engines of war, tanks, trucks, aeroplanes and such, become useless. Capture the Ukraine and you have the industrial resources of the USSR and open the way to the oilfields of the Caucasus. Then you can turn off the tap. No. This time it will be Kiev in the south-east and possibly Leningrad in the north, rather than Moscow.'

'But surely Moscow is the capital, the seat of government?'

'It's not the same kind of capital as Paris or London

266

where everything is centralised at a hub, transport links, telephonic and radio communications, and the complex gathering of peoples' representatives without which the government cannot function. It's more like the Moscow of 1812 or the Berlin of today. The seat of government is where the leaders are. The state bureaucracy and secretariats can be moved anywhere. Czar Alexander left the city but was still able to govern even though Napoleon found the Kremlin deserted, and I've no doubt our new German friend has this example set firmly in mind.

'Well I still think it would be a tremendous blow for the morale of the Russian people and a great propaganda victory if Moscow were captured.'

'So did Napoleon.'

She was still looking away. 'How long have you known I was so called in Spain?'

He was caught off guard by the sudden change of tack. 'Soon after we met.'

'You looked up my name in the files.'

He shrugged. 'You are famous.'

'But only under that name. That was the purpose of it. You looked me up, checked up on me. Why didn't you tell me?'

He felt uncomfortable and he knew he looked it. He wasn't sure himself, almost shamefaced.

'And why are you only referring to it now?'

He paused for a moment. 'Now seems appropriate.'

She raised her shoulders drawing in breath, and dropped them signifying an end to the matter for now at least, though she felt a twinge of disappointment in him for keeping his discovery close until he thought its revelation appropriate as if he were in a card game. Turning to face him she returned to the previous subject. 'You said, "this time".'

He narrowed his eyes quizzically.

'There is a non-aggression pact. Surely there will be no

267

"this time".'

Suddenly there was a surprising flash of lightning, bathing the battlefield in a second's blue-white brightness followed by a startling clap of thunder to the west. Echoing and re-echoing it seemed to roll over the plain toward them accompanied by a warm moist wind. At the splash of a large raindrop Miriam lifted her eyes to the roiling clouds. More raindrops pattered on her face. They turned and ran for the museum in the distance, pulling their tunic jackets over their heads. Breathlessly they reached the veranda of the building and looked out as the rain increased, deafeningly drumming on the roof, pouring in torrents from the gutters, and driven against the walls by the squall. They watched, faces dripping wet. Her hair had tumbled untidily from her cap when she pulled her tunic over it and hung around her face damply in dark, almost jet black ringlets. The clouds seemed to boil and swirl like a turbulent sea wracked by bolts of forked lightening tearing down through them. The cracking of thunder reached an ear-splitting crescendo, overwhelming the noise of the rain before booming overhead to be followed by yet more salvoes.

Dmitri put his mouth to her ear. 'I'm afraid our battlefield tour has ended before it's begun,' he shouted above the din. 'Let's take some lunch. There's a place in the village near the square.'

During their lunch the thunder continued rumbling and threatening another lightning storm while the heavy rain persisted. 'I wondered why the roofs of the village houses bristle with lightning conductors.' Miriam looked through the streaming windows. 'Now I know.' They waited indoors until the Moscow autobus arrived in the square, covered to the tops of its windows in cream-coloured mud from a road surface that had acquired the consistency of kasha. They ran across the cobbles, splashing through the rain to climb aboard.

The next day they lay in until the end of the morning, lustfully entwined in the pleasure of not having to report for duty. Eventually Dmitri rose to make some tea, leaving Miriam sensuously stretching out naked and slatternly on top of the coverlet. Dreamily half-awake she could hear him moving around. Things being picked up, the clink of glasses, the radio being switched on. The voice of the news announcer was muffled so that she couldn't make out what was being said.

She must have drifted off for a few seconds when she realised Dmitri was calling her. There was a note of urgency in his voice. 'Come in here quickly, quickly.'

Instantly awake she leapt off the bed. Moving with trained agility she joined him in the next room.

He pointed to the radio and turned up the volume. 'They keep repeating this special announcement.'

Miriam strained to listen. Above the crackling static she heard, 'Reuters news agency reports that since before dawn this morning, oh three hundred hours Berlin time, German troops have been crossing into Poland and are attacking on a number of fronts. News agency Tass confirms this and also reports that the German leader, Adolf Hitler, will make a speech to the Reichstag later today. All security and military personnel on leave are ordered to return to their units immediately.'

Miriam heard Dmitri spit out what she assumed was a colourful but untranslatable Russian expletive. 'That man has ruined our time together.'

'But there is an agreement. Why do we have to be on alert?'

'I suppose we have to ensure he keeps to his side of the bargain.'

Chapter Twenty-three

Moscow, September 27th 1939

She moved along within the great red walls of the Kremlin to pick up her detail of six NKVD men from the guardroom with a comfortable familiarity. She felt she was beginning to fit in, getting to know her way around in more ways than one as if she'd been there years. But the mood was dispelled when Dmitri entered her thoughts. He was never far from her mind as if the idea of him was always waiting in the wings. Continually on duty as she was it had been nearly three weeks since she last saw him.

Miriam and her squad were providing security for the aides and interpreters of visiting foreign dignitaries; mainly German, and the sudden change in her frame of mind made her especially anxious, for there was to be a glittering reception on their arrival this evening at the Great Kremlin Palace. This was her first time in the palace and she would be on duty in the anteroom of the reception hall itself. She went over the list: German Foreign Minister Ribbentrop, Gauleiter Forster of Danzig, and others. They were to be received by Comrade Molotov, commissar for foreign affairs, and she'd heard a whisper that possibly Comrade Stalin himself would attend, though the visitors didn't know it yet. She was yet to see either of them in person. It promised to be quite interesting.

When would she see Dmitri again? His card just said he'd been posted to somewhere in eastern Poland. That was over two weeks ago. No address for a reply. Eastern Poland, why there? Special duties, it said on the card. She'd heard on the radio that Soviet troops had occupied the region to protect Ukrainian and Byelorussian subjects of Poland from persecution. Perhaps it was to do with that. She hadn't been able to get in touch with Esther either despite her promise at their last meeting. No outside contact was permitted whilst on Kremlin duties. The current assignment ended tomorrow when the German party returned to Berlin. Then she'd attempt to get in touch using the time off due to her. She hoped Esther was getting over her ordeal, though she was uncomfortably aware that her real motive was to gain some information on what was happening in Poland. Perhaps she'd try phoning: it was getting easier to do so.

When they entered the large anteroom from a side door it was empty of people. She set her detail to check the room, examining furniture and searching behind curtains before positioning them as discreetly as possible on the side. Then she waited at ease, hands clasped in front, looking expectantly towards the double doors that opened into the great hall. However, after some time, it was the door through which they had entered that was opened. An aide came in and walked briskly to a small table without a glance to right or left, placed a folder upon it, turned to Miriam, and beckoned for her to come closer, signalling for her to stop when he was satisfied she was near enough, then waited at the side for some moments with his hands behind his back, his eyes lifted to the high and elaborately ornate ceiling with its crystal chandeliers.

They didn't have to wait long. Comrade Stalin appeared in the doorway almost at the same time as the second person with whom he was in conversation. As they both walked up to the table everyone stiffened to attention. Bareheaded, he seemed shorter than expected, with a slight belly showing under his mouse-coloured unbelted tunic buttoned up to the neck. The baggy trousers were tucked into soft brown calf-length boots. He turned his face to her. The sallow skin was pockmarked and his famed dark moustache was untidily spiky and flecked with silver. Permanently narrowed eyes – to her they were feline, almost oriental – flickered to the men positioned around the room and back so that he turned them on her. The deep brown orange-flecked pupils invaded her mind with a feeling of authority and power that seemed to make her catch her breath. He smiled so that creases formed at the sides of his mouth and he slowly inclined his head to her before turning to the folder on the table. Opening it with the right hand she noticed his left arm was held stiffly in an unnatural position and the braid on his tunic pocket was worn, even frayed. This was not a bit like the iconic figure on the posters. He spoke to the man at his side. She recognised him immediately as Comrade Molotov. In contrast he did look like his poster image, high forehead, clipped black moustache, and a dark grey-striped double-breasted jacket. Stalin's voice was surprisingly soft and high-pitched. It sounded tired, though she wasn't quite near enough to make out what he was saying, the aide had seen to that. Molotov took out his pince-nez and clipped them on his nose, looking even more like a professor of mathematics than his poster image as he followed Stalin's pudgy nicotine-stained finger down the first sheet of the folder, then briskly snatching them off and giving a dour nod he followed the Boss around the table as he signalled to the aide they were ready to receive their guests. Stalin stood expectantly, holding his left hand with a slightly amused expression, almost sardonic, she thought, as if he was about to enjoy a practical joke, especially as he twisted his head toward Molotov with a brief remark and a chuckle before turning back and composing himself for the gravity of the occasion. Molotov's face remained blank as he stood at his side.

The visitors were conducted into the room led by the German foreign minister Ribbentrop. He was taller than Stalin by half a head and fairly slim, with thinning fair hair. Wearing a sombre black suit with his Nazi Party badge in the lapel he looked much like an English gentleman in his bearing and appearance, giving off an almost arrogant air of confidence as he led the party toward Stalin and Molotov. At the door he had paused briefly in surprise. It was clear he wasn't expecting to meet Stalin in person on this occasion although they had met before. So this was the source of the Boss's amusement the thought occurred to her. Through the interpreter, a bespectacled Herr Hilger, Stalin and Molotov greeted them and then Ribbentrop introduced Gauleiter Forster, a rather portly figure in his brown uniform. The scarlet swastika armband set Miriam's teeth on edge. Taking him by the elbow Stalin led Ribbentrop toward the double doors already opening by unseen hands. They stepped into the glare of the full diplomatic reception followed by the whole party. The unseen hands closed the doors, leaving Miriam and her squad to an empty room.

She marched them back to barracks according to orders as her security detail would not be needed until early the following evening. They would be on duty at the banquet in honour of the German guests and later at the Bolshoi where Stalin was expected to attend a gala performance of *Swan Lake* with Ribbentrop as his guest, while Molotov had business with Gauleiter Forster. The invitation to the Bolshoi was supposed to be spontaneous but everything had been planned beforehand. Nothing was spontaneous with the Boss, she'd been told.

Moscow, October 1939

Esther had looked considerably better as she came into the Perlov. It had taken Miriam four days to arrange a meeting, longer than she expected, but luckily she had some free time due to her after the German visit. Now perhaps she could find out what was going on in the world, especially what was happening to Dmitri in eastern Poland.

Esther didn't need much prompting. Her face was flushed with excitement. 'There's been great unrest among the Ukrainian and Byelorussian minorities there, they've been persecuted by the Poles since Germany has invaded. You know the way it goes with minorities, not being patriotic, accused of treachery and the like. The Polish government, which is on the run, has encouraged this. So the Soviet Union has occupied that part of Poland to protect them, the part that once belonged to Czarist Russia. That's why Germany invaded as well: to protect German minorities and sort out Polish border disputes and the trouble over Danzig and so on. Much of it was once part of Prussia anyway. Their invasion is almost complete. It's now German territory. Some of it is part of the New German Reich as they call it. I don't know what they will do with the rest but they've agreed to a line between German and Russian occupied territory. It's all rather unclear but that will be why Dmitri is there. I believe there's a strong NKVD presence dealing with right-wing nationalistic reactionaries. You know the kind of thing: anti-Soviet groups among the intelligentsia, like we saw in Spain. I expect the region will have its own Polish government of some sort. I'm surprised you haven't heard something about it but it's been released to the press for publication by the end of this week. That's why I'm telling you now.'

'Well, that was a mouthful. Is that all? I did know from

the radio and the press that Polish territory had been occupied by Russian troops.'

Esther shook her head while she was drinking her tea, spilling some of it. 'Oh no,' she dabbed at her mouth with a handkerchief, 'There's more yet.'

'Well I've heard on the radio that Great Britain and France are at war with Germany. Let's hope the Soviet Union stays out of it as planned and let's hope there's no bombing of British towns, you know, like we saw in Spain. I keep thinking of Dad and – and Nikolai. By the way a very important German personage, I daren't say whom, was in the Kremlin some days ago.'

'Well that must be connected with what I was going to tell you before you broke in. The USSR has occupied Latvia, Estonia, and from yesterday, Lithuania.'

'Oh!'

'You'll be able to read about it at the weekend but can't you see? This is all going according to plan. Russia has regained all its former territory lost after the Great War and without a shot being fired while the democracies and the Fascists are at each other's throats. Don't you think that's clever on the part of the Boss? Even matters with Japan have been settled. A formal agreement has been signed over a week ago after the defeat of the Kwangtung Army.'

'Yes but I must say I'm surprised it's come to that.'

'I bet Herr Hitler is too. He never expected the democracies would fight.'

'Neither did we, remember? Their war could go on for years if it's anything like the last one, leaving Russia out of it altogether with years of guaranteed peace to get on with building the workers' state and securing its borders.'

'Agreed.' Esther lit a cigarette offering one to Miriam. 'Now, what are your plans?'

'Plans?'

'Well, for you and Dmitri in the long run, and in the

short, how are you going to get in touch with him?'

'I have no plans in the long run as you put it. It's not possible yet and anyway there may not be a long run so I haven't thought about it. In the meantime I suppose I'll see him when I see him. I must say, Esther, I don't know how there can be any sort of relationship if there's no contact at all without any idea of when I'll see him. Why are you asking me this anyway? You're going to tell me how I'm going to get in touch with him, aren't you?'

Esther held her elbow with one hand, drawing on the cigarette with the other, then gently lifted her chin to breathe out smoke at the lacquered chinoiserie ceiling.

'Esther, what have you got in mind?'

She lowered her head. 'Well, there are only two main units of NKVD involved in the Polish occupation, one based in Smolensk and one in Bialystok. There's a strong chance Dmitri is with one of those.'

'Smolensk?

'It's close to the Dnieper. I'm not sure whether it's Polish or Russian, the border's rather fluid there right now.'

'And the other place?'

'That's further south, near the border with Byelorussia.'

'So! What are you getting at?'

'There's someone at the office going on assignment to both places. He should be able to find him. Dmitri is a colonel after all. It shouldn't be too much trouble getting a letter to him. This man owes me a favour or two.'

'Indeed!' Miriam gave her an arch look but inside her heart jumped. A letter and maybe she could get one back. 'Esther, haven't you learned anything from the last time? It seems doubly dangerous to me. Is this man married?'

'No, actually. So you needn't worry on that score. It's common for letters to be passed on in that way now.'

'You mean sealed in an envelope?'

'Yes. I think the authorities are becoming more relaxed

about that sort of thing. In fact I've heard there's going to be an announcement to that effect soon so that people will use the postal service more. It probably reflects a greater feeling of security now that things are going well with Germany. I'm surprised you haven't heard about it in your line of work. Keep it short to start with. You'll have to anyway, the official envelopes are very small and a peculiar triangle shape; in fact they are the writing sheet itself, it folds into the envelope. Just include an official address for you and remember the censor. Ask if he can give you an address for him then you can correspond officially.'

A letter, oh, that would be wonderful. Perhaps they could start exchanging them if what Esther said was true. She had almost become resigned to an empty relationship going nowhere, just withering away, but now that feeling of tremulous excitement, of hopefulness, of a future, as if she possessed something precious, was renewed.

Chapter Twenty-three

Moscow, October 14th 1941

Miriam was hurrying past empty shops and offices. Her boots were splashing through the slush. It was nearly six in the morning and wet snow was falling from an overcast sky, keeping the bombers away. The streets were empty of buses and tramcars. There were few people about and the Metro was closed. The walls were newly pasted with posters. As she passed them a striking and graphic image of a mature firm-jawed woman with sheaves of bayonets behind her caught her eye. One arm was held high the other was thrust forward clutching a sheet of paper on which was printed the title of the military oath,and over her head was a banner the Cyrillic letters in crimson and gold stating, *RODEENA-MATZ ZOVET! MOTHERLAND IS CALLING*! Another poster took up the whole front of a building. A soldier of the Red Army was holding up his rifle, his cape billowing heroically behind him. *OTSTOEEM MOSKVOO! DEFEND MOSCOW*!

She had been ordered to join a unit detailed to control the escape routes to the east. She welcomed the urgency, the action, the chaos immersing her, sweeping her along deadening her feelings of loss and keeping the dark beast of her smouldering grief at bay, just as did Dmitri, a fragment of happiness.

But where was he right now? The question clouded her thinking. For two years they had been meeting sporadically, walking arm in arm through the Alexandrovsky gardens with suppers in his apartment, where they'd shared their astonishment at the defeat of the

British Army and the fall of France. It had all happened so quickly. It was supposed to be a long, drawn out war, taking years like the last one, and now with London being destroyed by bombing what would happen to Dad if Britain accepted Germany's terms? Although it now seemed as if they were trying to hang on, but most of all what would happen to Nikolai? Feeling particularly close that June evening after they'd heard Molotov's voice on the radio, hesitant and uncertain, announcing the shocking news of invasion and asking the Russian people to stand behind the government and Stalin, she'd told him about Sergei and about losing Nikolai. Knowing he'd have to go back next day she'd had to share her anxiety with him. She'd felt the need for some time it was not enough to talk to Esther about it, and later she sensed a feeling of calm, almost of relief. He recalled a poem he'd been reading. Wait for me, it said. As long as you do this, I'll be back.

This was it, Miriam thought, the final battle that Germany had wanted all along and we were all on the same side now, Nikolai and Dad.

The loudspeakers crackled, breaking in on her thoughts. 'This is the communiqué of the SovInformBuro, 14th of October 1941. The situation around Moscow has deteriorated during the night.' Then with a disconcertingly loud click the speakers went off.

As she made her way towards the Highway of Enthusiasts she became aware of a strong smell of burning paper and it seemed to be snowing black flakes. Curiosity aroused she held up her sleeve to examine them as they fell on it. Another fluttered down, then another. The air seemed full of them, like black snow. It seemed as if every office had a bonfire of papers outside in the streets. Burning away untended were files, documents, directories, and lists of party workers. On the parapet of a road bridge someone had daubed in crude red letters, 'The Jews have sold us to the Germans.' The Metropolitan Police had clearly lost control. The evidence of rioting was everywhere, broken glass, debris littering the streets, burned out trolley buses and shops, their doors pasted with tattered sheets of regulations and decrees, had been broken into and looted. Walking through the residential district of Taganskoe she could see the grey and white smoke of pyres sending more flakes of scorched and blackened paper swirling up from the courtyards and squares of houses and apartments, to be taken by gusts of wind and blown about the streets as people, taking advantage of the absence of policemen, burned their torn-up party cards, diaries, notebooks, roll books, badges, photographs, braided insignia, certificates, diplomas, anything that might link them with the regime. At the bakeries there were long queues. As she passed she saw a desperate anxiety upon face after face wet with melting snowflakes and everywhere she heard the howling of dogs left behind by their owners.

Eventually she was able to report to her unit at a checkpoint on the Highway of Enthusiasts near the eastern outskirts of the city. In contrast to the inner districts the Highway was lined with heavily loaded trucks and large cars carrying party officials and petty bureaucrats, their personal goods secured on the roofs with nets, crawling east nose to tail, splashing those on foot as they passed. Motorcycle messengers were weaving through in both directions, occasionally mounting the boardwalks, scattering people, overturning handcarts, and tipping furniture, bowls of household utensils, and wicker cages of geese onto the wet snow.

At the checkpoint those on foot were being channelled into many lines, moving along slowly, shuffling with short steps, slow-moving yet eager to get going. There was no clamour just silence except for the hollow clatter of pots and pans hanging from straps and belts, but Miriam sensed the tension like the feel of static electricity in her hair, betraying barely suppressed panic. Word was going round that anyone who was anything to do with the party would be shot out of hand when the Hitlerites arrived. There were many anxious glances at the sky, hoping the low overcast would last long enough to keep the planes away until they were clear of the city. Vehicles were divided into lanes and papers were checked. Many were turned back through the suburbs. Only those being officially evacuated were allowed to leave for Kuibyshev in the east.

Suddenly a car sped up, its tyres smoking as it attempted to accelerate away. Someone shot at it with a machine gun. Now there was panic. It seemed to Miriam the ordered lines suddenly exploded so that the whole area was filled with milling people, all trying to move at once, pushing, shoving, trying to elbow their way through, some silent and grimly dogged, some shouting, suitcases bursting open, clothes wrapping around feet, shoes being kicked along, birdcages rolling, baskets and boxes all spilling their contents. The car veered across the road, tipping on its side where it lay ignored by everyone except Miriam. A large dog leaping out of the vehicle through a shattered window captured her attention. She followed it with her eyes, momentarily spell-bound as it loped wolf-like across the snowy arctic-blue landscape to disappear into a forest of birch trees, briefly gleaming silver in the failing afternoon light. The vision stirred melancholic feelings deep within her.

Then in the midst of the turmoil she recognised her commanding officer, Major Volodin, standing on the cab of a truck, attempting to impose some control by shouting orders over the screaming and the bawling. She shouldered her way through the press, calling at the top of her voice to get his attention, 'Comrade Major.'

He turned and pointed, yelling, 'Get beyond there,

Captain, and take up a position with Raskova's group. There are certain cars trying to leave without proper authority. If any break through wait until they get up to you and fire at the windows.'

Bryansk, 18th October 1941

Dmitri jogged urgently alongside the slow-moving rail car. He must get back. He'd told her he would come back to her as long as she remembered him. Dodging the others doing the same he tried to time his leap as the train gathered speed, making several tentative but false attempts. Finally, discarding his pack, he made a last desperate grab for the handrail. The forward movement of the train swung him off his feet but he hung on, clutching and fumbling at the door until it opened and he fell through. Another man followed him, lunged for the handrail and missing it, lost his footing, falling with a cry of despair beneath the wheels of last train to leave Bryansk before it fell to the enemy. Lying face down on the floor, his breath coming in short gasps, the feeling of relief swept over Dmitri. He had been pulled from his command in the desperate final stages of the fighting and ordered to Moscow to take charge of a special unit with immediate effect. He couldn't believe his luck, to Moscow, to Miriam, just hours before death in battle or capture and inevitable shooting by the enemy as an NKVD colonel. It had been a constant series of postings since the disaster at Kiev. He could feel the stealthy embrace of battle fatigue but the two pistol shots, one after the other, dispelled it. As he lifted his head a pair of toecaps appeared before his eyes. He pushed himself up with his palms. An NKVD trooper stood over him, a smoking Nagant heavy pistol in his hand. 'You'd better have the correct papers and permits, Comrade Colonel, or you get the same as those other two deserters.'

Moscow, October 1941, the same day

Yaroslavl, only one hundred kilometres from Red Square, had fallen. The northern pincer of the enemy's claw was closing on the city. During the night, with the situation at the eastern checkpoints, under control, Miriam had been despatched with her whole division to the southwest to cover a sector behind the army itself as a backstop. Her formation held an inner ring from Kuntsevo on the right of the army to the Moscow River on the left, with orders to prevent enemy mechanised units from breaking through to the city and to shoot anyone under arms who was falling back.

She was falling down the well, down and down to her death and no one could help her. Waking with a start from an hour's snatched sleep, her tongue clinging to the top of her palate and her heart thumping she hauled herself out of the bunker.

Stretching stiff limbs in the keen air she became aware of the sounds of battle. The distant growl of artillery, the occasional howling and whooshing of the Katyusha rocket launchers and the telltale clinking of armoured tracks above the crackle of small arms was carried across the plain on the stinging wind now becoming dry as the temperature dropped. A grey dawn lit the snow-heavy clouds behind her. Suddenly, to the west, sunbeams struck through, illuminating far-off silver domes. Beyond there was Borodino, the Napoleonic battlefield, already in enemy hands. It seemed another age when they were there that thundery afternoon less than three years ago. She recalled her conversation with Dmitri. Then invasion was just a hypothetical topic. An enemy wouldn't go for Moscow, Dmitri had said, but now it was battering at the door in what had become a terrible reality. Things had not gone well, not gone well at all.

The mood overtook her, catching her off guard. This

was the start of her fourth winter in this land. She'd been watching other babies since she lost him. She still heard him crying, sometimes getting out of bed to feed him. She did not welcome sleep, for waking brought the deep sense of loss all over again, but she realised he was older now, no longer the baby she remembered. She had mementoes, his photograph and a small furry rabbit without ears kept in a tobacco tin. He will be three and a half, she realised with a start. She was always watching out for him in other children, wondering what he looked like. Sergei perhaps? The thought struck her, reminding her – oh my God! She banished it. Smothering the image by thinking of the dreadful cold soon to grip the fields either side of the road, ahead marked only by a line of frost-rimed telegraph poles. It was already disappearing under dry powdery snow, wind-blown and sweeping along in waves. Oh what a dreadful place this was.

With her eyes half closed against the fine driving flakes clustering on her lashes she watched a column of trucks moving slowly east to west at the crossroads of the Mozhaisk Highway silhouetted against the skyline slipping and sliding in the glutinous mud. With the coming of night it would set hard as concrete. A small furry creature caught her eye as it scuttled along the edge of a ditch to plop into the water through the thin skin of ice.

The hoarse sound of coughing and the rasp of vigorous throat clearing broke into her mood. She turned to the source, Sergeant Sarayev sitting at a distance on an ammunition box, eating his kasha off a sheet of newspaper.

She watched him for a moment. 'Sergeant!'

He turned to her, licking his fingers.

'Are you enjoying that?'

He nodded warily and noncommittally.

'Good. It'll be your last for some time, I think.'

He looked puzzled. 'Captain?'

'Take the men's rations from them, Comrade Sergeant, and put them in a single sack and bring it to me; that includes vodka, tobacco, and tea.'

He looked even more puzzled.

'We've been transferred to army command since early this morning. They're not obliged to feed us and I don't think they will, given that our task is to shoot any soldier with his back to the enemy, so we need to go on half rations for the next few days.'

'What about ammunition, Captain?'

'Oh, they'll keep us supplied with that, don't worry.'

'And, er, Comrade Captain?'

'Yes. What?'

'We've run out of cigarette papers.'

'Then use that newspaper you're eating from, Comrade Sergeant.'

He looked so dejected as he walked away she called after him, 'I'll ask for some when I send for the ammo but you know the chances of them taking any notice as well as I do.'

Zvenigorodskoe Shosse tram terminus, three days later

The phone rang in her detachment's new billet in the terminus for the first time since they had taken up this position two days ago, bringing Miriam dashing into the room. The nerve-jangling bell changed to a faint tinkling then stopped as she made a grab for the heavy receiver. Cursing angrily she kicked the table. Three days ago, according to some regular passengers interrogated by her, a German forward patrol of a few men had reached the terminus and stood watching curiously as a tram arrived and picked up passengers, then departed for the city centre. The patrol presumably withdrew west down the highway, so the front line must be close, but how close was a mystery. The lack of information or contact with the rear positions was unnerving and it didn't help that the phone was dead except for strange ghostly murmurings whenever she picked up the receiver and tried to make contact. During the last twenty-four hours there had been little to do despite the battle raging ahead of them, ever closer, and nothing to eat.

The phone rang again. This time she managed to pick it up in time. 'How far is the front line from your position, comrade captain?' a voice barked.

'Less than a kilometre,' answered Miriam uncertainly.

The voice barked again, 'They're on their way, should be at your position soon,' before cutting off.

Puzzled she rattled the cradle but there was no response. 'Who?' She shouted into the receiver before banging it down.

Almost as soon as she put the phone down her question was answered. The civilians arrived in tramcars, rolling up nose to tail, bringing food with them. They were followed by truckloads of sandbags and soon a great wall of them with steel-plated loopholes, welded in the railway workshops, had been thrown across the road, extending on either side to the buildings in the distance. It was turning white under a light fall of snow.

Two days later Miriam stood in the doorway of the billet, stirring a spoonful of jam into a glass of thick black tea. She watched the women, seemingly thousands of them, digging out the enormous anti-tank ditch in front of the sandbag wall with backbreaking toil, some with feverish energy, some with a dogged determination. It was like a great black scar creasing the whitening landscape for many kilometres. Her fingers unwittingly traced the furrows on her face.

That one over there, she singled out a bent-backed babushka, her feet and legs bound in sack-cloth, struggling up the steep loose side of the ditch dragging her burden, a wattle basket piled with spoil, to tip it onto the bank before descending for more. What was going on in her head? Why was she doing that? What had she got to lose or gain? Life would be just as hard for her no matter who won. Perhaps she had children, grandchildren? Suddenly the thought flashed into her mind: what had she herself got? What was she fighting for? Her child was not there, not in this land. He was far away. Suddenly she felt dizzy, outside of herself, as if the whole scene was revealed in some sort of truth. And what future was she fighting for, was it for him and for Dmitri? Could she have a future with them both? She struggled within herself to look forward, but she could see only mist rising before her. With her breath coming in shorts gasps and her mouth feeling dry so that her tongue clung to her palate she clutched at the doorpost until the sensation passed and her head cleared.

On Zvenigorodskoe Shosse, earlier that same day

Dmitri ordered his car to pull over. Glancing briefly at his map he opened the door himself and warily stepped out onto the treacherous surface, petulantly refusing the driver's offer of assistance. No one could tell him exactly where the enemy line was. The situation was fluid, he'd been told. They could run into it at any moment. He was irritable and anxious. Steadying his elbows against the vehicle he attempted to scan the horizon with his field glasses before impatiently tossing them back inside. They were useless against the freezing mist that was swirling around them, muffling all but the most strident sounds before clearing momentarily and treacherously revealing every detail of the landscape. Signalling to his bodyguard in the following half-track to deploy either side of the highway and follow him he motioned to the drivers of both vehicles to stay and keep their engines running to prevent icing up and to be ready for a quick escape.

On being recalled to Moscow NKVD Colonel Dmitri Ignatov had been assigned immediately the special task of organising forward posts for sending out patrols to snatch prisoners for the interrogation centres. He had failed to contact Miriam. There were no replies to his letters. It was doubtful they reached their destination or were ever despatched. In the chaos and disorder at the Lubyanka no one seemed to know whether she had been evacuated or posted to some part of the front, only that there was no address for her. Taking advantage of the eerie silence during a lull in the battle, he was going up to the enemy lines to get a close look for himself. They hadn't come far. Even in the treacherous road conditions it had taken less than thirty minutes to travel from Lubyanka Square to their present position.

Dmitri sent two men forward to report back on the situation ahead then he moved after them, stealthily followed by his group in their white camouflage over-smocks. They held pieces of ice in their mouths to chill the breath so that it didn't steam and give away their position to enemy snipers or patrols that may be in the area. Powdery snow was starting to lie on the rutted highway, marked by the poles of the tramway system. The frozen air carried a hazy mist that drifted across the open ground with a milky opacity, draping the birch trees in a melancholic stillness and the deep silence gave the unwary a false impression of being in a landscape empty of all other beings.

Suddenly each man became aware of the familiar sound of trams coming from the direction of the city centre. Exchanging glances with each other as if to confirm their senses were not playing tricks on them they took what cover they could find at the roadside. With the sound increasing they could see the flashes from the overhead power lines bathing the folds of mist in a blue glow, then two great columns, taking both east and westbound lines, of swaying cars emerged, rattling past endlessly with their cargoes of volunteer and dragooned citizens of all ages crammed aboard with bags of food and every digging implement that could be found.

No longer feeling the need for stealth they started to walk openly alongside the tracks but were soon forced off the road by a convoy of trucks continuously roaring past at amazingly high speed, using only their rear lights as red pinpricks in the murk.

Dmitri sent back for their vehicles to be brought up as soon as possible while they continued to move west toward the front line, which going by the traffic appeared to be further off than was formerly assumed. Eventually they met the two men who had been sent forward and they reported what was going on at the tram terminus. Dmitri decided to go up to the terminus and use it as a base from where he would take two of his bodyguards and get up as close to the contact point with the enemy as was practical, for him to assess the situation for setting snatch teams in place.

Cautiously moving along the shallow ditch that served as a trench, crouching double and flinching involuntarily at the occasional mortar round, they stepped laboriously over the legs of men positioned every two metres. Dmitri and his bodyguards were led to the hollowed-out hole that served as a bunker for brigade headquarters. Pushing aside the canvas sheet that hung over the tiny doorway they entered into the fusty, earthy smelling air and were met by the stench of the paraffin lamps hanging face height from the extremely low ceiling and the acrid reek of acid from the batteries powering the five-watt transceiver, and the twenty-five line switchboard busily operated by the women signallers. Elbowing through the bustle of messengers and aides and lifting aside the festoons of telegraph transmission wires their guide led them to the NKVD officer who was acting as the political commissar. He was seated at his table, an ammunition crate, and he looked up at his visitors warily.

Dmitri started to explain the purpose of his visit, setting out his map and placing a candleholder on it to give more light.

'Comrade Colonel, your men will have to wait outside. There just isn't room or air for more people than is necessary in here.'

Dmitri indicated with a movement of his head for his men to go.

'Now take a seat.' With his foot the commissar pushed a box towards him.

'First of all,' Dmitri started off, 'I need to know what position you're going to fall back to so that –'

The commissar brought his hand down on the map with a thump. 'There's no more falling back, written orders from the Boss himself. "'Not one step back,'" he quoted.

Dmitri raised his head, looking into the commissar's face. Outside he could hear a drum roll of artillery above the buzzing of the switchboard, the constant ringing of field telephones, and the urgent babbling of the signallers into their sets. Fine dark soil trickled down his neck through the gaps of the bulging wood-clad ceiling, and pattered lightly onto the map. The candle flame, already flickering low with the thin air, guttered, giving off a foul black smoke.

'The next time we move it will be forward. We counter-attack soon – with tanks.'

'Tanks! I didn't see any tanks when I came up.'

'They arrived from the factories two days ago, all under cover now, crewed up, fuelled up, and gunned up with the new eighty millimetre.'

'Nor did I see signs of preparations for a counter-offensive, only for defence.'

'Good! You weren't supposed to.'

Dmitri looked down thoughtfully for a moment, inclining his head to one side. Producing a smacking sound with his lips he exclaimed, 'Well! That makes my job a little easier. Explain things to me.'

The commissar swept his hand over the map. 'Here in this whole region we're facing Second Panzer Army under Colonel-General Heinz Gudarian. Opposite us on our left is Eighth Panzer Corps Bryansk supported by Thirty-Fifth Army Corps Metz, comprising Forty-Five Division and Hundred and Thirty-Four Division. As far as the enemy is concerned it's one more push and they're in Red Square.'

With his practised eye Dmitri grasped the situation. 'And you want to know the strength of their armour and their disposition.'

'That's about it, and how much fuel they're bringing up, where it's stockpiled, whether they can start their engines in the mornings in these low temperatures, or whether they have to keep them running all night to prevent icing up. I've had listeners put forward. Sometimes they think they can hear them but they're not sure. Our new tanks start with compressed air or nitrogen, no need to use the batteries, they're useless for starting when it's below minus twenty anyway and it always is. Also we need to know whether they've fitted the new guns yet, the eighty-eights instead of the seventy-fives, so I need tongues and someone to make them wag. That's where you come in, Colonel.'

Brushing soil from the map Dmitri moved the candle again, spilling some grease on it as he did so and together they worked with scale rule, dividers, trammel, and compass, assessing the most suitable areas for the snatch teams to operate and where to position them.

With his map secure in its case Dmitri gathered his two bodyguards. Crossing over the anti-tank fosse by a precariously slippery foot bridge they passed through a narrow opening in the increasing mass of the earth bank to the tram terminus, where the vehicles and the rest of his group were waiting. As his car was pulling away Dmitri sat back in the front passenger seat his thoughts, immediately sinking into the task ahead.

Miriam waited for the car to pass, almost brushing her overcoat as it slowly edged its way through the tram traffic onto the road. As the passenger side came up to her Dmitri's face framed by the window and staring fixedly through the windscreen, only centimetres away from her own, impacted forcefully on her consciousness so much so that for an instant she hesitated thinking she was mistaken, but no she was certain it was he. Her heart leaping she called his name at the top of her voice, but it was swept away in the noise of the trams and the half-track following close behind. She tried to catch up with the slow-moving car, to reach it with her outstretched arms and bang on the body but it was gathering speed and the following half-track was getting perilously close forcing her to step back. Desperately she waved her arms, attempting to get it to stop but it passed. The driver was too intent on manoeuvring the vehicle onto the main highway, where it disappeared into the mist, to see anyone waving. In a moment her heart was plunged from an ecstasy of delight into a trough of despair. Clasping her hands to her mouth emotion swept over her. She'd missed her chance. Oh, why did she let him go? Why didn't she do something, anything? She could have fired her pistol in the air, shot at the wheels. Was there anyone on foot who was with him? She looked about wildly but there was no one and no other vehicle with his car except the half-track. Now that too had gone with no way of knowing where they had come from or where they were going. Overcome with her feelings she lurched across the road, dodging around people, trams, and trucks and staggered into her small room in the terminus building, collapsing onto her bunk, the realisation crashing over her. She'd lost the chance of speaking to him, of saying what she'd so wanted to say all those weeks, months when she didn't know if he was alive. He'd come back and she wasn't there for him. Now it would go on, the aching, the waiting and the not knowing if she would see him again. Oh God, that may have been the last time she would see him.

Chapter Twenty-four

Moscow, January 1942

Miriam warmed herself at the brazier, keeping ice-free the great wood-lagged water tank for replenishing locomotive tenders at the end of the platform, where she knew the engine heading the train would stop. The main German attack had come in late November, just as the air temperature was plummeting and the ground froze so hard footsteps began to have the ring of walking on steel. When the counter-offensive that halted the German advance began, the meteorological department at the Smolny Institute regularly recorded the lowest November temperatures for thirty years: readings of minus thirty degrees Centigrade, occasionally falling to forty. The pincers threatening Moscow had been forced back at enormous human cost. The Great Panic was over; demolition charges had been removed from the bridges and important buildings. Miriam's unit was on duty at the Kazan Station, checking for German agents among the government officials returning from evacuation.

Neither the small huddle of market women, rook-like in their black kerchiefs pulled tight on their brows, hoping to sell their wretched-looking potatoes from their carts, nor the station staff, came near her to share the warmth of the brazier. Despite the intense cold the feared blue tabs on her shoulders and the blue cuff bands on her sleeves ensured she had it to herself. She watched the massive engine slowly rolling towards her, panting asthmatically as jets of steam spurted from the cylinders with each stroke of the pistons and puffed in clouds from the chimney. It made a powerful statement in its new coat of shiny blue-black paint, red and white wheels, and a red star on the front of the smoke box picked out in yellow. As it passed with squealing brakes, bringing the train of cars to a convulsive halt she saw someone had painted in white Cyrillic letters diagonally across the tender, *SMERT FASCISTI!* DEATH TO FASCISTS! The women in layers of clothing stuffed with old newspapers shuffled in their hessian-wrapped clogs through the steam, roaring and cracking as it met the frozen air, and lifting their arms as if in praise to the great iron beast they basked momentarily in its warmth.

Standing on a box Miriam made sure her men were in position. She watched the passengers coming towards her, the frozen snow screeching under their feet as they padded along. Some were staggering with their bundles and distended pillowcases gripped tightly over their shoulders. As they milled around the checkpoint she examined their faces, partly obscured by steamy breath, lined with exhaustion and hunger. Occasionally she referred to the spiroflex pages of photographs in her directory, added to daily, pointing out an individual to be held for questioning later.

Suddenly she saw him: a little boy barely old enough to walk, a cap too large pulled around his ears, a muffler around his mouth, and a long coat almost down to his booted feet. There was a cord around his neck like a lanyard with a spoon attached to it and with both hands he was clutching a strap. It was tied to the belt of a great-coated man in a fur hat with a scarf around his face. He was carrying a large bulging sack in both arms, obviously a civil servant, or that was what she thought.

She watched the boy as he toddled past her, his face a mask of urgency in his desperation to keep up, occasionally tottering when the strap was almost yanked out of his mittened hands, quickening her heart each time this happened. The man looked fixedly ahead as if indifferent to the boy. She signalled for him to be held at the exit. How dare he treat such a lovely little boy in that way? He doesn't deserve him. She would teach this bureaucrat a lesson. Grief and loss had turned to anger swelling within her.

When the platform was cleared she made her way to the truck and ordered the detainees to be taken away, 'Except for those two.' She pointed to the man and the boy. 'Put them in my car.'

With the detainees bundled into the back of the truck Miriam's car, a black Packard provided by the United States, followed it to the interrogation centre. The man's blood had run cold when he saw Miriam signal for him to be held. Now he sat unresisting and without protest, quietly comforting the child, sitting silently but with wide eyes betraying his alarm.

Miriam looked intently at him across the table with eyes cold and flinty. His papers were spread out in front of her under the light of a powerful desk lamp. Her fingers drummed them lightly. He sat hunched forward, his hands plucking at his now-empty sack, still in shock from being roughly searched. The windowless room was bare except for the table and chairs. A rime of frost rose halfway up the walls and a single unlit bulb hung from the ceiling. The boy was sitting beside the man, eating with his spoon from a bowl of American powdered egg snatched by Miriam from a militiaman. Sergeant Sarayev stood at the open door, his face blank and emotionless. The contents of the sack lay scattered on the floor behind him.

'Comrade,' Miriam paused perusing the papers, 'Lozovsky, correct?'

'Yes.'

'Georgi Lozovsky?'

'That is correct.'

Without looking up from the documents she asked,

'When were you evacuated, Comrade Lozovsky?'

Nervously he answered, 'October 16th last year.'

'Here I read the 15th, comrade. Why is that?'

He made to answer but his mouth was too dry. He tried again. 'I thought it had passed midnight when the train left.'

Miriam stared into his eyes. The desk lamp lit her face from below, giving it a menacing appearance. 'According to this certificate your rent was paid in advance. For how long does it say here?'

'Four months.' Nervously his voice broke into a hoarse whisper.

'What was that? You must speak up, Lozovsky.'

'Four months.'

'Yes it does. What is your rank in the ministry of finance?'

'I am a senior clerk.'

'You are the boy's father?'

'Yes.'

She leaned toward the boy. Tenderly her hand moved to his face but she held it back without touching, almost in contact with his cheek. 'What is your name?'

He stopped eating and drew away from her.

'He won't speak. He's been like that since we were bombed.'

'His first name?'

'Aleksei.'

She ran a finger over the papers, 'I do not find his certificate here, nor his ration card, nor his permit to return.'

Lozovsky swallowed. 'The train was bombed when we left. Some of our papers were lost.'

Miriam stared steadily at him for some moments. 'The boy's mother, this is her name on the evacuation certificate is it not?'

He nodded.

'Where is she?'

'She stayed in Kuibyshev.'

'Why?'

'She has not been recalled yet.'

'And her position is?' Miriam glanced at the papers.

'A typist in the ministry.'

Miriam collected the papers together. Carefully and deliberately she laid them aside. Lozovsky instantly recognised the significance of this, as she intended, and sat up. He wasn't getting them back. She watched the anxiety playing on his face. It fed her anger and her hunger for possession. She would seize the boy. The idea grew swiftly from a small seed in her mind. Who was this man to get in her way, dragging the child behind him on a lead like a troublesome dog? She fixed his eyes with hers for some moments before shifting her attention to the boy. Lozovsky put his arm around him and drew him closer. It was obvious and had been from the start, that there was nothing suspicious about this man but oh, the impulse to take hold, pull the child to her and put a bullet in this man's forehead. Even so there were steely calculations at the centre of her consciousness. NKVD had issued a specific order: no one was to impose the harshest punishment arbitrarily except in the case of a flagrant breach of discipline such as attempting to escape. This had come from the Boss himself.

Lozovsky could not understand why he'd been singled out for questioning. In his exhaustion his mind drifted. They'd been on the train for three weeks. Crammed in a stinking unheated car with walls sheeted with ice. The thirst and the hunger, all their ration coupons had been exchanged for bread, the long waits shunted into sidings as the troop trains passed on the main line, hurrying to the front and the terrible fear under the bombardments they brought in their wake.

'Lozovsky,' Miriam interrupted his thoughts watching

his reaction as she caught him off guard, 'if that is your name, I think you picked this child up, snatched him perhaps from his real parents, or perhaps they were killed or he was just abandoned, and you're using him as a cover.'

'No! That's not true. He's my son. He's mine.' Lozovsky drew the little boy even closer. The boy clung to his him, burying his face in his chest, something he had obviously been doing since he was a baby.

Suddenly Miriam's dormant anguish was roused. For a fleeting moment the vision of the diminishing end of the Red Cross train was evoked. She screamed, 'Do you really expect me to believe this child's mother would willingly allow you to take him from her and bring him back here?'

Georgi Lozovsky sat white-lipped. Desperately he sought an answer. How could he explain the conditions in Kuibyshev, a small town on the Volga whose population had swollen by half a million evacuees in a matter of weeks? The factories and their dormitories springing up on the edge of the town, everyone packed together in that old crumbling house without running water. The streets of frozen mud lined with antiquated wooden buildings with great icicles hanging from the roofs, most vehicles, apart from a few trolleybuses, drawn by horses or even camels. The crowds of people searching for food in the few shops, the reek of drying fish, the only food reliably available, and the stench of the privies. Above all the fear of typhus when the thaw came with no way of knowing when the child's mother would be released, or even if she would be released at all.

Miriam's words, now icily calm, broke into his thoughts, 'I'm minded to wire the NKVD at Kuibyshev to have the boy's mother produced. In the meantime he will stay here in my custody.' She leaned over to him hissing spitefully, 'If they cannot produce her, Lozovsky, you will be handed over to my NKVD colleagues as a suspected

Hitlerite agent.' Leaning back she picked up his papers. 'In the meantime I will keep these to me.' She called in Sarayev to give him his orders.

Sensing that something terrible was about to happen the boy clung to his father and started screaming. Wild-eyed, Lozovsky wrapped his arms around his son and rose to his feet, attempting to wrest him from the arms of the two militiamen who had come to take him. Another man tore the boy from his father, knocking the lamp to the floor in the struggle, casting their bizarrely elongated shadows on the walls and leaving the room with only the light from the doorway through which he carried him.

Miriam called to Sarayev loud enough for everyone to hear, 'Take this man to the Kazan Station in the morning and put him on the train for the interrogation centre at Lyubertsky under close escort. The boy is to go to my room. Put someone in charge of him and see that he's washed and fed. I'll make arrangements for him later.'

Sarayev turned to leave but in the bustle of general movement Miriam called him back to her, putting her mouth close to his ear. 'That man's not going to Lyubertsky. Do you understand?'

Sarayev looked at her quizzically.

'At the station tomorrow see that he's shot trying to escape.'

Sarayev nodded.

'And, sergeant, he must be seen trying to escape. That's important, you understand?'

He nodded again.

That night alone in her billet, sitting on the bed, Miriam slowly and deliberately placed the tumbler on the ammunition box that held her possessions and poured the vodka, carefully sprinkling pepper on the surface of the clear liquid. She smoked a cigarette as she watched the grains settle to the bottom, taking an oily residue with them. She would deal with the boy in the morning but tonight she would shut out the anguish, deaden the pain, steep her senses in alcohol and forgetfulness.

At daybreak, fully clothed, she gradually and painfully regained consciousness. It was not the pale dawn light that awoke her but the intense cold and the retching. Suddenly sitting up and knocking the empty bottle over she lurched to the bucket and vomited noisily and copiously, bringing up a foul-smelling liquid tasting of diesel fuel. Lighting a cigarette to ease the searing pain in her head she looked at her watch by the light of the match but her eyes would not focus. The leaden sensation in her stomach was overwhelmed by a wave of nausea. She slumped down on the bed and fell back, staring at the ceiling until it stopped spinning.

The vision of the boy filled her mind setting off the emotions of the day before. What was she to do with him? She couldn't look after him. What would happen when she was posted? Where would he go? What would become of him? He would be put in one of those institutions run by the political police. Then the dreadful nature of her action came sweeping over her in waves of revulsion. Oh God! What had she been doing over the past few years, in Spain and now here in Russia?

How had it come to this? She wasn't evil, but had she stayed a teacher or a farmer's wife, the things she had done, she would surely see them to be so. She would see them as monstrous. Was she a monster? Dad would think so, and Mam. But Esther didn't, did she? She wasn't sure. But surely if she was a monster she was made monstrous by these times, these events. She'd taken part in good works, the soup kitchens and the fight against Mosley, against right-wing authoritarianism and capitalism, but was that her motive, her reason for her actions? Well, it was at first but then it became – something else. Something to do with her underlying anger perhaps, something on which to work it out. Was it to overcome the evil regime of Franco when she took up Sergei's offer? Was it sheer ambition? Or was it an opportunity to inflict her wrath born of frustration, injury, and outrage at her disfigurement, of having this wreckage of a face forced upon her like some hideous battle mask on an ancient helmet, to inflict it upon the world that had rewarded her so when all she wanted was to improve it, to right wrongs, to fight evil. And now, had she in turn become evil? She had indeed done terrible things but small wonder considering the terrible things that were done to her. But did she really believe that, that she was made this way, that she had been compelled to do these things, that she had been made monstrous? But surely she was taking part in creating a new era and fighting against the forces that sought to destroy Russia and enslave all Europe, including Nikolai. That's what it had been about from the start. The final victory over the Fascists must be achieved if only for his sake. When it was over no one would quibble about what had to be done to accomplish it, and she was ready to do whatever had to be done.

These thoughts triggered the longing to hold him that was always lurking in the corners of her mind, rising to an intolerable intensity. And now she had lost Dmitri. Where was he? She hadn't seen him since that glimpse in the car. She fell upon the bed, sobbing deeply without any effort to control it for some minutes. Then she rose with a start, looked at her watch again. Lozovsky, there was still time. She snatched open the door and shielding her stinging eyes from the weak sun she called for her driver. 'Kazan Station as fast as you can.'

During the night Sergeant Sarayev had pondered hard on the task the Captain had set him. Even if they could trick Lozovsky into trying to make a break for it the platform would be crowded. There would be a stampede if shots were fired. Shot at the station packed with people while trying to escape, easier said than done. They could push him under a carriage; make it look as if he had fallen trying to run away. No. People might see, besides it would hold up the train. A single bullet was the answer, into the back of the head as usual, but how? Why not shoot him now in the cell in private? But that would go against the Captain's orders. At the station, she said, in public and that's what it will have to be.

As he lay on the damp sacking in his cell that night Georgi Lozovsky had time to think. They weren't going to wire Kuibyshev and send out a patrol of NKVD to look for some insignificant person just to confirm his story. They were going to shoot him in the morning. Of that he had become certain. When the door was thrown open at daybreak he thought his time had come, but he was mistaken for the time being at least.

By morning Sarayev had decided what to do. As their black van approached Komsomol Square he ordered it to draw into the goods depot on the edge of the Kazan Station. The sentries at the marshalling yard let Sarayev's party with their handcuffed captive through. He led them onto the tracks and they picked their way through the rolling stock and shunting engines towards the eastbound platform. They could see it in the distance through the steam and smoke packed with people anticipating the arrival of a train. Lozovsky stumbled clumsily as he stepped across an icy sleeper and was pushed forward. 'Where are you taking me?' He'd asked the question three times before but with no reply. This time the militiaman who'd pushed him smirked, 'To your death, comrade.' He pushed him again with the butt of is rifle. When a stationary train of wagons masked them from the platform Sarayev ordered a halt.

Miriam's car slithered to a stop on the icy approach to the three great arches of the station's main entrance, followed by a vanload of militiamen. Using her men she forced her way through the crowded booking hall and plunging into the mass of anxious people in the concourse steamy with the breath from thousands of mouths and nostrils she led them to the barrier of the eastbound platform and bawled at the guard over the echoing din of the great train hall, 'Has an escort with a prisoner gone through?' He shrugged shouting back, 'I don't know, Comrade Captain. I've just come on duty.' Miriam ordered him to open the barrier and led her men through pushing, shoving, and calling for people to move aside but no ground was gained. Exasperated Miriam ordered rifle butts to be used to clear a way so that gradually they reached the edge of the platform. Walking along with her men using their rifles like staves to force back the press with their backs dangerously close to the edge she searched the sea of faces, looking in vain for Sarayev's party.

Sarayev turned to his men and ordered them to sling their rifles. 'Bring him here and take off the cuffs.' Then pointing down the track leading along the platform he took Lozovsky by the arm and muttered in his ear, 'Go on, make a run for it. You've got sixty seconds before I give them the order to open fire. It'll take them another fifteen seconds to take aim.'

Lozovsky looked at him wildly.

'Go on. You can dodge across the tracks. There's plenty of cover. I'm offering you a slim chance. Take it.'

Lozovsky shook his head, taking a step backward, holding his palms before him, partly pleading partly attempting to ward off the awful violence that he thought was about to destroy him.

'Please yourself, but if you stay here you get a bullet in the belly and a long, hard death. If I were you I'd take a chance: at least if you don't make it it'll be quick.'

Lozovsky turned and looked at the wide expanse of the rail yard with flatcars slowly clinking and clanking along the metals gleaming in the pale light to fade away into the white mist of frozen air. He teetered on the edge of a desperate gamble. No thought of what to do if he did make it. Just to get away, to survive at least a little longer.

Miriam, distracted by freight cars moving slowly along the line behind her, glanced over her shoulder.

Lozovsky burst into a run.

As the brake van passed Miriam it unveiled the scene before her and everyone else at the platform's edge, just as Sarayev had intended.

Lozovsky was running, almost stumbling as he lurched across the tracks.

Un-slinging their rifles, taking their time, sure of their target, Sarayev's men were about to take aim.

Miriam screamed, 'Sergeant! Hold your fire.'

Immediately a train of passenger cars rumbled along the platform, screening Sarayev and his men and prompting a desperate rush of people even before it stopped. Miriam climbed down under the couplings between the cars, leaving her men to fight their way through the scrabbling mob to get around the rear of the train and onto the tracks. As she emerged from the steam on the other side of the train she was dreading what she would see.

Lozovsky ran, stumbling as he changed direction, desperately looking for a freight wagon to put between them and him but it was too far to go. He would never make it. Better to resign himself to the bullets that would hit him at any moment, but they never came. Had he made it? He kept running, his chest felt as if it was bursting with the pain. He had a chance. He wanted to live. He never saw the switch lever. He hit it, tripped, and fell onto the track. He scrambled to get to his feet.

'Lozovsky!' It was a woman's voice.

He looked back. The woman was walking towards, him fumbling in her tunic pocket. She was reaching for a pistol to finish him off but no; she pulled out his papers and handed them to him. 'Take these.' Lozovsky hesitated, 'Go on take them. Your son is safe. I will take you to him then you will be free to go.'

Georgi Lozovsky felt his knees give way with relief and he sat down heavily on the line, feeling the burning cold of the metal.

Chapter Twenty-five

Wrexham, 1957

'The next time we met was in the late spring of 'forty-two I think. Yes it must have been then because I remember most of the snow had gone from the streets. That's when she told me about the boy at the Kazan Station.' Esther draws her chair around so that she is cornering Nicholas, making him feel uncomfortable. 'She still didn't know at that point whether Dmitri was alive or not. It was to be a long time before we saw each other again, not until the July of 'forty-five. She'd been promoted by then, a major with the NKVD; in fact it had become the MGB, attached to Beria's secret police.'

Nicholas tenses visibly and Esther is quick to notice.

'So! That bothers you, does it? Well the business at the Kazan Station had changed her, I think.'

Nicholas gives her a questioning look.

'Yes. You might like to know that. In fact I think it's important you know that. I remember her telling me about something she'd seen on the streets about a month before. She would have told it, or even seen it, in a different way before the matter with the boy. Do you know what I mean?'

Nicholas shifts uneasily and leans back, still with a sceptical look that irritates her.

'No, I don't think you do. Well before that she would have told me what she'd seen without feeling, I suppose, or possibly not told me about it at all, but then she seemed to have gained – I don't quite know how to put it – perhaps some humanity. She had changed. What she saw got through to her just as it would to us or most other people in a way it would never have done before.'

'Nonsense!' Nicholas sits up, nearly toppling his cup from its saucer. He looks round for somewhere to put the irksome object that has been annoying him for some time.

'Oh for God's sake put it on the floor and stop fidgeting, you're making me edgy.'

He leans forward and puts it down with a rattle of china, then he sits up again, anxious to regain his decorum. 'Are you expecting me to believe that my mother was now transformed after what you've told me about her? If that was the case how would she be able to face her past, all the terrible things she had done? Any normal person in her position would have shot themselves.'

'You know, you can be too bloody precocious by half. Has anyone ever told you that?'

Nicholas makes to respond, his face darkening.

'Oh, don't bother to answer.' Esther stares at him for some moments. 'You do remind me of your mother when you get ratty. Her eyes used to widen too and there's that same firm line in the mouth.'

Nicholas feels his mouth twitching as he tries to change the expression on his face.

'Life is never that simple. It you want find out what your mother was like you're going to have to withhold judgement until you understand what it was like for your mother. I keep telling you that. You're going to have to let it sink in.'

Nicholas takes a deep breath. 'Just go on. Tell me what she saw on the streets that shows she had changed.'

'She was walking through the city near the Byelorussia Station.'

Moscow, April 1942

It was difficult for Miriam to move through the crowds lining the pavements. There was a cheerful and good-natured air. People were calling out to acquaintances just for the sake of it and chewing sunflower seeds sold by the gypsies mingling furtively among them. The atmosphere was infectious. Miriam knew this was to be a great spectacle. Some sixty thousand prisoners were to be paraded through the streets before being loaded onto the trains for the camps somewhere in the east. She didn't feel she wanted to see it but she gave up the struggle against the crowds and resigned herself to waiting until they'd passed by. It shouldn't take long.

Was that cheering? Yes. She could hear snatches and some patchy clapping rippling along the street towards her. Then a rider on a white stallion came into view. He was attempting to walk it along the middle of the street. It was General Sinilov. She recognised the commander of the Moscow Garrison. She'd seen him before at the Kremlin. It was obvious he hadn't ridden for some time. His attention was focused on reining in the high-spirited horse, its head pulling up and down with impatience against the foam-flecked bit drawn tightly into the corners of its mouth.

Then it seemed a carpet of silence unrolled behind him as the prisoners followed, shambling along in ranks twenty across. To Miriam it was a vision of dejection and despair that seemed to thrust through to her very being. She brought her hands to her mouth, stifling her anguished gasps. The mood of the crowd changed. The cheery chatter fell silent as the column filled the street in front of them. She saw feet swathed in sacking barely able to be lifted out of exhaustion and thirst. Tunics shabby with neglect, ragged, without battle harness, and often with trousers held up with grubby hands. Heads bare, faces grimy and

311

unshaven, hollow eyes downcast with humiliation and the anxiety and despair of knowing the freedom to exist was lost along with the knowledge of what the future had in store. Above all each man carried an overpowering stench.

Occasionally a prisoner would totter and stumble before clutching at his comrade, scrabbling to keep his feet, causing Miriam to flinch with compassion and sounds of sympathy to break the silence along the pavement, but no one moved to help.

Miriam stood for nearly two hours, locked in the crowd and unable to turn away. Finding it unbearable she closed her eyes with revulsion, almost retching so that her throat burned. She was part of this dreadfulness, not as a witness like these bystanders, but as a participant, and worst of all she was taking part in this horror by choice. Was this what bringing the final victory over Fascism was about? It had better be worth it. The idea of asking to be sent on frontline duties arose in her mind but that would be refused for sure and awkward questions would be asked. Apart from that Dmitri would expect to find her in Moscow. 'Wait for me and I'll return,' he'd said, quoting the recently published poem by Konstantin Simonv. 'Just wait for me. As long as you wait for me I will return.' It had been three years since she last saw him in that car, then joy of joys, a month later the brief few words arranging to meet scribbled on an active service chit slipped under her door while she'd been out.

What had he been doing in Soviet-occupied Poland before the Hitlerite armies invaded Russia? Actions, he called them, but he wouldn't say more than that. Did she want to know? No. Could she make a distinction between the violent and brutal police actions, often necessarily against the innocent, which were part of her day-to-day work and the fighting at the front? She hadn't done so. The enemy is not just at the front; she'd always thought that. They are around us, in the city, everywhere. When or if Dmitri came back did she accept what he was and how he was made by what he did, and in the same way did she accept what she was? The questions spun round and round in her mind. For her crucially it was the motive. She couldn't decide whether it was her injury, an issue of revenge and if so on whom in particular, or the end justifying the means? Before she accepted what she was she had to face the fear lurking within her that she may be doing it all because she enjoyed it, quite apart from the satisfaction gained. At that prospect a feeling of revulsion at herself welled up within her. She didn't want to be that kind of person. That kind of person was not fit to be a mother, not the mother of her Nikolai. But nevertheless she would stifle that feeling and since there was no way of knowing the answers to these questions what was important was the readiness to do what had to be done. That was all.

The water carts following to clean up the mess marked the end of the show and the throng began to break up.

PART FOUR

MOSCOW, 1945-1953 and WREXHAM 1957

Chapter Twenty-six

Miriam could see her death. She knew it had been following her as she walked over the mountain, and now the little creature was sunning itself on the bank of the stream, unaware she was watching. She took a sack and crept up on it. Sweeping her death into the sack she swiftly pulled the drawstring tight, shutting it in. She could feel it and hear it scrabbling and tearing with its sharp little hands, rustling and chattering with frustrated anger, but the sack was too strong. She would keep it tight shut and lock it away in Dad's tool chest so it could never come for her again.

Waking with a start in her bed at her old quarters at the Lubyanka barracks, her face was bathed in sweat as she came round from that persistent dream. It aroused thoughts of Dad. How was he, she wondered. It would be pointless trying to find out.

The Perlov Tea House, July 1945

At her request the waiter had been only too pleased to give Miriam a table facing the door. The medal ribbons on her tunic had ensured that. There was the Order of the Fatherland War for taking part in it generally, the Order of the Red Banner for her part in the Battle of Moscow, an Alexander Nevsky medal for partisan activity, mining roads, burning enemy-held villages, shooting those who helped the Hitlerites, and ambushing trains and motor columns. Then there was the Order of the Red Star for activity behind enemy lines on the First Byelorussian Front before Marshal Rokossovsky's thrust to the Prussian border last year. On formal occasions when she was required to wear the medals, it was a source of satisfaction and pleasure to feel the weight of the metal on her chest and to hear then jingling as she moved.

She let her eyes wander over the chipped and broken lacquer work of the almost-empty shelves and the unmatched chairs with not a tablecloth in sight. Instead the surfaces of the tables were covered in a fine layer of plaster-dust, contributing to an overall air of dilapidation. A far cry from the first time she'd set eyes on the Perlov. Calling the waiter over she asked him to open the once-elegant door now sheeted over with plywood, replacing the handsome bevelled glass that had been blown out in the November of 'forty-one hoping, with a thrill of anticipation she would be able to see Esther as she turned the corner of Myasnitskaya and walked toward the tea house. Her thoughts turned to the slip of paper in her pocket, just her name and Esther's with a phone number printed large in Latin characters. That was what had drawn her attention, standing out as it did from the Cyrillic notes on the board. She was prompted to read it again for the third time since she returned from East Prussia three days ago. She'd rung immediately but it had taken many frustrating attempts over the last three days until today she'd finally been given a line. Surprised at how Esther's voice was unchanged, still so familiar yet it seemed so long ago since she'd last heard it. Excitedly they'd arranged to meet within the hour. She should arrive at any moment.

The note had been fastened on one of the old newspaper boards in Lubyanka Square. Gently shouldering her way through Miriam had joined the searchers scanning the thousands of fluttering leaves pinned up in the forlorn hope that their loved ones had left information or that someone may have left answers to questions of their whereabouts. These unofficial message boards were all over the city, surrounded by women of all ages, emaciated figures rummaging with bony fingers among the curled photographs and tattered pieces of paper, chatting, smoking, desperately seeking news of a husband or a son, in limbo, unable to move on until they knew what was left to rebuild their lives.

She'd really been hoping to find something from Dmitri, intending to seek out Esther at her apartment later, but the fruitless search had left her dejected and she'd found Esther's block bombed out and no one at *Izvestia* would give any information. The impact of the immediate posting on the very day of the arrangement with no way of contacting him still seemed as fresh on her emotions as the day it happened. She'd been stopped as she left the building on her way to meet him, ordered into the truck with her squad then to the station for a three-day railway journey. What did he think when she didn't turn up? The question had tortured her ever since. Wait for me, he'd said, but that always assumes one is free to do so. In truth it would seem we are no freer to do such things than to choose when to be born.

'Hello!'

The greeting in English startled Miriam, snapping her out of her reverie.

Esther was standing at the table looking down at her.

For some moments Miriam sat back as she scanned her. Always slim, even thin, she looked even more so, especially her neck. Her eyes, though bright, were sunken; the skin on her face was grey and lifeless with the texture of parchment, and her jacket hung loosely about her shoulders.

'*Zdrastvooy*,' Miriam returned the greeting informally. 'So! It's been tough, yes?'

'You could say that.'

'Well, sit down. I tried to find you at your old apartment. Nobody at *Izvestia* would say where you were.

They refused to tell me.'

'If you didn't have official authorization to ask questions what did you expect? I was fixed up with a place. It's still near the office.'

'It was lucky I found your note.'

The waiter brought the tea and placed the glasses before them, leaving without ceremony.

Esther leaned forward. 'Before you ask, there's no sugar and no lemon.'

'Dmitri, you don't know anything about him?'

'Nothing at all. I'm sorry.'

There was a pause. Miriam felt deflated; the thrill of anticipation suddenly put to flight. The mood became leaden for her.

Then awkwardly Esther asked, 'How long has it been?'

Miriam told her about the last sight of Dmitri back in January 'forty-two. 'It's as long as the last time I saw both you and Moscow. I had no chance to get in touch. I've been behind enemy lines most of the time.'

'What do you think of the city now?'

Miriam shrugged dismissively, taking a sip of her tea and gazing absently out of the cracked and partially boarded plate-glass of the window. Then she turned back to Esther. 'It's been quite tough, you know, here and there, been shot at, shelled, bombed about a bit, but no more than most, wouldn't like to go through it again though.'

'Miriam,' Esther spoke out abruptly in English, 'Dad's dead.'

Miriam sat still. The stillness closed in on her. Somehow she'd never expected it. People were dying everywhere but not Dad. He would go on for ever but no – the last link with her past, gone. A deep sense of loss arose in her. 'When?'

The conversation continued in English. 'Over three years ago in 1942, April, a stroke. He's buried in the corporation cemetery in town.'

In town, when did she last hear that? In town, it sounded so strange now, so alien as if from another life, another time. 'How did you find out?'

'The Red Cross on one of their routine information exchanges through our Berlin office set up there last month. That's when I got to find out. It had been sitting with them all that time. Moscow won't have anything to do with the Red Cross, you see. It looks as if someone from the party branch back in Britain has been following our careers. I think they got in touch with the Salvation Army who passed it on.'

Guilt swept over her. When did she last think about him? She couldn't remember, but she recalled his face on the station back in 'thirty-six. He must have known he was seeing them for the last time. Quietly she sobbed for a few minutes as Esther held her hands, letting the tears tumble freely until they dried up.

'So you've been back three days, after how long? It must be over three years?'

Miriam nodded. 'And you, you've been here all through?' She spoke Russian again, as if to bring a curtain down on that part of the past.

'Yes.' Esther waited expectantly for Miriam to go on.

Instead Miriam let the conversation die. There was so much she'd wanted to ask Esther and so much she'd wanted to tell her but she felt the energy drain away. She'd expected they would be sharing the exhilaration of victory but she just couldn't find any enthusiasm. Suddenly she realised she was tired, so very tired.

They sat in silence, both falling under a mood of melancholy until Esther attempted to resurrect the dialogue. 'Well, now the final struggle against Fascism is over, will Franco be called to account do you think?'

Miriam looked at her blankly as if struggling to understand the significance of the words, before shrugging off the effort.

Esther decided to go on as if she'd answered. 'No. I don't think so either. He'll be too useful to the capitalist democracies.' After some moments of silence Esther gave up and simultaneously, as if by mutual consent, they made to leave after arranging to keep in contact.

The Byelorussia Railway Station, Moscow, July 1945

The Warsaw train was late, pulling in under the skeletal ribs of the half-repaired station roof after being held up by the threatened collapse of the bridge at the River Bug crossing. It was in danger of finally succumbing to the bomb damage received the previous autumn. An inspection had to be carried out and it was some time before the engine was allowed to draw the overlong train at a crawling pace over the twisted latticework. Then it bumped and rumbled noisily over the buckled members spanning the great trestles with the wounded bridge groaning and screeching in protest as it took the weight of a train crammed almost to bursting with starving verminous people, mothers with infants and homeless children prematurely aged by the horrors they had witnessed, all displaced by the recent hostilities. Many in their desperation were riding on the couplings and whole families were squatting on the roofs. Wrinkled old women in kerchiefs clung perilously to the sides, sometimes falling off from exhaustion. Amid clouds of steam and with driving wheels slipping, giving out streams of sparks in an attempt to gain traction on the undulating metals, the dilapidated engine had hauled its train across the kilometre-wide river, slowly reaching the relative safety of the opposite bank.

Dmitri shouldered his way through to the door and with relief stepped out of the rank air of the car, climbing down onto the platform. Slinging his bag on his shoulder and carrying his brief case in the other hand he pushed and thrust his way through the ragged throng aiming to get to the barrier, before the crush.

Sitting back in the seat of the commandeered cab he relaxed briefly, allowing himself the luxury of some reflection. After what had now become known as the Battle of Moscow he had been sent to organise partisan activity behind enemy lines south of Kiev. When Marshal Koniev's tanks had crossed the River Dneiper and broken through to Hungary in the middle of 'forty-four, last year, the whole partisan picture was altered and he had been recalled to Moscow. Then in early January as an NKVD colonel he was detached to Marshal Zhukhov's headquarters in Poland before the capture of Warsaw to sift out and eliminate aspiring Polish representatives deemed unsuitable for the coming elections to the provisional Polish government. In February with the systematically devastated city newly liberated he moved in to ensure that those who had actively shown a friendly attitude to the Soviet Union and were honestly prepared to cooperate with the Soviet State, dominated the emerging government administration. With the task completed he was now recalled to the Lubyanka for 'special duties' connected with the need to restore the pre-war thoroughness of communist society that had necessarily been relaxed during the Great Patriotic War. The Soviet Union and the Russian people must now be prepared for the great demands of reconstruction.

He laid his hand with some satisfaction on the briefcase chained to his wrist. The report it contained should make a good impression and some leave would be due to him. He allowed his mind to wander freely, something he did often since conditions had eased. The questions he'd suppressed for so long began to surface. What had happened to Miriam? Why didn't she turn up? Did she get his note? She may have been posted with no way of getting in touch with him, and if so was she still alive? Did she still think about him after all this time? So much had happened. Had it changed her? Was she still waiting for him to return like he said he would?

Chapter Twenty-seven

The Lubyanka, the end of August 1945

There was nothing dramatic about their reunion. Although accidental it occurred in normal circumstances and was surely inevitable, although neither thought so at the time. Shortly after they both arrived back in Moscow Miriam was crossing the main entrance hall of the People's Commissariat of Internal Affairs when she heard Dmitri's voice addressing her from behind.

'Major Moss!'

Her heart leapt as she stopped and turned. With a shyness alien to their previous relationship, as if it had been erased by the passage of time, she walked up to him.

'Dmitri Alekseevich!'

'Miriam!'

Her smile was hesitant at first but then it broadened.

Where are you going? Before she could reply he made to take her bulky document case. 'Let me carry this for you.'

Teasingly she drew it away from him, 'Have you nothing else to do with your time than to carry people's bags, Colonel?'

'I could use my time to take a short walk in the Alexandrovsky Gardens with a certain major. It's a beautiful day.'

She cocked her head on one side; 'I'll have to drop this off at the front desk. Come, you'll have to wait a moment while I sign for it.'

She stole a glance over her shoulder as she leaned over the desk. He looked different from when she last saw him, a little stooped; certainly thinner, but so was everyone else. He was still imposing in his well-cut uniform, his shoulders, the line of his back, and his smile. But was he angry with her for disappearing from his life? Would he accept her reasons? How much had his life changed? Was there no longer any room in it for her?

They walked to the gardens without a word passing between them.

She was slimmer, her cheeks a little sunken, and the loss of flesh enhanced her scars, but she was still how he remembered her, still the person he recalled so often for fear he would lose the ability to bring her to mind. Did she even want to meet him again or was this just a display of good manners, and anyway, what had they got to say to each other that hadn't been said all those years ago?

They chose a picnic table to sit at, rather than the intimacy of a double seat, and sought some pleasantries to exchange, but their attempts at small talk ended in awkward silence as if they'd started out on the wrong note.

Suddenly he blurted out the words almost accusingly, 'I came but you were out. I left a message, pushed it under your door.'

'I found it.'

'I see.'

'What do you mean, "I see?"'

'You wanted to end it.'

She shook her head. 'No.' Then she told him what had happened.

'I hoped it might be something like that, hoped for a long time that you were waiting for me to return. That if you were that's what would keep me alive. Then I stopped hoping, stopped feeling, didn't care whether I returned or not.' He took out a paper packet of cheap cigarettes and lit up, taking a deep draw without offering one to Miriam. 'You know I find it difficult to recall anything of the last three years, nor do I want to. In fact there's no memory, just emptiness.' He took another draw. 'I prefer it that way. Those times we had before then, before the invasion, it was another life, a life that has no place. There's no continuity, you see, separate existences that don't belong together, don't follow on. Sometimes I feel a dreadful sinking as if something has gone wrong. Everything seems grey. My arms feel so heavy as if I'm carrying the water for the cattle like I used to as a child.'

He used the Russian *vedro* for bucket, a word unfamiliar to her, but even so she pictured a little boy struggling with wooden pails slopping water over his muddy feet.

'And I'm almost overcome by a tiredness, as if I've aged a thousand years, then it passes and things are bright again, leaving me in dread of the next time. At first I used to think, like most people I'm sure, that afterwards we could pick up the threads, so to speak, but it can't be done. I've been changed. I see a different world. There are no threads to pick up.'

Miriam watched his hands strangely clasped together, shielding the tip of the cigarette as if by habit. 'I think it's like that with me. It isn't so much the four years, almost, when you say it like that it's not that long, it's what happened in that time that makes those years seem like decades.'

They lapsed into silence, each lost in their own thoughts Miriam stifling hers as images of events and actions she desperately sought to consign to oblivion were called to mind. Somehow she hadn't pictured a reunion like this. She'd expected they'd fall into each other's arms like she'd seen couples doing at the railway stations. Mentally shaking herself she decided she'd break the train of thought.

'You look different somehow. You've lost weight. Are you well?'

'I've been on a diet for my health.' He chuckled as he

realised how comical his words sounded, and a grin wavered around Miriam's mouth that turned into a giggle. Suddenly they both burst into peals of laughter that went on and on as if the tensions of the recent years were being released like a flock of doves. Gradually the laughter subsided until they self-consciously composed themselves, but now the atmosphere was eased so that they both felt more comfortable with each other prompting him to come out with the question that hung between them.

'And how has it been for you? Oh not the war. We know what we've both been through but what about –'

'I missed you, yes. I got used to missing you. It became part of me, as if it was a living thing following me. I used to imagine I could creep up on it, stuff it in a bag, and throw it away.'

He looked at her thoughtfully for a moment then he stubbed out his cigarette. 'I have to go soon.'

'Yes. So will I.'

'Shall we see each other again?'

'Will you be going away again?'

'I don't expect to. I'm based in Moscow.'

'So am I. We could meet just once and see what happens, perhaps a new beginning, but I don't want to get hurt, not again.'

'There is an inn near Pereslavl.'

She laughed. 'An inn! That sounds unbelievably Tolstoyan.'

'I've been there. It's very picturesque: they have piano and violin concerts in the evening. In two weeks I have some days' leave coming to me. If you can manage it also we can take the train, be there by the afternoon, walk in the countryside, spend the night, and be back next day.'

Chapter Twenty-eight

Lake Pleshcheevo, Pereslavl, mid-September 1945

They walked, without speaking, along the wide path of loose brown soil flanked by the enormous expanse of the lake. Its surface glinted metallically in the harsh light. The air was heavy with the scent of mimosa and the humming of insects. Some distance away sunbeams striking through the heat haze made luminous the eggshell blue onion domes atop the stark white buildings of the church rising above the ramshackle wooden railway station on the edge of the little town. It was almost possible to forget things were not quite what they seemed. The church had been a warehouse for many decades and from the station they'd seen the other side of the domes was disfigured by the line of holes stitched by heavy cannon fire.

He'd not touched her hand, nor taken her arm since they met that morning to go for the train, though she'd not shrunk from him, brushing his tunic comfortably with her arm as they walked. After leaving their bags in their room they'd followed the dusty rutted street, looking the worse for wear with the boardwalks pulverized by the tracks of armoured vehicles the previous autumn and empty of any signs of life, until they passed an open window with a large dog lying with its muzzle resting on its paws, taking in the breeze wafting off the cooling waters of the lake. The dog had lifted its head in acknowledgement to Miriam's greeting as they passed. When the road ended at the lakeside they'd turned onto the path and paused to gaze idly at a cluster of boats moored at the bank. There they'd come upon a man standing at an easel painting in watercolours, hunched intensely over his work. They drew no response from him as they paused to look over his shoulder before passing by as if they existed in another dimension of time.

Abruptly the sun moved behind a bank of cloud and the domes became shadows silhouetted against the skyline. It was then they heard the sonorous buzzing from clouds of flies rising into the air above the town, the sound rising and falling in a morose chorus. A sudden chill prompted them to turn away from the lake. They took a path leading through alleys, passing drowsing dogs with twitching ears, the backs of clapboard houses with peeling paint, broken picket fences, reeking privies, crumbling handcarts lurking in weed-choked plots of pumpkins, cucumbers, and huge sunflowers, their bowed golden heads heavy with seeds. Somewhere nearby they heard a tune being whistled, the sudden slam of a door, someone sawing timber, the hint of a footfall, but no sign of those responsible. They were out of sight as if they had just turned the corner. Their absence seemed to emphasise the feeling of emptiness hanging in the air, creating a mood of poignancy in Miriam, prompting the return of melancholy.

As they emerged onto the narrow main street a large flock of geese bore down on them with their heads held uncompromisingly low on necks urgently stretched to full length, as if moving forward with a single purpose. Pressing themselves against the timber boarding of a house they let the geese pass. For a moment Miriam felt a wave of panic. The low cackling from the collective throat of the flock seemed a sinister concerted sound threatening to engulf her in an elemental force. She felt she was in danger of being swept along by something uncontrollably powerful. Seeing her feelings reflected in her face Dmitri took her hand and held it firmly, so that she took comfort from it and returned the pressure. The flock was in the charge of a peasant woman shuffling behind, as oblivious to the presence of the couple as the geese themselves. Clad in black from the kerchief on her head to her boots despite the heat she was wielding with both hands a slender, springy wand of birch so long she was able to flick the heads of the leading birds with it and so keep the flock in order.

Presently they followed hand in hand. Taking the turning that led to their lodgings they climbed up the steps onto the veranda and stepped through the open double doors, plunging into the bustling noise of the inn's big crowded common room. Their eyes gradually adjusted to the dim light coming from naked bulbs glimmering weakly in the dense tobacco smoke. The innkeeper came over to meet them, a bent old man with a soldier's soft cap, gnarled hands, and a distinct limp that probably indicated a badly set broken thigh. At the sight of their MGB uniforms the babble gradually settled to a low muttering.

'Send tea up to our room,' ordered Dmitri, 'and see that a meal is prepared for later.'

Submissively the innkeeper bowed. 'The servant will bring it to your room immediately, excellency.'

They mounted the open staircase, their footsteps echoing on the bare pinewood treads in the tense air, both conscious of meaningful glances being exchanged behind their backs. A strip of Turkish carpet served as a runner along the landing that was open to the common room on one side. Miriam cast a glance over the balustrade, sweeping her glance over the room below, knowing she would meet the stares of many pairs of eyes. The wall of the landing was decorated in heavy yellow and green diamond-patterned paper with a series of faded black and white etchings depicting views of Tolstoy's estate at Yasnaya Polyana, ornately framed with suitable deference. There were pots of dusty aspidistra plants on tall stands and thick red velvet curtains hung before the narrow white-painted double doors of their room, held aside with swags of richly brocaded fabric. Curiously there were no handles or latches to the doors that closed of their own volition as if sprung or weighted. As the other rooms didn't seem to be occupied they weren't too concerned by this. The large bedroom was floored in yellow pine with a Chinese rug in front of the massive wooden bed opposite the entrance. In one corner was a stove shaped like a giant pepper pot standing on its bronze feet and soaring from floor to ceiling, resplendent in bright green tiles. The window was triple-glazed, with tiny opening panels and distorted green glass panes that rippled with movement as if rainwater was running down them. A photograph of Stalin in his plain white marshal's uniform without any medals except the gold star, the Order of Hero of the Soviet Union, hung on the wall above the bed. There was little else in the way of furniture except a green-painted pine table in the far corner with two towels made from large potato sacks neatly piled on it. On one of the double doors a mirror was fixed with most of its silvering lost. On the other was a framed notice boasting of hot water in the bathhouse every morning but only two people at a time, it commanded, were allowed inside.

Both prised off their dusty boots. Dmitri undid his belt and cradling the holster hung it over the only chair. Unclipping his tunic jacket he tossed it across the room onto the far table. Miriam, watching him, did the same shrugging off her jacket and self-consciously placing it on top of his. Then he drew from his bag a box of Balkan Sobranei cigarettes and a lighter, a trophy of war, embellished with the runic lettering of the SS and the swastika enamelled in black, red, and white. He placed them on a small arabesque side-table before recklessly throwing himself on the high bed. Rolling over he lit two of the black gold-tipped cigarettes, holding out one for Miriam. Going round to the opposite side she climbed up clumsily and they lay side by side in silence, each comfortable in the knowledge that nothing was expected of the other, at least for the time being, except to watch the scented smoke rise and await the tea.

Eventually the clattering of tea things and the thumping of boots on the stairs heralded its arrival. The doors flew open with a kick from the servant: a youth with coarse Kirghiz features and an empty sleeve to his blouse precariously balancing on the palm of his remaining hand a wooden tray with a large teapot, glasses, and a dish of jam with an aluminium spoon standing in it. He came over and placed the tray on the side table and then stood at the foot of the bed waiting respectfully with his one hand in front as if in his mind he was holding it with his phantom other.

Dmitri, tongue in cheek, inclined his head and dismissed him with a graceful wave of his hand, '*Spaseeba.*'

Bowing from the waist and mumbling, '*Gospodin,*' the young serving-man turned and left.

Scarcely had the doors swung to behind him and his boots sounded on the stairs than they both shared a laugh at his quaint behaviour that seemed so much in keeping with the old-style setting of the inn and the town.

After the tea they lay back on the bed side by side smoking another cigarette and listening to the high-pitched chirruping of the cicadas in the cooling air of early evening until Miriam realised she was beginning to doze.

With a start she woke. Dmitri was lying on his side watching her. The window was black and a single bulb hanging from the ceiling cast a pale light over the bed. The sound of raucous laughter and discordant singing drifted up from below.

She sat up suddenly. 'How long have I been asleep?'

'Some two hours. I let you slumber on, you must have needed it, besides I dozed myself.'

A tune was taken up on an accordion accompanied by

333

clapping and stamping feet.

'You said there would be piano and violin concerts.' She gave him a reproving glance.

'I may have pitched things a little higher than I should, painted the egg a little too brightly. So!'

She laughed at the odd saying. 'An egg is still an egg no matter how you paint it, and speaking of eggs –'

'I know! You're hungry, so am I. It's time we went down to find something to eat.'

First there was the need to use the primitive facilities of the bathhouse to freshen up. Although their long experience of soldiering left them with no qualms over communal ablutions there was a tension in both of them when they entered the large stark chamber carrying their towels. The tiled walls were bare except for a shelf holding two baskets for clothes, two newly cut blocks of soap, two wooden handled water pans, and a metal mirror for shaving. The entire floor was brick-paved. A large stone tank stood at one corner with a drain and two taps. At the opposite corner there was a screened squat hole with two sizeable vessels filled with water at the side of it.

She hesitated. To take off her clothes in front of him, to stand naked washing herself, was she ready to return to this closeness?

Dmitri sensed her feelings. 'I'll wait in the room for you to go first if you wish.'

There was relief at the decision partly made for her.

'Right now, I would like that.'

When they had both finished in the bathhouse they pulled on their boots and put on their tunic jackets, donning full uniform.

'So!' Dmitri sounded cheerful. 'Let's go and see what our friend the innkeeper has cooked for us.'

On the landing they looked over the balustrade at the gathering in the common room below, veiled in cheap

334

makhorka tobacco smoke where a tall man in a tawny-coloured soldier's tunic was dancing to the accordion music, the source of the stamping. The innkeeper came over to meet them at the foot of the stairs. Without a word he led them through the parting crowd to a passage and as he did so the music died away and the dancing stopped. A short way down the passage he pushed open the door to a cosy room with a bulbous tiled stove in one corner. On a wall where once an icon had hung was a plaster plaque of Lenin. A shelf below it held a candle whose flickering flame was reflected in a small cut-glass vase of dusty artificial cornflowers. A round table was spread with a white cloth and set for two with a small hand bell, an opened bottle of rough vodka, a jug of locally produced wine, and two glass beakers. There was also a small photo-frame holding a picture of Stalin as a centrepiece.

As the innkeeper bowed himself out of the room they could hear him shouting something down the passage. Soon afterwards the door was bumped open by a rickety trolley pushed by the young servant. From it he set out two miniscule vodka glasses, a small loaf of bread, and a large dish of zakuski made up of salted herring fillets, sweet onions, boiled potatoes, beetroot slices, hard-boiled goose eggs, a large pot of sour cream, smoked freshwater trout from the lake, blini with some kind of tiny dried fish, pickled mushrooms, pickled cucumbers, and rye bread. Setting them out he sprinkled salt on the loaf, poured the vodka into the glasses, and left. The strains of the accordion drifting down the passage told them the dancing had resumed.

Without a word they started to sample the *hors d' oeuvres*, hesitantly at first, awkwardly watching each other, taking care their forks didn't clash. Suddenly Miriam remembered she was hungry, very hungry, not having eaten since that morning. Dmitri put down his fork to use his fingers. She took this as licence to do the same.

Before any conversation started she'd just finish the zakuski. She gave herself up to it, picking at the morsels, stuffing her mouth with blini and pieces of smoked fish, crunching the cucumber pieces, savouring the pickled mushrooms, dipping into the sour cream, munching the onions and beetroot slices, sipping the vodka that was complimented perfectly by the strong salty and vinegary flavours, their hands touching as they fumbled, delved, and felt around for the food, prompting their eyes to meet fleetingly. Slyly he stole a glance at her fingers being drawn one by one through her lips shiny with sour cream. She caught him and smiled provocatively. He ran his tongue around his in answer. Soon the dish was cleared and Dmitri rang the bell. They drained their vodka, wiping their mouths with their hands; there were no napkins, as the table was cleared and the first main dish was brought in. Then the young serving-man poured the wine and left.

Now Miriam's taste buds were aroused and she felt even hungrier as she surveyed the dish. It was rassolnik: fish soup with pickled cucumbers and fish dumplings. They set to with their spoons. The soup was hot; almost scalding, so that with faces shiny with perspiration they slurped and splashed, trawling for the dumplings, all the time not speaking or even attempting conversation except with the swift flashes they gave each other with their eyes. As they wiped their plates clean with the rye bread Dmitri rang the bell.

This time it was cold borsch. They disposed of it, swiftly cooling their mouths with the sweet beetroot flavour and the sour cream. The serving-man arrived before the bell with osetrina: smoked carp from the lake, instead of the customary sturgeon, with pickled cucumbers. The crumbling flesh flaked under their fingers as now, losing all inhibitions, they gave in to their appetite and devoured the dish using neither knife nor fork while quaffing the wine to wash it down.

By now the young man was in step with their tempo and arrived with his trolley as they finished with a platter of pirozhki: savoury parcels stuffed with cabbage that they popped into their mouths one after the other without stopping and clearing the dish as he stood there ready with a plate of golubtsy: a dubious kind of minced meat and kasha seasoned with herbs, rolled in cabbage leaves, and baked. Now slowing to savour the moment and to prolong the pleasure of the meal they sat back, staring into each other's eyes as if drawing breath for another sally. Miriam was first to renew the assault, tearing at the cabbage leaves with her fingers and forking the contents between lips that seemed to Dmitri to have become full, voluptuous in a glossy way, and deeper in colour.

With their hunger still not assuaged they sat back, wiping their hands on the tablecloth as the serving-man attended on them.

'Is it now the main dish?'

'It is,' the serving-man answered Dmitri.

'What is it?' Miriam asked him.

'Kulebyaka.'

'Ah! You're going to like this.' Dmitri turned to the serving man, 'The long pie, is that so?' He received a nod then he explained to Miriam, 'A yeast pastry filled with salmon and rice.'

The serving-man shook his head. 'Kasha.'

'Kasha instead of rice. I might have known. What is the fish?'

'Fish there is but I don't know.'

'And hard-boiled eggs?'

'Goose.'

'And mushrooms,' Dmitri said to Miriam. 'Is that so?' He snapped at the serving-man who hastily nodded.

They sipped at the vinegary wine in anticipation.

The pie was brought in, served on a long narrow dish and cut into fine slices. They set to each, taking a slice at a time, beginning to match each other's reaching and eating, reaching and eating so that a rhythm built up to a heightening tension that aroused an echo within both, leaving it unresolved when the dish was cleared.

They sat back, still un-sated yet both knowing, as they waved away the dessert, this wasn't the time for a cigarette, Armenian brandy, or coffee.

Rising from the table and taking her hand, he drew her through the door, leaving the wine jug half full.

Afterwards she couldn't recall mounting the stairs. They'd posted up to their room and, surprised by the tremors of lust shuddering and contracting, they fell on the bed, seizing each other's jackets and stripping them off where they lay in a thrill of scrabbling, pulling, and tearing at ribbons and tapes, casting aside trousers and underwear. Their activity was prolonged, intense, fervent, even ferocious, plunging, thrusting like warriors locked in mortal combat. Each taking it in turns to initiate different positions, different ways of slaking their aroused passions. Their bodies shiny, glistening, slick with juices, each seeking to achieve profound depths, to lose oneself in the very spasms, flowing like waves of rippling flesh. And still it went on, making up for lost time, perhaps, loosing pent-up tensions of stress and anger. They strove through the night in the attempt to achieve release each time, exploding then, fanned by lust, the embers of the fire flared up into a further conflagration, until finally exhausted they both fell into the deepest slumber they could ever remember.

The next morning they had no trouble sharing the bathhouse, tenderly rubbing each other down with the coarse soap as they stood in the steamy room, pouring the hot sulphurous stream over each other by turns, and then the shock as each dipped a pan into the tank of icy water from the bottom of the glacial lake, pouring it onto their heads so that their breath came in short gasps and their skin grew taut over their flesh as rivulets ran down their cerise bodies, finding every crevice, leaving them tingling and the arousal of their senses obvious to each other. Hastily clutching their clothes they ran down the corridor to their room, savagely clutching and groping as they hurled themselves on the bed in a bout of urgent consummation.

After a simple breakfast of kasha, jam, and cheese they set off for the railway station and the Moscow train. With a compartment to themselves they both sat quietly facing each other, relaxed and at ease on the bare wooden seats gazing out at the vast fields of corn. To their experienced eyes the ominous deep golden russet stretching to the rolling cloudbanks on the horizon meant the fields were unharvested and therefore abandoned. If they had been harvested on time they would have been a much lighter colour. Dmitri imagined the over-ripe grain was already spilling to the ground, providing a feast for the mice. Inwardly he gave a sigh: such was war.

It looked as if things could get back as they were, she let her mind drift over the last few hours, although he did seem distant in some way, still almost detached, as if he didn't feel he was part of things. She understood his feelings to some extent from her own experience, but where would it lead from here? Would they be able to see each other regularly? What would happen when they got off the train? Would they go their own way?

He caught her looking at him intensely.

She started; unaware she had been doing so.

He smiled as if he could read her mind. 'So! The trip went well, yes?'

She returned his smile and nodded.

'And where do we go from here? That's what you're thinking, yes?'

She nodded again.

The train slowed almost to a walking pace before

juddering to a stop. Dmitri looked at her and shrugged before turning to the window again. Then the engine gave a startling shriek on its whistle and the cars jerked forward, rolling slowly on the suspect metals. He turned back to her. 'It looks as if we're being shunted onto a side line. There must be something wrong up ahead. Could be bridge trouble. We'll be late in.'

He took out his cigarettes and held them up, gesturing for her to come to him.

She rose and made her way across, steadying herself against the sudden rocking and jerking of the car as the train clattered over the switched points. A final jerk sent her against him shoulder to shoulder and he put his arm around her as he offered a cigarette with his free hand. She felt a warmth from his body and she snuggled up to him, nuzzling his hair with her face.

As he was about to take out his lighter she felt his body stiffen and his hand tighten on her shoulder. It was as if a cold blast of air had entered the compartment. Startled she turned to him and followed his eyes staring out through the grimy window of the car. What she saw brought a sharp intake of breath.

It was a deserted village, a large one by the look of it. Many of the houses had stood along the railway track. Only one or two were still standing. Burnt and blackened they were empty. Nothing was left of the others, or of the village itself but piles of charred rubble with brick chimneystacks, row upon row like a forest of pine trees stretching into the distance.

They didn't speak as the train rolled slowly on; both were lost in their thoughts and feelings as only the beat of the locomotive exhaust broke the silence between them. Given the region this must be the work of the Hitlerites, but it could just as well be hers or Dmitri's in enemy-occupied territory. The thought shocked her. Somehow when seen like this, dead, stark, silent, barren of life and movement, rather than in flames with people running about shouting, screaming, and the shooting in the heat of the action; the consequences were sharply outlined. Is this what she'd become, an agent of death and destruction? Seen like this there could be little difference between having your village burnt by the Fascist beasts or the NKVD – or even the Czar's Cossacks; little difference between a pogrom and a purging of succour to the enemy. What had she been doing? Perpetrating what happened to her grandparents' village?

The car went through a series of convulsive jerks that indicated the train was returning to the main line. Soon it was drawing into the Moscow suburbs and they reached their bags down from the luggage rack. As they pulled into the Yaroslavskiy station Dmitri turned to her. 'Then we shall meet again soon, yes?'

Briefly she was swamped with panic. This was it. Did they go on from here to become once more open to chance; exposed to whatever heartbreak the future may hold?

He felt his heart missing a beat, seemingly stilled as he waited on her reply, and, realising how important it was to him for this relationship to begin again, he pressed her. 'Yes?'

'Yes,' she blurted out, feeling the tension discharge. 'But we can't pick up where we left off. That won't work. We have to start anew.'

He smiled as he opened the door, throwing out his bag. 'Yes we shall.' He jumped down the steps and held out his arms for her.

Chapter Twenty-nine

Wrexham, 1957

'Well, their relationship did start up again. It went on for some years. They rented an apartment, if you could call it that, a shabby fifth-floor room with a communal bathroom in Golyanovo, a rather bleak suburb. Whenever they could get the time off together they would spend it out there. She took me to see it once but I never went back. We always met in the city, quite often actually.'

Esther finds it hard to keep going, her eyelids are heavy and they are beginning to droop. The gin is becoming unpalatable; she knows she's had enough but she needs him here until it's over. He mustn't go until then. She has to run it through to the end.

'Why didn't they marry, set up home in a proper apartment provided by the authorities?'

Nicholas's voice grates on her thoughts. 'I don't know why they didn't marry.' It was a question she'd always stumbled on and didn't like to be reminded of now. 'Somehow I don't think it occurred to them. It seems strange, I know, but they preferred to keep their relationship discreet. The authorities were rather puritanical about what they called loose relationships and the prevailing spirit at that time was to put things off until the future when the Soviet Union would be rebuilt. Reconstruction was the thread that ran through everything. Heavy industry was to have priority. The war was won but there were still dangers from outside and in. The state of siege was to be maintained.' She rises and stands over him. 'Look, I must get some sleep now.'

Nicholas starts. 'Is that all she did after, just had an – an affair? Surely there's more to it than that. How did she die?'

Esther lights a final cigarette, exhaling the smoke at the ceiling, 'You're not going to catch that train in the morning, are you?'

'Why not?'

'Because in the morning you'll still want to know whether she carried on thinking about you. It bothers you that she may have lived on happily without giving you a thought. You realise that, don't you? You might as well accept it. You can telephone, send a telegram or a note, say you've got a chill or whatever you people do in these circumstances. This has to take as long as it needs to take. Do I need to remind you there's more to it than just telling a story?'

Nicholas gives a resigned nod. Somehow he'd known for some time that catching the early train wasn't going to happen. College seems to have declined in importance, at least for the time being, removed as it is from the reality he is facing.

'I'm going to bed and you can shake down on that sofa. There's a dressing gown hanging over there behind the door. You can use it as a blanket to keep off the chill. The bathroom is down the hall. Sweet dreams.' She closes the bedroom door behind her.

He is woken by the pungent smell of toast threatening to burn. Opening his eyes cautiously and peering from under the dressing gown he sees Esther has placed slices of bread on a small electric fire that she's laid on its back in the fireplace. A porridge-coated saucepan is steaming on the gas ring, and going by the smell it too is about to achieve the same state as the toast.

With some dexterity she switches off the fire and snatches the saucepan from the ring, placing it on a small

344

oilcloth-covered table. 'You slept heavily, snoring like a train when I came in.'

In fact he'd taken a long time to get to sleep. His mind had been restlessly struggling to make some order out of the thoughts spiralling around in his head and each time he tried to close his hot and feverish eyes disturbing images rushed at him out of the darkened corners of the room. He must have finally dropped off just as the dawn light seeped through the now-opened curtains. It feels as if it was only an hour ago: it probably is.

She places a saucer with a knob of margarine to soften near the warmth of the gas ring. 'Keep an eye on that while I do the porridge. Don't let it melt.'

When he comes back from the bathroom he joins her at the table to share a plate of toast and marmalade from a margarine- and crumb-encrusted jar, followed by a bowl of porridge made with water, for which there was no sugar and no milk. It was too early, even for the milkman. He declines the proffered spoonful of jam so she puts it in her tea.

Afterwards he is left on his own while she washes the breakfast things at a sink in the corner of the room shielded by a curtain. Then lighting a cigarette she goes to the bay window and looks out, briefly smoking before turning to him to resume the conversation as if the night had not intervened.

'Did she go on thinking about you in those years with Dmitri? Of course she did. To her you were locked in time, still the baby she lost, although in 1945 you were seven and when she died in 'fifty-three you must have been, let me see – you were fourteen. She watched for you in other children as the years went by, constantly and desperately trying to imagine how you would look. She gazed at their hair, the way they walked and held their hands, how they laughed, how they smiled. She peered into their eyes, imagining how you would see the world she lived in.'

She draws deeply on her cigarette. 'I remember one particular occasion, she'd arranged for me to stand with her at the victory parade on Red Square in 'forty-five. In the middle of the pomp and ceremony when the banners of the German Fascists, the Nazis to you, were being hurled at the feet of Stalin and Marshal Zhukhov she suddenly turned to me and said, 'What would Nikolai have thought of this, and of what has happened to us over the last few years?'

For a tense few seconds Nicholas's eyes are fixed intently upon her face. 'What did you say?'

Esther hesitates and swallows through threatening tears, 'I said – I said, "He would think it a great adventure, Miriam."'

'Ha!' He spits out the exclamation in disgust.

She turns away sharply and goes over to the table. For a moment she fidgets with the tea things, then she turns on him, shouting plaintively, 'She gave her life for you.'

Taken aback he pales slightly.

'Can't you see that? Can't you find it in yourself just to accept that? What more does it take? What more do I have to say?'

Steadying herself she goes on quietly, 'Ultimately she put her life in jeopardy trying to contact agencies outside the Soviet Union and even attempting to leave to come and find you. I tried to persuade her against it but it was no use.' With a helpless shrug of her shoulders Esther stubs out the cigarette in a saucer.

In the silence that follows Nicholas becomes aware of the reek of tobacco that is starting to overcome the flat, charred smell of burnt toast. 'Shall we go out? I think I need some fresh air.'

'Come on. There's a patch of open ground with seats at the end of the street.'

It is a children's playground, deserted, with rusty swings and a broken roundabout. They sit facing each other at one of the rickety picnic tables. Esther pauses to gather her thoughts, giving a momentary shudder as if to shake off the chill of the damp early-morning air carrying a sulphurous smell of smoke from recently lit coal fires. 'I think they were reasonably happy in those years after the war, at least until 1950. I'll say as little as necessary about their work as it just seems to upset you, 'though I'll have to bring some aspects of it in.'

'Go on.'

'Well, from just before 1950 things started to get unpleasant for anyone who was in any kind of senior position as a Jew or even a half-Jew.'

'How could that be? I know that anti-Semitism was part of Russia before the revolution; "pogrom" is after all a Russian word, but this was the land where everyone was supposed to be equal.'

'Do you think I haven't asked that question of myself a thousand times? Over these last few months I've had time to think. It's surprising how you can go through life without doing that. Like being in a train charging through stations too fast to read their names. Well this is the way I've come to see it: after the break with the United States with its highly vocal and influential Jewish lobby the Soviet Union was becoming isolated from the rest of the world, like it is today. The Americans supported Zionism and the emergence of the State of Israel claimed the allegiance of Jews everywhere, including the Soviet Union, or that's how the Soviet government, in other words Stalin, perceived it. Just like in the thirties the call for vigilance against enemies of the people and traitors within was revived. Your mother was involved in much of the consequent operations, as was Dmitri, arresting whole families for deportation, sometimes trial and imprisonment. Jews in the highest echelons of Soviet society were being identified, when it was deemed convenient, as aliens, "Europeanised cosmopolitans", or

"Zionist agents of America". Believe me, I know. I didn't actually coin those phrases but I had to write them into much of my copy. I think Stalin had always shared this prejudice that has been so much a part of Russian history, but it was not until the late forties that he became as anti-Semitic as Hitler so that, as his physical powers diminished with age even though his power as a tyrant was as strong as ever, I think it began to set him apart from his closest cronies, and indeed from the party, especially when a group of doctors was arrested and charged with plotting to kill him by giving him a fatal dose of something or other. They all happened to be Jews, or most of them anyway. Ultimately and, when I look back; inevitably the arrests trickled down to your mother's level and everyone connected with her.'

Chapter Thirty

The Office of the Political Police at the Lubyanka, mid-January 1953

The MGB officer behind the desk paused as he took a paper from Miriam's ominously thick manila file. He adjusted his wire-framed spectacles and looked directly at her. 'I am Colonel Josip Ordzhonikidze.' Opening the file he looked at the top page. 'You are Major Miriam Moss, MGB, formerly NKVD, OMSBON. Born in 1901, Wales, England. Father's name Rabinovitz, called Rabin. You have lived in the Soviet Union since 1939 when you became a Soviet citizen.'

Miriam felt the blood drain from her face. As the officer moved his head his spectacles became mirrors, turned on her narrowing eyes and his oily shaven scalp gleamed in the sunlight streaming through the top of the bare, un-screened window behind him. For an instant the glare diffused by the grimy panes gave him a saint's halo, like those on the icons in the Tretyakov Gallery. He held the paper towards her.

Her mouth dried with apprehension as she saw it was her last letter applying for an exit visa. He picked three more letters from the file, holding them up for her to see, then dropped them back before pulling out her application for a Soviet passport. After holding it up also he placed it on top, then closing the manila folder he pushed it across the desk to her.

Sitting at the end of the long desk was a uniformed woman, an officer in the political police, whose almond-shaped eyes and high cheekbones revealed her Tajik

349

origin. The interrogating officer glanced momentarily at her but made no introduction before addressing Miriam in his thick Georgian accent that grated on her senses, 'Thank you for coming at our request, Comrade Major, but why you seem surprised that we have asked you to do so I can't think.'

Brusquely he waved aside Miriam's weak response. 'Now please open the file and look over the papers.'

Anxiety sharpened, Miriam's perception so that her eyes were drawn to the silver ring set with a yellow stone on the nicotine-stained fingers toying with a pencil. She opened the folder and lifted the papers out one by one. There, after her visa forms and the three letters addressed to the Red Cross and the child refugee organisations, was her application for Soviet citizenship back in 1938. Obviously taken from the bottom of the pile and placed with the most recent papers. Opposite the section asking for her family name and the section asking for 'father's original family name if different' was typed the word *Yevr'ey*, Jewish. Across it was scrawled in thick black crayon pencil the word Jewess. The shock of the derogatory Russian word used, *Zydovka*, left her skin tightening as if hit by a blast of arctic air. Somehow it seemed laden with so many notions, condescension, disdain, scorn, dislike, and hatred. Staring at it she ran her finger over the writing. The crayon wax smeared slightly, suggesting it was recently done.

'You see, Comrade Major, the question is –' the officer's words encroached on her consciousness, gradually gaining some meaning.

Slowly she raised her eyes to him.

He placed the pencil down with both hands and spoke to the desktop, 'the question is why did you make an application for an exit visa after you sent three communications to a Western agency between the August and the November of 1945, despite being refused each time. The first time we were prepared to overlook,' he shrugged placing his hands on the desk as if on a keyboard, 'stress, perhaps. In the Patriotic War you were under some strain,' he nodded in acknowledgement toward her medal ribbons, 'we all were. It takes time to work out, but to try again and again,' each time he stressed the word by lifting his hands up and down and looking at them as if playing a chord, 'that is determination.' He paused as long as it took to draw a single breath and lifted his eyes, 'Or something else, perhaps?'

The pale sun compelled her to move her head to screen her eyes. It was irritating, especially as she knew her chair had been placed for this purpose. She'd done it herself many times. Gradually the realisation dawned on her. It had been a trap. They'd let her send a number of letters, incriminating herself more deeply each time, letters that had never been allowed to leave the Soviet Union, and after waiting all these years, eight years, until it was convenient, they pounced. 'I explained in the letters. I have a son. He was six then, a little boy, taken from me in Spain soon after he was born. I wanted him to be returned to me. He was fostered. There was an organisation connected with the Red Cross that might have helped me to bring him back here to the Soviet Union, or at least let me know what happened to him.'

'Yes, that may be so. As you can see all your communications with Western agencies are in your file. The last one was in the November of 'forty-five. Is that correct?'

'Yes, I suppose so.'

'Yes you suppose so. Why did you stop your attempts at communicating?'

'They never replied. They're in there,' she pointed to the file. 'So now I know why.' Her voice broke slightly. 'They never even got them.' It was hopeless. The despair swept over her. It was quite a long time since she'd looked for him in other children. She couldn't remember when she'd last done that. With a shock she realised she'd given up. He was lost. The upsurge of grief almost overwhelmed her.

'Why did you wish to leave the Soviet Union?'

'It was to find him. I've told you, and then to bring him back. That's what I explained in my application letter.'

'Really! And if you had found your son you would have brought him back, so you say. Or would you? Would you instead have stayed in England? Perhaps hoping one day to get to the new state of Israel when it was founded?'

Puzzled she shook her head. 'To Israel?'

He leaned toward her. She sensed the cloying sweet scent on his tunic. 'Tell me, what do you think of Israel now it has become a lackey of the United States?'

She gazed at him, suddenly seeing her situation in a new light. So this is what it was about: not forms and letters from the past. They were just occasions, pretexts to conduct a purge against anyone who may now or in the future be likely to favour the state of Israel. Now her loyalty to the Soviet Union, to Russia, proven at great cost, was suspect.

The woman officer opened a drawer and took out a cardboard packet of English tea biscuits. Noisily she tore it open and began filling a jar on the desk, seemingly oblivious to them both watching her.

'You have your own national homeland at last. You are no longer without roots,' he said, still watching the woman.

'It has never crossed my mind.'

'Maybe not, but can you honestly say you haven't been tempted? After all, you people consider yourselves citizens of the world, not just of the Soviet Union, is that not so?'

Miriam's eyes flashed as she turned them on him. 'No more that you would, Comrade Colonel.'

The assistant officer froze, looking up for a moment her

hand holding a biscuit.

'It is you who wish to leave, Comrade Major.' There was an icy edge to his voice as he looked at her over the top of his spectacles for some moments.

The officer continued with her task, careful not to let the biscuits break as she lowered them into the jar.

To calm her heart thumping against her ribs Miriam fixed her attention on a cat sitting on the high wall outside, intently staring in.

When he spoke his voice was softer as he sought to draw her back. 'Maybe you wanted to become an agent of the United States.'

Miriam answered flatly, 'No. Of course not.'

'Yes. Maybe you didn't realise it but once out of the Soviet Union you may have decided to be so.'

Miriam refused to reply. She twisted her head to look out of the side window again, as much to cool her anger as to avoid the sun in her eyes. The cat was now grooming itself.

'This was just a preliminary investigation you have helped us with today. You will present yourself again when we send for you in due course. The next time we will want to talk to you about anyone with whom you may have discussed this matter, your sister, for example, or Colonel Dmitri Alekseevich Ignatov.'

Abruptly Miriam turned back at the significance of what she had just heard. 'I haven't talked to anyone about this.'

He held his open palms toward her, 'You may have done so without realising it, or someone may have planted the idea in your head for a sinister purpose. You know there has been a plot against the lives of certain persons at the highest level. It is possible you were unknowingly being used by enemies of the Soviet Union.' Clasping his hands he leaned forward. 'Now, Comrade Major, I'm sure you will want to work with us to get to the bottom of this matter.'

'Is that all? When do I have to come back?'

He gathered the papers and took the file handing it to the woman. 'It may be sooner or later.'

'Can't you tell me any more than that?

'Perhaps arranged so as not to interfere with your duties? At night, at short notice, or at any such time as is thought necessary.'

'Why can't the matter be sorted out now?'

'Good day, Comrade Major.' He rose and gestured toward the door. The woman walked over to it and held it open.

As Miriam left the room, striding along the familiar corridors with their grey carpet runners, one question dominated her thoughts: how long would they play this cat and mouse game before they came for her? She crossed the marble expanse of the main hall of the Office of Political Police, reverberating with the clatter of typewriters, and went through the great bronze doors out into the keen fresh air on Novaya Ploshchad.

As she rode the tramcar back to her apartment she could make out, through the frost-rimed window, the British Embassy in the distance across the prospekt. Perhaps that was the answer, get in and apply for asylum, but no, the MGB had plain-clothes security all around the embassies. By now her photograph would be widely circulated. She knew how the system worked, for she was part of it. What about Dmitri and Esther? They would both be taken in. For some moments cold fear took hold at the thought. She must contact them. Warn them. But her phone calls were almost certainly intercepted. She would have to keep clear to avoid contaminating them, but how? He would come for her and Esther would phone or send a card. She was probably being watched and followed even now. Involuntarily she glanced around, gripping the bare wooden slats of her seat tightly to control her trembling hands, becoming conscious of the curious gaze of a woman opposite.

When she got down from the car she found herself looking back at the passengers following her. This was futile of course. If she were being shadowed they would probably be waiting near her apartment block. Besides if they didn't want to be seen then she would never see them until – on the other hand they may want her to see them to soften her up for the next interview.

At the central reservation people were milling around the wide stair leading up to the huge cast-iron footbridge crossing the broad street and linking the tramcar platforms with the Metro. Joining the slow-moving throng Miriam allowed herself to be carried along the northward lane of the bridge. Her arms crushed at her sides she felt safe in the anonymity granted her by the flow of individuals packed tight like her, their breath releasing steamy puffs and their feet tramping in unison along the wooden boards, but when she descended and turned off the prospekt into the narrow canyon-like ulitsa leading to her block each solitary footfall jarred on her nerves. Out of the corner of her eye she examined the street cleaner as she passed. He was energetically sweeping the snow with his birch broom, perhaps too energetically to be authentic.

In the lobby the stony-faced concierge seemed more attentive than usual. The lift had not worked since 1941 so she climbed the stairs to her floor with increasing foreboding. As she walked along the wide wood-panelled corridor, passing each of the monumental doorways, she could feel her heart beating with trepidation, expecting to find her door ajar, for that's how she would do it. But it was closed and when she entered the apartment was empty. There was no one waiting for her. Everything was just as she left it.

Chapter Thirty-one

Moscow, early February 1953

She was not answering his phone calls. He was convinced of that. The phone just rang and rang. She couldn't be out every time. She was not calling him either nor leaving notes everyday as she usually did. He wouldn't be too hasty, going round to her apartment, nor try to contact her at her office. This was born of his analytical nature and habitual distrust engendered by years of professional experience, and if he went round to her apartment or to her office and she wasn't there what would that tell him? Nothing except something was wrong and it would raise suspicion. With some misgivings and against his judgement he gave in to his anxiety and decided to contact Esther. She wasn't at her apartment and the *Izvestia* switchboard cut him off when he gave his identity. Dread began to take hold, so that when they came for him he was almost relieved.

As Esther turned the corner into Myasnitskaya to keep her regular appointment with Miriam there was a black crow van standing outside the teahouse. Ice-cold trepidation immersed her, suffusing her whole being. Her steps faltered. Should she go on? She hesitated and almost took one step back before her arms were taken from behind. Without a word she was propelled to the opening doors of the van. Pushed forward onto the floor, hands cuffed behind her. She was held down by booted feet pressing in the small of her back while a thick cord was pulled across her mouth and drawn tight into the corners, bridle-like,

357

before being knotted tightly at the nape of her neck, trapping her tongue so that she could only make gargling sounds. The van leapt forward and within a short time it halted and the doors were flung open. Without a word she was dragged out, wrenched to her feet, and force-marched along a passage by two men roughly pushing her arms up her back from behind until the door opened into a room with a desk and a stout woman in the uniform of the MGB. At a nod from her the men tore at Esther's clothes, yanking them from her until she was completely naked, then they thrust her face down over the desk, holding her while the woman carried out an examination, brutally entering her with her fingers twice so that her breath was forced out in wheezing outraged gasps. Then one of the men crimped a slim metal band around her neck, holding a label denoting her identity. Finally both men signed the woman's register and dragged Esther through another door into a large windowless chamber reeking of disinfectant and perpetually bathed in harsh light where she was confronted by the sight of a cage in the middle of the concrete floor barely higher than the average person and holding at least fifty naked people of differing sizes and shapes without room for them all to sit down at the same time. At first glance they all appeared to be women of varying ages. A small gate was opened, her cuffs and gag were removed and she was forced through before it was slammed and locked. The men left closing the heavy door behind them with a boom.

In shock she fell against the bars, slowly sliding down to the floor as clammy bodies were forced aside by her weight. Trembling, her arms clasped around her head, she attempted to shut out her surroundings but to no avail as the ramblings, whimpering, and above all the continual coughing penetrated her consciousness, along with the stench of human filth and disinfectant.

Suddenly the door was flung open to admit barefooted

men in grey canvas overalls, looking like real criminals, she thought. Then despairingly she noticed they carried hoses. Oh no! Not again. She cowered into a ball against a wall of bodies, burying her head under her arms. Moving around the cage they jetted everyone with powerful stinging spurts of chlorine-laden water, driving them into a pyramid of tangled pallid flesh, laughing and jeering as they did so. Then they blasted the concrete floor, draining it into a grid in the centre of the cage as arms and legs untangled. This was followed by the arrival of a trolley carrying two tubs of kasha pushed by a bent, grey-haired man accompanied by a guard. He looked frail and ancient, though he probably wasn't. As he limped around the cage ladling, the thick mess into wooden beakers he leered at the women as he handed them through the bars. Five minutes was allowed to eat and get the water that followed the kasha into the beakers before they were handed back and the number checked. A discrepancy would mean everyone would miss a meal.

So it went on. For how long Esther had no way of knowing. There didn't seem to be a pattern to the hosing or the arrival of the kasha and the lights were kept on continually. She soon lost all sense of time. Nobody spoke or communicated in any way. Most just stared blankly into space. Sometimes the void was relieved as another prisoner would arrive through the door to be pushed bewildered and shocked into the cage. Occasionally they would come for someone, calling out a name and dragging them off after confirming from the neckband. In this way the population of the cage never fluctuated by more than one or two.

The Lubyanka Prison, Moscow, 2nd March 1953

The executioner adjusted his rubber apron and deftly eased the spring of the pistol. He took a certain pride in this aspect of his duties. This was to be the thirty-fifth today and it was only mid-afternoon. He insisted on using two cells alternately. One being cleaned out discreetly while the other was used. No sense in distressing the prisoner unnecessarily, besides it made things easier for all concerned.

Miriam sat in the chair facing the black-draped camera on its tripod. She stared hard at the lens. Nikolai may see this photograph one day. His work done, the photographer snatched up his equipment and left to set it up in the next room.

The muzzle felt cold on the back of her neck where her hair had been cut away. She heard the scrabbling claws ripping open the sack and at last her death tore free and found her.

Lefortovo Prison, Moscow, April 1953

He could hear the cell doors being opened one by one all down the passage, voices, the rattle of keys and footsteps. This hadn't happened before. It was always one at a time when people were taken for interrogation. His gums were throbbing again where two teeth had been yanked out with pliers. They promised to take two more out at the next session but that was perhaps weeks ago, he couldn't tell. There hadn't been anything recently. Over and over they'd taken him through their time together. He'd lost count of the sessions of continuous questioning, hour after hour with relays of interrogators. What did they talk about, they'd asked him? He was holding something back, they said. Perhaps he didn't realise it, they suggested.

Was it because of something Miriam had done, or Esther, or both? The question had dominated his thoughts throughout his interrogation. They'd told him nothing but he knew the form. Eventually it would become clear when he was presented with his written confession. They would never get a signature from him, he was determined of that. And what was happening to Miriam?

Footsteps approached; there was the familiar crash and rattle of keys in the lock. His heart started to pound. More interrogation perhaps, or were they were going to shoot him? The door was flung open and a colonel in a strange uniform pushed aside the guard and stepped in. 'Colonel Ignatov. I am Colonel Leskov, MVD. Follow me.'

With the guard self-consciously trailing after them Dmitri knew there was something different as he followed the colonel down the passage, for all the cells were empty their doors hanging open and there were no guards to be seen, and what was that the colonel had mentioned, MVD? He was taken to the bathhouse.

'Get yourself cleaned up and then come along to my office through that door,' the colonel pointed down the passage, 'and leave those filthy clothes behind.'

Naked and pink from the hot showers and cleanly shaved from the razor provided he entered the colonel's room. Immediately opposite on a chair was a complete colonel's uniform and accessories including polished shoes. 'I hope it fits, Colonel. You appear to have lost some weight. Now get dressed, then, after I've given you some news you will no doubt find profoundly shocking, I'll explain your situation to you.'

Dumbfounded, he found the uniform jacket had his complete set of medal ribbons on the breast. The habit of asking questions, so much part of his nature, had been beaten out of him to be replaced by almost blind obedience, at least for the time being. He did as he was told without query.

When he was dressed the colonel invited him to sit and brought a chair to face him. He leaned forward on his elbows. 'Do you know what month it is, Colonel?'

Dmitri was taken aback. He'd lost count of the days early on. He shook his head and shrugged.

'It is April, Colonel, April 10th. Comrade Stalin is dead.'

It seemed to Dmitri the air between them suddenly became still.

Colonel Leskov looked at him intensely for some seconds. 'His death was announced on March 5th. He was taken from us by a heart attack. His funeral was on March 9th.'

Dmitri was about to search for a response but Leskov, anticipating this, stilled him with a gesture. 'Since then things have been moving fast. Minister Beria ordered a review of all charges relating to the doctors' plot and to anti-Soviet activities. As a consequence all cases have been terminated, all connected arrests are cancelled, and all executed persons have been publicly exonerated in a list published last week. You are rehabilitated; your apartment and all your possessions are restored to you with full reinstatement of your rank. An investigation into the activities of those high-ranking officials in the MGB who took it upon themselves to further these activities behind Comrade Stalin's back has been instigated by Minister Beria, and because the leadership of the MGB had become isolated from the people, out of touch, embarking on treasonous deeds, it has been dissolved and those concerned with the decision making have been arrested. A new organisation under Minister Beria has been created of which you are part. It is called The Ministry of Internal Affairs or MVD.'

There was silence between them for some moments and then Leskov rose from his chair. 'I hope your stay was not too uncomfortable, Colonel,' he said wryly.

Tenderly Dmitri felt his jaw then the thought flashed into his mind, Miriam. He must find her. Making a brief farewell to Colonel Leskov and ignoring his advice to get something to eat he made to hasten out of the building and get over to her apartment. However the sudden activity was too much for his weakened frame and he found himself having to sit down for some minutes in the entrance hall of the prison until the strength returned to his legs and the dizziness passed.

Having forced himself to take a more leisurely journey he arrived at Miriam's apartment block. Riding in the tramcar he'd pictured the scene as she opened the door. He felt her lips on his, her arms about him as he swung her off her feet. Oh what joy, he felt it even as he rode in the rattling car, and despite his exhaustion there was a spring in his step as he climbed up to her floor though he had to pause on each landing to let the light-headedness settle. Her door was near the end of the corridor and in his eagerness he almost broke into a run but his legs were just too weak for the effort.

He was unprepared for the MGB seals still intact where

they had been fixed across the door and its frame. He stared at them, unbelieving at first, but then the implication slowly took hold. Why hadn't she been back? Surely she must have been released by now. He would go to the main entrance hall of the Lubyanka, make enquiries. Yes, that was it. He had his rank restored. He would use his authority.

After much fruitless searching in the release files the enquiry clerk suggested he look through the exonerated list in the glass case on the wall. No. He didn't need to do that. Perhaps they were slow releasing her. She must be on a holding list. The clerk should go through the records again but no, only the release lists were available. Her name wasn't there.

He went to the list on the wall, just to eliminate the possibility. He found her name quite easily with the note, Executed March 2nd. Exonerated April 3rd. The shock stunned him and the impact was intensified as he realised she'd died just three days before the death of Comrade Stalin, a death that had saved him but had been too late for her. A growing sense of guilt at not being able to save her and of evading the same fate was prompted deep within his consciousness. It would remain with him for the rest of his life.

The Lubyanka Prison, April 1953

The heavy outer door was thrown open. Suddenly guards carrying poles rushed in and surrounded the cage. 'Out! Out!' they shouted while they used the poles to drive the prisoners to the gate, relentlessly poking and pushing at them through the bars until a seething mass of naked bodies was crushed against it. Then the gate was opened so that the mass spilled out to be driven through the outer door into the adjoining chamber where a mountainous heap of clothing stood in the middle of the floor.

'Dress,' the guards kept shouting, 'Dress, dress,' while at the same time they used the poles to pitch the clothing into the air, scattering it and separating it out and kicking shoes about the chamber. With her mind numb and uncomprehending Esther clutched various items to her while she rummaged among the clothing, attempting to dress and instinctively trying to catch shoes at they flew past her.

Those that the guards considered were sufficiently dressed were dragged and pushed into a smaller room. The room with the desk, Esther recalled, from so long ago. There she was made to stand in the crush of bodies waiting until her name was called, then she was pushed to the desk where her identity collar was checked and removed before a clerk gave her a paper and made her sign for it. An officer standing behind pointed to the door and shouted at her, 'Go!' She walked freely down the passage among the others, expecting to be stopped at any time as she went through door after door until finally she found herself out in the street. She was free. Only then did she look at the paper she was holding. Squinting in the pale April sunlight she read that Comrade Esther Rabin was unconditionally discharged and fully reinstated in her post.

It was the same every morning. For a moment or two as he

struggled to wake he would think she was still alive, still waiting for him to call around, to spend time together. Then reluctantly as he let sleep fade he became aware of her no longer being there or anywhere, and the familiar emptiness rose up to meet him. The things they used to do together when he recalled them, they were gone, no longer part of his life, as if those things had happened to someone else. He sat hunched on the edge of the bed for some moments before he decided to rise and make some tea, light a cigarette, switch on the radio. Eventually he would have to dress, tunic, boots, they would feel cold as he drew then on. He found it difficult to go out but his duties awaited him. He'd put on his coat, his cap, and go down to the mess-room for some tasteless breakfast, then to the office, mechanically, to carry out his tasks for the day, without feeling, without heart, robot-like.

Chapter Thirty-two

Wrexham, 1957

'I saw Dmitri only once soon after I was released. I was posted to the Budapest office within weeks, you see. I was never completely cleared, always under suspicion, so was everyone else who'd been arrested, including him. He phoned me, wanted to tell me what had happened to Miriam, I suppose. He must have known I already knew about it. *Izvestia* had published the list on the front page. Anyway we arranged to meet at this bar. What was it called? Café Margarita, that's it, a foul place. Very little was said between us there was nothing much to say anyway. We just sat quietly. When he did speak his voice was weak, no strength in it. He looked thin, his hair was always very light, but it seemed to have whitened and he had a racking cough. He told me he'd asked permission to retire in two years. He was about fifty-eight then and that was it except, when I'd been in Budapest for about two years; I learned he'd been re-arrested. That wasn't unusual then. I didn't feel too safe myself, that's why I was keeping my ear to the ground. I heard from my source they'd caught him on his way to Kursk Province, going back there to take up farming, I think. The charge was unauthorised travel. He wasn't heard of after that.'

The early morning sun is strengthening and steam is rising in faint wisps from the crumbling tarmac and wild grass bordering the playground. With one hand Esther fumbles in her jacket pocket for her cigarettes, all the time holding Nicholas' eyes with hers. She takes out the crumpled

367

packet and feels for a cigarette with her other hand. Placing it in her mouth she pokes the matchbox open and cupping her hand strikes once with a downward motion. Lighting the cigarette as the match sizzles she shakes it until it goes out and casts it away.

Did she do the right thing? Getting him on that train certainly saved him and maybe she could have got his mother on it too, but she never intended for her to go. She had undertaken to rid her of the baby. That was her part of the deal with the Comintern. Could she have refused? No, but perhaps she could have got her out anyway, had her abducted. Yes, but she would have had to get out too to save herself.

She could have done that. Oh my God! She could have done that. For the first time the thought arises, striking her like a hammer blow. But she chose to stay. However Miriam may or may not have come to see things after is of no consequence. She chose to stay. She made her choice: to serve the Comintern, to keep Miriam in Madrid, and to gain her reward, a desk at *Izvestia*. She wasn't interested in the baby that it was saved was just an unintended consequence. And here it was, this young man, Nikolai. For the first time she is feeling the connection between the two while vainly fighting back the tears, and for the first time she's confronted by the hollowness of the story she's told herself over the years, stripped bare of pretexts and false intentions. The truth overwhelms her.

He sees her face crumpling as she discards the cigarette. Her flinty personality shatters. She is covering her face with her hands, slumping forward, her elbows coming to rest on the tabletop. He reaches out to her but stifles the impulse, letting his hand drop to the table. 'Is this because of my mother's death?'

She lifts her face and sits back, nodding her head twice. Let him believe that. Could she tell him the truth that she's just had to admit to herself, that she disposed of him for her own furtherance? Never. She could never to do that. It's too much to ask, just too much.

Now he knows about his mother, what kind of a person she was, everything. What she did in Spain and Russia. Can he understand what drove her, how much grief and loss played a part? If she'd found him and lived on in England what kind of a person would she have been, and what kind of a person would he have been? After all, he was seven at least when she started taking positive steps; by 1953 his childhood was behind him, and although nothing was inevitable the die was cast. In fact that was the case when he was put in that Red Cross train. If she'd come with him to England things would have been so different, or would they? She'd already committed atrocities. One day he may have found out about them, she may have confessed, and he would have been in the same position as he is now. Her acts would always be hanging over them both, ready to fall on their heads.

So could he live with the mother he discovered? She must have known that if she sought him out the system to which she was devoted would destroy her. Her love for him clearly played a part in her own destruction. In the end was that kind of love the only thing that counts?

It is midday, the sun is overhead, and children, let out of school, are taking possession of the playground. Esther nods to the fence, 'There's a bus stop. Let's take one into town. It's only a few minutes ride to the market. We can have some lunch before you go for your train, then I can walk up with you to make my usual visit to the police. It's on the way to the railway station.'

It's been a good lunch. For the first time they've felt at ease in each other's company, asking no more questions and no longer feeling the need to give guarded answers. Now they're walking up toward the police station with a warm afternoon sun on their backs. She feels a deep sense of resignation. In time she knows she will come to accept it. He is feeling more at ease with himself than he has done for some time, probably since he had received the envelope. Although they aren't touching, they both feel they're walking together as if they're linked somehow. Eventually they come to the police station where they are to part.

'I'm so glad I'm living now, and not through those times,' he is saying to her, 'because I don't know what decisions I would have made, nor what acts I would have committed if I'd lived as an adult then.'

'You can be grateful you will never know the answer to that.'

'Well, we can also be grateful we don't have to live through such times now, not here anyway.'

'No, but people are still living under those conditions in the USSR and in Spain.'

Nicholas feels reluctant to share such gloomy thoughts. 'Yes, but for how much longer?'

As they make their farewells the warmth of the bright sun captures his spirit and with a light step he sets off for the railway station.

Other Accent Press Titles

For more information about **Vic Evans**
and other **Accent Press** titles

please visit

www.accentpress.co.uk

Lightning Source UK Ltd.
Milton Keynes UK
UKOW03f0613071014

239707UK00001B/3/P